THE LAST MAN TO DIE

THE LAST MAN TO DIE

War Is Murder In Self Defense

A Novel Of World War I

BOB COLVIN

eleven point
publications

BOB COLVIN

ISBN 978-1-7364400-0-1 (paperback)
ASIN 1736440004 (paperback)
ASIN B08RS4Z9L2 (ebook)

Cover design by:
Dave Gjerness/Eastwood Creative
Caroline Stenz/Stenz Design

For Dave Gjerness, loving husband to Linda, talented artist, good friend.
R.I.P. buddy

TABLE OF CONTENTS

PART ONE

TROUBLED WATERS

BACK

They ask me where I've been,
And what I've done and seen.
But what can I reply
Who know it wasn't I,
But someone just like me,
Who went across the sea
And with my head and hands
Slew men in foreign lands …
Though I must bear the blame
Because he bore my name.

—Wilfrid Wilson Gibson

CHAPTER 1

APRIL 29, 1918
LONELY OAK BRIDGE, ELEVEN POINT RIVER,
RANDOLPH COUNTY, ARKANSAS

James Jedidiah "Jed" Martin shivered from the cold rain and his fear. Lightning had carved off an arm of a giant oak sitting by the Eleven Point River bridge. The log had fallen on the wooden bridge, knocking the near span into the river, wedging itself between the bank and the central pilings. It was wedged too tight for a mule and a rope to pull it free. Jed sat astride this log inching his way out to the bridge, chopping off small branches with swipes of his ax. He had a rope harness around his shoulders, the other end attached to a mule harness on the riverbank. Jed carried the ax, a satchel full of spikes, a large hammer, and a loop of rope through a pulley. His best friend, Mike O'Kean, held the ends of the pulley's rope.

He stopped and stared at the water streaming by. This river had swallowed his mother when he was eight years old. They had never found Rose Martin's body.

"Come on, get on with it," his uncle said, perched on his horse at the river's edge. James Enoch Martin squirmed in his saddle and rubbed the thigh of his stiff right leg. The family called him Enoch, based on the family custom of referring to male relatives by their middle names.

Jed ignored him.

At the bridge, Jed stood on the slippery wood and chopped the tree trunk jammed on the bridge. The wood was rain-soaked, and the ax glanced off, but he finally knocked the trunk free. It slid into the water leaving an open space between the bridge and the riverbank. The notches for the base beams were intact. He secured the pulley to the bridge with the hammer and spikes. Uncle Enoch's nineteen-year-old Negro foreman and mule wrangler, Theodore Roosevelt Stains, passed Mike the long wooden beams from a large flatbed wagon. Mike and Teddy pulled the first beam straight out to the bridge by the rope and pulley. Jed guided the beam into its notch on the upriver side, securing his end in place with the sledge and spikes. Mike hammered a twelve-inch spike through the other end securing it to the railroad crossties sunk into the roadbed. They installed the next three runners as the storm increased in intensity.

A strong gust of wind hit Jed, tossing his floppy farmer's hat onto the riverbank. He slipped and lost his balance grabbing for the hat and fell into the river. The rope harness tugged at him, preventing him from being swept downstream, but he sank deep into the water. His feet touched the bottom, the satchel of spikes an anchor. He forced the strap over his head, dropped the spikes to the bottom, and bobbed to the surface as his breath gave out. He gasped and got a lung full of the foam at the surface, coughed, and submerged again.

He feared he was going to drown but a white calm sprung from deep inside him.

Damn the water—fix the bridge.

He swam to the surface and gulped a clean lung full of air.

Teddy walked the mule away from the river pulling Jed toward the riverbank. Bottom silt swirled around him. A drowned and disemboweled pig embraced him before floating away.

Mike grabbed the rope harness and pulled Jed out of the water, helped him up the bank, and propped him against a wheel of the wagon. Jed coughed and sputtered, spitting out the river-bottom dirt that coated the inside of his mouth.

"Thanks, Mike," he managed.

"I'm glad we had your rope on the mule. Teddy did a great job."

"Thanks, Teddy."

"Are you all right, James Jedidiah?"

Jed coughed then gulped a full lung of air. "Yes, Teddy, I'm all right."

"Damned fool," Enoch said. "You made a mess of it."

Jed ignored him.

Mike reached under the wagon driver's seat and produced two bottles. The first contained clean water and Jed swished a mouthful and spat the grit from his mouth.

4

Mike offered the other jug.

Jed shook his head.

"A shot of this will help settle you."

Jed hesitated but accepted the jug and took a drink. The moonshine burned his throat and bored its way into his stomach and after a second, he retched and coughed up water and dirt. He grabbed the water bottle and rinsed his mouth, washing his face, and blowing remnants out of his nose. Mike offered him the moonshine jug again. Jed took a second burning mouthful, hesitated, and swallowed. The drink warmed his stomach as he relaxed against the wagon wheel and took several deep breaths.

The rain stopped.

A new storm rumbled to the southwest, marching over the horizon.

Teddy handed Jed his floppy farmer's hat then turned to Mike. "Michael Sean, we need to fix the bridge before that other storm comes."

A lightning bolt stabbed from the clouds to the earth. Jed counted the seconds to the thunder. The storm was two miles away.

Jed got to his feet. "We've got forty minutes, at the most." He walked to the riverbank and started across a beam to the bridge. He made it two steps then slipped.

Mike grabbed his arm. "You're the experienced carpenter but let me finish."

Jed pursed his lips and nodded.

Mike never missed a chance at a physical workout. He had a record of fifteen, one, and one as a semi-professional boxer, and had taught Jed how to spar with him.

Jed relied on Mike in tough situations.

Sometimes too much.

Mike ran out onto the bridge and he and Teddy set the last beam. Jed passed the cross planks to Teddy and he and Mike nailed them in place.

As they finished, the storm arrived.

The four men sheltered under the wagon bed. Jed and Enoch locked eyes. Enoch shook his head. Jed turned away.

It rained hard for ten minutes before tapering off into a steady drizzle as the thunder and lightning moved away.

Teddy secured the tools and unused lumber in the wagon bed. Jed draped a blanket over his head and wrapped it around his shivering body, looking like a half-drowned medieval monk. He sat in the wagon beside Teddy as they set off toward the farmhouse near Birdell, three miles to the south.

Teddy glanced over his shoulder at Jed's uncle riding his horse behind the wagon, rubbing his thigh, his walking cane stuffed into a carbine scabbard attached to his saddle.

"James Enoch should ride up here. His leg is bothering him again."

Jed looked back. Enoch sat taller in the saddle, looking around at the weather.

Jed turned forward. "He's got his pride. He wants to embarrass me."

Mike urged his mule forward next to the driver's seat.

"Why do you let your uncle treat you that way?" Mike asked. "You're not eight years old anymore."

Jed shook his head. "He's giving me a hard time because you finished my work for me. I want to get away from him, but I'd have to leave Aunt Bessie." He watched the storm march to the east. "I feel like I'm drifting along. There must be more to life than sitting on a mule watching croppers pick cotton."

"I heard stories about the war in Europe," Teddy said. "They say the artillery rumbles and glows along the horizon like the lightning there and, before you know it, the shells come and explode in a storm around you."

"It's not your war, Teddy," Jed said. "It's a bunch of crazy white men killing their cousins over who-knows-what?"

"They're taking Negro men for the army. Mister James Enoch pays me fair and never calls me names, but there might be a better future for me there."

Jed pondered this news. "If you think so, Teddy, I wish you the best."

"And you, Jed?"

It was the first time Teddy had used Jed's familiar name.

Jed shook his head. "Those Germans did nothing to me. Besides, most of my ancestors are German."

Teddy guided the wagon into the Martin mule shed. "The Good Lord will show you the way, James Jedidiah." He dismounted the wagon, unhitched the mules, and guided them to their stalls.

"I want out of this small town. It'd be an adventure," Mike said.

"You watch too many moving pictures. Do you think you're Douglas Fairbanks?"

Mike grinned.

"What about Linda Sue Anderson? You'd miss her."

"We're friends who get together to have fun sometimes." Mike winked. "We've stayed out of trouble so far. If I go, I suspect she'll be here when I get back."

Jed shook his head.

"What about Katie Flynn?" Mike asked. "I caught you two going at it right here in this shed. Did she get pregnant and go to a Florence Crittenton Home?"

"No. Aunt Bessie declared her a gold digger and ran her back to her father's illegal casino in Hot Springs. When she didn't get her hooks into our farm, she called me an inexperienced hick."

"Then there's nothing holding us here but our families and we can come back to them. We're both registered for the draft. If I'm called, I'll go and so will you."

"Yes, but I won't volunteer. The war is four years old. You could die right before it ended. Why risk it?"

"It's the ultimate gamble."

Jed climbed down from the wagon.

"I'll be going," Mike said.

"Why don't you stay here tonight?"

"Y'all don't have room for me. I'll stay at the family store in Pocahontas."

"I'll see you tomorrow. Thanks for helping."

Mike touched his hat brim and winked at Jed. He urged his mule down the road.

Inside the house a living room fire kept the house warm and dry.

Jed walked into the kitchen.

His aunt stood at the stove, stirring a pot. It smelled like homemade potato soup. She had on her blue cotton dress and white apron; her hair done up in a bun. She turned away from the stove. Her eyes widened, and she stepped toward Jed.

Jed put his hands on her shoulders. "We were fixing the bridge. I fell in the river. Mike and Teddy pulled me out."

She grabbed his hands and kissed them. "Thank God."

"Yes, thank God."

"You go put on dry clothes and I'll give you a bowl of your favorite soup."

Jed kissed her on the forehead and went up to his room. He felt better after washing up and putting on clean clothes. He went downstairs and stopped in the shadows outside the kitchen door. Bessie and Enoch were talking.

"He slipped and fell in," Enoch said. "He failed. The O'Kean boy finished the work."

"You're hard on him."

Enoch sat down at the kitchen table. "Before Seth died, I promised to look after Rose and Jed, but Rose died. I tried with Jed."

"Of course, he's your blood."

Enoch's shoulders slumped. "I wanted more children. If you hadn't miscarried—"

Bessie's back stiffened. "Don't blame me. You got wounded."

"I'm not impotent. At least we tried." Enoch stared at the tablecloth rubbing his inner thigh. "Those damned Moro bastards sliced me up and killed my brother."

"Don't swear so much." Bessie leaned on the table. "Enoch, talk to the boy about Rose, and you, and us." Her voice choked. "He's registered for the draft and could die in this war."

"Jed's not a boy. He's twenty-three years old." Enoch shook his head. "There's no sense in me talking to him. He doesn't like me much."

Someone knocked on the front door. Jed opened it. Old Man Pinkert, the postman, stood there, water dripping from his floppy hat, a rain slicker draped over his skinny frame.

"Hello, Mister Pinkert," Jed said.

"Hello, Mister Martin," Pinkert said. "I brought a letter for you. Whenever an important government letter arrives, I make sure I get it to the party as soon as possible. The army won't take me. They say I'm too old. I reckon delivering letters is my part in the war effort."

Pinkert handed the letter to Jed and departed.

Jed sat down at the kitchen table and laid the letter in front of his place setting.

Enoch stared at him.

Bessie set a glass of cool tea and a bowl of soup in front of him, her hands trembling.

Jed bowed his head and said a silent Grace. *Lord, thank you for help at the bridge. With this letter, Thy will be done.*

He picked up the letter and tore it open. He read it, set it aside, and took a spoonful of the steaming soup.

8

Enoch slapped the table. "What does it say?"

Jed blew on the spoon to cool the soup and relished the taste of butter, onions, and milk wrapped around the tender potato bits.

"Jed, *necken uns nicht so*—don't tease us," Bessie said.

"I'm going into the army. I've been drafted."

Bessie sat down at the table and wept into her kitchen towel. "I thought you were getting a deferment."

Jed patted her hand. "I'm going into town tomorrow to take the unused lumber back. I'll ask Mr. Jones. There may be a mistake."

She rose, held Jed's head against her waist and bent to kiss the top of his head. "I'm sorry to cause a scene, Jed. Wars tear up the lives of good young men."

Jed stood. "If I have to go, I'll do the best I can." He raised her chin and looked into her eyes, silvered with tears. "I'll be all right." She ran her hand along his face and kissed him on the cheek, then turned to the stove.

Jed sat back down and ate more soup.

Enoch held up the letter. "Says here you report for a physical on May seventh. If you pass, you leave two weeks later. Ain't they rushing it?"

"I guess they need men bad," Jed said.

"You can't even fix a bridge without someone finishing it for you."

Jed ignored him.

"And the way they fight now, burrowing into the ground like moles. Trench warfare, they call it." Enoch sat up straight, "In my day we stood back-to-back and presented cold steel, none of this hiding in the ground business."

Jed wiped his mouth with a napkin and reached for the glass of tea. "I suppose things have changed since you served, Uncle."

"At least I volunteered. I didn't wait for them to drag me away under threat of force."

Jed stared at his uncle. Before he could speak, Bessie pointed the soup ladle. "James Enoch Martin, this boy has put his whole life aside to help you with this farm. He has so much courage he almost drowned today helping you." Her voice caught. She turned back to the stove, talking to herself in German.

Enoch stood, grabbed his cane, and took out his pipe. He limped across the kitchen toward the door to the back porch. "For a small woman, you make a lot of big declarations," he said, "and half of them in a language I can't understand." He went out onto the porch and slammed the screen door shut.

Jed ate his soup in silence.

When he finished, Bessie surprised him with a special treat. She placed a slice of strawberry-rhubarb pie in front of him. The sugary crust and sweet strawberries contrasted with the tart syrup from the rhubarb. It was one of his favorites.

He finished the pie, placed the dirty dishes in the sink, kissed Bessie's cheek, and went to his room and read the letter again. He breathed deep and forced the air out through pursed lips. Someone else had decided if he should stay or go.

CHAPTER 2
APRIL 30, 1918
POCAHONTAS, ARKANSAS

After a night of restless sleep, Jed rose early to take the unused lumber back to the Jones warehouse. As he descended the stairs, Bessie sat in the overstuffed chair by the bay window overlooking the front porch and the view of their land stretching east. The rising sun shined through the window and outlined her small frame.

A cup of tea steamed on the small table beneath the window.

Bessie had her two most prized possessions in her lap: her family Bible, and her picture book, which contained all the photos of the family.

Jed coughed as he walked up behind her so he wouldn't startle her.

She inclined her head. "Come, sit by me and let me show you."

Jed pulled up a hassock and sat beside her. He knew telling the stories calmed and grounded her in this time of upset. It would help him, too.

Bessie handed him the Bible, open at the first page. There she had written, in her neat, tiny hand, the names, birthdays, wedding days, and dates of death of Jed's ancestors.

She turned the picture book to the first page. Staring out from an old daguerreotype was a fit and bearded man in full Confederate officer's uniform. He was the patriarch of Jed's family from whom Jed had received his name—James Jedidiah Martin, Major, Confederate States Army.

"Your grandfather distinguished himself at the battle of Cheat Mountain and General Lee promoted him to major."

Jed read the entry in the Bible, "Born October 15, 1819, Fauquier County, Virginia, died February 27, 1902, Randolph County, Arkansas, age 82."

"Many Virginians settled in Arkansas. After the war, Old Jed bought land and sharecropped it to whites and freedmen alike. He never owned a slave. Business was good, and he expanded to the three hundred acres we own today."

"If he didn't hold with slavery, why did he join the Confederacy?"

"The war wasn't only about slavery," Bessie said. "He was fighting for Virginia."

Bessie turned the page. Old Jed and a tall woman with two long blonde braids stared out from the page. "This is Old Jed and Grandmother Ilsa Moler, a German immigrant. They wed late in 1865. The next year Seth and Enoch were born." Bessie shook her head. "When Mother Ilsa died in 1893, it took the will out of Old Jed. When you were born in 1894, he perked up but it was like the last flare in a smoldering fireplace."

Jed remembered an old man with a cane in a rocking chair on the porch, gazing far into the distance. He died when Jed was seven and received a military funeral. An American flag stood by the gravesite but the Stars and Bars of the Confederacy draped the casket.

His sons Robert Seth and James Enoch went to war six months later. When Enoch returned from the Philippines alone and wounded, he resumed running the farm and often took his father's place in the rocking chair on the porch, his own cane across his lap.

Bessie turned another page. She caressed another tintype of a short man with a derby hat and an impudent smile under a handlebar mustache, standing next to a small, handsome woman with her hair done up in two severe buns on the sides of her head.

"This is mama and papa."

Jed remembered them as Papaw Hale and Oma Birgit—his grandparents Harvey Hale and Birgit Gruber—he an Irish railroad conductor for the Saint Louis, Iron Mountain, and Southern Railroad, she the daughter of a German immigrant railroad telegrapher.

"I remember sitting on Oma's lap as she shelled peas and taught me German."

"Enoch says we use the language to keep secrets from him."

When Jed was six Birgit and Harvey moved to California.

Jed's heart broke.

Bessie helped him write letters in German to his Oma in California.

Bessie turned to a picture of two beautiful young women in Gibson Girl dresses sitting on a picnic blanket: herself, Bessie Mae and her sister Rose Birgit Hale. Beside them sat identical twins James Enoch and Robert Seth Martin.

"They were as interchangeable as new metal plow blades," Bessie said, "but Rose and I could always tell them apart. Seth's eyes had a slight lavender luster while Enoch's are clear as water, like yours."

She looked away and picked up the tea cup, taking a nervous sip, her hands shaking. Her talkativeness, red eyes, and breath showed there was more in the cup than tea. "We loved them both and from the moment we met them we knew we'd marry them. The boys assumed Enoch and Rose would get together—they were the talkative ones. Seth and I were quieter. We girls picked our opposites and settled it."

She turned the page. The two couples stood on the front steps of the old Methodist church in Pocahontas, the girls resplendent in their white satin wedding dresses and flowing veils, the men wearing black frock coats. The caption, in white ink: June 1, 1889.

"Old Jed bought us the dresses so his sons would have proper brides."

Jed put his hand on his aunt's shoulder. "It's only right for the two prettiest girls in the county to have the best wedding possible."

She turned and caressed Jed's face. "I hope one day you have a day as happy as that."

He kissed the back of her hand and nodded.

"Before the Philippine war we were so happy. Sometimes Seth and I sat together by the river and watched it flow, not saying a word." She stared out the window. "Rose and Enoch took long walks together and chatted on for hours. The four of us were like different parts of one person. We loved being married, shared our deepest secrets, and forgave each other everything." She twisted the handkerchief in her hands. "The townspeople disapproved of us living together. We weren't welcome in church but we read from the Bible at our Sunday picnics. I favored passages on love and forgiveness." She sipped the strong tea. "When you came along, we determined to raise you traditionally so you wouldn't suffer their scorn."

"You taught me the Bible, German, and manners," Jed said, "but Uncle Enoch isn't talkative now. Most of what he does say I don't want to hear."

"War changed him," Bessie said. "He wasn't the same when he came home. He felt guilty that he lost his twin."

She turned to a picture of Seth and Enoch sitting in the back of a wagon with their suitcases. The caption read, "*Martin brothers—off to war.*"

"Why did they volunteer for the army?"

"They were patriots whose father had served," Bessie said. "They went off to the Philippines to fight the Moros."

Jed's uncle's words echoed in his mind: *At least I volunteered. I didn't wait for them to drag me away under threat of force.*

Bessie paged through other memories and pictures of relatives Jed had never met or remembered. She turned to a picture of eight-year-old Jed, standing on the bank of the Eleven Point River, a cane pole in his hand and a ridiculously large straw hat on his head.

"You were always such a sweet boy, Jed, always running along the river bank and dropping hooks in the water or swimming in the creek."

Bessie stroked her finger along a brown stain at the bottom of the photograph. "Seth had this picture of you in his pocket when he died. This is his blood." Her glistening eyes searched Jed's face. "Try to help people, even when you are afraid." She took his hands. "*kommen der feine junge Mann zurück, daß ich weiß, daß Sie sind.* Come back the fine young man I know you are."

Jed rode to Pocahontas on the lumber wagon, sitting on the driver's seat next to Teddy, who guided his two favorite mules, Hoss, and Old Clem, down the dirt country track. George Bradford Jones owned the local lumber warehouse and was on the staff of the draft board. Jed had expected a farm deferment, but they had denied it.

The army would get him away from his uncle but leaving Aunt Bessie would be painful. He wasn't afraid of being killed or wounded, but if he was, it would break her heart.

He turned and checked the wagon load. Tied to the back of the wagon was one of Enoch's mules with a deer strapped across its back. Jed had shot the deer that morning when it wandered onto the farm and foraged in Bessie's vegetable garden. Jed planned to stop by the shop of his friend Herr Kurtz, the local butcher, and exchange the deer for the succulent *Rotwildwurst*—deer sausage—Kurtz produced.

In Pocahontas, shopkeepers cleaned the fronts of their stores and filled in puddles and ruts caused by the heavy rains.

Teddy pulled the team up to the open double doors of the Jones warehouse.

The oldest Jones son, Alan, greeted them. "You returning extra lumber?"

"Yes," Jed said.

Alan motioned for two of his men to unload the wagon.

"Is Mister Jones here?"

"He's in his office."

Jed entered the warehouse. A dark blue, 1915 Cadillac seven-passenger open touring car sat on the concrete floor. Mister Jones was the father of four boys and two girls. Two of the boys, Bart and Clay, were childhood rivals of Jed and Mike. On fair-weather Sundays after church, Jones rolled back the long, sloping cloth top of the Cadillac and drove his family around town, his wife in one of her stylish New York dresses and a hat from Paris, the three youngest boys and their two little sisters in the wide back seat. It was an ostentatious display by the town's wealthiest man, who bragged he had paid the enormous sum of two thousand four hundred and seventy-five dollars for the car.

Jed crossed the warehouse floor and knocked on the open office door.

Jones stood up behind his desk.

"Ah, young Martin," he said. "How may I help you?"

Jones had a nineteenth-century Victorian air, parting his hair in the middle and slicking it back, the wax in his handlebar mustache vying with the hair oil for weight and shine. He wore high starched collars and a blue cravat with a three-carat diamond stickpin and—always—his suit jacket.

"We repaired the bridge out on the Eleven Point and I brought the extra lumber back. Alan is taking care of the accounts."

"Good. We'll need the bridge for the harvest."

"Mister Jones, why didn't I get my agricultural deferment?"

"The board considered your application. You help your uncle in administering the farm, but, as you don't own the farm, you will not receive one of the agricultural deferments. You will report with the others for your examination." He cleared his throat. "The board's decision is final."

"And your sons, Mister Jones?"

Jones looked Jed in the eye. "My two middle sons Bartholomew and Clayton are in the draft. I couldn't send other men to do their duty without expecting my family to do the same. I still have their older brother to run the business."

"Alan isn't going?"

Jones shook his head. "The board has a policy to exempt married men. We want to preserve the basis of a stable society and I don't think the government wants the responsibility of supporting millions of family members when the breadwinner is overseas." Jones put out his hand. "I wish you the best, son. With you boys pitching in, the whole mess will be cleaned up in a matter of weeks."

Jed shook Jones' hand.

When Jed returned to the wagon, the lumber had been removed and Teddy sat in the driver's seat waiting. "What did he say, James Jedidiah?"

"He said I'm to be a soldier."

Teddy nodded his head. He spat into the street and looked from side to side but the white workmen nearby stared in silence. "Makes two of us. I joined two days ago."

Jed scrambled up into the wagon seat. "Does my uncle know?"

"I told Mister James Enoch this morning," Teddy said urging the mules forward.

"What did he say?"

"Good luck in this changing world."

Teddy stopped the wagon at the butcher shop.

The O'Kean dry goods store was across the street.

Herr Kurtz stepped out of his shop.

"*Guter Tag*, Jed, Theodore," he said.

"*Guter Tag zu Ihnen*, Herr Kurtz."

Teddy touched the brim of his hat. "Good morning Karl Ludwig."

"Did you fix the Eleven Point Bridge?" Herr Kurtz asked in English.

"Yes, sir," Jed said.

"I knew you would do a fine job. The repairs you did to my shop after the fire left it better than new."

Teddy told Jed he was going to the blacksmith to check Old Clem's shoes. The mule had been limping since they got into town.

Jed untied the pack mule and secured the rope to a hitch next to a water trough.

As Teddy drove away the three youngest Jones brothers, Bart, 23, Clay, 22, and eleven-year-old Dennis, staggered around the corner of the butcher shop.

"This is a fine deer you have," Kurtz told Jed in German. "I will cut for you three fine venison steaks to take home to your aunt."

Bart Jones stopped, punched his brother in the arm and pointed at Jed and Kurtz.

"Clay, do you hear the Heinie jabbering over there?"

"I sure do," Clay said, taking a swig from a jar of moonshine and handing the jar to Dennis. "Hey, Herr Kaiser, take that Hun talk and go back where you came from."

Kurtz turned to face the men. "I come here from Germany to get away from people who wish to push me around. I let no man insult me."

Bart rolled up his sleeves. "We Joneses have been drafted into the United States Army and are gonna go over there and insult us a bunch of Germans. I guess we can warm up by kicking a little Kraut ass right here in our own home town."

As the men moved closer Jed stepped in their way. "Knock it off, Bart. Herr Kurtz is an American citizen and doesn't like the Kaiser any more than you do."

Bart stopped and grinned at Jed. "Boys, we have us a Kraut lover here. He even speaks the lingo. We might as well whip him too—again."

Clay rushed Jed, trying to take him by surprise, but Jed sidestepped and planted a solid poke on Clay's nose. He followed with a straight left and two more right jabs. Clay was the same size as Jed but was also the drunkest of the brothers. He staggered back against the tethered mule. The mule kicked and shoved Clay away.

Bart charged Jed and toppled him backwards over a kneeling Dennis into the horse trough. Jed kicked his legs in the air as his backside rested on the edge of the trough, his head and upper body submerged. He gripped the sides of the trough and pulled himself up, filling his lungs with air.

Clay joined in and tried to push him back down.

"His momma drowned herself in the river and he's afraid of water."

"Ma says his mama and aunt were loose women living in a house with two men and they got married to cover it up. They were Free Lovers and Bohemians," Dennis said.

"Shut up, Dennis." Bart released Jed and slapped his little brother. "You, too, Clay."

Jed kicked with his right knee and caught Clay on the side of the head causing him to release his grip. With a determined pull Jed rose from the trough and slammed his head into Clay's nose. As Clay

17

crumpled to the ground, Jed stood up. Bart landed a roundhouse right to his face. Jed went down on one knee and blocked Bart's kick with his arms.

Mike appeared and flattened Bart with a right-hand punch to the face.

The fight was over.

Bart shook his head. "No fair, hitting a guy when he's not looking."

"Like Dennis tripping Jed from behind," Mike said. "I saw the whole thing through our store window. Where's the little creep?"

Dennis hid behind Kurtz who was calming the mule.

Bart rubbed his jaw. "Sorry about my brothers, Jed. They're repeating a bunch of stuff Mother said. It don't mean anything."

"No more fighting," Kurtz said. "Save it up to fight those bad Germans over there."

"I got my draft notice," Mike said. "Who else is gonna fight those bad Germans?"

"Mister Jones told me this morning when he came for his breakfast bacon," Kurtz said, "all four of you are drafted."

"I'll be a blue-eyed baboon," Bart said. Mike helped him to his feet.

Mike winked at Jed. "Our great gamble begins."

Bart approached Jed and shook his hand. "I admire how you don't back down, Jed, like when we used to swim and fight down in Thompson Creek when we were kids, but it still took this overgrown heavyweight to finish it."

Jed didn't respond.

"Hey," Clay said, "doesn't anybody give a shit about me? I think you broke my nose, Jed." He stood up holding his hands to his face, blood running down between them. Bart grabbed Clay's nose and pulled. There was a snapping sound. Clay howled.

"It'll be straight enough. You'll pass your induction physical all right."

"What did your mother say about this draft business?" Mike asked Bart.

"There was hell to pay for Dad. She threatened to divorce him and go back to her family in New York, but he stood his ground. We registered, we're not married, we go."

Herr Kurtz produced a hip flask. "You Jones boys are rude but, since you will fight for our country, I will share a Canadian contraband schnapps with you." He winked and passed the flask around.

Jed swigged the schnapps but remained quiet. He had stood his ground but once again Mike had arrived and finished the job. It was foolish to resent his friend for helping him. He would need friends to face the unknown—this thing called war.

Jed, Mike, and the Joneses reported for their physicals on May 7th. They filled out forms, waited in line, were probed, scoped, and thumped by the assembly line physicians, and pronounced fit for service overseas.

Ten days later, Pinkert delivered little blue cards telling them to report for transport on May 24, 1918.

CHAPTER 3

May 24, 1918

RAILROAD STATION, POCAHONTAS, ARKANSAS

Enoch drove the family buggy into town with Bessie perched on the seat between Jed and him. Bessie held on to Jed's arm and sobbed. He patted her hand and told her everything would be all right.

"Jed, I'm so fearful. I think I may never see you again."

"Don't be foolish woman," Enoch said, "a fine way to send the boy off. Besides, we don't know if he'll make it through his training."

Jed kept quiet as he had done so many times before.

When they arrived at the station Enoch parked the buggy next to the long blue Cadillac with the Jones brood clustered around it. Everyone exchanged courteous greetings but the strain of the moment was palpable.

Teddy stood at the end of the platform where a group of field hands held the mules Enoch had sold to the army: one hundred dollars apiece for three-dozen mules, a price Enoch said was lower than he could have got from the British but which it was his patriotic duty to accept.

Mike wrapped his arm around his mother who kept repeating, "My beautiful boy." She turned to Mike's father, a tall, sandy-haired man like his son. "Don't let them take my only child, Patrick. Don't let them destroy my baby." She collapsed against her husband who struggled to keep her upright. The elder O'Kean's complexion was sallow.

"It'll be all right, Mother," Mike said as he stroked her hair. "The war will be over before we get there. Please don't carry on so."

"I hope so, son. I pray so," she sobbed.

Mike's father held his wife close and addressed his son. "I'd better get her back, Mike. You take care. Make us proud."

Mike nodded and patted his father on the shoulder. He turned to Jed and shrugged.

Bessie took Jed's hand. "I'm as upset as she is but I won't create a scene." Tears glistened her eyes. "You come home to me, boy."

"I will, Aunt Bess."

Jed lined up on the platform with Mike, the Jones brothers, and Teddy. Bart and Clay were drunk. Mister Jones and his wife stood apart from Enoch and Bessie.

"Where's Linda Sue?" Jed asked Mike.

"Yesterday she told me she's found another man who isn't going off to war."

A major from the 162nd Depot Brigade at Camp Pike stood before the men, beside a quartermaster sergeant, and a corporal who carried an American flag. The draftees raised their right hands and repeated the enlistment oath the major recited for them.

The major saluted them. "Welcome to the United States Army, men."

A long whistle blast sounded from a train approaching the platform. It had three stock cars behind two Jim Crow segregated passenger cars. As the train groaned to a stop, the stock car doors opened, and the animals were led in. Teddy's mule Old Clem refused to mount the ramp. The quartermaster sergeant beat him with a piece of rope.

Teddy hurried over.

"Step back, boy, the army is in charge here."

Jed started toward the sergeant but Enoch held his cane across Jed's chest to stop him.

"They're my mules. I'll take care of this." He limped forward and addressed the sergeant. "There's no call to berate the man, Sergeant. These are my mules and he is my foreman. He knows these animals and you would profit by his advice."

The sergeant peered at a medal pinned to Enoch's lapel. "Philippine service, I see. What was your rank, old timer?"

"My rank now is civilian, owner of those animals. I also pay taxes, so you work for me." Enoch stared him down. "Will you accept our help?"

"Perhaps we can benefit from the local expertise in this matter," the major said.

The sergeant braced to attention. "They say he's good with mules, sir." He stepped back and waved Teddy forward.

Teddy spoke to Old Clem, "We both in the army now old friend."

He loaded the animals into the cars.

The sergeant walked up to Enoch. "Thanks for the help, old timer."

"Thank Theodore. He did all the work."

The sergeant looked at Teddy then turned away and moved up the platform urging everyone to say their goodbyes, the train would leave in five minutes.

The major handed Enoch the bill of sale for the mules. "We inspected the stock and they are acceptable for our needs." The major regarded Enoch's medal. He had a similar blue and red ribbon on his blouse. "When did you serve in the Philippines, sir?"

"Oh-three."

The major nodded. "I served near the end in 1913." He looked at Enoch's cane, "Tough year 1903."

Enoch tapped his right leg with the cane. "Seems like only yesterday."

The major snapped to attention and touched the brim of his Montana campaign hat.

Enoch shifted his weight to his good leg so he could stand straighter and returned the salute. "You take good care of our youngsters, Major— colored and white."

As the major dropped his salute he nodded and joined the sergeant.

Teddy stepped in front of Enoch. "Mister James Enoch, you have always treated me fairly. Thank you."

"Good luck, Theodore."

Teddy turned to Jed. "I pray the Good Lord keep you safe, James Jedidiah."

"The same to you, Teddy," Jed said and held out his hand.

Teddy grasped Jed's hand. "Maybe one day we'll fight beside each other."

"I'd be honored," Jed said.

Jed walked back to Bessie who was crying. She grabbed his arm. "Take care my boy. I'll pray for you every waking minute."

Jed held her tight and whispered his love for her. He shook Enoch's hand. "I'll make you proud of me," he choked. "Take care of yourselves."

Enoch nodded his head, his face an emotionless mask.

The train whistle screeched.

Mister Jones stood next to his wife whose composure was gone. She wept into a silk handkerchief. After final kisses and handshakes, the men hurried to board as the train moved forward.

Dennis Jones ran along the platform and called to his brothers leaning out of a window beside Jed and Mike. "Don't win the war too fast. I want my chance to help out."

"Forget it," Bart shouted. "It'll all be over in a week after we get there."

Jed waved to Bessie who stood forlorn and small beside the wooden Enoch. She managed a feeble wave back as she dabbed at her eyes with her handkerchief.

The train wheels made a rhythmic racket.

The air crackled with excitement.

This was real.

Jed wondered if he would ever see his aunt and uncle again.

CHAPTER 4

May 25, 1918
CAMP PIKE, ARKANSAS

The train jolted through a series of switches and left the main line onto the grounds of Camp Pike, backing to a track between a warehouse and a passenger platform. A sergeant leaned in the door. "Grab your gear and get off the train. Line up in front of the platform and no talking."

Jed and Mike shuffled after the others across the platform and onto the ground. The Negro troops filed out of their Jim Crow car and stood near the stock cars. Mule hoofs clattered as handlers led the animals into the warehouse.

Their indoctrination into the army began with instructions from the sergeant, a burly man Jed nicknamed "Bruiser".

"Put those goddamn suitcases down in front of you. Now, dress up the line."

With much shouting and swearing Bruiser taught them how to dress their line and stand at attention. He had them pick up their belongings, faced them to the left and formed them into two parallel columns. They started off, Bruiser calling a simple cadence, "Left—left—left-right—left." They traveled over two hundred yards before all of them marched in step.

The Negro men followed another sergeant, struggling to stay in step.

Jed and the others passed through a grove of pine trees and emerged onto the main cantonment area, marching down a wide avenue flanked by two-dozen one-story wooden buildings. Behind the buildings stood endless rows of pyramid-shaped white tents. Bruiser halted them by a large warehouse and directed them inside.

Army clerks checked the new men in, confiscated their belongings, and assigned them their identification tags. Medics examined them and gave them an injection in each arm.

They passed by long rows of shelves from which they drew uniforms, hats, boots, web belts, canteens, packs, shelter halves, raincoats, overcoats, field manuals, toilet articles, pillows, blankets, and a duffle bag. The men staggered under the loads.

Bruiser led them through the maze of tents. Jed and Mike dumped their gear on two cots in a tent and assembled outside with the others.

The rest of the day consisted of lectures on customs and courtesies, wearing the uniform including wrapping wool puttee strips from boot to knee as leggings, then an hour of fatigue duty picking up cigarette butts in the common areas.

They spent the last hour of the day sitting on their cots studying their Soldier's Handbook with Bruiser there to keep them from falling asleep.

Bruiser turned the lights out at 10 P.M. and the men dropped back on their cots in exhaustion. Jed was asleep before the final note of Taps sounded.

Reveille was a jolt the next morning that started a dreamless instant after Taps. Before the first three bugle notes had sounded, Bruiser was in the tent, banging on a metal bucket and shouting for them to fall out, on the double, in their boots and underwear.

After calisthenics and a breakfast of beans, cornbread, and coffee, the training in the school of the soldier began.

They spent the next three weeks marching, digging ditches, making beds, polishing boots, saluting, assembling the field pack, more marching, digging trenches, filling sandbags, wearing gas masks, learning first aid and field hygiene, and more digging.

There were not enough rifles for everyone, so they used four-foot-long boards carved into the shape of a rifle. They used these "suitable substitutes" to practice the manual of arms.

Bruiser led them through the commands. "Present arms! Order arms! Right shoulder arms!"

The training was unrelenting.

There was always more marching.

Bruiser became a hated man.

Jed put on muscle and increased his endurance. He and the others became a team, marching to a synchronized cadence, a gliding rectangle of men responding to orders, shifting and changing direction as one.

CHAPTER 5
JUNE 19, 1918
CAMP PIKE, ARKANSAS

When he had free time, Jed visited a Salvation Army canteen and read a weekly tabloid, The Stars and Stripes, intended for the troops in France, but also available in the United States training camps. The newspaper contained tips on regulation changes, tales of battles "over there", cartoons, poems written by AEF soldiers, health issues, and reports on recreation and entertainment. There were also stories of the award of medals like the Distinguished Service Cross. Jed looked up the word posthumous in the library's dictionary and found that some awards for gallant action had cost the recipient everything.

The Stars and Stripes

AMERICANS HELP TO STEM GERMAN DRIVE ON PARIS

American machine gunners were called upon to join with the French in holding the ground south and west of Château-Thierry. To gain time for the defense of the Marne, they were hurried forward at top speed and had scarcely piled out of the lorries, and been jubilantly greeted by the battle-weary poilus, when they were bidden to cross the river and engage the enemy, then entering Château-Thierry.

Though the bridge was under enemy fire, one section of the gunners managed to get across by a series of rapid dashes and, once there, to clear the way for the rest and later for such a rush of French Colonials as drove the Germans clean out of the town.

"Courage Beyond All Praise"

In a French order dealing with the part that American machine gunners played in the battle for Château-Thierry occurs the following:

"The courage of the Americans was beyond all praise. The Colonials themselves, though accustomed to acts of bravery, were struck by the wonderful morale in the face of fire and the extraordinary sang froid of their allies."

THE STARS AND STRIPES: FRANCE, FRIDAY, JUNE 7, 1918, pages 1 and 2

CHAPTER 6
JUNE 28, 1918
CAMP PIKE, ARKANSAS

Bruiser harangued the men about the most minor of infractions. Jed's uncle had been a harsh taskmaster but even he went to sleep at night.

The army never slept.

Bruiser dreamed up a phony inspection failure by Jed and ordered him to run around the company area ten times with a nine-pound iron bar extended above his head. After he finished, Jed stood panting and sweating. He dropped the bar at Bruiser's feet.

"Pick that rifle up."

Jed was incredulous. "It's a bar of iron, not a rifle."

"It's the same weight as a Model of 1917 Enfield. You'll treat it as a rifle and will carry it with care and keep it off the ground." Jed hesitated. "Pick it up."

Jed picked up the heavy bar.

Bruiser took a half step back. "Attention." He ran Jed through the manual of arms with the iron bar then dismissed him with a rueful grin and the opinion Jed might finish the course of training. It was small consolation as Jed dragged himself to his cot and collapsed, his arms aching.

Mike came into the tent with the others from their detail digging rifle pits. "Come on, Jed, let's go shower and get chow before manual study this afternoon."

"I'm too beat up for food."

Mike stripped off his shirt. His muscles bulged.

"You're fresh for someone who's been out digging holes in the ground," Jed said.

Mike grabbed Jed's hand and pulled him to the edge of the cot. "You weren't the only one singled out today. Bruiser came along and said I wasn't digging fast enough so he ordered me to run around the rifle range for an hour holding two full sandbags. I did seven miles of roadwork pumping those sand bags up and down. It's the best workout I've had since we got here."

Jed stood up and undressed. "I did the same thing with an iron bar *rifle*."

Mike shadowboxed. "Bruiser says they'll train the boys how to box. He said it's good for balance and building aggressiveness. At the end, there'll be a tournament and the grand prize is a twelve-hour pass. If I keep getting in Dutch, I ought to be in fighting trim by the tournament." He feigned a few more punches. "Let's go."

Mike had a talent for turning mule shit into fertilizer. Jed grabbed his towel and followed him to the showers.

After chow, Bruiser led them to a warehouse with iron bars over the windows. A sign stenciled over the door read ARMORY. The group's sullen attitude changed to one of excitement as they filed into the warehouse and deposited their "broomsticks" in large bins. They were each issued a factory-new Model of 1917 Enfield rifle. Jed relished the feel of the smooth black walnut stock and cool metal barrel, the tool of a soldier.

The Enfield was a bolt-action repeating rifle loaded by stripper clips of five rounds pushed down through the space left by the open bolt. An ordnance sergeant demonstrated the loading technique. After dismantling, cleaning, and reassembling the rifles three times, the platoon assembled outside and ran through the manual of arms until they performed with precision and snap. They returned the weapons to the armory and spent the rest of the evening studying the rifle manual.

In the morning, they retrieved their rifles and marched to the firing range where they received a safety briefing on the commands and rules of the range. They proceeded through a course of fire from single shots to full magazines of five rounds. Jed had fired over the plain barrel of a shotgun or through the open sights of his grandfather's cavalry carbine. He preferred the Enfield combat sights.

At the end of the course, they fired ten rounds for qualification. Jed worked through the ten rounds and grouped his shots near the center of the target.

Mike shot a wider group but all of his bullets had hit the target.

Bruiser declared them both qualified.

"You won this contest, Jed."

"Your best bullet is your right hand."

Mike winked. "It's hard to miss from two feet away."

CHAPTER 7

JULY 4, 1918
CAMP PIKE, ARKANSAS

The Stars and Stripes

STALLING BANNED IN ARMY MATCHES
Real Honest Boxing Called For in American Training Camps

[BY CABLE TO THE STARS AND STRIPES.]

AMERICA, June 27. - Real boxing matches, not the kind where one boxer and then the other stands back and waits for his opponent to do the leading and fighting while he stands back on the defensive, are the kind wanted in the Army training camps.

It is this type of boxing that will aid the boxers in their real warfare, and the War Department's Commission in charge of camp activities has promulgated new boxing rules, putting a premium on aggressive attack as against defense and discouraging backstepping, covering up and other purely defensive tactics.

THE STARS AND STRIPES: FRANCE, FRIDAY, JUNE 28, 1918, page 6

The trainees marched to the warehouse area where they formed up in line of platoons parallel to a railroad siding running the length of a long warehouse platform decked out in red, white and blue bunting. A mile away behind a stand of trees, a steam engine chuffed puffs of smoke. The pure white noon sky dazzled a promise of the heat of July and a warm breeze stirred insects and weeds in small dusty tornadoes.

The company commander, Captain Baldwin, and Bruiser stood at ease in front of Jed, Mike, and the Jones brothers in the front rank of Second Platoon at the center of the formation. A squad of Negro soldiers stood at rest near the end of the tracks with coils of rope and buckets of water.

Teddy nodded to Jed across the gap between them.

Colonel Fine W. Smith, the camp commander, waited on the platform with a stuffy-looking man in an ill-fitting suit.

The brigade band stood to the right, brass instruments gleaming in the sunshine.

Three whistle blasts to the right preceded the snarl of the steam engine backing slowly. Two stock cars, a Pullman car, a flatcar, and a mail car coupled behind the tender and engine emerged from the woods. Two large wooden crates and a blue 1915 Cadillac seven-passenger open touring car sat on the flatcar.

"Now, I'm the blue-eyed baboon," Clay Jones said.

After the train stopped, Teddy and his squad moved to the stock cars and guided a dozen mules down a ramp at the end of the platform, gave the animals a drink of water, and led them to the stables.

A squad of men from First Platoon untied and opened the wooden crates on the flatcar while men from the training headquarters loaded bags of mail onto a horse-drawn wagon and disappeared toward the post office.

Alan Jones left the passenger car followed by his little brother Dennis. They untied their father's car and jumped in. Alan backed the car onto the platform and drove it down the ramp the mules had used, whipping it around the end of the train and parking it in front of the assembled company. He climbed out of the car and wiped the dust off the fenders with a towel. Dennis waved to his brothers who stood red-faced in the front row. He came to attention and threw an exaggerated salute at the assembled soldiers.

The captain ordered present arms, and the band played a flourish as the elder Jones exited the Pullman and greeted the senior officers. He wore a white linen suit topped by a yellow straw skimmer. His red brocade vest glowed like the throat of a hummingbird and vied with the gleam of the three-carat diamond stud nestled below the dimple of his cobalt blue cravat. He looked like a Dixie Democrat on a whistle-stop campaign.

Colonel Smith returned the salute of the company. Captain Baldwin commanded order arms and then rest.

The colonel stepped forward onto the flat car. "Men, on this glorious summer day when we celebrate our country's independence, I am accompanied by two distinguished gentlemen who will have a positive impact on your training. To my left is Mister Joseph Lee, the local chairman of the Commission on Training Camp Activities, the CTCA."

"He's the one closing the whorehouses in North Little Rock," Mike whispered.

"To my right is Mister George Bradford Jones of Pocahontas, Arkansas who has made a generous donation of 200 pairs of boxing gloves so we may keep physically fit and promote the aggressive fighting spirit we will need in the offensives to come."

Bruiser led the applause as Jones stepped forward and waved to the men. During a short speech, Jones took the credit for his gift but acknowledged James Enoch Martin for providing many needed animals for army work and thanked Patrick Sean O'Kean, Mike's father, for helping to pack up the boxing gloves for their shipment to Camp Pike. It was too bad, he said, those other two prominent citizens couldn't be there to receive the accolades of the soldiers, but he would pass along their thanks.

He ended with a reference to the noble goal of victory they were all working toward. He saluted the colonel and invited the men to gather around, inspect the gloves, and take a ride in his Cadillac.

Captain Baldwin dismissed the formation, and the men surged toward the car. Alan Jones rolled back the cloth top and took the wheel. With Dennis perched on his lap, he took groups of soldiers on a tour of the nearby camp area. The men waved their hats as they skittered past the milling crowd. Dennis beamed beneath Bart's campaign hat, the front brim folded up and back by the wind stream. The band played patriotic music and a rolling kitchen served lemonade and cookies.

Mike and a civilian Jed didn't know joined Jones and the colonel beside the flatcar where an army photographer took a picture of the four men. They all shook hands, then Mike led the stranger to where Jed stood to the side. The man looked as if he'd been carved out of an oak stump by a sharp ax. His brown-eyed gaze was clear and direct, his handshake commanding but not overbearing. His twisted nose marked him as a boxer.

"Jed, I'd like you to meet Richard 'Dickie the Decker' Parks: sixteen, one, and one in his professional career with fourteen knockouts."

"Pleased to meet you, Mister Parks."

"Most folks call me Decker."

"I fought Decker to a draw last year over in Little Rock," Mike said.

Decker grabbed his chin and worked his jaw back and forth. "This big, dumb Irishman has a bomb for a right hand. We call him Thunder Fist O'Kean."

"I never went full pro like you," Mike said.

"You made money betting on yourself."

"Then I lost it at the casino in Hot Springs."

Jed glanced at Mike who shrugged.

Decker slapped Mike on the shoulder. "You're in good shape, Irish. We'll have fun training these lads."

"Decker's in charge of the boxing training," Mike said. "I'll assist him and I put in a good word for you as an assistant too, Jed."

"I'm not good enough, Mike."

"You're better than all these other guys. It'll be fun."

Jed sipped the tart lemonade and watched as Mike and Decker stood with easy confidence, relaxed yet alert, two athletes, immense power under careful control.

Mike's close identification with Decker left Jed with a twinge of jealousy, but he also felt pride that Mike found him worthy to join the training cadre.

After an hour, the bugler sounded assembly, and the company formed ranks. The Cadillac sat tied down to the flat car. Mister Jones and his sons Alan and Dennis leaned out a window of the Pullman car. Jones waved his skimmer and beamed like a candidate who had won all the delegates.

The band played The Stars and Stripes Forever and the men presented arms.

The engineer slipped his brakes and drove the train down the spur.

As the company marched away, to the command "Squads Left— Forward March," the train whistle saluted them. The chugging of the engine increased in tempo as the train sped off into the distance.

35

For the next two weeks Decker led the afternoon physical fitness sessions. His friendly and direct approach appealed to Jed and most of the other men. Each night Mike gave Jed another lesson and with the new knowledge Jed stayed one step ahead of his students.

For most of the men, the boxing sessions degenerated into a general melee with men throwing wild roundhouse punches or cowering behind gloves held before their faces. Decker swam through the sea of bodies exhorting individuals to assume an aggressive stance and punch their opponent. "Pershing wants aggressors not defenders," he shouted. "The best way to keep from getting hit is to hit him first."

Engineers constructed a boxing ring outside the gymnasium with bleachers around it. Decker created a list of the more promising members of the company with the goal of declaring a camp champion. Mike demurred because of his semi-pro status but Decker would have none of it.

"I want these men to go up against some real skill."

Jed also tried to keep out of the tournament. He preferred the role of assistant coach and instructor. He also wanted to avoid the chance of having to fight Mike.

Decker insisted he take part.

"Jed, you're one of the top men in skills and I need you. Your only real weakness is you fight defensively. You need to learn to take a punch and retaliate. Be more aggressive if you expect to win."

"I've been telling him that all his life," Mike said.

Jed reluctantly accepted.

"Did you select Bart and Clay Jones, too?" Jed asked Mike.

"No, they're brawlers, not boxers."

Decker had selected 16 men to compete for the camp championship. He refereed with Colonel Smith, Captain Baldwin, and Bruiser as judges. Bruiser also kept time.

Colonel Smith addressed the assembled troops. "Men, General Pershing and the officers and men of the American Expeditionary Force in France are urging us to send them more men as soon as possible. Therefore, we will complete the tournament in one day. The preliminary bouts will be two rounds, the semifinal bouts three, and the championship bout will be four rounds. Beginning tomorrow, drill, maneuver, and marksmanship will be our primary concerns. The war is not waiting for us. Good luck, gentlemen and let the tournament begin."

36

In his two preliminary bouts Mike won on points but allowed the weaker men to get in a shot or two.

Jed asked him why.

"I don't want to humiliate the guys. If I can give them a little confidence, maybe they'll do better in the war."

Jed made it to the semifinals winning both bouts on points. He was nimble enough to move in, score effective jabs, and bounce away.

Decker wasn't happy. "Be more aggressive."

Jed's semifinal opponent was a red-headed Irish kid from First Platoon named Finney, who was Jed's size and one of the better students. If Jed won this next bout and Mike won his, he would have to fight Mike.

Jed fended Finney off for two rounds scoring hard jabs but not committing.

Mike approached Jed before the third round began. "You're ahead on points. Hit this guy hard a couple of times and he'll quit. Be more forceful."

"You want to clobber me in the finals?"

Mike's gaze was level. "I want to see you survive, Jed."

The bell rang.

Finney bull-rushed Jed, who backed away from the jabs and ducked a roundhouse, rising and planting a hard, right-hand punch to Finney's face. Jed followed with a hard left and right combination.

Finney flopped back on the canvas and lay gasping for air.

Decker motioned Jed to a neutral corner and counted.

Finney waved him off. "No more."

Decker waved the fight over and raised Jed's gloved right hand. Second Platoon erupted in applause and whistling.

Bart and Clay Jones sat on their hands.

Jed climbed out of the ring and walked past Mike.

"I told you so," Mike said.

"I don't need you solving all my problems for me." Jed walked away, untying his glove laces with his teeth.

He sat on the first row of bleachers and watched Mike enter the ring. One recruit acting as Jed's second gave him a bottle of water.

"Why so glum, buddy? You made it to the finals."

"Yeah," Jed said spitting water on the ground. *Then, why do I feel like shit?*

In the ring, Mike's opponent, a well-muscled heavyweight named Hunt, advanced with confidence. The two men felt each other out with stiff jabs for half a round until Mike moved in with a series of lefts and rights. Hunt covered up and then backed Mike off with a strong counterpunch. Hunt pressed forward without finesse and hammered at Mike with wild roundhouses and uppercuts, one of which stunned Mike. Mike responded with a wicked right cross that staggered Hunt as the bell rang.

In the second round Hunt was more cautious and jabbed, wary of Mike's right hand. Mike landed solid body blows but when the bell rang ending round two, Jed figured the bout was even on points.

Mike sat on the stool in his corner and took a sip of water from the second, who wiped off his face with a towel. "How are you doing, Mike?"

"I need to finish this guy quick before he hurts me."

The bell rang and the two fighters met Decker in the center of the ring. Mike attacked with a rapid series of strong jabs which caused Hunt to back into a corner and cover up. Mike hit Hunt in the body to lower his guard then followed a stiff left jab with a right cross. Hunt fell to his knees then sank to all fours, breathing hard and shaking his head. He sat on the canvas as Decker counted him out.

Decker finished helping Hunt from the ring and took up his position at the center of the canvas. "We'll take a fifteen-minute break and then begin the final bout: Martin versus O'Kean."

Mike approached Jed, who stared at the ground. "Let's show them some good boxing. I won't go to the body. You're not trained for it" He turned and climbed into the ring.

Jed's second laced up his gloves and gave him a sip of water. Jed took several deep breaths trying to quiet his nervous stomach and then climbed into the ring. Mike stood relaxed in his corner.

Bruiser rang the bell.

Decker motioned the two to the center of the ring and gave his instructions. "Four two-minute rounds scored on points for an effective punch or knockdown. The three-knockdown rule is in effect. At the sound of the bell, come out boxing."

Jed looked into the crowd. The Jones brothers glared at him and shook their heads.

Mike held his gloves out. Jed touched them with his gloves and returned to his corner. When Jed turned back toward the ring, his stomach had settled. He felt calm and resigned.

The bell rang and Jed advanced on Mike, his guard raised. Mike started in with a series of sharp left jabs. Jed fended them off with his own left hand. Mike threw two hard lefts and started a right cross. Jed stepped back and dodged left and Mike missed, but Jed was out of position and off balance and couldn't counterpunch.

Mike moved in.

Jed backed off.

The sequence repeated with the same result, the crowd murmuring its disapproval.

Bart Jones booed. "Come on ladies, fight."

Jed gathered himself and blocked Mike's jabs. He faked a blow to the body forcing Mike's glove down then hit Mike above the left eye with his right, ducking under Mike's left counterpunch. It wasn't a full force punch but Jed had scored.

The crowd stopped grumbling and applauded.

Mike came in again. He opened Jed's guard and planted a solid left jab over Jed's right eye knocking Jed flat on his back. When Decker counted to four, the end of round bell rang.

"Are you OK?" Decker asked.

"First time he ever hit me so hard."

Decker helped Jed to his feet and steadied him as he sat down, looking into Jed's eyes. Jed stared back, his head throbbing.

"You're all right. Keep boxing and don't back step. Mike is giving you an honest match." Decker slapped Jed on the shoulder.

Jed accepted a sip of water from the second who sponged off Jed's face and wiped him down. A few deep breaths cleared Jed's head. Mike had played it straight, taking what Jed gave him.

The bell rang and Jed stood up. He supposed there were worse things than getting your brains beat out by your best friend but couldn't think of any right then.

Jed approached Mike, covering up. Mike jabbed and Jed backed up, jabbed again and Jed backed up again.

Mike's shoulders slumped and his hands lowered. "Come on, box."

Mike was stronger, but Jed was quick. He jumped forward and hit Mike in the face with a right, left, right combination. Jed pressed his advantage as Mike backed into a corner and covered up, allowing Jed to punch his arms and gloves, to the cheers of the crowd. He lowered his aim and gave Mike a hard shot to the ribs with no clear effect.

Bruiser slapped the canvas. "Ten seconds."

Mike moved forward out of the corner and, when Jed missed with a right jab, hit him in the ribs with a left. The air exploded from Jed's lungs and he collapsed onto the canvas as the end of round bell rang.

Jed flopped onto his stool, gasping for breath.

Decker came over. "The bell saved you twice but you have two knockdowns. One more and you lose by a technical knockout."

Jed's body ached and his head throbbed, the surroundings spinning and indistinct. He wanted no more. As the second wiped Jed's face, Jed grabbed the towel and tossed it into the center of the ring.

The crowd booed.

When Decker raised Mike's hand in victory, they cheered.

The second untied Jed's gloves and gave him a long drink of water. "You put up a good fight, Jed. No sense getting beat to a pulp."

Jed shook his head. He had quit, unable to beat his best friend.

Mike tossed his gloves to his second, walked over, and kneeled down. "Why?"

"I'm done."

"You did well. You tagged me good a couple of times."

"I wanted to win at least one round but I can't beat you."

Bart and Clay Jones rushed up. "I knew you were chicken," Clay said.

"No wonder I've been whipping your ass since we were kids," Bart said. To Mike, he said, "You should have knocked him out like you did Hunt."

"This is a boxing exhibition," Mike said. "Hunt thought it was a prize fight."

"You still let Jed off easy," Clay said.

"If either of you want to come in here and finish the bout, I'm available."

The Jones brothers said nothing. As they turned to go, Bart said to Clay, "He'll surrender when the first shot is fired."

Jed stared at the canvas between his feet and flinched as Mike reached toward him.

"I feel bad, Mike. Leave me alone for a while, OK?"

"Sure, Jed, sorry about the body blow. I just reacted."

Jed waved him off. "My mistake…"

Mike climbed out of the ring. Men from Second Platoon shook his hand and patted him on the back.

Jed showered, dressed, and ate chow in a corner by himself. At mail call, he received a letter from his uncle. Jed sat on a packing crate behind the chow hall and opened the envelope.

Mike sat down on the other end of the crate. "Nothing for me today," he said.

"My uncle is bringing the last of our mules he sold to the army," Jed said. "He'll be at the North Little Rock train station at noon Sunday, the 28th."

When Jed looked up Mike was holding a folded piece of paper toward him.

"What's that?"

"It's the twelve-hour pass I got for winning the tournament."

"I can't take your pass."

Mike grinned. "I have no reason to go into town. They closed down the whorehouses and poker rooms. Take it. Visit with your uncle. I'll clear it with Bruiser."

Jed hesitated, but took the pass. "Thanks."

"You did OK, today, Jed. It was good to see you get aggressive." Mike slapped Jed on the knee. "We'll pull through this war all right, the two of us helping each other."

"Sure, Mike," Jed said. *I hope so.*

CHAPTER 8

JULY 23, 1918

CAMP PIKE, ARKANSAS

The colonel asked for privates to volunteer for immediate duty in France. Volunteers were relieved from fatigue duty and would get two weeks of intensive weapons and maneuver training. Their units in France would finish their training.

"Come on, Jed, let's go now before it's over. Our guys over there are kicking the Kaiser's ass." Mike shadow boxed Jed. "The Jones brothers are going. Do you want them to get all the glory?"

"What glory? Men died. They need us to replace them."

"This is a replacement training camp."

Jed didn't like the idea of volunteering but Mike had never led Jed astray. He was always right about everything.

"OK, Champ."

Bruiser approved the transfer of Mike's pass and on Sunday morning Jed started for the Camp Pike front gate, a haversack hanging by his left hip.

As he crossed the camp, he walked by the boxing ring where Mike and Decker instructed a group of trainees.

Mike jumped down and trotted over to Jed. "Say hello to your uncle for me."

"I will, Mike. Thanks again for the pass."

"Don't look so glum, pal."

"My uncle can be a hard man, but I really need to see him before I go." Jed had a letter for Aunt Bessie in the haversack. In it he had told her he loved her, that he would take care of himself, and that she shouldn't worry. He knew she would, but he needed to tell her. "Anything I can give Uncle Enoch for your family?"

"I dropped a letter in the post office this morning."

"I'll be back before Taps. See you then."

Mike jogged back to the ring, light on his feet as the space between them widened.

Jed shuffled to the camp gate and showed his pass. As he started down the road, a truck pulled out after him. The driver stopped and offered him a lift. Jed climbed in.

"Where are you going?" The driver had the five stripes of a battalion supply sergeant.

"I'm headed for the North Little Rock train station."

"I'm going right by there." The sergeant looked over at Jed. "You're Martin, right? You fought in the camp boxing final."

"Yes, Sergeant, and I quit." Jed turned away and stared out the truck window.

"You put up a decent fight. It was clear O'Kean was more experienced."

"He used to box semi-pro."

"You know him?"

"He's my best friend."

They drove on in silence.

"Are you going over soon?" the sergeant asked.

Jed nodded.

"Good luck. Keep your head down."

They stopped in front of the train station.

"Thanks," Jed said as he climbed out. The truck pulled away leaving fine dust hanging in the air.

Jed entered the Choctaw Route Station and passed through the lobby out to the passenger platform. He sat on a high-backed bench facing the tracks, pulled a canteen out of the haversack and took a drink of water.

He had a copy of the latest Stars and Stripes. At the top center of the front page was a picture of a Marine named John Kukoski who earned the Distinguished Service Cross at Chateau-Thierry for charging a machine gun alone and capturing the gun, crew, and an officer. Another article was an account by a soldier who lost his captain and 15 men of his unit to a single artillery shell, a shocking and sobering story.

The Americans were always depicted as upright, determined and heroic, the Germans as small, hollow-eyed, brutish cowards.

The sun rose higher, and the air grew warmer.

Jed dozed off.

He woke to the sound of a train whistle to the north, stood, straightened his blouse, and put the canteen and newspaper back in the haversack.

A group of six Negro soldiers, led by a white captain and sergeant on horseback, stood at the far end of the platform. They carried halters and ropes.

Teddy wasn't with them.

The whistle sounded again, and the train glided into the station, the engine panting and blowing a strong odor of burned coal and hot oil. The train was short: a passenger car, a flat car loaded with lumber and a stock car at the end.

Enoch climbed gingerly down from the engine cab. He waved to the engineer, limped over to Jed, and laid a wrapped package on the bench. He didn't offer his hand to shake.

"I'll be back directly," was all he said.

He hustled as fast as his game leg and cane allowed toward the lone stock car at the end of the train. The Negroes unloaded the mules, and the sergeant dismounted and inspected them. The captain saluted Enoch and dismounted as well. They conversed for a few moments, Enoch gesturing toward the lumber car with his cane. The sergeant approached the captain and spoke. The captain nodded and handed Enoch some papers then mounted his horse and led the detail around the end of the station toward the camp.

Enoch walked back, stuffing the papers into the inside pocket of his jacket. He was wearing his Philippine service medal. "This is a special train, not on the schedule," he said. "Mister Jones sold the army some lumber and asked me to be his agent."

The train engineer sounded the whistle. The steam cylinders wheezed, the wheels slipped, and then dug in. The train lurched forward and out of the station.

"The engineer is an old friend of your grandfather Hale," Enoch said. "He let me ride up front. They're going over to the freight yard to unload the lumber and change crews."

Enoch looked tired, his three-day stubble darkened by coal dust, his eyes red-rimmed from smoke, but the deep silver centers still clear and unblemished. Jed smelled moonshine on his breath.

Enoch sat on the bench. "Would you get me a cup of coffee?"

44

Inside the terminal was an urn supplied by The Salvation Army with free coffee for past and present service personnel. Jed filled two cups and returned one to Enoch. He sat on the bench two feet from his uncle.

Enoch pushed the package toward Jed. "Bess sent you a tin of rhubarb pie."

There was a message on the package. *"Mit diesem Paket kann ich meine letzte Pflicht, mein kleiner Junge, bis er zu mir zurück."* (With this package, I do my last duty to my little boy, until he returns to me).

Jed couldn't speak.

He swallowed hard and found his voice. "How are you?"

"Tolerable, I suppose. I expect only half a bale per acre this season so I can spare the mules. I don't know if I'll go ahead next year. I may sell the farm and retire."

"I'd stay and help you but I got drafted."

"You did," Enoch said. He reached into his coat pocket and pulled out his pipe.

"We're shipping out in two weeks."

Enoch paused with a lighted match. "Is your training over so soon?"

"They asked for volunteers and will cram as much training into us as they can before we go. We'll get the rest of our training over there."

"Sounds like the army." The pipe flared to life. A cloud of sweet smoke drifted on the slight breeze. "You say you volunteered. That's a first for you."

"Mike suggested it. He said we should get over there before it's over."

Enoch stared into the distance. Whistles sounded far away, steam engines chugged, and couplings rattled open and closed. The sun was overhead, and it was hot, even under the station awning. Jed pulled his canteen out and offered Enoch a drink. Enoch drank a sip, handing it back. Jed drank, the water refreshing though warm.

"If you're training hard, how did you get off base?"

"Mike got a pass for winning the camp boxing championship. He gave it to me."

"Mike's a good boy," Enoch said. "You and Mike remind me of Seth and me at your age." He reached into his lower left jacket pocket and produced a silver flask. He glanced left and right. The Newberry Act had passed in 1915 outlawing the manufacture and sale of alcohol in Arkansas and the rest of the country was debating prohibition. Enoch

45

poured a shot of moonshine into his coffee cup. He handed the flask to Jed who did the same and handed the flask back.

"You should never volunteer," Enoch said drinking the spiked coffee.

"I should never volunteer?" Jed stared open-mouthed. "You gave me grief for waiting to be drafted."

"Seth and I volunteered and look what happened to us. He's dead and I'm crippled."

"I'll never understand you," Jed said snatching the flask out of Enoch's hand. He didn't care if some temperance minded busybody saw. He tilted the flask up and drank the moonshine straight. Enoch took the flask back, drained it, and put it back in his pocket. He pulled another flask from the left back pocket of his pants, drank again, then put the flask away. "I'll save the rest for the ride home."

Jed picked up Bessie's package and ripped it open. The pie tasted sweet and sour and warm and made him smile.

He finished the pie and coffee, his mind buzzing from the moonshine, his guard against his uncle relaxed.

He turned and confronted Enoch.

"Tell me how my father and mother died—no bullshit, no family myths."

Enoch took his time to refill and light his pipe and then leaned back and started in. "I don't like to talk about Seth." He took a deep breath, his gaze far away. "Seth's death was as pathetic and heroic as anyone's. We were fighting the Moros on the Island of Mindanao in the Philippines and Seth and I fought back-to-back in a Moro ambush. I killed two of 'em but not before one sliced me in the groin and another one stabbed Seth in the chest with a spear. I reached under Seth's shirt for this." He pulled out a small pistol with a loop of leather thong tied to a ring soldered to the pistol butt. "It's a .41 caliber Remington Model 95 rimfire Derringer, two-shot. Seth always carried it around his neck under his shirt." Enoch's eyes misted. "I blew the Moro's head off, but it was too late. Seth died in my arms. He made me promise to look after your mother."

"And me," Jed said.

"I had to look after my blood kin."

Enoch showed how to load the pistol then unloaded it and showed Jed how to fire it. He put the two bullets into a small leather pouch and handed it and the Derringer to Jed. "You have four bullets. Don't let the army know about it. They'll take it away from you."

Jed repeated Enoch's demonstration and dry fired the pistol twice. Satisfied, he put it in his haversack. "Thank you. I hope I never have to use it."

"I hope so too."

The train growled back from the freight yard.

Jed and Enoch stood.

"What's it going to be like?" Jed asked.

Enoch shook his head. "It will be bad, I'm sure, but every generation has its own type of war." He looked Jed in the eye. "War changes everything for everybody—for the worse. It will change you too. How? I don't know."

The conductor called all aboard. As Enoch started away, Jed reached out and stopped him. "What about my mother?"

Enoch stared at the ground. "After Seth died, depression took Rose. She may have fallen in the river by accident or killed herself. I don't know."

"Aunt Bess knows. She was there."

"She won't say. It's the only important thing she ever kept from me."

"What do you think?" Jed insisted.

"I hate to say it. I think she killed herself, Jed."

"Why would she abandon me?"

Enoch paused then said, "Maybe the pain was too much."

"Aunt Bess said you all had a beautiful life."

"We did when we were carefree kids, but, when you get married, have children, go to war, and lose someone, things change."

Jed stuck out his hand.

Enoch took it. "Take care of yourself—son."

Jed pulled his letter to Bessie from the haversack. "This is for Aunt Bess."

Enoch took the letter and put it in his jacket with the army papers. "Write when you can and let us know how you're doing."

"Some say it'll be over soon after all of us are over there," Jed said.

"I wouldn't bet on it. We took years to get the Moros to behave. I doubt that these Germans will be different and listen to reason."

"When do you think it'll be over?"

Enoch stared into the distance. "When the last man who's supposed to die there dies."

The engineer sounded his whistle, and the conductor called all aboard again. Enoch hobbled as fast as he could and climbed to the passenger car step. The engineer slipped the brakes, and the train started up the track.

Jed came to attention and saluted Enoch who stood straight and saluted with his cane as if it were a sword. The train disappeared around a curve and behind a stand of trees.

Jed's departure for war brought back painful memories for Enoch, but one thing hadn't changed. Enoch always referred to his brother as Seth, never as Jed's father.

Over the next two weeks the volunteers spent every morning at the rifle range and afternoons in the field learning hand signals, small unit tactics, and defense against gas attack. They threw hand grenades, qualified with the 12-gauge Winchester Model 1897 Trench shotgun, and did bayonet thrusting drills against straw-stuffed dummies.

They received their travel orders, packed their gear, and marched to the train station in North Little Rock where they began their travel east.

CHAPTER 9

AUGUST 13, 1918
ON THE TRAIN TO CAMP MERRITT, NJ

The Stars and Stripes

MENTIONED IN ORDERS
NEW HEADGEAR

The "Oversea Cap," the latest thing in military headgear, has been officially adopted as part of the uniform for officers, soldiers and other uniformed members of the A.E.F. ...When the cap is issued to a man, he will be expected to turn in his service hat to the nearest Quartermaster depot.

THE STARS AND STRIPES: FRANCE, FRIDAY, FEBRUARY 8, 1918, page 4.

The train ride cross country was tedious. Jed read back issues of The Stars and Stripes and stared out the window. He was glad that Bart and Clay Jones had selected a different train car and that he had Mike to keep him company.

Jed pulled out the latest letter from Bessie.

July 29, 1918
Dearest Jed,

I wanted to write to you since I don't know when you'll be going overseas. Enoch says it will be soon.
I'll pray for you every day and ask the Lord to bring you back undamaged in body, mind, and soul.
Enoch fell off his horse last week and re-injured his leg. I fear something is wrong but he won't tell me about it. All I seem able to do is pray and hope my prayers are heard.
Take care of yourself. Avoid sick men and wash your hands often. I'm helping out at an influenza clinic in Pocahontas two days a week and this is the advice the doctors give us. We wear masks and gloves and so far, all of my coworkers are well. Remember that we love you,
Aunt Bess

Jed tucked the letter away and settled back for the long ride.

They ate doughnuts and drank coffee and on two occasions had roast beef sandwiches provided by the Salvation Army. The train made no stops except for water and fuel.

The country rolling past the window in the rural areas seemed familiar, but, in the cities, like Saint Louis, Chicago, Cleveland and Philadelphia, Jed marveled at the vast warehouses and manufacturing plants, huge rail yards packed with thousands of cars to carry equipment and supplies, and tall buildings, ready to topple over from their great heights.

Jed gazed out the window wondering what he had gotten into by volunteering.

CHAPTER 10
AUGUST 17, 1918
CAMP MERRITT, NJ

When they got to Camp Merritt, New Jersey, the scale of the effort exploded before them. Tens of thousands of men moved in groups in all directions. Trucks piled high with cargo plied the streets amid herds of horses and mules being driven toward the docks.

They boarded a ferry that took them down the Hudson River to the pier in Hoboken where swarms of soldiers crowded up the gangways onto an enormous ship.

The SS George Washington left the dock and joined several other ships and escorts in a convoy that headed out into the Atlantic Ocean. Jed was seasick for the first two days but then adapted to the swaying deck. Mike adapted a day later.

The voyage settled into tedium: cramped quarters, average food, calisthenics, physical exams, and study of army manuals.

The ten-day trip was uneventful except for one supposed sighting of a submarine periscope. Destroyer escorts accompanying the convoy circled the pod of ships whooping sirens. At one point a destroyer fired a deck gun three times and dropped two depth bombs. Some wags adopted "periscope off the port bow" as a signal for senior officers or NCOs in the area.

A lookout sighted the coast of France on August 27.

They were in the war zone

CHAPTER 11

AUGUST 27, 1918

BREST, FRANCE

At the bustling port of Brest an administrative corporal gave them their travel instructions.

"You're going to Brouville, the headquarters of the 147th Infantry Regiment of the 37th Division. You'll take a train to Azerailles. After that you hitchhike."

At the train station Jed and Mike settled into a second-class compartment. The train rolled for a half hour and stopped to load more men, the pattern for the next two days.

Jed read a headline from The Stars and Stripes. "*Villages linked in record time by railway unit.* It seems they laid 2.69 miles of track in just over seven hours."

"They must be out in front of this train," Mike said.

The French countryside sliding by the window reminded Jed of home, with rolling hills, small stands of trees, and herds of cows grazing in pastures, but no cotton fields, only grass and summer wheat.

At Azerailles they hitched a ride in the cab of a supply truck going to Brouville.

As they traveled, the surroundings changed. Fields under cultivation became burned-out houses poking up through weeds, small towns reduced to piles of rubble.

"What happened here?" Jed asked the driver.

"War happened." He spat out the window. "See the higher ground to the northeast? Those are the Vosges Mountains. Back in 1914 the Germans swooped down out of there and overran this whole area. They did a lot of damage and killed a bunch of civilians before the French kicked them out. Old men, women, and children run the farms.

Sometimes, when they're plowing, they run into an unexploded shell and wham, it's all over." He shook his head. "They love this land. Lots of Frenchmen died to take it back."

They rode in silence for a few minutes.

"This was a quiet sector," the driver said. "The two sides sent units here to rest. But now we're here and Blackjack Pershing has another idea. We're to dominate no-man's-land and the Boche don't like it. They thought it was live-and-let-live around here."

"Boche...?"

"What the French call the Germans, not a loving term."

In Brouville a clerk directed them to the Second Battalion headquarters in Merviller.

The driver drove them the two miles to the ramshackle assembly of knocked down houses and piles of blackened bricks wreathed in the stink of burned lumber. They got out of the truck in front of a row of ancient stone buildings with low thatched roofs and tile smokestacks.

Someone had chalked the number 2/147 next to one doorway.

Jed and Mike set their bags beside the open door.

Jed knocked twice.

A soldier came to the door. He had the five stripes, three pointed up and two rockers down, of a Battalion Sergeant Major. Mike and Jed stiffened to attention.

"Well, you're so formal to knock. People usually come barging in with their problems." He struck a match and lit a pipe. "Relax fellas. What can I do for you?"

"We're replacements," Jed said, handing over their orders.

The sergeant major studied the papers, puffing on his pipe. The sweet smell of the briar swirled out the door overlaying the general funk in the air. "I'm Sergeant Major West of Second Battalion." He looked at a clipboard hanging by the door. "I'll send you over to my friend Les Trask. He's First Sergeant of Company G." He turned into the room, stamped the orders and signed them. "Company G is around the corner three blocks up the street. They'll check you in and assign you your billets." He shook their hands. "Welcome to the Buckeye Division, men. Tell Cain, the company clerk, that Abel said to take good care of you."

Jed and Mike stared at him.

"Okay," he said. "Billets are a place to sleep. We call the division Buckeye for the State of Ohio, and our insignia is from the state flag, a white circle for Ohio and a red circle inside to represent a buckeye nut from our state tree."

"Cain and Abel?" Jed asked.

"My name is John Able West. People call me Abel, like in Genesis. I guess they think I've been in the army since the Creation. You'll meet Cain when you join Company G."

"We have a lot to learn," Mike said as they picked up their gear.

"Boche, billets, and Buckeyes—Cain and Abel—they speak a whole different language here," Jed said.

They walked up a cobblestoned street between two rows of brick houses, many with half roofs and front walls tumbled onto the sidewalks. Camouflage netting extended out from the buildings to poles in the middle of the street.

After one block, they passed a rolling kitchen backed into a shed with soldiers lined up in front. A sergeant, wearing a piece of an army blanket as an apron, motioned the men to the kitchen. "Come on, boys, the slum's ready." The sergeant glanced up at a thin stream of smoke rising from a hole in the roof. "Dubman, you red-headed idiot, keep the fire hot so's it don't make no smoke. Those Heinie airplanes will see it."

"Yeah, yeah, Smitty."

Two blocks farther along a corporal sat at a small table under a camouflage net studying a stack of postcards. Ledgers and papers lay on the table with a steel helmet and a small typewriter acting as paperweights. A rifle leaned against a doorway leading to a basement. A cardboard sign tacked to the front of the table read: G/2/147.

Jed and Mike walked up to the table and dropped their bags on the ground startling the corporal who dropped a postcard. Jed picked it up. The picture was of a bare-breasted woman kneeling before a turbaned man with a large scimitar strapped across his back, his pantaloons down around his knees. She had his manhood in her mouth. The caption read, *Sultan and Harem Girl.*

Mike whispered to Jed, "Remind you of anyone?"

"Shut up," Jed said.

The corporal snatched the postcard out of Jed's hand. He lifted his helmet and tossed the cards under it. "French love", he said. "Twenty million Frenchmen can't be wrong."

"Where did you get those?" Jed asked.

The red-faced corporal ignored the question. "What do you want?"

Jed presented their orders. "We're replacements. Abel said to report to Company G."

"You've found it," the corporal said reading the papers. "Let me see your identity tags." They pulled their tags out and the corporal examined them. He opened a ledger and picked up a pencil. "I can put you in Second Platoon and Third Platoon."

"We were hoping to stick together," Jed said. "We grew up together and have been together since basic training."

"I can't play favorites for buddies. I'm supposed to balance things so we don't have a lot of new men in one unit."

Mike reached across the table and lifted the edge of the helmet but the corporal slammed his hand down on it.

"Does Abel know about your picture collection?" Mike asked.

The corporal's eyebrows shot up. "You just got here and you're putting the squeeze on me already?"

"Look," Jed said, "what's it to you? You've got to put us somewhere."

The clerk's eyebrows knitted together. He was still unconvinced.

"What's your name?" Jed asked.

"Goldson, Chaim David. Most call me Cain."

"Cain and Abel." Mike nodded his head.

"Yeah, and when Abel gives me a hard time, I remind him of Genesis 4:8."

Jed knew the verse. "Cain rose against his brother and killed him."

"I say 'Cain slew Abel'".

Mike patted the helmet. "It would've been 'Abel slew Cain' if Abel had known it was coming." Mike raised an eyebrow. "What can you do for us, Cain?"

Goldson looked at Mike, then the helmet, and sighed. "I've got two spots in First Squad, Rifle Section, of First Platoon, all men from the original Ohio Guard. You can replace Walker and Darnell who we lost last week."

"Were they killed in action?"

"No, James, they came down with influenza. The major shipped them off to the hospital before they infected everyone else."

"I go by Jed. My family calls all the adult males by their middle names."

Cain wrote in the ledger and flipped it closed. "O.K., Mike and Jed, you are assigned to First Platoon, Company G, 147th Infantry

Regiment." He leaned forward. "No mention of postcards, right? Most are pictures of naked girls but some are rare like the one you saw. They're a lot more valuable, say, the difference between a nickel and a quarter."

"The only postcards we know are the YMCA cards we send to the folks," Mike said.

Cain closed his eyes and nodded his head.

"Thanks, Corporal," Jed said.

"You may not thank me when you meet your section leader, Sergeant Brock."

A breeze shook the camouflage netting above and a few drops of water fell onto the table. Cain brushed them away.

"What are you doing outside, anyway?" Mike asked.

"When it stops raining, I try to get up out of the mole hole they keep me in." He pointed to the basement entry.

The three men looked upward as the faint drone of an airplane engine became louder. "German observation plane," Cain said. "He's been up there all afternoon since the weather cleared. We put this camouflage netting up to keep them guessing. Try to stay out of sight of enemy planes and observation balloons. At the front those planes and balloons can cause real trouble."

Cain looked down the street then picked up his helmet and put it on. He stuffed the postcards into a white envelope and then into the haversack suspended by a shoulder strap at his right hip.

A captain, second lieutenant, and two NCOs walked up the hill from the kitchen shed.

"That's Captain Brown, First Sergeant Trask, Corporal Joe Collins, and the new First Platoon commander," Cain said. "The captain is from a rich family in Cincinnati. He's been with the unit ever since it was the Sixth Ohio Infantry. He trains the company hard but takes good care of us. The lieutenant is George Samis. He was a corporal and returned from officer school last week."

As the captain approached, Jed and Mike came to attention and saluted. The captain saluted in return.

"These men are replacements, sir," Cain said. "I've assigned them to First Squad, Rifle Section of First Platoon."

"Well then, here are your Platoon Commander, Squad Leader and Company First Sergeant: Lieutenant Samis, Corporal Collins and Sergeant Trask," the captain said.

He excused himself, returned their salutes, and departed.

"Welcome to the Buckeye Division, men," Lieutenant Samis said. "Collins will take you to your quarters and exchange your campaign hats for overseas caps. Get a meal and bed down for the night, we march to Gelacourt for small arms training in the morning." He accepted the enlisted men's salutes and walked away.

"Boy lieutenant," Collins said.

"He was a good corporal," Trask said. "I've seen a lot worse."

Sergeant Trask was six feet tall and was as broad in the shoulders as Mike. He carried himself with confidence and Jed got the impression his light green eyes didn't miss much. "The trip to Gelacourt starts at six o'clock. I'll see you in the morning."

Cain watched Trask walk away. "He's the finest NCO in this army. You can call him Top, for Top Sergeant. If you do what he tells you, you might survive this mess."

"How would you know, clerk?" Collins said.

"I spend plenty of time in the line running messages. The address on those whiz-bangs is, *to whom it may concern*."

"Yeah, yeah."

Collins led them to a warehouse with six rows of ten cots, most piled with packs and other personal gear. A sergeant with curly black hair and glasses sat at a folding table reading The Stars and Stripes.

"This is Sergeant Lipsitz, we call him Lips," Collins said. "He's the assistant to the platoon commander. Lips knows everything going on around here."

"Put your things on any empty cot," the sergeant said. "Keep your helmet and gas mask carrier handy at all times up here."

Jed and Mike put their packs on two adjacent cots.

"Have you had chow yet, Lips?" Collins asked.

"Andy Watkia will be along any minute to relieve me."

"Will you show these new guys where to eat? Looks like slum and punk again."

Collins noticed the look on Jed's face. "Slumgullion is a kind of stew. Punk is bread."

Jed and Mike exchanged a look.

A soldier hurried into the room holding a bundle of white envelopes. He glanced at Jed and Mike.

"This is Private First Class Andy Watkia. He's in your squad," Lips said.

Watkia nodded to them. "Can you guys excuse us a minute?"

Jed and Mike retrieved their mess kits and waited outside until Sergeant Lipsitz came out slipping a white envelope into his haversack. "I'll be back right after chow to pull the rest of your detail, Andy."

"Don't be late," Watkia called from inside the barracks.

Mike smiled. "Postcards. There's more than terminology to learn in this outfit.

CHAPTER 12

SEPTEMBER 7, 1918

GELACOURT, FRANCE

Reveille rolled the platoon out of their cots at 4 A.M. After breakfast First Platoon lined up in full marching order: overcoats, full packs, gas masks, and weapons.

Collins scanned the sky above the camouflage nets. The droning of airplane engines drifted down. "Those are our guys patrolling up there. Gelacourt is only two miles away. We'll be safe on our march."

"Where's Brock?" Lips asked.

"Don't know—don't care," Collins said. "He'll show up. He always does."

They moved out in a column of twos followed by a rolling kitchen, water cart, and an ammunition wagon. They marched for two miles in the open, entered a stand of trees, and then pitched pup tents in a meadow covered by camouflage netting. Rifle fire and dull explosions echoed through the trees.

First Squad did calisthenics with other platoon squads not at the rifle range.

When Jed and the squad approached the range the hand bomber section was leaving. In the group were Bart and Clay Jones.

"What are you two doing here?" Jed asked.

"We got here last night," Bart said.

"Watch out, you might find a grenade rolling around in your pup-tent, courtesy of the Jones brothers," Clay said as they walked away laughing.

"Let's see you outrun a rifle bullet," Mike said.

A soldier with British sergeant stripes stood nearby. "Don't mind the lads. Their leaders have pumped them up with their mission. I say, I agree with the French, when clearing Hun machine gun nests, hand bombers come in handy. We British prefer the bayonet." He snapped to attention. "For those who have recently joined the unit I am Sergeant Bertram McClardy, British Army. I have seen action on the Somme and elsewhere and have been with this division as an advisor since June."

McClardy led them into a short trench next to a deep pit with rifle targets at the other end. "At this station, you will throw American Mark II hand grenades and practice rifle marksmanship."

They spent the next hour and a half throwing and shooting.

The next item McClardy showed them was a German Model 1917 or M17 stick grenade. The grenade resembled a bean can with a hollow wooden handle extending from one end. "We Brits call this a potato masher." He pointed to writing inscribed on the handle below the warhead. "It is inscribed as a five and one-half second delay." He removed a cap at the free end of the handle and pulled a ceramic ball on the end of a string that dropped out. Smoke flowed from the handle. Jed began a slow count. McClardy threw the grenade into the pit. They crouched down and after Jed's count reached five, the grenade exploded.

After an hour of bayonet drill, they were dismissed.

They lined up at the rolling kitchen manned by the red-headed cook.

"What's in the pot, Mess Sergeant?" Jed asked.

"I've got stewed vegetables with beef. My name is Clarence Dubman and I'm not the mess sergeant, just a cook. The sergeant, old Smitty, doesn't like to go out in the field so he sends me and stays in the rear."

Jed and Mike received their stew and joined the other members of First Squad sitting together under a tree at the edge of the woods. As they ate, the squad members relaxed and made introductions.

The first to speak was an Italian named Anthony DiNiccola.

"Yes, I am American citizen. They line us all up on the last day at Camp Sheridan and swear us in. We raise our hand in front of Judge Clayton and take the oath. Right after, we march to the train and travel to Camp Lee and then get on the boat for France." He laughed. "I steal three years of life from United States since I do not have to fight Austrians in Italian army, and America draft me and send me to fight Germans."

"If you weren't a citizen, they couldn't force you to serve," Jed said.

Tony nodded his head. "I declare I'm'a not intend to become citizen and should not be drafted. I do not know I must fill out exemption form.

60

So, when they tell me to go, I go." He waved his arm to take in the rest of the squad. "They assign me with these fine National Guardsmen. I fight for them, for my family, for America. Those three years of extra life I do not waste. I get busy selling musical instruments and teaching piano." He leaned toward Jed. "My Sophia and me we get busy too. *Io chielo due ragazzi.* I have two little boys."

"You should see his wife," Corporal Collins said. "The kiss she gave him on the platform when we left Cincinnati for Camp Sheridan still has those Salvation Army ladies' knickers in a knot."

Tony passed around a photograph of a pretty dark-haired woman holding two miniature Tony's on her lap against her ample breasts. He grinned as his squad mates gawked at the picture.

"I thought they weren't drafting married men," Jed said.

"They call me alien slacker and make exception." The picture made the rounds back to Tony. "I am first one to sign up for the maximum war risk insurance. If something happens to me, *mio bellissima moglie,* my beautiful wife, and boys have something to keep them going."

The smiles on the faces of the squad members disappeared.

"He's not the only one with a story to tell," Collins said, breaking the spell by grabbing a young soldier around the neck and rubbing the bristles of his close-cropped blond hair.

"Stop that, Corp," the boy said, pushing Collins away.

"Timmy Smith here is only sixteen," Collins said. "He lied about his age to get into the Guard. When we were up at the front last month, he showed plenty of guts. He killed a grenadier and captured a Kraut lieutenant. He can patrol with me any time."

"Here, here," a handsome soldier said raising a canteen in a toast.

"Hey, Bunny," a dusty soldier with an Appalachian accent said. "What you got there, son? You followin' our section sergeant's lead and carryin' wine in your canteen like the Frenchies do?"

"That's against Black Jack Pershing's rules and regulations, Doody," Bunny said wagging his finger, a lit cigarette dangling from the corner of his mouth. "Today it's only water." He reached over and poured some on Timmy's head. "I'm baptizing a virgin."

"We know you're no virgin, Bunny Love," Doody said.

"Bunny Love?" Jed asked.

"My name is Benjamin Lev Steinmetz. Some call me Benny Lev. Sergeant Brock called me Bunny Love, and it stuck."

"And our Bunny is quite the lover," the soldier called Doody said. "How do you maintain your health with all those cigarettes you smoke and all those gals you poke?"

"Well, Doody, old boy, the cigarettes give me energy and, when wading in unfamiliar waters, always wear your galoshes." He held up a condom package.

His squad mates laughed.

"What does it cost you, you know, to get some?" Doody asked.

"A lonely widow will take food, wine, or cigarettes. A pro wants fifteen francs, about three bucks."

"Shoot, you can get it back home for two."

Bunny shrugged his shoulders. "War profiteering, I guess."

"Periscope off the port bow," Timmy said.

The men stood as Lieutenant Samis walked up followed by a burly sergeant and Andy Watkia. "Break time is over, men. Sergeant Brock and I will lead the platoon in field exercises with the rest of the company."

Sergeant Brock was the same size as Mike and Sergeant Trask but was softer and non-athletic. He wore a M1911 automatic pistol in a covered holster on his right hip and two canteens on his web belt. His posture was one of casual disinterest, but his bloodshot eyes glared from beneath his helmet, a livid scar above his right eye.

Sergeant Lipsitz arrived with the platoon's hand bomber, rifle grenade, and automatic rifle sections, and Second Squad, the other half of the rifle section. They ran simulated attacks on machine gun emplacements. Jed dry fired his rifle laying down covering fire for the hand bombers as they flanked the mock machine gun nests, using stones as grenade substitutes.

During these scenarios, Sergeant Brock stayed well back behind the section, urging the two rifle squad leaders, Collins and Kraft, to lead their squads from the front.

The platoon stumbled back to the bivouac at sundown.

After more stew, Jed and Mike slept in their pup-tent, the rattle of the firing line replaced by distant thumps of artillery and the occasional buzzing of German night bombers looking for careless campfires or unguarded lights.

In the morning, they packed up and marched back to Merviller.

Andy Watkia went ahead on an errand for Sergeant Brock.

"This Brock fellow is an odd duck," Jed said.

"How about Andy Watkia with those postcards?"

"The rest of the guys seem all right," Jed said. "They all sound like they're from the city, except for the Italian guy and that hillbilly Doody."

When they got back to Merviller, they unpacked their gear and met outside the warehouse with Sergeant Brock and a few members of First Squad. Brock leaned a wooden chair with one front leg missing against the back wall of the barracks. He sat slumped on his perch, a sullen look on his face. Jed and Mike sat side by side on an empty crate across from him. Bunny sat on a barrel of nails whittling on a stick with a pocket knife, throwing the shavings at Doody who lay sprawled on the ground before him resting back on his elbows.

Corporal Collins, Timmy Smith, and Tony DiNiccola were asleep in the barracks. They had been up all night on a guard detail with the lieutenant.

Andy Watkia was absent again.

Doody turned to the two new men and asked, "So, you boys are from Arkansas?"

"Yes, I'm from O'Kean, a small town my granddad founded," Mike said. "Jed's from Birdell. Both towns are near Pocahontas, Arkansas."

"Hey Sergeant, what was the name of the puke bucket we came over here on?"

"The USS Pocahontas," Brock said. "I'm amazed a dope like you could remember such a detail, Doody."

Doody smiled, all cornpone.

"Do you want to know how Doody got his nickname?" Brock asked.

Doody sniffed; the smile gone. "My name is Steven Foster Dodd, thank you."

"Because he did doody in his pants on his first night patrol," Brock said.

"The food here gives me diarrhea," Doody said. He turned to Jed and Mike. "You can't get any good greens here. Y'all are from the South, you understand, greens keep you regular."

Brock wouldn't let it go. "Doody did doo-doo because he got no greens. Hah!"

"Don't take no notice of this banter. We veterans kid each other a lot."

"Veterans?" Brock said, rubbing the scar over his eye. "The only thing you're a veteran of Doody is pud-knocking."

"See what I mean? We're always kidding. A lot of the boys let loose the first time a shell lands close."

"You've all seen action?" Jed asked.

"Each time we was up in the line we got a fair dose of shelling," Doody said.

"Did you run into any Germans?" Mike asked.

"We killed two of them on night patrol four weeks ago when Timmy got his Kraut." Doody brushed a few splinters off his uniform blouse. "And it makes us veterans. They was tough but I guess we was tougher. We did what we had to do." He turned to Brock. "Weren't it a sad thing to kill them Sarge?"

Brock leveled his gaze at Doody. "You haven't seen any real war yet, Dodd."

"Well, whatever it was, real war or not, I can say I been through it, didn't get a scratch, but I was scared. You boys will be too, nothin' to be ashamed of. It wouldn't be right if a man weren't scared when someone's trying to kill him." He stopped and pondered for a second. "Why, oh, why Lord, do we have to risk it all and kill all those German boys?"

Bunny flipped another splinter at him. "We kill them because they're trying to kill us, you dunderhead."

"If we weren't here, we wouldn't have them so mad at us."

Brock leaned forward balancing on three chair legs. "We are here to help our friends the Frogs and Belgies, who happened to get themselves invaded." Brock spat on the ground. "The only thing the Frog men are good at is making wine and the only thing Frog women are good for is French love." He stood, his chair toppling. "Speaking of wine, where the hell is that stupid Polack Watkia?"

He walked a few yards away looking right and left.

Doody rolled onto his side toward Jed and Mike and motioned them closer. "I'm from West Virginia and moved to Cincinnati for a job. I joined the National Guard for the extra money." He glanced over his shoulder. "Y'all watch out for Brock. He's a mean one. Rumor has it he raped a woman and got away with it. Now, all he does is drink and fool around with any female he can find. He claims he got the scar over his eye from a Moro sword stroke. He and Sergeant Trask have served in the same units since the Philippines and he hates Trask enough to kill him."

Bunny leaned forward. "This long-winded piece of donkey shit makes sense. Brock is a coward, and he's a survivor, but don't cause him trouble."

Andy Watkia sauntered around the corner of the building away from where Brock was looking. He walked up to Bunny and pulled two bottles of red wine out of a canvas bag slung over his shoulder. He handed them to Bunny and Doody then leaned down and whispered something in Bunny's ear. Bunny nodded his head and pointed to Jed and Mike. He handed Watkia two ten-franc notes. Jed and Mike each got a bottle.

Watkia walked over to Brock and tapped him on the shoulder. Brock turned, grabbed the bottle Watkia offered, and headed down the street into town. Andy shook his head, turned to the squad members and pulled out a bottle of cognac identical to the one he had given Brock. He tucked it under his left arm, saluted, did a precise right face, and marched off in the direction opposite the one taken by Brock.

Bunny stood. "Gentlemen let's relax for a few hours. We'll need the rest. We move up to the front day after tomorrow and relieve First Battalion."

CHAPTER 13
SEPTEMBER 10, 1918
SUB-SECTOR MONTIGNY,
BACCARAT SECTOR, FRANCE

The men of Company G, in raincoats and full packs, shuffled in a soaking rain along a muddy road snaking past churned up fields and pools of water of unknown depth. In the four miles they had marched, the land had changed into a tragic mess. Debris of all types floated in pools of water and mud. There was no remnant of a building over three feet high.

The air held a familiar odor that twisted a knot in Jed's stomach. It smelled like the garbage cans behind Mr. Kurtz' butcher shop—blood and spoiled meat.

Captain Brown halted the company and consulted a map. The road changed to a duckboard track, slats of wood nailed crossway on runners that skimmed the swampy ground and disappeared into the mist.

Brown climbed onto a fallen tree trunk. "This track will take us to our assignment in the line. Stay on the duckboards. Don't get off of them for any reason. If you're sucked into this quicksand, we'll not help you. I won't lose three men trying to save one." He paused for a deep breath. "If the Krauts shell us don't jump off the duckboards and run for cover. Stay on the path. With all this mud, it'll take close bursts to hurt you so don't panic."

The men formed an elephant walk, holding the pack of the man in front, a human train following the wooden track.

They moved down the duckboards for a half hour before a few harassing rounds landed in their vicinity. Brown was right. The mud absorbed most of the blast but there was a lot of the slimy stuff flying around, making the wooden track more slippery.

The men passed a large shell hole filled with the gooey mud.

A shell whooshed in and landed in the hole, the explosive gasses bubbling to the surface. Timmy Smith slipped off the path, but Tony DiNiccola caught him and pulled him back onto the duckboards.

"We almost made a virgin sacrifice to that mud volcano," Tony joked.

After another hour, as the sun set unseen behind the overcast, the column left the duckboard track and halted on a stretch of road running by smashed piles of bricks that may have once been houses.

The men fell out, slumping down in the rain. Jed sat down and leaned against a small mound of bricks. He pulled his overseas cap off and fished his farmer's wide brim from under his raincoat. He pulled the hat down over his eyes and wrapped his rifle under his raincoat, pulling the front of it closed. His hat did its usual job of keeping the rain off his face and the wool uniform and raincoat made him as comfortable as possible under the circumstances.

After a minute his mind relaxed, and he dozed. He bobbed on the surface of a river, soaked and cold, drifting toward an unknown danger.

Something hit Jed's foot, and he woke up.

Lieutenant Samis kicked his foot again. "On your feet, Private."

Jed scrambled to attention.

The lieutenant glared at Jed, blinking as raindrops hit his face. His overseas cap offered no protection.

Sergeant Trask walked up. "Excuse me, Lieutenant. What's going on?"

The lieutenant turned to Trask. "General Pershing has outlawed the wearing of campaign hats in theater." He pointed at Jed, "This man still has one. I want him punished per the General Order."

"We told you boys about that when you got here," Trask said.

"I turned in my campaign hat, Top, right after the lieutenant told us."

"Then what's that on your head?" Samis demanded.

Jed bent his head forward so the lieutenant could see the domed felt hugging the top of his head. Accumulated water ran off the wide brim and splashed at Samis' feet. "Lieutenant, it's not a peaked campaign hat."

"Then what is it?"

"It's the hat I wear back home on the farm to keep the sun and rain off my face, like the campaign hats at Camp Pike. All the boys would rather have the campaign hat."

"It's an order, no campaign hats. If I can be confused by it, so can a senior officer and then we'll all be in Dutch. Get rid of it." Samis spun toward Trask, "Sergeant Trask, I expect you and the other NCOs to enforce orders."

"Yes, sir," Trask said.

Samis hesitated a moment. "Well, carry on men." He pulled the collar of his raincoat tighter around his neck and trudged toward the head of the column.

Trask watched him with a wry half grin. He looked at Jed with one raised eyebrow.

Jed looked down at the mud around his feet. "Am I going on report, Top?"

"He didn't mention punishment a second time. Keep the hat out of sight and he'll forget all about it."

Jed put his farm hat in his haversack.

Brock walked up. "What's up with Samis? He didn't look too good."

Trask shook his head. "I feel sorry for him. He wants to do well, but he's just a kid."

At the head of the column the company commander spoke with Samis who turned back toward the platoon. As he walked, the men beside the road stirred. A wave of rising men followed in the lieutenant's wake.

Trask glanced at Jed. "Put your helmet on. It'll help with the rain." Trask addressed the whole platoon, "We're moving up closer to the Kaiser's guns. You'll need your helmets for sure then. Brock, make sure these idiots keep those rifles clean." He strode toward the front of the company formation.

Brock glared at Trask, his hand on his pistol holster. "Keep it up, asshole. One day when we're alone..." He glanced at Jed. "Put your helmets on and get ready to move. And keep those goddamn rifles out of the mud."

Artillery murmured on the horizon.

Jed hefted his pack onto his back, slung his rifle, and moved forward.

Captain Brown suspended the ten-minute break every hour, and the company trudged forward, some men sleeping as they walked, pulled from in front, pushed from behind.

The rain stopped but the darkness only deepened and the sounds of artillery strikes increased with every step.

As the company entered the third line reserve trenches, platoons and sections peeled off to the flanks.

First Platoon continued forward, descended into a zigzag communication trench, and walked for several hundred yards in water up to their chests, holding their equipment over their heads.

"I don't like all this water," Jed said.

They climbed out of the end of the trench and down into a drier one, slinging their packs and rifles and shuffling forward, halting fifteen minutes later near the second line support trench parallel to the front. Jed flopped down on the trench bottom and sagged against his pack, too tired to take it off.

This section of trench was perpendicular to the front lines and ran down a slope. The whole panorama of the front lay before them. Bright white parachute flares drifted down illuminating no-man's-land. Green, red, white, and purple signal rockets raced into the clearing sky from the German trenches and red flares added multiple balls of color arcing through the air. The distant horizon glowed orange and soon artillery shells rushed in and detonated along the American front, the golden flashes and yellow sparks erupting like brief flowers.

Mike leaned in close. "It looks like the Fourth-of-July picnic back home."

"This ain't no picnic," Doody said.

An explosion ripped the air overhead and bits of shrapnel slapped into the sandbags above Jed's head.

Sergeant Lipsitz peeked around the corner of the support trench. "Why are you guys sitting out in the open? Get in here, now."

Jed and the others scrambled into the trench.

Lips turned to Corporal Collins. "Joe, you know better than to leave these men exposed."

"I thought they were with Trask."

"Don't make your lazy excuses. Take care of your squad." He glared at Doody. "You experienced men know better."

"I stop where I'm told, Sarge."

"Yeah, brainless hick," Brock said, squatting nearby.

69

Jed crouched next to Brock and followed his gaze as red and white rockets rose behind the German lines.

"What does that mean?" Jed asked.

"I think they're calling for artillery to increase range." Brock turned to the rest of the section. "We're in for it. Stay low against the forward edge of this trench."

Several shells arrived with a rising shriek and a sharp detonation.

The Brit, Sergeant McClardy, lay face down and held his helmet tight to his head. "Whiz-bangs, the hate begins."

A storm of shells engulfed the area. Jed lay on his left side with his head and knees against the trench wall, his fingers in his ears, his helmet covering the right side of his face. He slid his pack up onto his right shoulder and hip for added protection.

The barrage lasted for one-half hour, the noise blending into a solid entity permeating everything. The ground vibrated, the air sang, his chest thumped with each explosion.

A shell landed in the trench fifty feet away. Someone screamed.

A shell burst near Jed tossed dirt over him as his ears popped and protested. He prayed, *Help me, Lord. Thy Will Be Done!*"

The barrage stopped.

Sergeant Brock bellowed over the ringing in Jed's ears, "Third Section, riflemen, First and Second Squads, sound off." Jed sat up and responded in his turn. Everyone was still there. Mike was grinning at him and brushing himself off.

Lenny Gurr, from Second Squad, trotted down the trench and tripped over an outstretched leg, sprawling beside Brock. "Where the hell are you going?" Brock asked.

"I'm going for stretcher bearers."

"Who got hit?"

"Jimmy Lane, from Second Section, ripped his guts out." Gurr moved away.

"Rifle grenadier, he came up here right after we did." Mike said.

Jed remembered a shock of white-blond hair above deep green eyes. He shook his head. "Close…"

"Too close," Mike said.

"It'll get closer," Brock said.

The men dozed until the sergeants roused them and ordered them to recheck their equipment and prepare to move forward.

A low bank of clouds moved in covering the sky like a sponge, wringing dirty water out into the trenches as the rifle section splashed toward the front, slipping in the mud, balancing themselves against the sandbagged walls of the trench.

A grimy corporal with a five-day growth of beard and caked-on layers of mud and charcoal camouflage stood near the entrance to the front-line trench. Eight members of his section huddled together, passing cigarettes to each other, shivering in the cold rain. The whites of their eyes and the wiped-clean lips holding the cigarettes were the only light color on their darkened faces. They looked like a minstrel show on break.

"Are you Second Battalion?" the corporal asked.

"Yeah, Rifle Section, First Platoon, G Company," Brock said.

"What's the setup here?" Kraft of Second Squad asked.

"Your section assignment is to the left and right between this communication trench and the next ones down on either side." He took a deep drag on his cigarette. "I need four men to replace my sentries."

Kraft designated two of his men to go to the right and Collins selected Smith and Doody. When the relief was complete four men jogged into view, splashed around the corner into the communications trench and continued out of sight in the misty rain. The other First Battalion men threw down their cigarettes and set off after their section mates.

"The Krauts man their sectors with patrols, and only sometimes with a permanent presence like we do," the corporal said. "You never know when they're there." He took an anxious drag on his cigarette and shook his head. "Sometimes they lay on a barrage. We lost three men and our section sergeant during the shelling this morning. We didn't find any part of them, not a tooth, not a stitch."

The corporal walked backward up the trench, offering his final briefing. "And keep your sentries awake. Those Huns are sneaky. Sometimes they'll crawl right in with you at night and you never wake up." He turned and jogged after his men.

Kraft moved his squad into the main trench and turned to the right. Collins led his squad to the left.

Two German shells had landed in the trench. One had hit the parapet and carved a ten-foot wide hole extending six feet out into no-man's-land. The other had landed in the trench bottom digging a six-foot deep hole full of rainwater. Two box periscopes perched atop steps to either side of the pool. Timmy Smith and Doody peered through them at no-man's-land.

The rain changed to a drizzle.

"Let's work fast before the rain picks up again," Collins said. "Watkia, you and Tony fill sandbags. Martin and O'Kean bail out this hole." He tossed them two French collapsible buckets. "Bunny, establish contact with Second Platoon on the left. I'll try to find some duckboards."

Jed removed his pack and leaned over the hole to fill a bucket. Something shoved his backside, and he tumbled headfirst into the murky water. In a panic, he stood up in the stinking hole, sputtering and coughing, the water up to his armpits.

Brock and Mike stood face to face, Brock smirking, Mike red-faced, right fist white knuckled. "Why did you do that?"

Brock's smirk changed to a sneer. "You can't bail out the hole from up here. This is faster. Get in there with him. We don't have all night." Mike clenched his jaw in defiance. Brock touched the flap of his pistol holster.

Mike slid down into the hole.

Bunny trotted back from the left. "We're linked up, Sarge."

Corporal Collins returned and dropped a loose bundle of duckboard slats in the trench's bottom.

"How many sandbags do you have?" Brock asked.

"Twenty dozen."

"Not enough." Jed and Mike shivered in the hole. "Get busy down there. Bunny Love, you and Collins help them." He scanned the trench. "Throw the water over the back of the trench. If you throw it over the front, the Huns will know where you are and start the hate. I'll be back with more sandbags." Brock hurried away.

"One of these days there won't be any witnesses," Mike said when Brock was out of sight.

"You can't get the son of a bitch," Bunny said, reaching down and taking a full bucket from Mike. "He rides you and rides you and, when you stand up to him, he pulls rank." He handed the bucket to Collins who poured the water out of the back of the trench through a wide notch in the parados.

"Sergeant Trask has known Brock a long time," Collins said. "They served together back in 1913 in the Philippines. Even he can't get the goods on Brock."

"Brock's a coward who knows how to survive," Doody said from his perch at the periscope. "Going back for sandbags, shee-it, he could've sent me."

They worked their bucket brigade for several more minutes until the water was only knee deep. Jed leaned toward Mike. "How's this for the glory of war?"

"We're covered in glory." Mike grinned and wiped mud from his face.

"For a minute there, I thought I was back in the Eleven Point," Jed said.

They worked until they scooped buckets of mud.

Sergeant Brock returned. "We got lucky. The engineers are here to help."

The engineer sergeant was a tall man named Patterson with a hound dog face and a bushy, non-regulation mustache. He led a dozen enlisted men carrying shovels, lumber, and sandbags.

The engineers scooped out a wide space in the damaged wall on the no-man's-land side of the trench, filling the bailed-out hole with the dirt. They built a rectangular wooden box, lined the bottom with planks, put ten-foot poles across the top and piled sandbags three deep. They shoveled dirt over the whole structure to blend it in with the parapet. Other engineers nailed together framing at the bottom of the trench and attached duckboard slats to them.

Jed helped with the wood work.

"I could use a man as good as you with a hammer and nails," Sergeant Patterson said.

Jed looked at him. "Forget it. I want to stay with the infantry."

Patterson nodded his head.

The rising sun brightened the overcast.

"That space is your new squad bunker," Patterson said. He turned to his men. "Let's go before it gets light enough for the Huns to see us moving."

"Good work, Patterson," Brock said, stomping his foot to test the duckboards. "Buy me a beer when we get back to the rear, yeah?"

Patterson stared Brock down. His men picked up their gear and disappeared up the communication trench.

Captain Brown ordered the men to "Stand-To" on the firing step, weapons ready. It was routine at sunrise and sunset, times when an enemy attack was most expected.

After Stand-To, the squad settled into a routine using the shelter of their new bunker to rest and dry out, swapping sentry duty at the periscopes.

German artillery rounds landed throughout the day sending steel splinters zipping across the top of the trenches, cutting sandbags open. A few of the shells contained gas, and the Americans donned their gas masks and took shelter in dugouts or one-man funk holes carved into the sides of the trenches.

By midday the gas had cleared, and the battalion air observer spotted a German aircraft approaching. His bugler sounded the four-note "attention" call, and everyone took cover. The German plane made a long run down the length of the American line, firing machine guns and dropping four bombs, then sped away. Three bugle blasts signaled the all clear.

The bombs killed two men. First Squad was so far unscathed.

After dark, Jed and Doody crawled through a narrow trench to a listening post dug fifty yards into no-man's-land. The Germans sent no flares up, a sign that German patrols were active. Jed watched and listened but there was only a setting first quarter moon for light and his ears still buzzed from the artillery bombardment the night before.

Doody rubbed his face. "Damn, boy, I'm fallin' asleep. I need coffee. Watkia's got a pot on. You want me to bring you some?"

"Good idea," Jed said.

Doody slipped out of the listening post and left Jed alone, rubbing his eyes and the back of his neck trying to stay awake.

He whirled around at a noise in the trench behind him. A figure stood in the gloom.

"Were you asleep on post?" Brock said.

"No, Sarge. Listening and waiting for some coffee."

"You know what I can do to you for sleeping on sentry duty?" He drew his pistol.

"I wasn't asleep—"

"Shut up."

Brock hurried toward Jed, raised his pistol, and fired.

Jed ducked away.

Brock peered out of the listening post. "I think I shot a Kraut with a grenade."

The American lines came alive. An illumination flare bloomed over no-man's-land showing a small group of Germans scrambling back toward their lines. An American machine gun fired a long burst at them.

Doody arrived with a canteen cup full of coffee.

Brock fired his pistol again. "You two assholes give me some help here."

Doody dropped the coffee. He and Jed fired their rifles at the shifting shadows thrown by the flare. Jed didn't know if he hit anything but fired, reloaded and fired again.

The fire along the rest of the American line stopped.

The flare died out. "Martin, go see what's going on."

Jed crawled out into no-man's-land his gut churning. He probed in the darkness but didn't find a body. His hand slid through a warm puddle and touched a hard object. It was a German grenade. He grabbed it and crawled back into the listening post.

"Nobody's out there, Sarge. There's a lot of blood but they must have dragged him away." Jed handed the grenade to Brock.

"You got lucky this time, mister." He waved his pistol at Jed. "Next time I put one in your ear." Brock started down the narrow trench. "Now I gotta talk to Samis."

"Sorry, Jed, I didn't think it would hurt to go for coffee," Doody said.

Jed washed the blood from his hand with coffee left in the dropped cup. He shivered at the memory of Brock moving toward him with the pistol.

"Brock is dangerous."

"Yes, he is, son, yes he is."

At 2 A.M. Jed and Doody joined Sergeants Brock and Lipsitz as they assembled a raiding team. Brock had his .45 and a bolo knife. Mike carried a canvas bag full of hand grenades. Doody and Bunny had pistols and bayonets. Jed carried his Enfield rifle.

"A raiding party of two hundred men will attack in Sub-sector Badonviller two miles to our right an hour before sunrise," Lipsitz said. "A barrage of artillery and machine gun fire will keep the Germans from reinforcing. Your job is to be in front of the enemy positions across from here and, during the confusion, move forward through the enemy first and second line of defenses and capture prisoners. The Germans man their front-line trenches randomly but we know Germans patrol this sub-sector." He passed out black knit caps. "Leave your helmets and wear these."

"We're going out through the listening post and straight across," Brock said. "Keep in physical contact with the man in front of you. Bunny and Doody, you stay right by me on point. O'Kean, as we go forward to the second trench you stay twenty yards back. If we need to get out quick, wait until we pass, then slow down the pursuit with hand grenades. Martin, you are drag. Don't let anybody get behind us. Questions?"

No one had any. They darkened their faces and hands with charcoal sticks.

DiNiccola and Smith manned the listening post. The only light came from German flares fired at random along the front.

The raiding party crawled out of the listening post and across the tortured ground, Jed holding on to Mike's boot as they moved forward. When a flare blossomed overhead, he froze with the others his face buried in the stinking earth. After the flare died out, they inched forward and made it to the German wire gathering in a large shell crater.

"We'll wait here until the ruckus starts," Brock whispered.

They had no canteens and sucked on lemons to assuage their thirst. The sloshing sound of a half-filled canteen might give away their approach.

Brock hissed in Jed's ear. "Stay awake and be here when we get back."

"I'll be here," Jed shot back.

Bright sparks of light erupted far to the right followed ten seconds later by the booms of impacting artillery rounds. Machine gun fire underlay the sharp accents of the artillery.

"Let's go," Brock said. He led the patrol through a wire gap and they jumped into the German trench.

There was no one there.

A zigzag of empty trenches ran to the right and left. Brock led the others forward down a communication trench toward the German second line.

Jed settled into his position, sitting on the firing step of the main trench and shivering as the temperature dropped. The machine gun and artillery fire to the right raged on.

After ten minutes, several pistol shots rang out where Brock and the patrol had gone.

Nervous minutes later, five figures appeared out of the gloom. Brock urged a German soldier along with pushes to his back. Mike stood next to Brock and Doody covered the trench, pistol in one hand, bayonet in the other. Bunny moved to Jed's side.

"We got one," Brock said, "quiet as eternity. Then their sergeant came by to check on him and raised the alarm. They'll send a patrol. We've got to move."

A flare lit overhead and German soldiers raced down the communication trench toward them. Doody shot the first one who dropped, skidding in the mud, and then parried the bayonet thrust of the second and drove his bayonet deep into his chest. Brock shot the third one and swiped at his neck with the bolo knife. The man fell into the mud, blood spurting from his neck. Another German squeezed past the hand-to-hand fighting and advanced toward Jed and Bunny with his rifle. Brock grabbed him from behind in a bear hug. Mike smashed the German in the face with his fist as the man fired. The bullet traveled high over Bunny's head as the German went limp, his neck broken. He dropped his rifle. The original prisoner grabbed the falling rifle and swiped at Bunny with the bayonet. Bunny danced back, but the bayonet caught his arm. The German whirled, advanced on Jed, and raised the rifle to fire. Jed couldn't fire his own rifle; Brock was behind the German.

The German pulled the trigger and nothing happened. He worked the bolt to load a live round into the chamber. Jed raised his rifle ready to parry a bayonet thrust but he couldn't parry a bullet.

He was calm inside. *So, this is how it happens.*

The German groaned and his eyes rolled up as he crumpled face down into the bottom of the trench.

Bunny wiped his bayonet on the German's pant leg. "Kidney, it's quick and painful."

More illumination flares blossomed overhead.

Doody searched the pockets of the dead Germans.

Another German raced up, skidding to a stop in the mud. He glanced at the Americans and his dead comrades then sprinted away. Brock fired at him but missed.

"Now they know their patrol is dead, they'll either come in force or use artillery." Brock cursed and then turned to Mike. "Why did you kill him? I had him under control. We could have had two prisoners, now we have none."

"He was going to shoot Bunny."

Brock turned to Jed. "You did nothing."

"You want me to shoot him this close? I'd have hit you behind him."

Brock raised his bloody bolo. "You babies will get me killed. If you chicken out on me again, I'll kill you myself." Brock turned to Bunny. "What's your story?"

"He was going to kill Jed. I took him down as quick as I could."

Doody pushed past Brock. "If y'all are gonna jack jaw like this, those German fellas will be along directly. Let me see your arm, Bunny."

"How is it?" Brock asked.

Doody tied a bandage around Bunny's arm.

"It doesn't hurt at all, Sarge," Bunny said. "I'll be all right."

The concern on Brock's face disappeared. He grabbed his stomach and winced.

"You all right, Sergeant?" Doody asked.

"This goddam food out here has my guts roiled up."

"We got no time for shittery."

Germans shouted to each other nearby.

"They're calling for artillery," Jed said.

"Let's go," Brock said. "Cover us, Martin. Can you?" Colored rockets soared over the German lines. "They'll rain holy hate on this position any minute." Brock looked at the dead Germans with disgust. "Damn, no prisoner."

Brock, Bunny and Doody climbed out of the trench.

Mike turned to Jed and held out his right hand. He was holding a hand grenade.

"Thunder Fist," Jed said.

Mike pulled the pin and tossed the grenade as far as he could toward the Germans. It exploded with a satisfying crunch.

Jed and Mike climbed out of the trench and jumped into the large shell hole with the rest of the patrol.

A red rocket climbed from the German lines.

Distant artillery barked.

"We go now," Brock said. The men crawled out of the hole and back across the open ground toward their starting point.

Artillery shells landed in the trench complex and splinters whizzed overhead but no one was hit. They found an old section of a communication trench and stood up, making faster progress. The sky grew lighter as dawn approached.

Halfway down the trench, a bout of intestinal cramping hit Brock. He halted the patrol and pulled something out of the muck. It was a battered German helmet with a mess of scrambled hair and brains inside. He attempted to shake the matter out but the gooey mass stuck inside the helmet. He shrugged his shoulders and pushed the helmet into the mud, pulled down his pants, squatted over the upturned helmet and relieved himself of his diarrhea. He pulled up his trousers and strode down the trench.

Doody stepped past the putrid bucket and called out to Brock, "You need to eat some greens, Sarge. Clear that right up for you."

Bunny spat into the helmet, "If the Boche see that they'll know what we think of them."

As the raiding party approached the listening post, the sun rose above the horizon.

"DAYTON," Timmy said out of sight in the listening post.

"TOLEDO," Brock replied.

The men crawled into the hole.

"Did you get a prisoner?" DiNiccola asked.

Brock hooked a thumb at Mike. "Irish broke the neck of the one we should have had."

"Killed him with one punch," Doody said.

Watkia washed Bunny's wound with iodine and closed the cut with three stitches.

The men moved to their own shelter under a bright blue sky.

Jed looked to the east, beyond the vile scar of no-man's-land. The terrain sloped up into the foothills of the Vosges Mountains, green and purple and gold above the stain and waste of the combat zone. He looked through a box periscope. The view revealed grass and flowers growing in the churned earth. In this so-called quiet zone, with the enemy on constant watch, it was too dangerous to pick flowers or mow the lawn.

Jed spread his gear on the firing step in the sun to dry and then flopped down in the squad dugout and pulled his blanket around him. In the afternoon, he'd join a detail to go to the rear and get lunch.

CHAPTER 14

SEPTEMBER 12, 1918
SUB-SECTOR MONTIGNY,
BACCARAT SECTOR, FRANCE

At noon, Jed, Bunny, and Tony sat on Marmite cans in the reserve trenches next to Clarence Dubman's rolling kitchen. They had made their way to the rear through sporadic harassing German artillery fire only to learn that they'd have to wait until the food was ready.

Tony scratched under his arm. He dropped his cartridge belt, took off his gas mask carrier, and stripped off his blouse and shirt. He sat down searching the garment seams for the ever-present lice. "I can't stand it anymore. I'm going to get rid of these freeloaders." He scraped the cooties out of his shirt with his bayonet.

Jed and Bunny took off their blouses and joined Tony.

"This won't do much good," Bunny said, lighting a cigarette and passing the pack to Jed. "They've been at it laying eggs since we got up here. By tomorrow, we'll be crawling with them again." Bunny used the smoldering tip of his cigarette to chase down the pale gray lice and incinerate them one by one, seeming to get great pleasure in seeing them sizzle and pop under the hot ember. Jed took a cigarette and tossed the pack back.

The Germans continued their random harassing fire on the reserve trenches directed by balloons behind their lines. Most of the rounds landed out of harm's way and Jed watched Bunny and Tony for clues as to the danger from the shells. Once, Bunny looked up as a shell whistled toward them. Jed tensed, ready to throw himself onto the ground, but after listening for a second, Bunny turned his attention back to the seams of his shirt. The shell whooshed past and landed with a groaning roar a half-mile beyond them. A few minutes later, Bunny and Tony yelled, "Down". The men flattened themselves in the trench's bottom. The shell went off outside their trench.

Dubman calmed the mules hitched to the mobile kitchen. He checked the fires under his cooking pots and replaced items shaken out of their storage bins. Another shell landed nearby, but he didn't seem to notice. He made sure the lids sat on top of the pots.

"Don't you think you should take cover, Dub?" Jed asked. "Those German balloons must see your red hair."

"The Lord will take care of me."

Their British advisor, Sergeant Bert McClardy, walked up and stood beside Jed. He lit a match and touched it to Jed's cigarette, used it to stoke his pipe, and threw the spent match in the mud, saying, "Only two, bad luck for three." He observed the Americans searching the seams of their clothing. "Our lads call this chatting, sitting around having a chat and a smoke and battling the little buggers." He drew on his pipe and squatted down next to Tony. "There's a better way, you know."

"What you have in mind, Bert? I try anything," Tony said.

McClardy reached into his haversack and pulled out two bars of soap. He broke each in half and tossed one half to each of them.

"We can't take a bath up here," Jed said.

"It's not for bathing lads. Moisten it and rub it into the seams of your clothes. Lifebuoy soap is a strong disinfectant and the little blighters can't stand it. Soon they'll be marching right out your shirtsleeves and collars in formation, mark my word."

Jed sniffed the bar's strong chemical odor. "Will this work?"

"You don't see me scratching," McClardy said.

"Don't you need these?" Bunny asked, holding up the soap.

"My wife sends me a few bars every couple of months. I have plenty stored away." He knocked the dead coals out of his pipe. "When I launder my kit, the tunic and trousers clean up like new. It takes a bit of rinsing, mind you, what with all the soap and sweat soaked in, but it works."

McClardy waved off Jed and the others' thanks. "Think nothing of it, lads. I'm glad to help out."

Dubman announced the stew was ready.

The men dressed and lugged the cans to the rolling kitchen. A large steaming pot containing a thick, greasy stew sat at the back of the kitchen wagon. "Today's slum has meat, turnips, and carrots," Dub said.

Tony peered into the pot. "What kinda meat?"

Dubman filled the Marmites with a large ladle. "One of the supply train horses got hit by a shell yesterday," he said, not looking up. As the men groaned, Dubman paused. "If you don't want it, I've got plenty of hungry soldiers to feed."

"Just fill us up, all right?" Bunny said.

Jed poked Tony in the ribs. "From now on, don't ask what's in it."

Dubman filled the Marmites and helped the men into the canvas harnesses holding the fifty-pound cans. He filled two large sandbags with bread loaves, tied the open ends together, and draped them around Tony's neck.

"The punk's a little stale," Dubman said, "but it's all I've got."

A German shell rushed in and detonated fifty yards away. After the dirt and mud stopped falling around them Mess Sergeant Smitty appeared in a dugout doorway. "Dubman, pack up so's we can move." He disappeared underground.

"You'd think the fat bastard would help me," Dubman said. "The major found him loafing in the rear and ordered him up. He's not happy."

Bunny took the lead. They moved as fast as their loads allowed into a communication trench and started toward the front.

A rising shriek engulfed them.

The shell landed at the edge of the trench as Jed squatted, balancing his load. No one was hit, but part of the sodden trench wall collapsed and knocked Tony down, burying his legs in mud. His Marmite can lid opened and half the contents spilled out into the trench. Jed helped Tony get out of his straps and dug his legs out of the muck. Bunny set his can down and scooped the stew off the ground, putting it back in Tony's Marmite.

"What are you doing?" Jed asked.

"We need all of this. A little dirt won't hurt anything." Bunny put the can lid back on. "Are you all right, Tony?" he asked as he hoisted the can onto his back. The Italian nodded yes. "You take my can. I'll give this one to those First Section hand bomber dopes."

They arrived in the front-line trenches a half hour later. The hungry men of the platoon filled their mess kits and spread along the trench.

Bunny returned from his delivery. "Those bomber boys were dubious about the slum but I told them it was the same thing we had." He winked at Tony who grinned and dipped a crust of bread in his own stew.

The poor quality of the rations and the difficulty of keeping contaminants out of it had an insidious effect on the men of the platoon. It caused severe indigestion and widespread bouts of diarrhea. Doody continued his relentless pursuit of "greens" and was unsuccessful. He suffered as much as anyone. Latrines in isolated saps were in constant use and, when the wait in line was too long, men found a shell hole and relieved themselves in its bottom adding to the mess and discomfort of life at the front. Jed spent his share of time waiting in line, his gut rumbling.

The men emptied the latrine cans five or six times a day. It was the most hated duty. Narrow trenches had been dug to a huge shell hole behind the front-line trenches. The refuse was supposed to be buried in this hole but the blue cloud of flies, which could be seen from a mile away, caused the sanitary detail to throw the buckets as far as possible and retreat. In the far rear areas, kerosene was pumped in and the contents burned, but this near the front it wasn't practical. It was one more misery the men had to endure.

Jed and Watkia relieved Doody and Collins at the periscope in the listening post at midnight.

Sergeant Lipsitz and the Brit advisor McClardy were on patrol in no-man's-land with Bunny, Timmy Smith, Tony DiNiccola, and three men from Second Squad: a tall man named Arliss Howe and two other riflemen named Tommy Pricklin and Phil Zyren. Their job was to capture prisoners.

Jed asked Watkia, "You're experienced and do a lot for the squad, Andy, why aren't you a sergeant?"

"They made me a PFC because I've been in the Guard for a while but I don't want stripes." He took a drink from his canteen. "They say I have leadership qualities but all I do is make deals. I have no conscience. I can ask anyone for anything, and if I don't get it, I have other ways." Watkia leaned toward Jed. "I want to survive this and go back to Ohio to the family business. My Polish ancestors were Jews. They wouldn't work in the mines or steel mills, so we sell furniture, good stuff, all made in North Carolina and shipped to us by train. My granddad named the business Watkinson's Furniture because it sounded more American. My uncle took over the business after my dad died."

Watkia drank from his canteen and passed it to Jed who took a long drink of water mixed with wine.

"My drill sergeant, Henry Bonner, we called him Bruiser, said it would be hard here," Jed said, "but things like this make it better." He handed the canteen back.

"Bonner was right. It's tough, so we ought to have whatever small luxuries we can find. That's my department." Watkia looked through the periscope. "I hear you're a farmer. Are you going back to the land?"

"I don't know what I'll do." Jed stared between his feet. "I wanted to get away from my uncle, he's bossy and bitter. I got drafted, so that took care of that, but I miss my aunt Bessie something awful." He picked up a few pebbles and tossed them into a puddle. "If I don't go back, he won't be able to work the farm alone."

Watkia drained the last drops from the canteen and put it away. "Family is important but they don't always want what you want. I'm lucky. My whole family is as cynical and mercenary as I am. Come here and watch for a while."

Jed sat at the periscope. Nothing moved in no-man's-land. The only light was from the Milky Way slashed across the sky, amazing beauty amidst the mud and filth.

A flash lit up no-man's-land followed two seconds later by the dull boom of a German stick grenade. Someone screamed then went silent. An American Enfield barked.

Watkia joined Jed at the periscope. "What do you see?"

"Nothing," Jed said.

The Germans sent up three flares in quick succession but there was no gunfire.

"What do you think happened?" Jed asked.

"Somebody got stupid." Watkia leaned back and closed his eyes. "Wake me when the patrol gets back."

Jed stared into the periscope for the rest of the hour and saw nothing until a shadow moved at the corner of his vision.

He picked up his rifle. "AKRON."

"YOUNGSTOWN."

"Come on in."

Lips slithered into the listening post followed by the others. Arliss Howe and Phil Zyren lowered Timmy Smith's body to the ground. His face was bloody, his right hand missing.

DiNiccola kneeled beside the limp form and arranged the boy's arms across his chest. "I'm sorry for the virgin sacrifice joke, Timmy," he said, making the sign of the cross.

"He wasn't a virgin," Bunny said. "We hiked over to Brouville the night before we came up here. I know a widow there."

Watkia left the listening post and soon Samis, Trask, and Brock arrived.

"What happened?" Samis asked Lips.

"A nervous German sentry heard us and tossed a grenade. Timmy tried to toss it away, and it went off in his hand." He paused, considering the still form at his feet. "Tommy Pricklin shot the German, and we pulled back without a prisoner."

Samis, his eyes hard and his mouth pressed into a severe line, stared at Timmy.

"We ought to recommend a medal Lieutenant," Trask said.

"The lad did a brave thing," McClardy added.

"Yes," Samis said. "I'll make sure to mention his action in my report."

Brock wiped the blood off of Timmy's face with an empty sandbag.

Jed had seen a dead man before. His grandfather, dressed in his major's uniform, was placed for viewing in his open casket in the farmhouse living room and then buried under two flags and a volley. But Timmy was too young to even be in the army and his volley was the distant drumming of artillery, his flag the sandbag Brock draped over his face.

Sergeant Trask picked up Timmy, cradling him like a baby. He said a silent prayer then carried the body away.

Two automatic riflemen entered the listening post.

"The patrol is dismissed," Samis said. "Watkia and Martin, you are relieved. Go get some sleep."

Jed went to the bunker. Mike was there. Jed told him that Timmy had died saving his buddies from a German grenade, the first man of the squad to die, to "go west."

CHAPTER 15

SEPTEMBER 13, 1918
SUB-SECTOR MONTIGNY,
BACCARAT SECTOR, FRANCE

After Stand-To at dawn, Jed was on sentry duty. The bugler sounded "attention". A German plane droned along the American trench line, disappearing into the scattered puffy clouds hanging over the battlefield, then reappearing into clear air making no move to attack. The division anti-aircraft gunners took a few shots at it but missed.

More engines buzzed and two planes approached the German from behind the allied lines. The German turned his plane toward one of the larger clouds, ducking out of sight. The allied planes, with the roundels of the American air service on their wings, stayed out of the clouds, circling.

Three additional specks appeared high above and swooped down. The American fighters climbed toward the diving planes, the rattle of machine gun fire drifting down.

Mike, Bunny, and Doody climbed out of the bunker into the trench and looked up.

"What's going on?" Mike asked.

"Two of our guys chased a German plane away, but he had friends up above."

The two flights of planes passed close by each other, guns chattering. A thin stream of smoke trailed from the American leader. One of the German craft staggered and stalled, spinning down until the pilot recovered his plane before hitting the ground. The American anti-aircraft guns fired again. At least one round found its mark as part of the plane's tail separated from the craft and fluttered to the ground in no-man's-land. The German jerked his plane around and, with engine screaming, streaked back to the German side of the lines, the black crosses on his wings showing clearly on the white rectangular backgrounds. The other two Germans climbed toward the American planes who were diving straight down firing their guns, smoke now pouring from the leader.

Neither German plane was hit.

The American planes continued their dive then pulled out and drilled their way toward the platoon trench, flames flicking from the engine of the lead plane. The two green and brown fighters streaked fifteen feet above the ground, the pilot of the stricken aircraft scrunching his face in concentration, his eyeballs white behind his goggles as he side-slipped the plane to keep the flames away from the cockpit. The pilot of the second American fighter craned his neck scanning for threats but the German planes had disappeared.

The American craft roared over Jed and the others, the planes' prop wash blowing trash, and filling the air with choking oil fumes.

"Wow, I'd like to fly in one of those things." Mike said.

"I don't know," Jed said. "It looks dangerous."

Bunny swept his arms to indicate the trench. "Dangerous?"

They laughed.

Brock stumbled up the trench buttoning his pants. "What's so damned funny?" Above the background odors of ashes, gas, and putrefaction, Brock reeked of alcohol, and shit.

"You smell like the shithouse at the brewery exploded," Doody said.

Brock sneered. "You ought to know, hick asshole." He clutched his gut and ran back toward the latrine.

"He'll get caught drunk up here and tossed in the slam," Jed said.

"The slam's where he belongs," Mike said.

Doody spat. "He don't eat right and drinks too much."

"None of us eats right, and I'd like to drink more," Bunny said. "The cooler's better than living with rats and whiz-bangs."

At 11 P.M. Jed took his place at a periscope in the main trench. Another patrol had formed up to check the American wire. DiNiccola, Watkia, Collins, Doody and Mike, led by Lieutenant Samis, started to climb out of the trench when a single red rocket rose from the German trenches opposite them.

"Hold on, sir," Jed said.

They watched as the rocket burned out high above the German trenches.

"Call for artillery," Samis said.

A single white flare rose into the sky. Two field pieces barked from the woods behind the German lines. The shells whistled across no-man's-land and exploded fifty feet apart, bracketing the latrine sap. A freshening breeze bringing rain clouds into the sector cleared the smoke away.

The Germans fired two more colored flares into the gathering clouds. As the German guns spoke again a figure stumbled around a zigzag toward the squad position cursing and holding up his trousers with both hands. The two shells obliterated the latrine sap and knocked the running man onto his face in a puddle. Tony and Collins rushed forward and picked Sergeant Brock up out of the mud. He shrugged off their help, grabbed his falling pants, staggered forward, and sat down on the firing step, shaking. "Those Heinie bastards tried to kill me on the shitter."

"I reckon ol' Fritz found your helmet toilet, Sarge," Doody said.

"They can't know I shit in it."

"Shoot, Sarge, they must have figured anybody with a big case of diarrhea must spend a good part of the day on the can. They picked the nearest latrine sap to where they found the helmet. You've been sittin' on the shitter all day. Odds were, they'd get lucky." Brock glared at him. Doody grinned.

A booming thump reverberated from deep in the German woods and a large sparking shell arced up into the clouds. It made a mad whoof-whoof-whoof sound, pin-wheeling red sparks as it arced out of the clouds and landed behind the American lines.

"Everybody down!" Samis yelled. Jed dove off the firing step and sprawled on duckboards slimy with mud.

A blinding flash lit up the trench followed by an ear-splitting roar. Jed's body bounced off the duckboards and dropped back into the bottom of the trench. The sound reverberated through the trenches and echoed off the woods behind the German lines. Jed hugged the ground for several seconds but, as there was no more German fire, he picked himself up and wiped off the mud.

It started to rain.

Gobs of filth splattered down.

"Jesus Christ," Brock said, "they hit the shit dump."

Everyone scrambled to get under cover to avoid the filthy downpour. The shit rain lasted ten seconds.

Jed scrunched under the corrugated tin roof covering the periscope but couldn't avoid all the mess. When the shit storm stopped, a stench engulfed the area worse than any Jed had experienced so far. Several men vomited. It was all Jed could do not to join them. Soldiers groaned and cursed all along the American lines.

Samis motioned for quiet. "Listen…"

The men climbed onto the firing step and eased their ears toward the top sandbags, straining to hear. Brock, miserable and shivering, heard it. "Those slimy Hun bastards."

Waves of laughter drifted across no-man's-land from the German lines.

"*Amerikanische Soldaten.* You need not worry about an attack. We do not want those trenches now."

It rained, water from the clouds this time, but the showers didn't improve the situation. The rain washed the filth and stink into the sumps under the duckboards and into concentrated puddles. Jed moved out from under the periscope's protective tin roof.

Doody climbed up to relieve him. "Why are you sittin' out in the rain, boy?"

"Trying to wash this stink off me," Jed said.

"You could stand out here naked and not get clean," Doody said. He exchanged places with Jed and scooted back under cover. "This war stink will never wear off."

Jed peeled off his blouse and left it hanging in the rain beside other garments on a wire someone had strung across the trench then joined his squad mates sleeping under rain slickers and shelter halves along the firing step. They would take a chance on a random German shell rather than suffocate in the bunker.

The rain stopped after Stand-To. They bailed out as many puddles as they could and Mike and Jed dug a new latrine sap.

Brock walked up. "I think I'll test out this new commode for our Frog buddies. The French 14th Infantry is relieving us." Brock's gut rumbled. "Go get your gear ready to move out."

Two hours after sunset, a French captain and two of his men in clean horizon blue uniforms arrived in the front-line trenches accompanied by

Captain Brown and Lieutenant Samis. The squad stood together awaiting Samis' order to withdraw. They looked like the First Battalion men had looked four days before: charcoal blackened faces, filthy uniforms, and hollow eyes from lack of sleep.

The two enlisted Frenchmen grumbled.

"*Merde partout.*"

"*Américains dégoûtants.*"

"*Attention!*" The French soldiers braced at their captain's order.

"Yeah, shit everywhere," Brock said. "You'll be disgusting in a few days, too."

"Your tour here has been a difficult one, Captain," the French officer said.

Brown explained what happened.

"I see. The Boche are a nasty bunch, no?"

The Frenchmen walked up and down the trench with a shaded flashlight. One man made careful notes as the captain dictated. At length, he returned and said to Brown, "We will be here two hours before first light."

"We'll be waiting, sir," Brown said. The French captain saluted and the blue coats disappeared up the communication trench.

"Sir, do we wait seven more hours to leave?" Mike asked.

Captain Brown scanned the mess, his nose wrinkled in disgust. "I'm sorry, but yes. If it's any consolation, a load of this stuff ran down the steps into the company dugout and the staff is sleeping out in the open." To Samis he said, "Set your sentries and have the men get as much rest as possible." He left the way the French had gone.

Jed took a fitful nap. At three in the morning, he took his turn at the periscope. A light rain fell, and he gathered it in his hands and washed his face, breathing in the clean mist.

When the rain stopped, Jed pulled out a Red Cross postcard and wrote:

> *Sep 14, 1918*
> *Dearest Aunt and Uncle,*
> *I am dirty and cold but I haven't been hurt.*
> *Our casualties have been light.*
> *Please don't worry.*
> *Jed*

A half hour later, the French captain returned with a section of riflemen weighed down with empty sandbags, picks, shovels, and collapsible buckets. Captain Brown, his face haggard from lack of sleep, returned the Frenchman's salute.

"I relieve you, sir," the Frenchman said.

"I stand relieved, sir."

Brock led the rifle section up the communication trench past the arriving French soldiers. "I left a nice welcoming present for you in your new latrine, Froggy," he said. The Frenchmen recoiled from the smelly American and Brock roared with laughter.

CHAPTER 16

SEPTEMBER 15, 1918

MERVILLER, FRANCE

They lined up at the laundry and delousing station as the rising sun peeked out beneath low clouds. Quarter Master Corps officers relegated all items of the platoon's clothing and equipment to destruction except rifles, bayonets, and helmets. They dumped the rest into a large trash bin. Jed received a towel and a canvas bag for personal items. He hid his Derringer there.

Their filthy condition earned them twice the initial thirty seconds under a hot shower, then a half minute of cold rinse, then two minutes of soaping under warm water and thirty seconds of warm rinse.

Jed felt human again. He rubbed a fresh coat of Lifebuoy soap into the seams of his new clothes.

After he dressed, he sat on a wooden bench outside the delousing station with Mike and Doody. They watched flashes on the horizon and heard the delayed fump-fump of American artillery and the chump-chump of shell impacts in the German lines.

"Well, I reckon some other poor bastards are gettin' hit and not us," Doody said.

A wagon drawn by two mules stopped next to where the men sat.

The driver sat staring at Jed.

"Teddy!" Jed jumped up and hurried to the wagon. Mike and Doody joined him.

Theodore Roosevelt Stains looked down from his perch on the driver's seat. "James Jedidiah, Michael Sean, sir," he nodded to the three in turn.

"Theodore Roosevelt Stains," Jed said, "this is Doody, Steven Foster Dodd."

"Steven Foster." Teddy touched his overseas cap in salute.

Doody returned the salute. "Private Stains."

"Teddy, what are you doing here?" Mike asked. "We haven't seen you since Pike."

"We got some infantry training at Camp Pike then they shipped us over here. Most of the boys ended up in the Pioneer Battalions building roads and digging trenches and graves. My captain found out I could get these old mules through mud holes none of the other boys can. He said he would send me to a supply unit supporting the engineers. I wrote to James Enoch and he told me your division. I asked him to send me here and he did."

"That's great," Jed said.

"I even got the rating of Wagoner." Teddy indicated a round patch with an embroidered wagon wheel on it sewed to his right sleeve. "I found Old Clem there and claimed him. We run supplies between the division dumps and the engineers near the front."

Jed patted the familiar old mule's neck.

"I'm doing what the white wagoners do and they don't like it, but they can't do anything about it." Teddy glanced at Doody then went on. "There's two all Negro infantry divisions, the 92nd and 93rd, but the 93rd's four regiments are attached to four different French divisions. They wear French uniforms and equipment but are at the front training and will probably see action." He looked down dejectedly. An awkward silence passed until Teddy raised his head, "I wanted to get into the fight at the front. I'm too good at driving these stubborn old mules."

A supply truck careened around a corner and roared toward the wagon. The driver swerved past and sounded his horn.

"Get out of the road, boy!"

As the truck sped away an empty wine bottle splashed into the mud. Teddy grimaced as he struggled to hold the mules steady. A dirty rag wrapped his left hand.

Jed and Mike climbed into the wagon seat and sat on either side of him.

"What happened to your hand?" Jed asked.

"You infantry don't have all the danger." Teddy said. "A big shell hit near the division dump and I got a bit of steel going by."

"Sounds like action to me," Mike said.

93

"Dangerous enough, but it's not what I had in mind."

"Why didn't they put a proper bandage on it?" Jed asked.

Teddy stared hard at the backs of the mules. "The supply sergeant said he didn't have time to tend to me. I had to get this wagon load forward right away."

"Cargo can wait for a wounded man," Mike said.

Teddy raised an eyebrow. "I guess old supply sarge will do anything to get the 'stain' out of his lily-white wagoner's world."

Jed removed the blood-soaked bandage. The back of Teddy's hand was laid open as if cut by a sharp knife.

"This ought to be stitched up." He turned in the seat. "Doody, go get Watkia and his bag." Jed pressed the wound closed with the bloody bandage. "You're not missing out on anything Teddy. Up there it's nothing but mud and shit, going crazy waiting for a shell to mash you into the earth. You're in enough danger in what you're doing."

Watkia and Doody hurried toward them. Watkia stopped short when he saw Teddy.

"Andy, come up and help this man. He's a friend of ours," Jed said.

Watkia took Mike's place and examined the wound. "I'm not a real medic but I can stitch this up for you if you want." Teddy nodded and Andy pulled a small surgical kit out of his bag. He cleaned the wound with iodine and closed it with six stitches. Teddy sat mute with tight pressed lips. Watkia tied a fresh bandage around the hand and handed Teddy two small bottles of iodine and two extra bandages. "Change the bandage every day. As soon as you get to an aid station, you should get a real doctor to look at it."

"Thank you, Mister Andy."

Watkia waved him off. "A friend of theirs is a friend of mine. Good luck." He changed places with Mike, rejoining Doody next to the wagon.

"They should give you a wound chevron," Mike said.

"Michael Sean, they won't even treat me, how they gonna give a chevron?"

"Not everybody's like your supply sergeant, Teddy," Jed said.

Sergeant Brock came around the delousing building corner. "What the hell's going on here? What are you doing messing around with this darkie?"

"Yeah, but some are exactly like your supply sergeant," Mike said.

Jed and Mike jumped down and stood beside Doody and Watkia. Brock looked hard at Andy. "Get out of here, Watkia. You know what you're supposed to be doing."

Watkia hurried off.

Brock turned to the other three. "I asked you babies a question."

"Teddy's a friend of ours from back home," Jed said. "He's hurt, so we helped him."

"Hurt?" Brock's right eye twitched as his normal sneer battled with a concerned frown. "Does it hurt much?" he asked Teddy his hand going reflexively to his canteen.

Teddy maintained a deadpan expression. "No, Sergeant, it don't hurt any at all."

The sneer won the battle on Brock's face. He turned to the white soldiers standing before him. Brock feigned an exaggerated southern drawl, "So you Arkansas hick farm boys have darkies for friends? Bless your heart. What about you Doody? You got any of them you hold hands with down in Virginia, or wherever you're from?"

"Well, Sarge, I can't say the folks back home, in *West* Virginia, don't have certain opinions about the coloreds but we only hold hands with the local gals and the colored folk go on about their business."

Doody stared Brock down.

Brock waved dismissively at Teddy. "Go on about your business, boy."

Teddy took a deep breath. He nodded to Jed and Mike then hitched his reins and started the wagon on its way.

Mike took a step forward. "You don't talk to our friends like that, Brock."

Brock squinted at Mike. "So, you want to take a poke at your old sergeant, huh?" A smile cracked across his puffy face like a split in an overripe tomato. "If you want to fight, I have the answer. I entered you in a boxing match scheduled for tomorrow. You go up against Wiesnetsky from M Company. He's from Massillon, Ohio but, instead of going to high school, he worked in the coal mines of West Virginia." He sneered at Doody. "I hear he can push a loaded coal car up a staircase and not break a sweat."

Mike shook his head. "I ain't fighting for you, Brock."

Brock leaned forward. "Oh, yes you are my fine, Mick, hick friend. I've had Watkia out rounding up enough wine to kill fifty Frenchmen and I bet it all on you. You've got the most brawn of anybody in the company and I saw what you did to that big Kraut with one punch." He stepped back, raising his chin in challenge. "You won't let us down. If you lose, it better be by death, because if you lose and live, your life will be one pain-pissing hell, courtesy of me. Martin and Doody, you're his corner men. The same goes for you if he loses."

"You're a filthy pig, Brock," Mike said.

"I'm a filthy pig? The three of you aren't out of the delousing house five minutes and you're crawling all over some lousy darkie."

"I told you about talking about our friend."

"Touch me and you'll spend the rest of the century in the stockade."

Mike stared hard but relaxed his shoulders.

"Good decision, Irish." Brock shook his head. "You babies fail inspection. I want you clean for the match tomorrow. Get your sorry asses back in the cootie-cooker, on the double." They hesitated. "On the double, I said."

The three men grabbed their gear and trotted toward the delousing station.

"Save up all that anger, Irish," Brock called. "Use it on that M company Polack."

As soon as they rounded a corner out of sight they slowed to a walk.

"Brock is pure scum," Jed said.

"He'll get his one day," Mike said, calmer now, his face still red.

"Are you some kind of fighter?" Doody asked.

"I've done some boxing where I made a little money."

"Well, a professional." Doody slapped Mike's muscled arm and squeezed his square shoulder. "You could take a doughnut-faced asshole like Brock with no problem."

"Maybe so," Mike grinned, "but I don't want to spend the next eighty-two years in the stockade." The two men laughed.

Mike halted in front of the delousing station doorway.

"Do you fellows feel dirty?"

"I reckon I'm as clean as I been in a month," Doody said. Mike and Doody headed toward their billets and the chow line, joking about what Mike would do to Wiesnetsky.

Jed followed, not laughing.

CHAPTER 17

SEPTEMBER 17, 1918

TRAIN STATION, BACCARAT, FRANCE

The war and the army interfered with Brock's plans for the boxing match. The 37th Division was ordered to move by train to a new area near Robert Espagne, France, to be available, if needed, to support the assault on the Saint-Mihiel salient begun on September 12th. The Rifle Section filed to a rail siding at three in the morning and stood beside a stinking French forty-and-eight boxcar, designated for forty men or eight horses.

Thanks to Watkia, the Rifle Section wasn't as cramped as the rest. Andy called the French train conductor to the side, held up two packs of cigarettes, and shined a flashlight into a white envelope he held part way open. The Frenchman scanned his immediate surroundings as Andy spoke in his ear. The conductor said *Oui*, tucked the envelope and cigarettes into his inside blouse pocket, and walked away.

Watkia waved toward the shadows beside the station house. Brock, Bunny, and Doody appeared pulling a cart piled high with cases of wine. They loaded the wine and cart into a dark rear corner of the boxcar. First and Second Rifle Squads scrambled aboard and slid the car door shut. It was relative luxury, sixteen men in a space normally reserved for forty. They laid out shelter halves on the dank straw as mattresses, used their packs as pillows, and huddled under their blankets. The air reeked of manure and sweat but after the eruption of the waste dump Jed didn't mind too much.

When the conductor and an American transportation sergeant appeared a half hour later, the men crowded toward the door in a dense clump. Brock reported all present and accounted for. The American seemed unsure but the French conductor urged him along pointing to his watch. Brock closed the door. Watkia lit a kerosene lantern and opened the ventilation hatch in the roof. The interior of the car became cozy despite the smell.

Someone knocked on the door. Brock cracked it open. Dubman stood there holding a steaming kettle. "I've got stew here, Sergeant," he said.

The train engineer sounded the whistle, and the car lurched as the engine took up the slack in the long train. Brock slid the door farther open and grabbed the kettle of stew and a ladle from Dubman's hands, handing them to Jed.

"What're you holding?"

"The pot for the next car up."

The train inched forward.

"Give it to me and get in."

"I've got to get it to the other guys. This is the last one."

Brock snatched the second pot from Dubman.

Mike leaned out and hauled Dubman inside as the train began to roll. "You can ride with us, Dub. Thanks for bringing us supper."

Dubman protested but Brock shut him up. "If you get off now, you'll be left behind."

Dubman took the pot from Jed and served the stew into the men's mess tins. Brock took his share and sat with one leg dangling out the door. Mike sat in the open door too, next to Bunny. Watkia woke Doody up and gave him his share. The golden light of the lantern and the warm stew lent a sense of peace and safety to the stark interior of the car.

"Where is your kitchen and mules?" Jed asked Dubman.

"They loaded them on a car further back."

Watkia produced six bottles of wine and passed them around. Brock claimed one and drained half of the bottle in one giant gulp.

When the first pot of stew was empty Jed handed Dubman the other.

"Give me some more," Brock demanded.

"Do you like it, Sarge? It's real beef."

"It's the best thing I've eaten all day."

Dubman slid into a corner, a dejected look on his face.

Jed leaned toward him. "The stew is really good, Dub." Dubman's eyes lit up, and he smiled revealing a swollen lower lip and a missing tooth. "What happened to you?"

"One of my mules kicked me yesterday."

"Looks bad," Jed said.

"I'll be OK." Dubman pointed at the wine cases. "What's that?"

"The wine we're betting on Mike for the division boxing championship," Watkia said. "We have the Company M bet here too. I worked a deal. I'm holding the whole jackpot and it'll be paid out when the match is over. Our contender," he pointed to Mike sitting in the door, "is gonna murder that coal-mining Polack."

Brock slammed his hand down. "He'd better."

"Here, Dub. Have a drink," Jed said, offering one of the wine bottles.

"It'll make the pain go away," Brock said.

Dubman took a long drink. "I'm glad you liked the stew, Jed. I know army food ain't great, but I try to serve up the best I can with what I have." He drank again. "Some boys accuse me of not caring what they eat." He looked intently at Jed, his eyes glistening. "I do care. I'd never deliberately serve anything bad for the guys."

"We know, Dub." Bunny said, holding an unlit cigarette.

Jed struck a match, lit Bunny's cigarette then one for himself. He held the still burning match up by Dubman's face. A curving bruise sat under Dub's right eye and a cut seeped blood under his left eyebrow.

"What's the real story, Dub?" Jed asked.

Bunny moved in closer, "Tell us, maybe we can fix it."

Dubman glanced at Brock who was staring out the door. "It's no surprise that a lot of the guys had diarrhea up in the line, the place was filthy, but the boys blamed me. Corporal Claggett and two of his hand bomber squad accused me of deliberately putting shit in their stew." He was wide-eyed. "I would never do that, but Claggett wouldn't listen. He and his boys worked me over pretty good."

Bunny and Jed locked eyes drawing hard on their cigarettes.

"There was a mistake, Dub," Bunny said. He looked as disgusted as Jed felt. "We'll see if we can fix it for you."

Dubman shook his head. "I don't want you fighting men getting into trouble over me. Besides, Jed, Claggett's men are friends of yours, Bart and Clay Jones."

"Don't worry Dub. I've had trouble with those two all my life."

Dub leaned back and fell asleep. Jed rolled a blanket and put it under his head.

"We'll have to take care of Claggett eventually," Bunny said, "but, there's something more pressing. Brock is determined to have this boxing match as soon as possible. Do you think Mike can take Wiesnetsky?"

"Yes," Jed said. "He'll do it for us."

"For all our sakes, he better." Bunny flipped the butt of his cigarette past Brock sleeping with his legs dangling out of the door, then lay back on his straw.

The car swayed gently and a cool breeze drifted through the door driving away much of the mustiness and stale smoke.

Sleepless, Jed pulled out the most recent letter from Bessie. He read it by the lamp light.

> *September 1, 1918*
> *Dearest Jed,*
> *I hope you are safe and not in much danger. I wish you would write more often so I would know you are all right, but I know you are busy and appreciate every letter or postcard.*
> *We are getting many cases of influenza in the clinic. It's so sad to see young people grow weak and die, but we do everything to help them. Older folks don't seem to be vulnerable but I take my precautions.*
> *Please don't worry.*
> *I feel when I write this to you, you are here in spirit.*
> *Take care of yourself, Jed. Come back to us.*
> *I pray the Good Lord keep you safe.*
> *Gott beschütze dich,*
> *Aunt Bessie*

CHAPTER 18

SEPTEMBER 18, 1918

LONGEVILLE, FRANCE

At noon, the jolt of the train slowing woke them up. Brock slid the door closed, and the men prepared to debark. The train stopped and Brock opened the door and peeked out. They dropped down from the car and stretched the cramps out of their muscles, mingling with men from other cars so they couldn't be counted.

Their billet was a large house with a solid roof. An artillery shell had traveled horizontally through one outside wall and blown out an interior wall but there was running water from a pump in the kitchen and the fireplace kept the house warm. Sergeant Brock and the corporals chose the small bedroom in the back. It had cots, mattresses, and a table and chairs. The privates occupied the larger front room. They hauled in straw to form makeshift mattresses for their cots. They hid the cart with the wine cache in a shed out back. The rest of the day they drilled and stood to an inspection.

Abel rescheduled the boxing match. Overnight, the engineers erected a ring under camouflage netting with crates and boxes around it for bleachers. Dubman and the other cooks made a breakfast of beef stew, punk and strawberry jam, canned peaches, and fresh coffee. With full bellies, and local wine and cognac, five hundred members of the division arrived for the match, mostly from 2nd and 3rd Battalions of the 147th Regiment. Abel declared it the division boxing championship.

The combatants were Mike "Thunder Fist" O'Kean from Company G and Stanislaw "Big Stan" Wiesnetsky from Company M.

"Are you ready for this?" Jed asked.

"I came out of basic training in great shape and the marching we've done has kept my legs fit," Mike said. "He can't have trained much more. I've seen him. He's my size, a little taller and heavier. I'm hoping he's long on strength and short on speed and agility."

"There's a lot at stake, Mike."

"Are you afraid of eight decades in the stockade?"

"No, but Brock—"

"I'm not going to lose. I'll know how to win in two rounds."

Doody brought Mike's boxing gloves. "We're countin' on you, son. The platoon has bet a month's pay on you."

"More pressure," Mike said with a wink. "You two be ready with a water bottle and a towel. I'll do the rest."

Doody finished lacing Mike's gloves as the bell sounded. The two boxers and their seconds gathered at the middle of the ring. Sergeant Bert McClardy officiated. "According to Marquis of Queensbury rules," he sniffed. "This is for the division championship: five three-minute rounds. Colonel Galbraith, Lieutenant Colonel Fife, and Abel West are the judges. No low blows or any other funny stuff." He braced at attention. "Don't let the side down. Touch gloves and at the bell come out fighting."

In their corner Mike looked at Jed, "Any advice?"

"Yes, win!"

The first round began slowly each fighter wary of the other. Every time Wiesnetsky landed a solid punch, Mike countered with a hard right stopping his adversary's attack.

At the bell Mike returned to the corner shadow boxing and full of energy waving to the First Platoon men who shouted their encouragement.

Doody propped the stool on the canvas and plopped the spit bucket between Mike's feet as he sat down. Jed wiped Mike's face with a towel and dabbed at a bloody cut on his chin. Mike pushed his hand away. "Give me some water."

Mike drank then leaned over the bucket and spat. "Watch Stan closely. Every boxer has a pattern although this guy's more a fighter than a boxer." He took another swig of water. "I can't wear him down in only five rounds. The guy's in great shape. I've got to get him to make a mistake."

The bell rang. Mike bounded to the center of the ring and let Wiesnetsky come to him. Mike darted in and landed a good combination and then backed out before Wiesnetsky could tag him with a left-right-left combination. As he backed out, he misjudged and was caught with his back to the ropes. Stan pounced, landing a good left-right combination. Trapped, Mike counterpunched and caught his opponent on the chin with a solid left jab. Wiesnetsky smiled and started a long, circling roundhouse with his right. Mike easily ducked under it and moved forward to attack the body but Wiesnetsky had been carrying his left low after the combination and now flattened Mike with a vicious left uppercut. Wiesnetsky moved away raising his arms in victory and McClardy started a ten count over the sprawling Mike.

Brock cursed Mike from ringside. Jed's stomach was in a knot but Mike sat up and winked at him. He was up by five and stood working his jaw and flexing his shoulders. Wiesnetsky went after him and landed a left-right combination. Mike ducked back this time and didn't counter punch. The big man stood still with a puzzled look. His corner called for him to fight and he stepped forward to go after Mike who stepped forward also and landed two sturdy left jabs. Wiesnetsky hit Mike with the left-right combination and started the slow decoy right roundhouse again but the bell rang.

Mike returned to the corner and sat shaking his head, blinking his eyes.

Mike turned to Jed. "Well, sparring partner, do you see it?" he asked, working his jaw and slapping his gloves together in anticipation.

"It's the decoy right roundhouse and left uppercut."

"Partly. He's no simpleton but is only so smart. He alternates his combinations: left-right then left-right-left. He doesn't use the decoy trap on the three-punch because he needs to keep the left back for the uppercut. Also, I always counterpunch when I'm hit and when I don't, it confuses him."

"You've got this whole fight under control, don't you?"

"It should be over by the end of round four."

The bell rang. Mike jumped forward to the center of the ring and began to jab incessantly at his opponent with his left and then punched hard with his right. Wiesnetsky's head snapped back, and he retreated to a corner. He held his jaw and winced in pain.

Mike concentrated on Wiesnetsky's left side adding to the damage to his jaw. Mike let his own left down a fraction and Wiesnetsky stepped forward and hit Mike with a right cross. Mike spun and landed face down on the canvas. He was up by the three-count. McClardy checked Mike's gloves and wiped them on the front of his shirt. He stepped back and signaled for the fight to resume.

The bell rang and Mike returned to his corner and slumped onto the stool. He took a large gulp of water.

Brock leaped through the ropes. "You're losing this fight on points, you stupid Mick. If he knocks you down again, you're dead."

Mike spat the rinse water onto Brock's boots. "If you're so smart, why don't you fight him, Brock?"

"I've got a lot riding on this fight and so have you. Use your right hand more. I saw you kill that big Hun bastard with one punch and you can knock this asshole out the same way. You've got thunder in your right hand and you had better use it." Brock took a deep breath and focused on Mike's face. "Win this goddam fight, O'Kean." He staggered back out through the ropes and sat beside Watkia.

Mike stared down into the bucket breathing hard.

"You're taking an awful pounding, Mike," Jed said. "Are you sure you know what you're doing?"

"Look at Stan sitting over there grinning," Mike said not looking up. "He thinks he has me beat, but he's in pain and has lost the left side of his body protecting his broken jaw." Mike rose to the round four bell. "Don't worry, Jed." Mike pounded his gloves together. "It's almost over. Besides, I bet 500 francs on myself at three to five and 100 for you. Watkia's giving eight to five on Stan. If I lose, he goes broke."

The fighters approached each other cautiously. Wiesnetsky fended off Mike's jabs backing away from his right hand then stepped forward with a left-right. Mike countered hard and Wiesnetsky started the decoy right. Mike ducked under it and, when he saw the left start to unload, quickly backed away. Wiesnetsky completed the right cross and continued up with the left flailing wildly when it didn't connect with Mike's head. His arms were helplessly crossed in front of his face. Mike stepped in and hit Stan with three hard right hands to the ribs. Wiesnetsky gasped, pulled his arms down to protect his body and Mike hit him with his own right-left-right combination to the head. Wiesnetsky sat down on the canvas to the raucous cheers of First Platoon.

Wiesnetsky's Company M supporters screamed at him to get up and he did, slowly, blood running from his nose. "Good one, Mike."

Mike kept up the pressure, backing Stan into a corner. Wiesnetsky brought his hands up to his shattered jaw. With a flurry of solid left and right hands Mike worked on his arms and torso.

Brock stood up. "Use the big right again."

Mike backed off slightly and Stan gamely followed him to the center of the ring. Mike jabbed solidly and barely ducked back from a vicious right. The force of the swing disrupted Wiesnetsky's balance. As he staggered forward, Mike hit him with a smashing right hand to his face. Stan collapsed onto the canvas and flopped onto his back, eyes closed, moaning softly. He made no effort to get up.

Mike winked at Jed. He had kept his promise and ended the fight in the fourth round.

McClardy counted Wiesnetsky out and First Platoon erupted, pushing past Jed, trying to get into the ring all at once. They nearly trampled the prostrate Wiesnetsky and marched Mike out of the ring into the surrounding crowd. Doody led the parade, his water bottle replaced by a bottle of wine, waving his towel as a banner of victory.

"He's got a bomb for a right hand," a beaming Brock declared to Watkia who stood nearby, his arms loaded with bottles of wine and cartons of cigarettes.

Jed climbed into the ring and went to where Wiesnetsky's handlers had him sitting up and drinking water. "Are you all right?"

"I'm all right." His voice slurred from his swollen jaw. "Mike is your friend?" Jed nodded. "Most men I hit go down and stay down but not Mike. He's as tough as steel. He will do well in this war, stay close to him." He struggled to his feet and with the help of his handlers climbed through the ropes.

Jed stood alone in the center of the ring, the losing side walking soberly away, the victors marching triumphantly away his best friend on their shoulders.

"Hey, slow down," Mike said. "All y'all talk too fast."

"Y'all say y'all all the time," Watkia said. The Ohio men laughed, intoxicated, especially Sergeant Brock, who was drinking directly from a cognac bottle.

"What's wrong with sayin' y'all? Everybody we know says it, right Doody?"

"Look, I've been tryin' to talk with these here mid-western Yankees for a while now," Doody said, shaking his head. "They go on yammerin' at each other and me. I nod my head and pretend I know what they're sayin'."

Brock's euphoria after the fight had faded with every drink and his disposition had turned foul again. "Bunch of ignorant hicks."

"I forgot you graduated from Ohio State University," Corporal Collins said.

"And there's another one, John Stuart Jackson Hill, a real Johnny-Reb, from Old Virgnny," Brock said pointing to a new replacement who had arrived that morning.

"Where did they find the snake egg you hatched from, Brock?" Collins asked.

"It would be Asshole-tabula, Ohio, Corp," Doody said.

"Shut your face, Corporal," Brock said. He glanced at Doody. "I was born in Cincinnati." He faced Mike again, "I moved to Ashtabula later on. I enlisted in the Guard there and it's my home of record."

"Yeah, after the Sheriff ran him out of New Orleans," Collins said.

Brock's face flushed. "I'll bust your lazy ass out of squad leader."

"Don't do me any favors," Collins said. "You can't help being you, Brock." He tipped his overseas cap forward and leaned back feigning a nap.

"You're as ignorant as these Southerners."

Mike stood up clenching and unclenching his fists. "That's enough."

Brock stood too. "Are you threatening an NCO? I told you what would happen."

"No threat, Sarge." Mike said straight faced. "Would you like to participate in another bout?" Corporal Goldson looked on. "Hey, Cain, do you think Abel can set up another boxing match? Brock wants to prove a point."

"You stay put," Brock said to the company clerk. "It's Sergeant Brock to you, hayseed," he said to Mike.

"Yes, sir, Sergeant Brock," Mike made a show of saluting, slow and exaggerated.

Jed jumped up beside Mike. "Come on, it's chow time."

"Yeah, go get chow," Brock said. "Maybe I can arrange a lot of shit details for you two rednecks."

Mike took a half step forward. "You're a foul-mouthed ignorant idiot, Brock."

Brock wavered while putting on a tough expression. He sat down abruptly and looked away. "Go on. Get out of here before I put you on report."

"Yes, sir," Mike said, "right away. Would you care to join us, Sergeant?"

"Thank you, no," Brock said. "I must help the supply sergeant for an hour, so I regret I cannot join you."

Mike turned and walked away. "Some people should watch how they talk about others, especially when they can't back it up."

After the squad moved away from Brock, their mood lightened. They vied for Mike's attention as they recounted his exploits in the ring. They wolfed down their supper and shadow boxed each other, dancing around Mike's table.

Watkia sat down between Jed and Mike and handed Mike 900 francs. He held out sixty for Jed.

"I didn't make that bet."

"Mike made it for you. He got his stake back and here's your profit."

"Take it, Jed, and put it to good use," Mike said.

"You really do like to gamble," Jed said as he put the notes in his pocket.

Mike shrugged. "It's good when you win."

As the group exited the chow hall Mike pointed to the company supply shed down the street. "Hey, fellas, I'm going to stop into supply and get a new haversack."

"I'm starting a crap game in the Salvation Army hut. Come on down, Mike, and risk some of that money," Watkia said.

"I'll send most of it home. My dad's real sick and can't work. I'll join you fellas after I see the supply sergeant."

"I'll come with you," Jed said.

Mike smiled. "Sure."

Inside the supply shed the only light was from two candles sputtering on the supply sergeant's desk where Brock sat. He grabbed a bottle of cognac off the desk and put it in the bottom desk drawer.

"What do you babies want?"

"Where's the supply sergeant?" Mike asked.

"He's up at the replacement depot. I'm sitting in for an hour."

"I need a new haversack."

"Where's the one we issued you when you came out of the line?"

"Lost it." Mike was relaxed, leaning slightly forward, his fingertips on the desk.

Brock stood up, opened the storage room door and went inside.

Mike winked at Jed.

Brock came out with a new canvas haversack and tossed it on the desk. He pointed to a receipt and pencil on a clipboard. "Sign here."

As Mike signed, Jed asked. "How about the fight today, Sarge? I knew Mike would win."

"He got lucky," Brock said as he leaned over to fill in and sign the issue receipt. "If that Pollock hadn't got his jaw broken, he would have murdered your asshole friend."

"Brock..." Brock raised up and looked Mike in the eye. He started to raise his hands but was too slow. Mike hit him with a right cross and Brock sprawled on the floor.

In the dim shadows behind the desk, Brock rolled over and propped himself up on one elbow. "Why?"

Mike hooked a thumb at Jed. "For picking on him, for calling our friend Teddy a dirty name, and generally for being a jerk."

Brock looked at Jed. "Do you want a piece of me too?" Jed shook his head. "Yeah, I guess not," Brock said, sitting up. "The big Mick is the fighter between the two of you."

Jed's face tingled.

Brock rubbed his face. "Now I know how you beat Wiesnetsky."

Mike offered his hand to help Brock up. Brock slapped it away.

Mike picked up the haversack.

"Go," Brock said waving his hand. "Get out of my sight."

When they got into the street Jed said, "You didn't need a new haversack, did you?"

"No."

Jed shook his head. "Brock could make trouble."

"Brock's not gonna say anything. He doesn't want to draw attention to himself." Mike leaned toward Jed, his jaw set. "Brock's a bully, but he'll back down in private or in public when he doesn't have a weapon. I proved that today."

"I don't know," Jed said.

"This isn't fighting the Joneses or a basic training boxing match."

"You think I'll throw in the towel again? You sound like Bart and Clay."

"You fight hard when you want to. Out here you can't ever back down."

It wasn't like Mike to speak to Jed this way but Jed knew he was right.

Doody hurried up the street. "Come on, Mike. Watkia's starting the crap game. The new Reb from Virginia is bragging how he'll break us."

"Come on. Let's have some fun," Mike said. "It's exciting."

"You go on. I'm not much of a gambler."

Mike slapped Jed on the shoulder "You'll do fine, Jed. Besides, I'll be there to help you." He walked away with Doody.

The sun set behind a gray curtain of clouds, the gloom surrounding Jed.

He walked into a warehouse across the street from the supply shed, sat on a crate in the shadows inside the open door, and lit a cigarette. The smoke slammed his lungs, but he was becoming accustomed to the sensation and immediately felt more relaxed. He sat for several minutes staring at the smoke drifting up from the cigarette.

The supply sergeant returned. After a few minutes Sergeant Brock came out, stumbled to a bench in front of the shed and sat down, taking a drink from the cognac bottle, and setting it down next to him. Brock sat hunched forward, hands clasped, elbows resting on his knees, head down. After a minute, he took another drink. A tear ran down his swollen left cheek and dripped off his chin.

Sergeant Trask strode down the street and stopped in front of Brock.

Jed froze in the shadows and watched.

"What happened to you, Leo?"

"I deserved it." He rubbed his cheek. "I've always deserved it, Les. Dad used to wallop me as a kid. Why should anything be different now?"

"Leo, you had it rough—"

Brock stood. "You're not my keeper, Les. Forget all that happy shit when we were kids. One of us is probably going to die in this war and, if you push me, I'll make sure it ain't me."

He grabbed the cognac bottle and strode away.

Sergeant Trask shook his head and walked the other way.

Jed lit another cigarette and thought about Mike.

CHAPTER 19
SEPTEMBER 20, 1918
LONGEVILLE, FRANCE

The Stars and Stripes

MENTIONED IN ORDERS
HARD LIQUORS

"Soldiers are forbidden either to buy or accept as gifts from the French, any whisky, brandy, champagne, or, in fact, any spirituous liquors. Commanding officers are charged with the duty of seeing that all drinking places where the alcoholic liquors thus named are sold are designated as "off limits.""

THE STARS AND STRIPES: FRANCE, FRIDAY, FEBRUARY 8, 1918, page 4.

The next day the platoon had no drill or inspections. Mike and Jed explored the town.

Longeville was far from the front lines and a few French civilians had set up shops all run by women. One shop sold postcards and lace handkerchiefs, and there was a bakery and a cheese shop.

Jed and Mike stopped by the Salvation Army hut, got a basket of doughnuts, and walked down the main street.

Sergeant Brock sat at a table in the alley by the cheese shop. Bottles of water and the squad's wine sat on the table beside bread and cheese.

Bunny and Watkia sat quietly in the shadows, drinking from small glasses. Mike tossed each of them a doughnut and set the rest on the table. Brock had a bruise on his left cheek but his face was so flushed from drink it was barely noticeable.

Bunny sat up straight. "Whoa, look at her."

A French girl of nineteen or twenty emerged from the bakery across the street carrying a basket. She had long brown hair, and a fresh scrubbed beauty startling to Jed who had seen nothing recently but mud and filth. She acknowledged the soldiers with a shy duck of her head and a nervous smile. Bunny started to rise but Brock pushed him back into his seat. He rose and hurried after the girl to the end of the block, stopping her and speaking to her in French. Jed couldn't hear the conversation, but the girl responded with constant negative shakes of her head. Brock pulled a sheaf of francs out of his pocket. The girl spat an emphatic, "*Non.*" and stormed down the street.

When Brock returned to his seat Watkia handed him his wine. "Nice try."

"Shut up." Brock took a long drink.

"Maybe your French ain't as good as you thought," Watkia said.

"Yeah," Brock said. "I always have trouble with irregular verbs like fuck."

"Where did you learn to speak French, Sarge?" Jed asked.

"My mother moved from Ohio to New Orleans after my dad died. I grew up in a whorehouse and bar in the French Quarter. Most of the girls who worked there were Cajun, and I learned French and a little Creole from them. My mother ran the bar." He looked sharply at all of them. "She wasn't a whore." He drank more wine. "When I turned eighteen, my mother moved back to Ohio, but I stayed on. I liked it there. They made me the bouncer, gave me a room, and paid me in booze and poontang. The madam was a pretty good Creole cook, so I had everything I needed."

"Until he ran back to Momma in Ohio," Watkia said.

Brock glared at Watkia. "Shut up, asshole."

Bunny scooted to the front edge of his chair. "You must have been king of the place, *beaucoup* free pussy."

Brock shook his head in disgust. "They weren't lonely farm girls whose boyfriends were overseas or busted up French widows like you've been picking off here. They were whores—black, white, Chink, or Creole, they were all the same." He ate half a doughnut. "All women

111

are whores. If you marry one, you pay all of your life and eventually, when she's settled in and in control, she'll stop putting out. Others you rent by the half hour. Every woman has her price, Bunny Love, every goddam one."

Watkia poured more wine into his glass. "The French call this *pinard*."

"The Brits say plonk," Brock said, chewing the rest of the doughnut, "for cheap, inferior wine."

Watkia tasted the wine as he sat down and shrugged, "Tastes all right to me."

They poured more drinks, and sat comfortably, chatting, and working on the wine, bread, and cheese.

"Periscope off the port bow," Bunny said.

The French girl walked down the street her arm crooked in the elbow of Lieutenant Samis, her basket filled with several tins of food and three bottles of wine.

Samis thumbed through postcards.

At one point the girl covered her mouth, giggled, and, pointed saying, "*Vous et moi?*"

"*Oui, Mon Cheri*, you and me, soon, I hope."

Brock glared at Watkia.

Watkia ignored Brock.

Mike and Bunny hid the wine bottles. Jed grabbed a water bottle and filled his empty glass.

As the couple approached, Samis slipped the postcards into the basket and waved them to stay seated.

"Good afternoon, men. May I introduce Mademoiselle Angelique Farrar?"

The men touched their caps and nodded.

Angelique's smug expression made Brock's lip curl in disgust.

Samis smiled. "It's a shame you don't have something stronger than water to drink with your bread and cheese." He looked up and down the street then took a wine bottle from the basket and set it on the table. "Don't tell the captain." He winked at Watkia, "I can get more later, can't I Andy?"

Watkia glanced at Brock then nodded.

Angelique stepped up to Bunny and took the cigarette from his fingers. She took a demure puff, staring intently into his eyes. She returned the butt to him, stepped back to Samis, and slipped her arm in his.

"Enjoy, gentlemen." Samis smiled at Angelique and the two walked down the street and around the corner.

Bunny stared after them.

"What did I tell you? They all have their price," Brock said. He turned on Watkia, "You stupid Polack. How did he find out about the postcards and wine?"

"He caught me at mail call. One of the postcard packages was damaged in transit. He found it, opened it, and I had to tell him the whole story." Brock glared at him. "He's OK. As long as he gets his cut, he'll look the other way. He's another layer of protection for us."

"Until he gets his second-louie ass shot off like all the rest," Brock said. He picked up the lieutenant's bottle, popped the cork with his bayonet and poured a round for the group. Raising the bottle, Brock declared, "Here's to our shave-tail louie. May he get pleasure from fucking the little French harlot and lead us on to victory."

Mike begged off having any more to drink. "I celebrated too late last night. I need a good night's sleep. See you later, fellas." He squeezed Jed's shoulder as he left.

"Andy, where do you get those postcards?" Jed asked.

"I get them from home. My brother-in-law owns a photography studio and owes me a lot of money. He takes the pictures, prints up the postcards, and mails them over. I sell them or barter them for stuff we need." He pulled the cigarette out of Bunny's mouth and took a heavy drag on it. "I have two male cousins who run a brothel in Parma, Ohio. The nudes are of their girls and the men are my cousins."

"One postcard had a Sultan and a harem girl."

Watkia chuckled. "My sister and her husband. She's not a whore and only does it with her husband but likes to show off. They once did a series of a nun and a Bishop. Some French priest found one picture and raised Hell. I had to destroy half of a shipment but saved a few of the postcards. They bring the best prices."

"Oh, shit," Brock said.

A small boy walked down the center of the street carrying a German M16 stick grenade. The woman who owned the cheese shop hurried out onto the stoop. *"Claude, no!"* she screamed, and then turned to the Americans. *"Soldats, aider Mon petit-fils!"*

Brock jumped up and started forward. "It's her grandson."

The boy tossed the grenade up into the air and watched as it turned over and arrowed back toward the ground. Giggling, he caught it by the handle and launched it straight up into the air again the porcelain ball on the end of the arming string trailing behind the grenade like the tail of a kite. This time he misjudged his catch and grabbed the porcelain ball. The grenade head bounced off the cobblestoned street at his feet, smoke spewing from its hollow handle. The boy stared at the string and arming rod in his hand.

Brock ran forward. "Everybody down!"

Jed and the others crouched in the alley as Brock wrapped the boy in his arms and threw himself on the ground kicking at the grenade. The lethal object rolled thirty feet away, spun in place, and continued to smoke.

The grenade went off spitting cobblestone fragments against the store fronts.

Jed jumped up and darted into the street.

The grandmother picked herself up off the stoop and ran to her grandson who sat in the middle of the street screaming and holding his bleeding right foot. "*Mon pied!*"

Brock was uninjured. He pulled his handkerchief out of his pocket and wrapped it around the child's foot. He seemed remarkably sober despite how much he had drunk.

Watkia staggered over to Brock holding out a wine bottle. "Jesus Christ, Sarge, doesn't this war shit ever stop?"

Brock ignored the question and grabbed the bottle. The grandmother looked on as Brock gave the boy a drink of wine.

"I'm going to take him to the regimental aid station," Brock said picking the boy up and cradling him in his arms. The grandmother crowded close, crying and praying. Brock spoke to her in French as they hustled down the street.

It was getting dark.

"I've had enough excitement for one day," Jed said.

"We're starting another crap game down at the Salvation Army hut," Watkia said. "Do you want to come?"

Jed shook his head and waved no thanks. "I'm going to turn in and sleep while I have the chance."

As Jed approached the platoon house, the replacement from Virginia sat on the front stoop smoking a pipe. Jed stuck out his hand. "I'm Jed Martin."

The newcomer stood and shook. "John Stuart Jackson Hill."

"That's quite a Southern name."

"I'm named after Confederate generals. My pappy's distant cousin was General A. P. Hill. Most just call me Reb."

"Why are you all by yourself?"

"Most of you are veterans and I'm brand new, hard to fit in." He puffed his pipe. "I never was around so many Yankees and Jews."

"A lot of guys are from the big cities in Ohio."

"I don't like that Jew boy. Watkia would have sold tickets at The Crucifixion."

"He's all right. He gets us a lot of extras," Jed said. "There's a crap game going on at the Salvation Army hut."

Reb kicked at the dirt. "I did too much braggin' last night. They busted me. I think Watkia uses loaded dice."

Jed said nothing.

"Leastways you're from Arkansas, you understand about Jews and Yankees."

"Look, it's tough out here and we rely on each other," Jed said. "The Civil War ended a long time ago."

"Not for some of us."

Jed shook his head. "I'm going to sleep. I'll see you later." He hurried into the house and upstairs.

He found Mike asleep on his cot. Jed took off his boots and blouse and sprawled atop his own cot and was soon asleep.

He awoke later, not to the sounds of a drunken squad returning, but to the soft sound of a woman's voice and the heavy tread of a soldier's boots as they moved into the NCO bedroom across the blown-out wall. Sergeant Brock lit a candle perched on the table and took a long drink directly from a cognac bottle.

Mike woke up and Jed silenced him with a hand raised to his mouth. The two rolled over on their cots hidden in the shadows.

Brock set the bottle down on the table and turned his attention to the woman. Jed recognized the blue shawl the woman wore as the one the grandmother of the injured boy had been wearing.

Brock whispered something into the woman's ear in French.

She shook her head. *"Non."*

He grabbed her firmly by the shoulders and whispered louder.

"Mon petit-fils?" she asked.

"The docs are taking good care of your grandson," he said. "Now you can thank me."

He pushed down with his hands. She resisted, and he slapped her face. He pushed down again, and she complied, kneeling before him. She glared up at him then pulled her blue shawl up over her face into a cowl as he unbuttoned his trousers.

Mike jabbed Jed in the ribs. Jed slapped his hand away.

She applied her mouth to Brock's body.

"Like the postcard," Mike said.

"Yeah, but she's no harem girl."

"And he's no Sultan."

Her head bobbed back and forth and his pale hips gyrated. He grabbed her head with both hands and let out a long moan.

Brock pushed her away. *"Merci beaucoup, Grand-Mère."*

She stood up and spat on the floor. She picked up the cognac bottle and took a drink, swishing the liquor in her mouth, and spitting it out. *"Dégoûtant Bâtard."* She kept the bottle and strode out the door.

Brock laughed and pulled another bottle from under his cot. He took a drink and held it up in salute. "Twenty million Frenchmen can't be wrong." He sat down on his bunk and corked the bottle, chuckling to himself. He lay back on his cot and passed out.

"What a show," Mike said.

"He shouldn't have slapped her."

Mike pulled his blanket up to his chin. "Brock is a miserable human being, but he did nothing to us."

"You're the one who slugged him."

"That was personal," Mike said. "This is just Brock being Brock, and you'd have traded places with him, like with Katie Flynn. She turned you into a man."

"She came after me, I didn't force her to do anything. What Brock did was rape. Remember what Doody said."

"If it bothers you that much talk to Trask."

The next morning, Jed approached Corporal Collins.

"Why are you asking me to see the Top?"

"You're chain-of-command."

116

"I don't care about that. Go ask Brock."

"I can't."

"Then go see Trask. Leave me out."

The first sergeant was in the company supply shed inventorying the spare equipment. Jed walked up and stood to the side, in Trask's field of view.

"What do you want?"

"Sorry to bother you, Top."

"Let's have it."

Jed hesitated. "What if one guy was violating the general orders?"

"Lots of the guys violate the general orders." Trask checked off an item on a clipboard. "I got my bottle of cognac. Watkia's not stupid."

"It's not the cognac, it's about a woman."

"You caught brother Brock with one of his ladies, right?" He looked at Jed. "Don't look so shocked, I've been watching him ever since we were kids back in Ohio. He hates me and I can't stand the asshole."

"Why do you keep serving in the same units?"

"I want to keep that bastard right where I can see him. I promised someone I'd keep him out of trouble. He's bound to screw up big and I'll be there to stop him."

Jed swallowed hard. "What are you going to do?"

"Was she an adult?"

"Kind of old." Jed said.

"You're a grown man. You understand what drives men."

"But he forced himself on her and slapped her. It was rape."

"Did she fight him or yell for help?"

"She said no at first, but then went along with it."

"If she doesn't file a complaint, there's nothing I can do."

Trask signed his name at the bottom of the form and tossed the clipboard onto the pile of equipment. "Everybody's got their demons and Leo Brock has more than his share. Do what he tells you and stay out of his way when he drinks."

"Yes, Top, but I don't understand why you don't do something."

"It's not for you to understand. Keep your mouth shut. I'll deal with Brock."

Jed was trying to take a nap when Bunny stuck his head in the door. "Come on, Jed. We've got work to do."

Mike and Tony waited in the street. Bunny gave Jed a cigarette, took one himself, and lit them with a match.

"What's going on, Bunny?" Jed asked.

"We're headed over to the chow hall."

"Chow isn't served for two hours yet."

"Yeah, well, Dubman's cooking right now. Corporal Claggett and your friends the Joneses volunteered for kitchen police; can you beat that? I think they're going to make another move on Clarence."

Bunny dragged on his cigarette, thinking. "When we get there, I'll do the talking. Mike, you weren't involved. Hang back unless we need you." To Jed and Tony, he said, "Be prepared to fight. We have to force the issue and end it now."

"Why don't you let us handle this?" Mike asked. "Jed and I have been fighting those boys all our lives."

"I'm'a one who spilled it," Tony said. "I'll fight them all."

Bunny shook his head and looked at Mike. "We three need to fix it for Dub, but I won't hesitate to call you if I have to." He threw the cigarette into the mud and started toward the chow hall.

Jed turned to Mike. "Let us handle this."

"I'm here to help, Jed."

Bunny led them through the back door to a darkened storage room behind the kitchen. Clarence Dubman was stirring a large pot and glancing nervously at Corporal Claggett who was standing nearby. Bart and Clay Jones sat on counters on opposite sides of the kitchen tossing a potato back and forth.

"What are you boys doing in here?" Dub asked. "You're supposed to be out back peeling those spuds."

"We're here to see that nothing nasty gets into our slum like it did before," Claggett said, peering into the pot.

"I told you I didn't have anything to do with it."

"We want to make sure. Maybe the thumping you got didn't take and we have to remind you what can happen."

Bart and Clay eased down off the counters.

Dubman backed away. "You fellas are wrong."

"I agree," Bunny said as he stepped into the kitchen followed by Jed and Tony. Mike stayed in the shadows.

"What are you guys doing here?" Bart asked.

"Setting the record straight," Bunny said.

"Are you here to defend this asshole?" Clay asked.

118

"Yeah," Claggett said. "He put filth in our slum. He probably laughed his head off while we shit our brains out."

Bunny shook his head. "Dub didn't do anything."

Tony stepped forward. "I spill the stew, was my fault."

"Stupid grease ball," Bart said.

"I scooped it up," Bunny said. "You guys were hungry, and I didn't think it mattered."

"Well, it does matter," Claggett said. "Come on, boys."

Bart rushed Tony and knocked him to the floor. Jed punched Claggett, knocking him against the counter, but then received a painful blow to the left jaw thrown by Clay. Jed counterpunched then jabbed twice following up with a solid right to the jaw. Clay staggered back against Claggett.

Tony was up and had Bart pinned to the counter. Dub punched Bart in the face followed by a punch from Tony. Jed held Clay off with his guard up.

Claggett grabbed a large knife from the counter and advanced on Jed holding it point down like a dagger. In a flash Mike was there. Claggett turned to Mike and struck with a downward slash. Mike danced away and grabbed the knife hand in his left forcing the tip of the blade down into Claggett's thigh. His scream was snuffed out as Mike crushed his face with a right. Claggett dropped to the kitchen floor and lay silent.

Clay pointed at Jed then Mike. "You still need him to finish your fights for you."

"I had it under control," Jed snapped at Mike.

Mike stood silent.

Jed turned away and caught movement at the corner of his eye. Sergeant Trask stood in the shadows of the storage room. He nodded to Jed, then turned and walked away.

Bunny tied off the wound in Claggett's leg with a kitchen towel. "Looks like a kitchen accident to me." He addressed the Joneses. "When he wakes up, tell him it's over. Dubman has friends."

Jed went outside, lit a cigarette, and walked away to be alone.

PART TWO

MURDER IN SELF DEFENSE

THE FEAR

To meet death in the fight
Face to face, upright.
But when at last we creep
Into a hole to sleep,
I tremble, cold with dread,
Lest I wake up dead.

—Wilfred Wilson Gibson

CHAPTER 20

SEPTEMBER 23, 1918
SOUTH OF AVOCOURT, FRANCE

The Stars and Stripes

FIRST ARMY, A.E.F., NIPS OFF SALIENT IN OPENING DRIVE
Swift, Successful Blow at St. Mihiel Nets Over 15,000 Prisoners

The First American Army, commanded in the field by General John J. Pershing, struck its first blow last week.

It was a blow sudden, swift and beyond all shadow of a doubt successful.

Supported by French Colonials, that Army closed like a giant pair of pincers on the old, heavily entrenched salient which the Germans had held ever since they dug themselves in after their failure at the first Battle of the Marne—closed in and in less than two days obliterated that salient from the fast-changing German war map…

THE STARS AND STRIPES: FRANCE, FRIDAY, SEPTEMBER 20, 1918, page 1

The St. Mihiel operation was such a rapid success that the 37th Division was not needed in support and was ordered to move again. Company G rode in crowded trucks past the ruined land that defined this part of France, the roads busy with men and animals moving in all directions, piles of supplies and equipment dumped at random along the roads. Two days of miserable travel ended with a skidding stop. They sat in a featureless plain of churned earth and devastation.

Sergeant Trask walked down the convoy from the lead company vehicle, whacking the fenders of each truck as he passed, repeating his bellowed order. "OK, out of the trucks. Come on, snap to it. We march the rest of the way."

Jed pulled the tarp open at the back of the truck and jumped down into the mud.

A stone church steeple rose from the rubble of a smashed village at the head of the column, a wooden cross jutting defiantly out of the decrepit tower. A sign at the side of the road pointed to the right toward Avocourt, 7 km away.

The truck drivers, small brown Asian men called Annamese, from French Indochina, gathered in a cluster, inhaling cigarette after cigarette, muttering in their strange language, flinching at the muffled crack and crump of artillery echoing in the distance.

Sergeant Trask walked back toward the front of the column. His helmet had the division patch painted on the back: the white and red circle Abel had described.

As Trask approached, Reb asked, "Hey, Sarge, what about your bullseye there? You gonna go up with that target in full view?"

"I'll be out front with Captain Brown. This helmet should be bright enough for you to follow. And, by God, keep your intervals. If you cluster up, they may get a bunch of you." He marched to where the captain was assembling the company staff.

"We've already been up to the front," Mike said.

"This ain't crawling around in no-man's-land," Brock said. "You follow Trask and don't do anything stupid and you might make it."

Jed rubbed the back of his neck and stretched onto his toes. Mike caught his eye and gave a crooked grin. Jed tried to relax, rolling his shoulders under his pack straps.

A stray German artillery round landed a mile away.

The Annamese drivers sprinted to their trucks, climbed aboard, and raced away.

A whistle sounded, and the captain pumped his arm up and down.

The company column moved out and turned right at the ruined church.

A half-mile in front of them stretched a wall of leafless trees.

"*Gesù Cristo*, what is this place?" Tony asked.

"That garden of sticks is the *Bois de Récicourt*, woods to all you hicks," Brock announced.

"The hell you say," Doody said.

"Hell, probably," Brock said.

"There's hardly a stick or brick higher than five feet for miles," Jed said.

"Thousands of artillery rounds," Brock said. "Stay off the road, and walk in the ditches, it's safer there."

The stench the men's feet kicked up from the bottom of the ditches was an overpowering mix of mustiness and putrefaction.

A tearing rush filled the air and Jed threw himself down at the side of the ditch. A white flash erupted in the center of the road. Splinters whistled overhead a fraction of a second later along with the deafening concussion. Another shell screamed in and detonated in a pile of brush setting it on fire. A third shell arced over the road and landed in a swampy area, the subdued blast spraying the area with mud and moss.

No more rounds landed nearby.

Corporal Goldson and Lenny Gurr from Second Squad moved down the road from the head of the column and kneeled opposite Jed and Mike.

"You guys OK?" Cain asked.

"I'm all right," Jed said.

"Me too," Mike said. "Hey, Lenny, you don't look so good."

Gurr's face was pale and his voice trembled, "The first shell landed fifteen feet from me and I didn't get a scratch."

"One of the company runners, Pete Gilbert, is missing," Cain said. "He was crossing the road when the shell hit."

Gurr lowered his head and shook it from side to side.

"You'll be all right, Lenny," Jed said. "It wasn't your time."

The captain's whistle sounded. Cain sent Gurr down the road to check out the rest of the company.

"I'm keeping him busy," Cain said.

When he returned Gurr had calmed down. "Thanks for the kind word, Jed."

It started to rain.

The sun set behind the overcast and soon it was fully dark. Jed grabbed a strap on the back of Mike's pack and slogged forward, trying not to trip over tree limbs fallen into the ditch.

After an hour of marching, they were guided off the road onto a path leading into a large stand of intact trees. Jed and Mike built a tent with their shelter halves and scraped fallen leaves into a pile in the center. Jed threw his blanket over it for a mattress. They used their packs for pillows and crawled under Mike's blanket, back-to-back, tossing their raincoats on top.

Jed lay down and fell asleep to the growling artillery lullaby.

CHAPTER 21
SEPTEMBER 24, 1918
FORÊT DE HESSE, FRANCE

At 5 A.M. Lips woke them. "Get your gear ready to move out. Put on dry socks. Marshal Foch has postponed the offensive one day, but we're moving to our final staging area today, anyway. You have one hour to shit and shave and get a hot breakfast, bacon and beans by the smell of it."

"Bacon and beans are better than anything I've had to eat in two days," Jed said.

Mike sniffed. "I smell coffee, too."

They found Dubman stirring a pot on his rolling kitchen under trees that had half their leaves. When Jed and Mike stepped up, his face lit up.

"Here you go," Dubman said as he ladled beans with bacon bits into their mess kits. As they started to move on Dub stopped them. He leaned forward and spoke in a low voice. "Thanks for what you done for me. Claggett limped by and I told him I wasn't taking his guff anymore. He hobbled away without a word."

"You take care of us really well, Dub," Jed said.

Mike patted Dub's shoulder. "It's the least we could do."

"Help yourself to some coffee." They dipped their cups into a steaming pot. Dubman looked around then pulled a tin box from a wagon compartment. "I only have a little sugar." He dropped a spoonful into their cups, closed the tin, and pulled a bottle out of another hidden compartment. He poured a generous dollop of brown liquid into each of their cups then put the bottle away. "No charge."

Jed took a sip. The coffee and sugar masked the liquor, but he felt an extra warmth travel down to his stomach.

He glanced at Mike, who shrugged. "Watkia is everywhere."

After breakfast, they marched north beside the road to Avocourt. As the column crested a ridge the terrain to the north spread out before them: two miles of forest descending into a valley, then a churned no-man's-land with tall grass stretching north to the Montfaucon Wood, the front line of the German defenses. Above the woods, the smashed buildings in the town of Montfaucon glowed white in the mist shrouding the high ground.

The column filed by a flat wagon with shivering, miserable mules in harness. An artillery officer issued each man 120 rounds of rifle ammunition in bandoliers and two fragmentation grenades.

The column then turned left off the road and in single file started up a duckboard track made slippery by a thin drizzle.

French soldiers directed them off the duckboards down a beaten path through the woods to a flat clearing where they built pup tents again and dug latrines.

After dark, traffic on the road nearby increased. Wagoners cussed, mules brayed, and artillery rumbled by.

Jed hoped the artillery would blast the Germans so there wouldn't be much fighting but knew that it was merely wishing. Still, he found the noises along the road comforting.

CHAPTER 22

SEPTEMBER 25, 1918

FORÊT DE HESSE, FRANCE

They were awakened at 9 A.M., took care of personal hygiene, did one hour of calisthenics and ate a breakfast of canned salmon, stewed tomatoes, and strawberry jam on stale crackers. At noon it stopped raining, and the sun came out.

Lieutenant Samis approached the rifle section with his notebook and briefed them on what to expect. The 37th Division was in the center of nine American Divisions stretching from the Meuse River in the east to the Argonne Forest in the west. When they went over the top, they would advance behind a wall of artillery strikes called a walking barrage. They were not to stop and help the wounded. If they encountered a strong point that was too formidable, it would be bypassed and cleaned up later by troops from the brigade reserve. Everyone was expected to repair breaks in telephone wire. Runners with red brassards on their left arms would carry messages in the right breast pocket of the blouse. If a runner became a casualty, they were to check that pocket and give any message to an officer. Souvenir hunting was forbidden. Many attractive items could be expected to be booby-trapped.

Samis took a deep, shuddering breath. "We will lead the assault. I expect the squad leaders to keep you on line and moving forward." He stalled out then remembered something. "We'll get hot chow this afternoon and move to our jump off point by midnight." He paused again. "Are there any questions?"

"No, sir," Collins said.

"Thank you, Lieutenant," Jed said.

Samis relaxed a bit but kept clamping his jaw.

"I guess that's all for now." He turned and walked away.

Brock walked up. "I give him, maybe, twenty minutes to survive after we go over tomorrow."

"If that," Collins said.

The men went through another hour of calisthenics, ate the hot meal, and policed up the area as it got dark.

Jed and Mike squirmed into their tent and tried to keep water from dripping in. The musty odor of wet equipment and oil wrapped itself around them.

Artillery rumbled in the distance.

"The big day comes tomorrow," Mike said. "How are you doing, Jed?"

"I'm a little nervous. This feels so real. It's going to be a lot different from anything we've been through before."

"We've done fine so far. We'll keep our heads down and be alright." Mike rolled over. "Come on, let's get a couple hours of sleep."

Jed lay thinking of Bessie and her picture book. Everything in his past led to this time and place. He would know soon enough how it would turn out. He said a short, silent prayer, and went to sleep.

At 10 P.M. the men were roused and urged to use the latrines. A thick fog lay on the ground and NCOs with flashlights marked the path to the slit trenches.

The division chaplain, Captain Hewitt, held a brief service over a small prayer rug and cross propped on the back of a rolling kitchen.

Jed had been baptized and raised a Methodist but kept his faith private. He considered himself devout but didn't normally attend church. He decided to join in this service.

Hewitt had thick glasses, a toothy smile, and pure white hair. He delivered his message in a deep, confident voice. Aunt Bessie would be out of place in the stark surroundings but would recognize the verse Hewitt recited from Joshua 1:9:

> *Have not I commanded thee? Be strong and of a good courage;*
> *Be not afraid, neither be thou dismayed: for the LORD thy God*
> *Is with thee whithersoever thou goest.*

Hewitt's verse comforted Jed. He would try to be strong and of good courage, but the unknown was daunting. He was keyed up but not afraid. That would likely come later.

After the service, the men packed their gear and formed up by platoons for the move to the assault line.

At 10:45 P.M. the order came to move out. They employed the elephant walk technique again and trudged blindly through the fog toward the jump off point. The French troops had laid out lanes through the forest and stood at intervals along the line to help the Americans who shuffled forward in the darkness, guided by the accented English of the French soldiers, tripping over large stones, tree stumps, and strips of old barbed wire.

They eased to the right as a line of shadow figures trudged past them going in the opposite direction, Americans who had been manning the defensive sector.

"Who are you guys?"

"Thirty-third Division. Who are you?"

"Thirty-seventh."

"Good luck."

"Thanks."

"Better you than us."

"You'll get your chance."

The terrain leveled out, and they moved forward on the road through Avocourt hidden by the fog.

They stumbled into a trench and sprawled on the firing step.

At precisely midnight, a single French 75 opened with an air-rending crack. The rest of the artillery, arranged in depth behind the trench, erupted in a soul splitting roar turning the air above into plasma.

Jed was engulfed in the violent storm of fire. It swelled from a roar to a presence, a thing hanging over him. The air and earth encased him in a welded metal shell. A giant beat a steel hammer on the metal cocoon. His ears had little part in it. The shock waves thumped his chest, and he had difficulty breathing. Sleep was impossible.

Watkia brought wads of cotton and Jed stuffed them in his ears. It helped but the sheer vibrating presence of the noise was still there.

The barrage continued for one hour, then two, then three. Jed wondered how long the artillerymen could maintain this volume of fire. The gun barrels must be melting.

CHAPTER 23

SEPTEMBER 26, 1918

MEUSE-ARGONNE OFFENSIVE – **DAY ONE**

The bombardment was still in progress at 4:30 A.M. when Collins roused Jed from a fitful nap. He sat on the firing step beside Mike and the other squad members.

The area was still covered by a thick fog.

Sergeant Trask walked along the company line. The noise from the shelling was so loud he shined a flashlight on a piece of paper. It said: *Fix bayonets. Guide on me. First objective is woods straight ahead.*

Jed's hands trembled as he snapped his bayonet onto the front of his rifle. While the core of his being cowered in terror, a remarkable sector of his consciousness looked at the world and watched. This was real, immediate, and tangible. It seemed he had been sleepwalking through his prior life. He had never felt so alive—because he was perched on the precipice of death.

He hated the waiting. He wanted to get on with it.

Bunny tapped him on the shoulder and held out a lit cigarette.

Jed inhaled. His trembling subsided.

The officers spaced themselves along the trench by their units. Samis had removed his officer's Sam Browne belt and rank insignia. Trask was crouched beside him talking to the young officer who nodded and swallowed hard.

Twenty seconds before the assault began, smoke shells erupted along the division front mixing with the lingering fog to create a thick screen. The attacking Americans wouldn't see their objective but the German gunners wouldn't see the Americans.

At 5:30 A.M. the officers blew their whistles and ordered the men forward. They rose with a shout, scrambled up out of the trench, and walked toward the smoke screen through the thigh high grass. Several tripped and fell, tangled in old, barbed wire and the brush and undergrowth growing up in no-man's-land. They picked themselves up and stumbled after their comrades. The American artillerymen adjusted their range and kept the barrage one hundred yards to their front as the division flowed forward and the long lines of squads held their formation.

The barrage chewed through the woods cutting down trees and throwing steel and wood splinters in all directions. Jed didn't know how anyone could survive that threshing machine. The air was filled with every size of flying steel: tiny buzzing bits, sizzling splinters, tumbling chunks, and whooshing slabs. The horizontal metal rain was everywhere, regarding nothing sacred, mowing down everything in its path.

As the Americans approached the edge of the woods, a German Maxim machine gun sputtered behind a thick tangle of barbed wire. Jed and the others threw themselves prone in the tall grass. The flame of the Maxim stabbed through the mist, the bullets carving their way through the stalks of grass making a hissing sound.

"Sounds like snakes," Mike said.

Sergeant Trask and a rifle grenadier named Billings crawled forward.

Sergeant Patterson and three engineers carrying Bangalore torpedoes threw themselves onto the ground next to Jed. "What's the holdup?"

"The gun and that wire," Jed said.

"We can take care of the wire if you get the gun," Patterson said.

Trask looked at Billings and pointed forward. "There's your target, behind those muzzle flashes."

Billings grounded the butt of his rifle, aimed it nearly vertical, and pulled the trigger. The grenade arced high then plunged down and exploded in the nest. Patterson and his men rose and moved forward, set the torpedoes under the tangle, moved back, and blasted a hole in the wire.

Jed and the others poured through the gap.

Many Germans had survived the artillery barrage, and the Americans advanced into the woods against heavy fire. Bullets struck flesh with sickening thumps. Trench mortar rounds rained down spewing splinters and shards.

Some men, when hit, sprawled on the ground as though tripped, some crawling to a shell hole or depression in the earth to get below the invisible slivers and bullets. A few writhed and screamed, cursing and crying in shock or disbelief, many lapsing into tortured groans, whimpers, and gasps as their mangled bodies tried to function. Others dropped like sodden mops, ending in grotesque tangled heaps of flesh.

A man in front of Jed disappeared in a fountain of mortar flame and smoke. He disappeared without a trace: no rifle, helmet, nor flesh. Vaporized.

Jed ran forward leaping clear of the smoking spot where the soldier had vanished, advancing up a shallow draw moving toward volleys of gunfire hidden in the misty woods. Machine gun bullets struck around him. He dove onto the bottom of the ditch.

Sergeant Kraft and four men from Second Squad were pinned down in a shell hole a few feet to his front. On the far-right flank Bunny crawled low. The German gunner saw the movement and turned his gun.

Kraft pointed his pistol forward. "Get up and go that way."

The five bounded up out of the shell hole and ran up Jed's draw. A second machine gun, sighted to cover the first, chugged to life. The five Americans fell and lay still.

Sorrow clutched Jed's throat, but he took heart as Lenny Gurr clawed his way back to the shelter of the shell hole.

A rivulet of bright red blood ran down Jed's gulley.

Two American grenades exploded to his front and, to his left, the chung-chung-chung of a Chauchat automatic rifle sounded. The fire from both machine guns stopped.

Jed checked the Second Squad dead, his spine tingling, then walked up the slope to where Trask, Mike, and a hand bomber friend of Lips named David Lewin kneeled beside a smoking machine gun pit. Mike showed Jed the grenade safety pin and ring wrapped around his left index finger.

Trask pulled out his compass and sighted carefully. "Seven degrees west of north is that way." He pointed toward a large rock outcropping sticking up above the shredded timber. "Looks like a perfect place for more machine gun nests. Let's go." He led off, the Buckeye patch on the back of his helmet clearly visible.

A German machine gun fired from the head of every ravine. Jed and Mike crawled forward and stopped behind a row of small boulders flanking a shallow gully leading to the right toward the rock outcropping

Trask had sighted on. The other side of the gully was lined with battered trees still shrouded in fog. A Maxim at the top of the hill, only forty yards to the right, fired down the nearly straight gully to discourage anyone from entering the low cover. Another gun across the gully fired long bursts across the top of the ditch. Shapes moved within the fog but Jed couldn't see any of the Germans clearly.

A burst of automatic rifle fire erupted at the top of the hill silencing that gun.

Lieutenant Samis ordered David Lewin to enter the ditch and try to get a grenade into the nest on the other side. Lewin slid into the ditch and inched forward, a canvas bag of grenades around his neck. Jed and the others hugged the ground behind the boulders, bullets splattering against the rocks and whining away.

The fog cleared revealing the denuded tree branches overhanging the gully and a new hazard. The Germans had wedged potato masher grenades into the crotches of the tree branches. Slack wires trailed away from the hollow wooden handles.

The wire attached to a grenade directly above Lewin grew taught and the grenade exploded, sending wood shards into Lewin's back. He tried to rise but collapsed, a shaft of tree branch pinning him face down.

Samis ordered Jed to enter the defile. As Jed slid down into the ditch, another grenade went off and he felt a stab in his right calf. A three-inch wood splinter stuck out of his leg. He pulled it out and blood oozed from the hole in the puttee.

Jed crawled to the wounded bomber, whose face was ashen, his fists clenched.

"I'm sorry, Mother," Lewin said. His body convulsed, and he was gone.

Jed said a silent prayer then removed the sack of grenades from the dead man's body.

Mike and Bunny scrambled down beside Jed, the German gunner firing a long burst but missing them.

Jed handed each man a grenade. The three pulled the pins and tossed the grenades toward the gunfire. They ducked as the grenades went off.

The firing stopped.

Samis pointed to Reb and a Chauchat automatic rifleman. "Hill and Forbes, check it out."

Reb leaped across the ditch followed by Forbes and his loader. A rifle shot echoed through the trees followed by the stutter of the Chauchat.

Reb signaled the all clear.

Watkia crawled into the ditch. He unclipped the canteen from Lewin's belt and put it in a canvas sack around his neck. Mike pulled the tree branch out of the dead man's back, then pulled several ammunition strippers out of his belt pouches.

"It feels like we're looting," Jed said.

"He doesn't need this stuff anymore and we do," Watkia said.

Sergeant Lipsitz kneeled beside the body and retrieved a bloody pay book. He checked his watch, made a notation in the pay book, and placed it in his shirt pocket. He stabbed Lewin's rifle and bayonet straight up in the ground and placed Lewin's helmet atop the rifle butt in a battle cross. "He was from my neighborhood in Cleveland," Lips said. He put his hand on Lewin's shoulder, "David Lewin, *Alav ha-shalom*."

"May peace be upon him," Bunny repeated. He looked sharply at Watkia, "*Alav ha-shalom*, Andy."

"I'll say a '*shalom*' over you when you finally get it, whoremonger."

"Better a whoremonger than a thief."

"I'm no thief. I pay for everything I get for you guys."

Corporal Goldson jumped into the ditch.

"What are you doing up here, Cain?" Watkia asked.

Cain pointed to Captain Brown who was organizing the company into a skirmish line in the ditch. "I go where the captain goes."

Watkia looked around. "Well, we got all the Jews here: Goldson, Steinmetz, Lipsitz, Watkia, and Lewin. Sounds like a law firm, with one member retired, permanently."

"Lots of Jews," Reb said standing with Doody and Collins at the side of the ditch.

"Shut up, asshole," Collins said. To the others, "You've all done your rituals over the body, so let's go."

"Where's Brock?" Watkia asked.

"Probably somewhere safe," Collins said.

They joined the middle of the skirmish line and continued the advance.

The platoon encountered a concrete German bunker and flanking machine gun nests covering a wide, shallow ravine. They took cover behind fallen logs. Yellow flames flashed from the nests and the low bunker opening. Bullets slammed into the protective tree trunks.

Lips and Bunny tried to flank the guns but were forced back.

The only way forward was straight across the killing ground.

Lieutenant Samis shook his head. "Advance by rushes, men."

Bile rose in Jed's throat and he swallowed hard.

Samis had his whistle in his mouth when a group of men moved forward from the woods behind the platoon. A one-pounder gun crew and Vickers machine gunners from the machine gun battalion moved forward with their heavy weapons. The crews perched their guns over the fallen logs and began to fire on the fortifications across the ravine.

The one-pounder barked and a high explosive shell splattered against the face of the concrete pill box. The next round arced through the ground level opening and exploded inside. Gray smoke curled out of the opening and the machine gun went silent. The Vickers gunners raked the German positions and rifle grenades thumped into the machine gun nests. When the German fire slackened whistles sounded, and the Americans vaulted from cover. Jed ran across the broken ground, Mike to his right, and Sergeant McClardy to his left.

They approached a silent machine gun pit when a German soldier jumped up.

"*Kamerad, Kamerad!*"

The Chauchat gunner Forbes hurried forward. The German let him get close then jumped into the pit and fired the machine gun. Only six shots rang out before the gun jammed but Forbes collapsed with a shattered leg and his loader fell dead. The German immediately threw up his hands.

"*Kamerad!*"

"Not bloody likely, mate." McClardy shot the man in the chest with his pistol.

The rest of the German gun crew were dead.

Jed and the others crawled snake-like through cloying mud, chopped through endless tangled brush and wire, and passed shredded corpses, and the quivering wounded they could not stop to help. At every ridgeline and rock outcropping, another array of German guns waited as they advanced, yard by yard, new danger by new danger.

As Jed crawled through a small clearing carpeted with a cluster of shell holes, something tugged at his right leg. The puttee had separated at the puncture and was caught on half-buried barbed wire. He cut the wool strip with his bayonet.

A German soldier peered over the edge of a shell hole three feet away holding a potato masher grenade. He pulled the arming lanyard. Jed threw himself across the ground and stabbed at the hand holding the grenade but missed. His momentum carried him forward and his bayonet hit the German's right eye. The eyeball exploded, and the bayonet penetrated until it hit the back inside of the man's skull. Jed drew back in horror hanging onto the bayonet. The German screamed and dropped the grenade. Jed hugged the ground as it exploded and the German's screams stopped.

Jed dry-heaved from his empty stomach, lying for a full minute, his hands shaking.

Mike rolled out of a nearby hole and scrambled to where Jed lay. "Your skin's as pale as your eyes. Are you hit?"

"Not in the body." He took several deep breaths and concentrated on wrapping the shortened puttee around his calf. He fixed the bayonet to his rifle and followed Mike as he crawled back into the battle.

Jed and Mike lay behind a fallen log as a German barrage began. Several low order detonations mixed with the high explosive blasts. Yellow-brown clouds of mustard gas boiled up and spread on the light breeze. Officers blew frantic blasts on their whistles. Jed pulled his respirator from the carrier on his chest, held his breath and squeezed his eyes shut until the mask was in place. The mask restricted his vision but he would have to suffer through it to survive the far worse danger of the gas. His hands trembled as he wiped mud off his boots onto the backs of his hands to protect them from the droplets of mustard.

Mike had his mask on and gave Jed a thumbs up.

Footsteps pounded to their left and someone leaped over the log as a high explosive shell detonated nearby. There was a sickening splat, and the man collapsed between Jed and Mike, lying face down, unmoving.

A masked and hooded soldier carrying an automatic pistol moved from the right. He took a knee, glancing at the dead man. His voice was muffled by his mask. "I'm Lieutenant Samis. We're pulling back because of the gas. The rally point is at a stream."

Samis moved away.

Jed rolled the dead soldier over. He stared into the blank green eyes of Corporal Claggett, his face still bruised from Mike's punch.

"Poor bastard," Mike said as he hoisted Claggett across his shoulder. They started back toward the stream.

Brock stood between the stream and a large shell hole. "Keep your goddamn masks on and come over here." The muffled bellow came from beneath Brock's mask.

Mike laid Claggett's body well away from the rushing stream.

"Who's that?"

"Claggett from the hand bomber section," Mike said sucking hard for breath.

Brock made Jed bend over the shell hole then scooped his helmet in the stream and poured water over Jed's head washing the dirt and mustard into the shell hole. He scooped again and washed down the rest of Jed's uniform, rifle and equipment.

"Move up the hill to that trench."

A cloud of white cigarette smoke wafted up from the trench. Bunny and Cain sat on the firing step. Jed removed his mask, took the lit cigarette Bunny offered, and sat beside Cain. "Claggett from the hand bomber section was killed by artillery."

Cain pulled out a notebook and made a notation.

Mike sat bedside Jed.

Cain pointed to the blood on Mike's uniform. "Are you hit?"

"No, this must be from Claggett."

Brock strode up his mask in his hand. "Come on, we're going forward. The wind has cleared the gas out but watch out, bubbles of mustard can cling to the underside of blades of grass or in air pockets in the mud."

The lieutenant blew his whistle, and they started off again.

Jed crawled up beside a tree stump. Thirty feet away a German machine gunner fired at the platoon moving up on Jed's right, loaders squatting beside the gunner readying new belts of ammunition. It had taken the platoon over an hour to creep 50 yards. The yellow flame of the German gun was answered by the pink stabs of fire from the Enfields.

Jed raised his rifle and sighted on the gunner. He had a clear shot but hesitated. Jed had the power to end another man's life.

It was murder.

He willed himself to pull the trigger but could not.

To his right, Sergeant Trask inched forward. The sound in Jed's ears was strangely muted. The gunfire was much louder than Trask's voice but he could clearly hear Trask.

"Can you see them?"

Jed nodded yes.

Trask nodded back.

Jed sighted again.

He pulled the trigger. The gunner sagged forward onto his gun. The rest of the German crew jumped out of the pit and ran away.

Lieutenant Samis low-crawled out of a shell hole and waved the platoon forward. Jed stayed low and followed.

Jed moved forward into a clearing near the northern edge of the woods. Smoke rose from two destroyed German machine gun nests on the other side of the clearing. Mike sat beside Doody who was talking and shadow boxing. Lieutenant Samis and Sergeant Trask kneeled to one side with Captain Brown consulting a map.

Sergeant McClardy sat with his back to a six-foot tall tree stump lighting his pipe. He patted the ground next to him. "Have a seat."

As Jed took a step forward, a low-flying shell whistled in and hit the ground twenty feet behind McClardy burrowing under the surface. It hit the base of the tree and exploded, the concussion knocking Jed onto his back. He sat up and crawled to McClardy. The Brit sergeant sat stunned, his pipe smoldering unnoticed in his lap, a red mess dripping from under his chest mounted gas mask.

Captain Brown rushed over.

"Goodbye, lad," McClardy said to Jed. "Captain, see the lads through. Tell my old girl I was thinking of her." He collapsed to the side and died.

Jed thought of Aunt Bessie fretting back home on the farm.

More German shells screamed in.

"The Boche have these woods zeroed in," Brown said. "Let's go."

As the company moved out of the woods, a long expanse of rolling terrain, pocked with shell craters and the ruins of houses and outbuildings, stretched before them. The crumbled town of Montfaucon perched on the high ground to the east, a church sitting at the highest point, its steeple gone. Yellow smoke rising from the center of town made the mound of rubble resemble a volcano.

Jed had crossed no-man's-land at night when it seemed vast and mysterious, able to swallow a man and keep him unseen. In the full light of day, it seemed smaller but deadlier. There was no place to hide.

The squad moved forward, Bunny to Jed's left, Mike to his right; his jaw tight. To Mike's right, Brock and Watkia stepped past the rubble of a farmhouse.

A long burst of machine gun fire sizzled through the group. Brock tumbled into the cellar of the obliterated house. Jed felt a tug at his pant leg but wasn't hit. Mike fell to the ground clutching his left thigh. Watkia dragged him into a shell hole.

Jed started to move toward Mike but Bunny pulled him out of the line of fire behind a low stone wall. Bullets shrieked off the top of the wall.

"I need to get to Mike," Jed protested.

"Andy will fix him up," Bunny said. He crawled to the left. "Give me some fire on that gun."

Jed peeked around the right end of the wall. The gunner and his assistant were in a shell hole. Jed fired three rapid shots and they ducked. Bunny ran forward, shot the assistant, and then ran his bayonet into the gunner's chest. He stood shaking for a few seconds, then moved away.

Watkia ran from the shell hole and threw himself down beside Jed.

"How's Mike?" Jed asked.

"Bullet wound high on his left thigh. I put a field dressing on it. He'll be all right."

"Brock went down," Jed said.

"He'll turn up." Andy got up and followed Bunny.

Mike waved Jed forward. "I'll be all right, go help the squad."

At least if he wasn't hurt bad Mike would be out of danger for a while.

Jed ran after the others.

As he skirted a giant shell hole a German shell hit near a man in front of him. The man's left arm hit Jed in the chest, chopped off at the shoulder socket.

The soldier fell to the ground wailing in pain, a fountain of blood spurting from his shoulder with every heartbeat.

Jed grabbed the wounded man by his cartridge belt and dragged him to the edge of the shell hole. He stepped into the hole. The mud crumbled under his feet and he and the wounded man tumbled through the mire. They came to rest in a heap near the bottom.

The hole had three feet of dirty rainwater in it and was so large his loft bedroom back at the farm would have fit inside.

The wounded man was semi-conscious and breathing in gasps, blood still flowing from his shoulder socket. It looked like when Jed pulled the drumstick off of a Thanksgiving turkey, gleaming pearl white, pristine, and obscene. The compress in the individual medical pouches was too small for the massive wound. He searched in the man's haversack and found a clean pair of socks and underwear. Jed bundled one sock and the underwear into the other sock and stuffed the wad into the cavity where the arm had been. He unrolled the man's blanket and, using his bayonet, cut off a strip two feet wide, placed the hasty bandage over the sock, and tied a knot under the soldier's right armpit. This stanched the blood flow. The man sank into a deep sleep. Jed eased him up the side of the hole, excavating a step to lay him on to keep his feet out of the water in the hole's bottom. He used the blanket corner to clean blood and mud off the man's face.

It was Tony DiNiccola.

Jed covered Tony as best he could with the rest of the blanket but didn't know what else he should do. He wanted to go search for Mike but Tony needed him too.

The machine gun and rifle fire had moved into the far distance but artillery shells continued to fall.

A shell hit nearby and Tony opened his eyes. "I'm'a guess it's time to pay America back for my three years."

Jed reached out to comfort him but Tony shook his head. "Don't touch, Jed."

"Someone will be along soon, Tony. Hold on."

"No, Jed." Tony labored for breath. "In my pocket, there is a letter to my Sophia."

Jed found the envelope in Tony's left breast pocket. "Are you sure?"

"Time is short, it will be over soon. You are not Catholic but we have no priest. Will you make the sign of the cross over me while I say my last Our Father?"

Jed raised his hand high and slowly brought it down. Tony murmured in his native tongue, softer and softer until he lay silent as Jed crossed his hand from left to right. Jed pulled the blanket over Tony's face, whispered his own prayer, and wiped his eyes.

A group of men approached. They sounded like the butcher Kurtz.

Jed's pulse quickened.

The worst must have happened. The battalion had been wiped out by a German counterattack.

He didn't know what he could do with only one rifle. He would have to either fight or surrender. He would certainly die if he fought, but he didn't want to be taken prisoner.

He leaned back against the side of the hole and pulled his helmet low over his face so he could peek out from under the brim. He held his rifle loosely across his belly.

A shell shrieked in and landed fifty feet away.

Someone dove into the hole and splashed into the muddy water at the bottom. The man who rose sputtering out of the water wore the bucket-shaped helmet of a German soldier.

Forgetting his ruse of playing dead, Jed sat up and aimed his rifle at the man who raised his hands in surrender.

"*Kamerad, Schiessen Sie nicht, Schiessen Sie nicht. Ich bin ein Gefangener.*"

The man claimed to be a prisoner.

Jed held his fire.

Another German appeared at the edge of the hole. He had no weapon. "*Karl, komm schnell. Hans ist verwundet.*"

The wet soldier forgot about Jed and his rifle and scrambled up out of the hole, calling, "*Hans, mein Gott.*"

The second German had a broad face cut by a large handlebar mustache and no helmet. His uniform was splattered with mud, his hands and face darkened by grime.

He spoke in English. "Karl's friend Hans was hit by that shell, one of our own, no doubt. His wound is very bad. He may die."

Jed put all the bravado he could muster into a question for the German. "What are you boys doing wandering around on the battlefield with no weapons?" He got to his feet, slipping in the mud, but keeping his rifle steady.

"We were a Maxim section left behind to slow your advance. We saw your men killing our comrades in the other machine gun positions. After we were surrounded, we could either fight and die or surrender. I ordered my men to surrender."

"Are you an officer?"

"I am their sergeant."

"Where are the Americans who captured you?"

"Your army could not spare men to escort us. They pointed us toward your rear area and said that we would there find medical assistance and food."

The German reached into his tunic.

Jed tensed.

The German froze. "You need not fear me. I have no hidden weapon." He produced a pack of American cigarettes.

"How did you get those?" Jed asked.

"One of your men took my Luger pistol and gave me this pack in exchange. He said it was a reasonable deal. He could have had it for free."

That sounded like Watkia.

A shell landed nearby. The German flopped down on the ground. "May I join you?"

Jed pointed his rifle at the other side of the shell hole. The sergeant scrambled in and scooped out a funk hole. He offered a cigarette to Jed who shook his head and sat down himself. The sergeant lit a cigarette and inhaled deeply, held the smoke, then let it out in a long sigh.

A highly agitated Karl returned and spoke intently to the sergeant. "He says they have stopped the bleeding but they have no clean bandage to dress the wound. You would happen to have an extra bandage?"

Jed considered for a few seconds. The men were technically prisoners of war and must be cared for. He reached into Tony's dressing pouch and tossed the package to Karl.

Karl ducked his head in a curt bow. "*Danke, Vielen Dank.*" He disappeared.

"*Sie Sind willkommen,*" Jed said after him.

"You know German," the sergeant said.

"My grandmother was from Koblenz and I have a friend at home, Herr Kurtz, the butcher. I practice with him." He didn't mention Aunt Bessie.

"You have a passable accent. I am originally from Lahnstein, a town near there. Perhaps we are distant cousins?"

"If you go far enough back, we're all related."

The German nodded then stared past his smoking cigarette. "What will you do now?"

Jed shrugged. "I don't know." He pointed to Tony. "He's gone but I have a friend who is hurt out there." He waved toward the top of the hole.

The German gazed up at the swirling smoke and clouds. "So many are gone." He shook his head. "We must get Hans back to your aid station and turn ourselves in to your military police. For us now, the war is, I think, over. It is a good thing for the war to be over." He looked at Jed with a wry smile. "Too bad the wrong side will win."

He stood up and threw his cigarette butt out of the shell hole. "This will settle nothing. You will hear from us again. Of this I am sure." He came to attention and clicked his muddy heels. He nodded his head in salute, climbed out of the hole, and was gone.

Jed sat back. The tension was gone. He had been carrying on a civilized conversation with an enemy soldier. He was happy to discover his unit hadn't been wiped out and was taking prisoners but he had no idea where they were. He wasn't wounded and should keep moving forward but he couldn't wander around a battlefield and hope he found his unit. Plus, he needed to find Mike.

Jed ducked as a pair of shells screeched in. They landed close, but with low order detonations. A cloud of mustard gas drifted away on the breeze. Jed looked out of the hole but could not see Mike.

He felt justified in staying put. The light was fading, and he didn't want to wander around after dark.

Jed dozed for a while but awoke when flares erupted in the darkness overhead and a voice called to him.

"Jed, are you there? I can't see."

It was Mike.

"Yes." Jed scrambled up to where Mike lay at the edge of the hole.

"Can you help me drag my busted butt in there with you?"

Jed helped Mike down into the funk hole the German had made.

"Is it bad?"

"I got hit in the ass." Blood stained Watkia's bandage on Mike's left thigh.

"I looked, but you weren't where I last saw you."

"I saw a bunch of Germans so I moved and hid. Then they threw in gas. I almost drowned pushing my face into the mud to wash the gas off but can barely see. I remembered seeing you get in this hole and have been inching along since dark. I'm glad I finally found you."

145

Jed used canteen water to wash out Mike's eyes. "Does that help?"

"A little, thanks."

An artillery shell landed two hundred yards away. Soon, bits of dirt and mud rained down on them. Something landed on Mike's stomach. It was nine inches across and looked like a soup bowl full of steaming pudding.

"Oh, my God," Mike said. "It's the top of someone's head." He slapped it away and the skull fragment landed in the bottom puddle and sank from sight.

Jed knew body parts of a blasted man had to go somewhere but shuddered at this proof.

Mike lay back and moaned. "I need sleep." He dozed off.

With Mike asleep and Tony dead, Jed was once again alone. Guilt vied with his sense of loyalty to Mike and Tony. What if the rest of the squad had needed him? Was he listed as missing? He hadn't tossed in the towel. He was needed here.

A shell screamed louder and louder. Jed threw himself over Mike to shield him. The shell landed in a hole a few feet away. The mud in the hole muffled the detonation and large clumps of dirt and mud rained onto Jed.

A burly man with an American helmet on his head scrambled into Jed's shelter after the shell exploded. He scraped mud off his arms and neck and cursed toward the German lines. "You shit-bird sausage eaters didn't get me."

It was Sergeant Brock. He squinted suspiciously at Jed in the shifting flare light.

"Martin? What the hell are you doing here? Are you wounded?"

"No, Sarge. I'm OK."

"If you're not wounded what are you doing hiding in this hole?"

Jed pointed to DiNiccola, pathetic and limp, already melting into the earth. "Tony was hit and lost an arm so I pulled him in here and tried to help him but he died. Mike came along a while later. He has a leg wound, can't walk, and he was gassed."

"You know orders are to not stop and help the wounded."

"Yes, Sarge, but Tony needed someone and I've known Mike all my life. I couldn't leave them."

Mike moaned and woke up. "Jed, are you there?"

"I'm right here, Mike. Sarge is too."

"It's starting to hurt, bad."

146

Brock moved to Mike and unwound the field dressing. He examined the wound by the flare light. "It didn't hit the bone. Is he hit in the gut too?" he asked Jed.

"No, just the leg."

Brock uncorked his French canteen and lifted Mike's head. "Drink some of this." Mike took a tentative sip. "Drink more, it eases the pain." Mike took two large gulps. Brock took a long drink himself and re-corked the canteen. He reached into his haversack and produced a small bundle of string. He tied one end to a pencil and the other end to a wad of gauze he tore from a bandage pack. Brock saturated the pencil, string, and gauze with iodine. A new flare blossomed and in the brighter light he found one of the holes in Mike's thigh. "This will sting." He thrust the pencil into the wound and grabbed the end when it emerged from the other side of the leg. Mike flinched but didn't cry out. Brock pulled the string through until the gauze was near the wound, added more iodine, and pulled the gauze through the wound channel. He placed the remaining pieces of gauze over the wound holes and wrapped Mike's thigh with the bandage ties.

"It's not bad, just hurts like hell. They'll sew it up and you'll be back in the line in a couple of weeks." He gave Mike more of the contents of his canteen.

"Give him some water."

Brock took another drink. "It's mixed with water like the Frogs do it. They know how to cope with this shit."

Jed had a question of his own. "What are you doing here? I thought you were wounded or killed."

"I was pinned down in a basement by a machine gun," Brock said.

"The gun had me pinned down too, but Bunny bayonetted the gunner." Jed began to suspect what the others had said was true, Brock was a coward. But what did hiding in this shell hole mean for Jed?

Brock crawled over to Jed and leaned in close, the brims of their helmets touching. His breath smelled like spilled wine. "I don't buy your Florence Nightingale story about helping the dead Dago or your Mick friend here. You're a fucking coward."

Jed put his foot in the middle of Brock's chest and shoved him away.

Brock started to lunge toward Jed. "I'll kill you for that—" He stopped when Jed held up his bayonet.

Other men approached, scrambling on either side of the hole whispering in English.

Brock pushed the bayonet aside and grabbed the front of Jed's blouse. "Don't get any ideas about talking to anybody about me because you don't know shit. Keep your fucking mouth shut or you'll end up like that Wop over there."

A face under an American helmet peeked over the rim of the shell hole, "SHAKER."

"HEIGHTS," Brock responded as he pushed Jed away.

The soldier turned away. "Lieutenant, we've got a couple of men here."

Another flare bloomed overhead.

Samis slid into the hole. "Are you men wounded?"

"No, sir," Brock said. "We've been out looking for stragglers like you. We found these casualties and moved them into this hole for protection."

Jed said nothing.

Sergeant Trask slid down into the shell hole.

"It's getting pretty crowded in here," Brock said and backed away from Trask.

"Where have you been?" Trask asked.

"Trying to find you."

"Sergeant Trask has been with me," Lieutenant Samis said through tight lips.

Mike groaned.

Samis turned to him and asked how he was feeling.

"It's starting to hurt bad lieutenant. There's fire all up and down my left leg."

Trask moved over to where Mike lay. "It's a good sign. It means your leg is still trying to work. If you couldn't feel anything it'd be much worse." He pointed to a face peering down. "Steinmetz go get Gurr from Second Squad, he's walking wounded, and those two Heinie prisoners. They can take O'Kean back to the dressing station."

Bunny nodded and disappeared.

Samis patted Mike gently on the shoulder. "We'll get you to the docs soon, O'Kean."

Mike held his gas-burned eyes tightly shut.

Bunny reappeared with the other three men.

Samis ordered everyone out of the hole. Jed picked up his rifle and, with a final glance at Tony's body, followed Brock up to the surface.

Lenny Gurr crouched between two grimy Germans, covering them with a pistol, his hand shaking. Jed squatted beside him. "I saw your squad charge the machine gun nest."

"Corporal Kraft and three of my squad are dead." Gurr took a deep breath. "I don't know where Phil Zyren and Tommy Pricklin are. Arliss Howe disappeared and I can't find him either." He wiped a tear from the corner of his eye. "Jesus, Jed, my whole squad was wiped out." He grabbed his side grimacing in pain. The bandage covering his ribs seeped blood.

"Your guys will turn up. Everybody's scattered to hell and gone," Jed said.

Gurr shook his head. "I want to go see my mom." Jed tried to comfort him, wrapping his arm around Gurr's shoulders and squeezing gently. He longed to see Bessie.

Trask motioned the two Germans down into the hole. One of them carried a six-foot piece of wood plank. In a few minutes, they struggled back up out of the depression and placed Mike on the plank in front of Jed.

Mike opened his watering eyes and turned his pale face to Jed. "Jed, are you still here?" His voice was weak but clear.

"I'm here, Mike. Lenny's going to get you back for some help, right, Lenny?"

Gurr wiped his eyes and took a firmer grip on the pistol. "You bet, Mike. We'll get back there together, get fixed up, and come back and kick Heinie ass."

Mike smiled. Gurr rose and motioned for the two Germans to pick up the board and move out. The four of them disappeared into the darkness.

Jed stood, slung his rifle over his shoulder, and walked over to Bunny and Brock.

Lieutenant Samis spoke to Bunny, "Lead Sergeant Brock and Martin to the platoon dugout and wait until we get there."

"Yes, sir," Bunny said. "Good to see you, Jed." He started forward.

"I'm glad to see you too, Bunny Love," Brock said.

Bunny pushed ahead, not looking back.

"Fucking Jew asshole," Brock said.

Under the rising moon and shifting flares, the landscape was spooky, with crumbled buildings, water-filled shell holes, and old wire and trash strewn everywhere.

Several dead men were marked by battle crosses for later recovery and burial.

As they stumbled forward over ground other men had bled to take, Jed's sense of failure grew. He had stayed out of sight, in a futile attempt to save Tony and comfort his best friend. His only wound was a small spot on his calf.

Shadows shuffled past them. Prisoners and stretcher bearers carried wounded to the rear, squads of stragglers, rounded up by officers and NCOs, moved forward, and medics responded to plaintive cries for help from mysterious, dark shell holes.

They approached a built-up section of trench. A sentry challenged, Bunny answered, and the three were motioned forward into a gap in the sandbags and down into the German trench system.

Brock leaned in close to Jed. "Remember what I said." He slinked away.

Bunny led Jed down a long flight of steps into a German dugout where a candle provided comforting light and some heat. The dugout was dry, had a wooden floor, and a table and chairs. Doody lay on a wood framed straw mat facing the wall, snoring softly. Collins, Watkia, and other platoon members sprawled on bunks in an adjacent room.

Jed and Bunny sat at the table. Bunny lit a cigarette from the candle flame, and stared down at the tabletop, eyes wide. He took a deep drag on his cigarette and shook his head.

"Rough day today, wasn't it?"

"What about the squad, Bunny?"

"With you here and knowing what happened to Tony and your buddy Irish, I guess we're all accounted for. We found this dugout and Doody declared squatters' rights. The lieutenant agreed."

Jed lit a cigarette with the candle and let out a long smoky sigh.

Bunny's left eye twitched. All morning he had been out front flanking machine gun nests and helping the hand bomber teams finish the gunners off with grenades while the rest of the unit gave them covering fire.

"You were very brave today, Bunny."

Bunny shook his head. "I was so scared I can't shit. You'd think you'd shit yourself." He looked at Doody. "Some do, I guess." He took another drag on his cigarette. "It was so random. One guy gets hit and not another?"

He flicked ash.

"You have to disconnect your mind and kill and move and kill and keep going. If you're going to get hit, there's nothing you can do about it. You stay low and hope a goddam piece of steel doesn't have your number on it."

Jed smoked quietly as Bunny stared at his cigarette. "Sorry to hear about your friend Irish. Was he hit bad?"

Doody half sat up. "Did you say Mike was hit?"

"Yes," Jed said. "Top says he'll be OK, but Mike was hurting pretty bad when they took him away. He was shot in the hip and got caught in a gas attack."

"Mike's a great guy. I hope he'll be all right." Doody began to roll back to sleep but turned back. "Are you OK, Jed?"

"I'm all right."

Doody was already asleep again.

The cigarette smoke gathered in a dense layer at the ceiling, swirled, and rushed up and out a ventilator shaft as cooler air sank down the entryway. It looked like a bathtub drain turned upside down. Bunny crushed the butt of his smoke against the floor with his boot and lit another one. "The lieutenant should be along soon. They're still trying to find out what happened to second squad."

Jed told Bunny what Gurr had said about second squad and what he had seen.

Bunny shook his head and stared at the wall of the dugout. He pulled gently at his left blouse pocket flap. It had been cut diagonally, and the button was missing. His uniform had other nicks and ragged tears.

"Looks like the wire cut your uniform up a bit," Jed said.

"Look at this." He pulled out his canteen and water splashed from two holes. He unscrewed the cap and took a drink, water splashing on the table. He slammed the canteen down. "A couple of inches left, and I'd have no liver." He looked at Jed. "You're not much better."

Jed's uniform had several nicks and holes in it. He'd heard the bullets snapping by but hadn't known how close they'd come. Two bullets had passed through his right sleeve and one had pierced the cloth of his wool breeches next to his left thigh. None had caught his flesh. He shivered at how close they had been.

The puttee around his right calf had come undone again. He swabbed iodine into the wound, wrapped the puttee tight, and tucked what was left of the tape down into the windings.

Bunny ran his right index finger into one sharp-edged canteen hole. "I've been with a lot of women, mostly whores. They only want money, they aren't committed, only present, no intimacy." He sucked hard on the cigarette in his left hand then blew a long column of smoke up at the ceiling drain. "Today I stuck that German gunner in the chest with my bayonet. He was committed." He met Jed's eye. "I ain't any homo, Jed, I never did it with a man, but when I put that blade in the guy's body it was more than sex, more than intimate. I heard him moan, not the fake moan of a whore, but the deep moan of someone in the throes of life itself," he blinked hard, "death itself. We were connected like no pussy I ever had, even the nice Catholic girls back in Akron who could fuck a Jew boy and then go to confession." He held Jed's eye. "More personal than putting your body into a woman." His bloodshot eyes held a silver shimmer. "God help me—I want to do it again."

He pulled his finger out of the canteen hole. A drop of blood spotted the table top.

Lieutenant Samis stepped into the dugout followed by Sergeant Lipsitz. The lieutenant waved Jed and Bunny to stay seated and sat down in a third chair pulling papers from his map case. He grabbed a pencil and looked at Lipsitz.

"What's the casualty report?"

Lips consulted his notebook. "The best I can figure, Lieutenant, the platoon had sixteen casualties: eight killed, seven wounded and one missing. Their names are listed here." Lips handed a piece of paper to Samis who wrote in his report as Lips talked. "Second Rifle Squad is combat-ineffective. They had four killed, one wounded, and one missing. I'll put the remaining two, Zyren and Pricklin, in with First Squad until we can get replacements."

"Private Howe is missing from second squad?" Samis asked.

Jed looked up. *Howe, yes, he was the one.*

"Lieutenant," Jed said, "I think I saw Howe killed. A mortar shell hit him." Jed shuddered at the memory. "I don't think you'll find anything left of him."

Samis looked at him. "Are you sure? It's important."

"Yes, sir. Howe was tall and thin. One second he was there, the next, he was gone."

Lieutenant Samis studied Jed's face. "Sergeant Lipsitz, list Howe as missing, presumed dead, based on Martin's report."

Lips made a note. "Nine dead and seven wounded. Platoon strength is forty-three."

"Nine dead, seven wounded," Samis mumbled to himself, "under my command."

The dirt and ash smeared over his two-day stubble added years to his appearance, but his eyes showed the changes were not superficial. He stared into space, swallowed hard, and returned to business. He made a final note and signed his report. "We'll continue the fight with what we've got." He folded the papers, the back stained with Bunny's blood.

Jed held out Tony's letter. Lips took it gently and put it in his pocket.

A major from the brigade staff stepped into the dugout, his leather boots and raincoat spattered with mud, rain dripping off his helmet. He scanned the room then called up the stairway. "Sir, this one's fine for the Post of Command. Sergeant, get your telephones and the staff equipment down here." He turned into the dugout and said, "Sorry, fellas. I've got to run you off. We need this dugout for the brigade P.C."

Samis nodded. "Yes, sir, we're just finishing up." He motioned his men out. Bunny roused Doody and Lips woke the other platoon members. As they exited, several staff officers and NCOs hustled in carrying spools of telephone wire, another table, lamps, and map cases.

Outside a light rain fell.

Bunny slapped Jed on the shoulder. "I'm glad we found you and you're all right. I've got a hole staked out up this trench. I didn't figure we'd be allowed to keep the dugout. I'll see you in the morning." He walked a few paces up the trench and sank into a funk hole low in the wall. Doody sat down on the firing step, tossed his helmet down as a pillow, and curled up sideways on the ledge under his raincoat. The rest of the platoon disappeared into refuges in the earth.

"It was too good to hope we could keep such a cozy hole," Samis said to Jed. "Find some cover and get what rest you can. We attack again in the morning."

CHAPTER 24

SEPTEMBER 27, 1918

MEUSE-ARGONNE OFFENSIVE – **DAY TWO**

Jed found an empty funk hole in the north edge of the trench thirty feet from the brigade P.C. He hung his raincoat over the opening and placed a loose sandbag as a pillow. He slipped in and lay down in the relatively dry interior. He was soon asleep.

The rain continued to fall as did German shells.

Images of the battle the day before appeared in his dreams. Men fell around him, blood flowed across the ground, torn bodies lay everywhere, discarded, pathetic.

He awoke inside his musty shelter shaking. How could men, who cherished their lives, march willingly into machine gun fire, risking all they had? Jed had done it and couldn't explain it other than he wanted to help the unit and not embarrass himself.

To clear his mind and make the dreams go away he used a trick Aunt Bessie had taught him when he was little. He rolled onto his other side. This had always worked to make him forget the drowning nightmares he had as a child. It worked this time as well. The images receded and the thrum of the rain soothed him back to sleep.

A pair of large rats barged into Jed's shelter. One of them woke him up by gnawing his hand. He grabbed the rat by its throat, skewered it with his bayonet, and held the body out to the other rat who sank its fangs into the meat. Jed threw them both out into the trench.

When he dozed off, he dreamed again. He ran from a giant rat trying to snap him up with terrifying jaws. He tripped on barbed wire and crawled through a field of slime, the rat catching up and, clamping its jaws on his foot, shaking him.

He woke in a panic.

Something shook his foot, but it was a human hand.

"Come on, Martin," Brock said. "Wake up."

Jed pulled the raincoat down, sat up, and wrapped himself against the rain. He didn't know which smelled worse, his own stink after being closed up in the funk hole all night or the rotting odor of the open air. It was still dark, the only light a German flare.

"What time is it?"

"Three-thirty," Brock said. Jed had slept less than two hours.

Watkia stood by Brock with a bucket. "Here, drink some of this." Jed pulled out his cup and Watkia filled it with coffee. Jed swished it around trying to wash away the foul taste in his mouth.

"Andy, go away," Brock said. Watkia dipped another ladle of coffee into Jed's cup and walked down the trench.

Brock moved close to Jed, his eyes reminding Jed of the rat in the dream. "I've got a job for you. The brigade runners are all shot up and the colonel asked for volunteers."

"I didn't volunteer for anything. I want to stay with the squad." Jed reached into his shirt and touched the Derringer.

"I volunteered you. If I keep you running around and away from here, maybe nobody will start asking stupid questions about yesterday." A German shell landed nearby. "Maybe one of those shells will catch up to you and my worries will be over."

Jed took a sip of coffee, swished it around in his mouth and spat it into the bottom of the trench, splashing Brock's boots. "You're a filthy rat, Brock."

"You watch yourself, mister." Brock patted the pistol at his belt. He pulled a piece of red cloth from his pocket and tossed it on Jed's lap. "Get your ass down to the brigade P.C. Wear the brassard on your arm so you don't get stopped by some nosy officer." As Brock turned away, he said, "It'll make you easier for the Kraut snipers to see." He stomped away laughing.

Jed finished his coffee, checked his rifle, made sure all of his other equipment was in place, then headed for the P.C.

He started down the stairs to the dugout and put the red brassard on his arm. As he went down, Abel West climbed up.

"You're Martin, right?"

"Yes, Sergeant Major."

"Watch out for that red flag. We lost a bunch of runners yesterday. Keep it in your pocket until you get to your destination. The German snipers won't be able to see it."

In the dugout, several hollow-eyed officers and NCOs perched on chairs. Cigarette butts and pipe plugs littered the floor.

Brigadier General Jackson, the 74th Brigade Commander, sat at the central table with a lantern, maps, and papers. His thin features were pinched by fatigue, but his jaw was square and resolute. He removed his wire-rimmed glasses and rubbed the bridge of his prominent nose. Colonel Galbraith, Jed's regimental commander, also sat at the table. He had the kindly, handsome face of a preacher but his tough demeanor supported the rumor he had been a sailing ship's captain. Colonel Lynch, the 148th Regiment commander sat to the side smoking a pipe.

General Jackson replaced his glasses. "General Pershing has reiterated his order. We of the brigade staff remain as far forward as possible, here with the troops. We'll push off at five-thirty and press the attack toward the town of Ivoiry. The 73rd Brigade, on our right, will move to flank the village of Montfaucon on the high ground and, with the 79th Division on the far right, take the town and relieve the pressure of machine gun fire on us." He looked around the room. "Colonel Lynch, Colonel Galbraith, keep the men of your regiments moving forward. Be stingy with their lives but keep them on the attack." Jackson turned to an NCO working with a telephone set on another table, "Anything with the phone, Ryan?"

"I get 20 seconds and then it goes dead again, General Jackson. It takes ten minutes to find the break and repair the line."

"Keep at it. Damn this German shelling." He signed a paper in front of him, folded the message, and handed it to Jed. "This finalizes our support plan for the assault. Get it to General Zimmerman over at 73rd Brigade as soon as you can. He's in this same trench a mile and a half to the east."

Jed took the message, put it in his blouse pocket, and glanced at Colonel Galbraith.

"Off you go, soldier."

When Jed exited the P.C., it was still raining but getting light. He hustled along, slowed by men emerging from their shelters and preparing for the morning's assault.

He made good time for almost a mile then approached a section of the trench only four feet deep, the sides of the trench piles of sandbags set above ground arcing over a stony outcrop. He crouched and duck walked through the section.

A dead American sprawled on his back in the center of the trench, the red brassard of a runner on his left arm and a bullet hole below his right eye. A pool of blood and brains spread around his head. He hadn't been dead long and a few of the black flies had found him, but his bowels had released when he died, and it wouldn't be long before scores of the vermin arrived. His right breast pocket was unbuttoned. Jed hesitated but stuck his fingers into the pocket. The message wasn't there. The flap of the runner's pistol holster was open, and his Colt automatic was missing as well.

The flies were getting more numerous. Jed pulled a sandbag down from the wall of the trench and, using his bayonet, slit the bag open and dumped out the dirt. He swiped the cloth above the man's head to shoo the flies off and then wrapped the dead runner's head in the sandbag. The covering might delay the inevitable long enough for a sanitary detail to arrive.

"God bless you, buddy," Jed said as he crawled away.

He snaked his way through the traverses of well-constructed trenches with firing steps and duckboards, sentries keeping watch through periscopes, men preparing to Stand-To.

Twice he found cut telephone wires and repaired them with an overhand knot and a twist of the copper cores after the insulation was stripped off.

He waded through a section of shell holes with shallow ditches linking them together like a string of beads, full of water and shivering soldiers. The trenches gradually curved to the right, the foreboding hulk of Montfaucon to his left, yellow glowing smoke rising from fires in the town. The trench complex continued south toward the Montfaucon Woods then turned back to the east.

Jed pulled the red brassard from his pocket and approached an officer who gave him directions to the 73rd P.C.

An officer stood in the middle of a shell hole carved into the edge of the trench. He surveyed the situation, brown eyes peering from under a plain steel dishpan helmet. General Zimmerman was a medium tall man in his fifties with a round face and a double chin. He wore a regulation pistol belt across a slight paunch and high-laced leather boots. An American colonel and a French major stood by him.

A Signal Corps private ran down a communication trench toward the front-line positions trailing the wire from a reel. He had traveled fifty yards when a shell landed under him and tossed him out of the trench.

"Damn," General Zimmerman said. He turned to Jed and held out his hand. The general read Jed's message and then scribbled a note on a message pad and handed it to Jed. "See the large tree trunk lying over the communication trench down there?" Jed nodded. "It's the regimental P.C. for the 145th. Take this down there. They'll pass it on." He consulted his watch. "We have five minutes to get this show started."

The rain stopped as the sun began to rise.

Jed removed his runner brassard and ran down the communication trench. When he got to where the signalman was writhing in the mud outside the trench, he reached out, grabbed the man by the arm, and pulled him down into the trench. He wrapped the man's individual bandage around his shattered leg.

"I'll be back for you," Jed said. He grabbed the wire reel and continued on.

As he neared the regimental P.C., he passed an American Hotchkiss machine gun crew firing at the German fortifications. The assistant gunner tossed the hot spent brass casings out of the pit with a shovel.

Jed reached the P.C. under the tree trunk, delivered the message and the wire reel, and hurried back toward the brigade P. C. shell crater. As he passed the machine gun nest, the assistant gunner shouted over the roar of the guns. "Tell them we need more machine gun ammunition."

Jed hefted the wounded signalman into a fireman's carry and hurried up the trench toward the brigade P.C. through a downpour of shells. His ears popped and his breath was sucked out of him by the near misses.

Medical orderlies met him at the P. C.

A Signal Corps captain hung up his telephone. "General, the lines are out again."

Zimmerman consulted his watch then ordered the captain to fire a green rocket. Whistles sounded in the front-line trenches, the Americans surged forward, and rushed toward Montfaucon from the west and south.

German machine gun fire roared.

A quartermaster corporal arrived leading a mule loaded with four crates of Hotchkiss and rifle ammunition.

"Sir, the Hotchkiss crews down there need more ammunition," Jed said.

The colonel waved his hand. "Use it where it'll do the most good."

Jed started down the trench, but the corporal didn't move. Jed turned to him. "You heard the man, let's go."

The corporal reluctantly pulled the mule after Jed. "What's the big idea? I'm ordered to deliver this stuff to the reserve dumps and you slobs are supposed to carry it forward."

Several German bullets snapped over the trench and two shells landed nearby. The corporal stopped and ducked down. "Do you want me and my mule to get killed?"

"What makes you think you're any more valuable than the rest of us?" Jed said. "Let's deliver the ammo and then you can take your cousin back to the safety of the rear."

They started forward again. "We get plenty of artillery back there, you know."

Jed ignored him.

When they arrived at the Hotchkiss, it stopped firing. The assistant gunner threw a last shovel full of brass out of the pit and leaned on the handle. "Shit." He glanced toward Jed and the mule, whooped for joy, and clambered out of the pit. He helped Jed unload two crates of machine gun ammunition and manhandled them into the gun pit.

A shell landed in the trench behind the mule and peppered its hindquarters with splinters. The animal reared up and pulled the lead rope out of the corporal's hands then jumped out of the trench and started running toward the rear. A shell landed on its back, flattening the mule. Rifle bullets sprayed in all directions.

The corporal yelped, ran up the trench and disappeared around a traverse.

Jed ran back toward the brigade P.C. through another storm of German shells.

Halfway to the P.C., the quartermaster corporal sat in the bottom of the trench, his individual bandage wrapped around his left arm above the elbow, one end in his right hand, the other in his teeth, pulling hard to form a temporary tourniquet. He relaxed his hold and tried to tie the bandage but blood spurted out of the wound to the rapid pulse of his heart. Jed grabbed the ends of the bandage and tied it tight stopping the blood flow. The man wasn't otherwise injured. Jed helped him up and draped the man's good arm over his shoulder.

"I'm sorry about your mule," Jed said.

The corporal said nothing.

The two men stumbled into the brigade P.C. and were met by the medics.

"Major Bernard, this soldier has had quite a day and it's not yet six o'clock," Zimmerman said.

The French major wrote on a pad. "I am making special note of the courage of this *bon soldat, mon général.*" He addressed Jed. "What is your name, rank, and unit?"

Jed hesitated. The major pointed with his pencil and nodded his head.

"My name's James Jedidiah Martin, Private, First Platoon, Company G, 147th Infantry, sir."

The major finished his notes. "Your name and exploits will be mentioned in my report to your Commander-in-Chief, General Pershing, and to my superiors in the French Army."

"But, sir, I did what anyone would have done. Heck, I've been scared right down to my socks for two days."

"The definition of courage is doing what must be done in spite of your fear. I watched you carry two men through barrages as heavy as any in my experience."

Jed noted the service stripes on the major's sleeve and the war cross on his chest. He also remembered his hiding in the shell hole. All this talk of mentions in reports worried him. What if people began to ask questions he didn't want to answer?

The Signal Corps captain motioned Jed over and offered him a seat on a crate. "It's the Croix de Guerre with palm for you," he said. Jed shook his head, not understanding. "The French War Cross with a palm leaf pinned to the ribbon, if it gets up to First Army Headquarters."

General Zimmerman watched the action around Montfaucon through binoculars. "The 145th is getting chewed up but the 79th Division on our right is finally moving forward. I think we'll have Montfaucon by sunset."

A runner hurried up and handed the general a message. Zimmerman read it and composed a reply. The runner ran off.

Zimmerman scribbled another message and handed it to Jed. "This one is for General Jackson at 74th Brigade headquarters."

Jed started to leave but the French major stopped him. "General, would you endorse my recommendation for Private Martin?"

Zimmerman looked Jed in the eye. Jed didn't know what he was supposed to do, so he met the general's stare straight on. Zimmerman nodded his head and signed the Frenchman's paper. Bernard folded it up and handed it to Jed. "Take this to General Farnsworth. He's temporarily with General Jackson at the 74th Brigade P.C. He'll forward it to First Army headquarters."

"Well done today, lad," Zimmerman said.

"Thank you, sir." Jed ran his fingers along the crease of paper. He didn't want a medal, he wanted to get back to his unit.

With the troops in the all-out assault and the German artillery concentrated elsewhere, Jed made good time to the 74th Brigade P. C.

General Jackson, took the messages, read them, and passed one to General Farnsworth. They consulted maps and spoke with the staff officers gathered around.

Jed slumped on a spool of telephone wire.

A corporal sat at a typewriter table and dug into a can of beans. He saw Jed staring at the can. "Would you like some? It's all we have here." The corporal tossed him a can.

"The boys in my squad are pretty hungry," Jed said.

The corporal tossed Jed three more cans. Jed put them in his haversack.

Jed opened his can with the tip of his bayonet, pulled out his mess kit fork, and gobbled down the contents.

General Farnsworth was watching. "I'm sorry, soldier. We are having the devil's own time getting artillery and ammunition forward on these impossible roads. The field kitchens are having equal difficulty and we are doing our best to support you men."

Jed set the bean can down and stood. "We know, sir. Things are tough all around."

Farnsworth turned to his aide. "Let's go." To General Jackson he said, "Bill, keep the men moving forward. We'll work on getting artillery for you, but you must not fall back." As he exited the door he said, "At ease."

Jed sat down.

The bell on the field telephone clattered and General Jackson picked up the handset. "74th Brigade, General Jackson." He listened for two seconds then slammed the instrument down. "I heard five words from a major of artillery and then the line went dead again." He motioned two young lieutenants over to his table. "Go and see if you can find any supporting artillery. If so, direct the commanding officer to report here at once."

The lieutenants hurried up the stairs.

Jed leaned against the wall, closed his eyes, and dozed.

Someone clumped down the stairs. Cain came into the P.C. pulling a red brassard onto his arm. He handed a message to the general then flopped down next to Jed.

"How's it going, old scout?"

"I've been running messages all morning. Where's the company?"

"Two of our battalions made it as far as Ivoiry. Company G is brigade reserve south of the Montfaucon-Ivoiry road. Not sure what's next."

The field telephone rang again. The general listened for several seconds then consulted a map. "I'll send the brigade reserve, hold on."

Another runner arrived. The general read the message. "Colonel Lynch, commander of the 148th has been wounded." He wrote a long message and handed it to Cain. "Take this to Colonel Galbraith. He is to use his reserves to repel enemy counterattacks, hold the line on hill 265, and take command of the advancing troops if Colonel Lynch has been evacuated." He turned to Jed. "You are released back to your unit, Private. Thank you for your bravery today."

Jed followed Cain up the bunker stairs.

"What bravery?"

"Nothing, I was just doing my job."

CHAPTER 25

SEPTEMBER 27, 1918

WEST OF IVORY, FRANCE – **DAY TWO**

Company G advanced on hill 265 moving through evidence of the 148th Regiment's assault earlier in the day. Long wooden planks and wide strips of chicken wire fencing had been thrown over the German defensive barbed wire to allow men to run across without being tripped. The company used these passages and made good progress at a fast walk. Fresh, dry shell holes dotted the area and rifle and machine gun brass littered the ground, glinting in patches of sunlight stabbing down through fast-moving clouds. The wounded had been removed to dressing stations but several dead men still lay in pathetic heaps or hung tangled in the wire. A lieutenant lay face down, his pistol in his hand and his whistle still in his mouth. Men hurried by other pulverized lumps of khaki and slimy red without looking.

The 147th regimental commander, Colonel Galbraith, had ordered the 134th Machine Gun Battalion to fill a gap between two of the division's regiments and wait for Company G to reinforce them.

First Platoon led the way up a shallow ravine below the ridgeline with Jed, Trask, and Brock on point. Enemy artillery fire fell on the ridge and on the southern slopes where the company made its advance.

When the company reached a point fifty yards from the ridgeline, the enemy artillery stopped abruptly. An American machine gun atop the ridge opened fire toward the other side of the hill.

Trask turned toward Captain Brown, pumped his arm vertically, and then pointed forward. The captain blew his whistle and the men double timed through the obstacles toward the hill.

The American machine gun ceased firing and the two-man crew jumped up and ran down the hill toward Jed and the others. As the two fleeing gunners approached, Brock grabbed one and swung him into a water-filled shell hole. Trask stepped forward and smashed his hand into the chest of the other. The man left his feet and landed flat on his back, gasping for breath.

Three Germans jumped into the American machinegun pit, swung the gun around, and fired at the Americans coming up the slope. They couldn't depress the gun enough to engage First Squad directly below.

The rest of the company took what cover they could in shell holes.

Jed was closest to the machine gun and crawled up the side of the ridge to within ten feet of it. The muzzle blast slapped his face.

Trask sprawled beside him and held out a hand grenade. "Go ahead."

Jed held the grenade spoon down with his right thumb and pulled the pin. He edged closer to the gun, hugging the ground to stay out of sight of the Germans. When he was within arm's reach of the trench, he released the spoon. The fuse on the grenade left a smoke trail as he flipped it into the machine gun pit and scrunched down.

The grenade went off and the machine gun fire stopped.

Trask smacked Jed's shoulder. "Go—go—go!"

Jed leaped over the parapet. He stopped, stunned by what his grenade had done. A German officer sat on the gun pit floor, moaning and holding his stomach. He raised a pistol. Trask pumped a shotgun blast into the officer's chest and the man flopped backward, his head submerged in the puddle at the bottom of the gun pit. His final breath bubbled out of his lungs and he lay still.

Another German pulled the headless gunner away from the machine gun.

Trask pointed. "Hit him!"

Jed stepped forward and drove his bayonet through the man's chest under his left arm. The man coughed and turned his head toward Jed, a pathetic expression on his young face.

Jed withdrew the bayonet as the boy fell to his knees.

"Hit him again!"

Jed plunged the bayonet downward toward the boy's heart. The soldier collapsed.

Jed felt Bunny's ecstasy but it quickly disappeared. The man lay still, his blue eyes and mouth open wide in death, blood running down his cheek.

Jed swallowed bile down hard.

Trask grabbed Jed's arm. "Are you alright?"

"It's murder."

"Yes," Trask said. "Murder in self-defense."

A German soldier appeared at the bottom of the steps that led up into the gun pit. He approached Jed, en-garde. His expression changed to shock as he looked down at the bayonet point that had popped out of the front of his chest. He dropped his rifle and crumbled into the bottom of the trench. The First Battalion corporal they had relieved in the Baccarat sector more than two weeks before stood where the German had been. He pulled his bayonet out of the back of the German, nodded to Jed, and turned, leading his squad up the communication trench from which the German had emerged. Furious gunfire erupted. No more Germans came down that trench.

Captain Brown and the rest of the company scrambled into the trench. Sergeant Brock hustled the two retreating gunners forward by the scruff of the neck and pitched the men head first into the mud at the bottom of the gun pit. "You two shit birds clean this mess up and get that gun back in action." The two gunners threw the German bodies out of the back of the pit, checked the machine gun, and swung it back around.

A light rain started to fall.

Jed and Sergeant Trask peered toward a stand of trees 400 yards away. The last of the retreating Germans disappeared into its underbrush.

"The Bois Emont, Emont Wood," Trask said.

The ground sloped down into a marshy depression and then up again to a line of trenches skirting the near edge of the forest. Communication trenches crossed the low-lying ground. The collapsed town of Ivoiry sat to the right of Company G's position.

The squad lounged in the bottom of the trench smoking cigarettes.

"Stay alert," Trask said. "The Germans will counterattack counting on you to relax."

Artillery rounds whistled in and detonated around the Company G trenches.

A group of German soldiers emerged from among the trees and jumped into the trench at the edge of the forest.

"Here they come," Trask said.

The Germans had coordinated the hasty attack well.

When the barrage lifted, Captain Brown ordered, "Commence firing."

The Americans stood up and discovered the Germans only fifty yards away.

The machine gun coughed to life. Jed sighted on the nearest German, hit the trigger, and the gun smacked him in the shoulder. The man fell but Jed didn't know if it was from his bullet or the machine gun. He worked the rifle bolt and fired again as the Germans pressed forward falling right and left.

Time slowed to a crawl, the air dense with sound, the rain hitting the hot barrels of their weapons sending a thin mist wafting through the trench.

Jed jumped down from the firing step and reached for a stripper clip at his belt. Watkia was standing there, his rifle slung across his back.

"Why aren't you firing your rifle?"

"Shit, I'd just have to clean the son of a bitch." Watkia handed a five-round stripper to Jed. "You guys are doing all right."

Jed pushed the rounds into the rifle magazine, closed the bolt, and climbed up onto the firing step. A German soldier stood before him, twenty feet away. The soldier was a grenadier with two stick grenades shoved into the top of each boot and a bulging sack slung over his shoulder. The German raised his rifle. Jed covered him with his own rifle, the white calm spreading through his chest and into his mind. The German had silver-gray eyes, a thin face, and brown hair pressed down by his coal scuttle helmet. The two enemies hesitated and lowered their rifles, staring at each other.

The spell was instantly broken as the American machine gun traversed toward the German who dove into a shell hole.

Immediately a potato masher sailed over Jed's head and splashed in the mud. Bunny jumped down, grabbed the grenade, and threw it away. The explosion was a dull thump somewhere in the mud. Another grenade flew in. Bunny caught this one in midair and threw it back.

Jed couldn't see the grenadier hiding in the crater.

An arm appeared above the shell hole and another grenade flew into the trench.

Bunny pitched this one out too. "Get the son of a bitch. I can't shag fly balls indefinitely."

With clenched teeth, Jed climbed up and sat sidesaddle on the sandbags, trying for some elevation and sighting on the hole. The grenadier popped up and pulled the lanyard on another grenade. His lips moved silently as he counted off the seconds on the fuse so it wouldn't be thrown back at him. He saw Jed as Jed pulled the trigger, his eyes wide. The bullet hit the German in the neck and he dropped out of sight. As he fell, he reflexively tossed the grenade out of his hole where it detonated harmlessly.

Brock grabbed Jed's leg and pulled him down as several bullets hit the sandbags around where Jed had sat. Brock fired several rounds over the lip of the trench then ducked down, the slide on his .45 locked back. He dropped the empty magazine and slammed a full one into the pistol and released the slide stop.

Brock grabbed Jed by the arm. "Don't try to be the hero we both know you ain't."

"Let go of me."

Brock waved his pistol in Jed's face. "At least you saw your old sergeant fighting."

Jed resumed his position on the step, ignoring Brock.

The surviving Germans retreated into the woods dragging their wounded.

Captain Brown ordered the company to cease firing.

A runner handed a note to the captain. He read it and signed his acknowledgement.

"Lieutenant Samis, Sergeant Trask, check for casualties and set sentries. We're staying here tonight."

The squad crowded into a small bunker like the one the engineers had built for them back in the Baccarat Sector. No one in the squad had been hurt seriously.

Collins lit a candle.

Bunny lit a cigarette. "You think they're going to get food up to us tonight?"

"It would be a miracle," Doody said. "Anybody got any water?" The men shared their canteens until everyone had a drink.

Watkia entered the bunker with an armful of white packages. He tossed one to each man. "I looked around and found a German dugout with a pot of hot coffee and a bunch of these packages. They're German emergency rations. Crackers, I think. Naturally, I helped myself. I also found these." He reached into his haversack and pulled out four fat German sausages. He passed these and three canteens full of coffee to Collins.

Jed pulled two cans of beans from his haversack. The squad seared the sausage in the candle flame, spread the beans over the crackers, and washed them down with coffee.

Sergeant Brock stuck his head into the bunker. "What are you guys up to?"

"Here Sarge." Watkia held a piece of sausage out on the tip of a bayonet.

Brock took a bite and chewed. "Not bad." He eased himself into the shelter and finished the piece of sausage and three crackers with beans. "You babies are a bunch of trouble but you take care of your old sergeant." He checked his watch. "We take over sentry duty at midnight. Collins, set up a schedule. We're attacking again in the morning." He stepped out of the shelter then stuck his head back in. "Douse that candle."

By midnight it had stopped raining. The sky was clear, and it was cold. Star shells slowly descending along the front line overpowered the light from the waning crescent moon rising in the east. Watkia, Bunny, and Jed put overcoats on, buckled on their cartridge belts and gas mask carriers, and picked up their rifles. The sentry post was a short distance away, and they relieved two tired hand bombers. Bunny stretched out and was instantly asleep, his smoker's snore muffled by a blanket he pulled over his face. Jed and Watkia settled into the warm depressions the other men had vacated. Andy watched the trench and Jed looked through a box periscope at no-man's-land.

Artillery from both sides kept up an intermittent rumble but for now no shells landed near their position.

A low moan, then soft gurgle, rose from in front of their post. After a moment, the sound repeated. It came from the shell hole where Jed had shot the grenadier.

Watkia scooted as high in the hole as he could without exposing himself. "Do you hear a noise?"

"*Oma, Oma.*"

"I think it's a German I shot in the neck. He's calling for his grandma to help him."

"He'd better stop all that dying noise or it won't be his Granny who helps him."

The boy's moans grew louder. He started wheezing and coughing.

Watkia cursed. He dropped his cartridge belt and pulled his bayonet off of his rifle. "Stay alert."

"Should I wake Bunny?"

"Let him sleep," Watkia said. He waited for a nearby flare to go out then slithered into no-man's-land. "Stop that dying noise."

Jed shuddered at the memory of shooting the man. Looking at his face, with his clear silver eyes, was like looking into a mirror.

The gurgling cries stopped.

Two minutes later Watkia whispered the password, crawled into the sentry post, and sat behind the periscope.

"Andy, did you—"

"Shut up."

"What happened?"

Watkia paused for a second. "He died. Get Bunny up and go to sleep."

Jed exchanged places with Bunny who stood with his rifle at the ready. Jed pulled Bunny's blanket around his neck to ward off the cold and drifted off, thinking about Andy Watkia, who wouldn't fire his rifle in battle, but would silence a wounded man.

CHAPTER 26

SEPTEMBER 28, 1918

BOIS EMONT, FRANCE - **DAY THREE**

Through the rest of the night the artillery bombardment increased in intensity. When Jed was able to sleep a dream swirled through his mind about a noise—a dying noise.

The rising sun hit Jed's face providing pleasant warmth after the cold night, but the sun also boiled mist from the saturated ground carrying the odor of death and decay.

First and Third Battalions moved into the trench. They would lead the day's assault with Second Battalion in support.

Ten small tanks crossed the trench line and idled to the left of the company sector.

"French FT-17s," Lips said as he and Collins settled down nearby. "Looks like we get support this morning."

"Every Kraut gunner this side of Montfaucon will try to hit one," Collins said.

At 7 A.M. First and Third Battalions jumped off and moved toward the woods following a walking barrage. The tanks spread out in the field to the left of the Bois Emont and paralleled the infantry advance. A platoon of infantry from First Battalion supported them.

After the lead battalions advanced one hundred yards, Captain Brown gave the signal and Jed stumbled out of the trench with the rest of Company G. They passed west of what had been the town of Ivoiry walking at a steady pace, descending the slope, bayonets fixed. Captain Brown and Trask advanced near Samis in the middle of First Platoon with Collins to the left and Lipsitz anchoring the right end of the platoon rank.

Jed drifted toward Trask. "Where's Sergeant Brock?"

"He'll show up," Trask said.

The lead battalions crossed the trench at the edge of the woods and disappeared among the tree stumps. Machine gun fire greeted them, answered by rifle shots and grenade blasts.

Jed jumped over the trench and glanced down at a mess of guts and blood in the bottom. He hurried into the woods.

To the left, German artillery fell throughout the tank formation. One shell landed on top of a tank. The fuel tank over the rear engine exploded and engulfed the hulk in an orange fireball. Another shell hit in front of a tank and tossed it six feet into the air, flipping it upside down. The two crewmen scrambled out of it but a German machine gun cut them down. Another tank turned its turret and silenced the machine gun position with its 37mm gun.

One of the machines crawled into the trees near where First Squad had stopped to watch the action. Its engine smoking badly, it clanked to a stop in a thicket. The crew opened the hatch and dove for cover under the brush. Collins waved them over, and they low-crawled to his side. The commander was a young lieutenant, the driver a sergeant.

Collins pointed south, "You two better head back to your command element."

The tank officer pulled his pistol from its holster. "I want a shot at those bastards."

Collins shrugged. "Suit yourself, sir. Be careful where you point that pistol."

"I'm qualified with this weapon, Corporal." He nodded to his driver who scrambled out of sight as the three surviving tanks backed out of the kill zone.

The tank officer followed First Squad as they crawled forward.

Lieutenant Samis and the rest of the platoon were pinned down by a Maxim. Samis signaled First Squad to move to flank the machine gun.

Jed crawled forward and spotted the flash of the gun fifty feet away. A hand bomber corporal named Stevens along with Bart and Clay Jones joined him.

"I guess you need us Joneses to pull your ass out of a tight spot," Clay said.

"There's a first time for everything."

Stevens and Clay rose and ran forward with grenades but the machine gunner saw them and turned his fire. Stevens clutched his left arm and dove behind a tree stump. Clay fell face first into a pile of leaves.

Bart jumped up and rushed toward Clay.

Jed grabbed for him but missed. "Come back here, Bart, you can't help him."

Bart hoisted Clay onto his shoulders, stood up, and took two steps. The machine gunner fired again. The brothers fell together and remained motionless.

The gunner resumed his sweeping fire.

Jed smelled the metallic heat of the machine gun bullets snapping inches above his head.

The gunner's head was four or five inches above the muzzle flash. Jed looked down the length of his rifle barrel, at this close range more an act of pointing than sighting. He placed the front sight above the muzzle flash and pulled the trigger.

The machine gun fire stopped.

After a moment, the snapping of the machine gun bullets resumed. Jed held his front sight above the flash three more times and silenced the gun every time.

When the fifth crewman grabbed the gun, Jed called for the gunner to stop and spare himself. *"Anhalten, sparen Sie sich."*

The German stood and called, *"Kamerad."*

He was a boy, maybe sixteen.

As Jed and the others rose to their feet, a five-man gun team popped up from a well-concealed pit to their left and raised their hands. *"Kamerad, Kamerad."*

The tank officer spun and fired his pistol hitting one German in his upraised arm.

Captain Brown walked up behind the tanker and pulled the pistol from his hand. "In my company," he said, making the pistol safe, "we don't shoot surrendering men." He handed the pistol back to the officer. "Put this away."

Sergeant McClardy would have agreed with the captain. Killing surrendering men was murder—with exceptions.

Brock and Watkia joined the squad.

"Brock always shows up eventually," Bunny said.

Brock tended to the wounded hand bomber Stevens. Watkia wound a bandage around the arm of the injured German. The other Germans stood with their hands clasped on their heads scowling at Jed who covered them with his rifle.

"Captain," Samis said. "There's a lot of ordnance lying around. These unhappy fellows need an escort."

Brock spoke up. "I'll make sure the prisoners and our wounded get back to the rear."

Samis shook his head. "I need you here with me."

"Good point, Lieutenant. You," Brown pointed to the tank lieutenant, "make sure these men get to the rear safely. Don't let them pick up a rifle and shoot you. If they try, then you can fire your weapon."

The officer's jaw tightened, but he nodded his head, pulled his pistol out again, and waved the Germans forward. Stevens wobbled to his feet and followed.

Sergeant Trask approached. "Captain, the company is falling behind the battalion."

Brown led them forward.

They caught up with the rest of the unit and advanced with no further resistance. When they reached the northern edge of the woods, Major LaForge halted the battalion. The men took positions behind fallen trees and waited.

The woods ended along a ridge running from west to east. The ground sloped down then leveled off across a miniature no-man's-land. A second, lower ridge ran west to east halfway across the valley. The terrain dipped again and finally rose to the town of Cierges, 1000 yards away, collapsed like Montfaucon and Ivoiry.

First and Third Battalions crossed the central ridge and entered the village.

Bunny was sprawled next to Jed. "Boy, could I use a cigarette."

Collins scooted by. "No smoking, be ready to move out. There's no German artillery on the town so it's a cinch the Heinies are in there."

Jed shook his canteen, but it was empty. He searched but found no corpses with canteens, only severed body parts.

After ten minutes, a roar of machine gun fire rose to a crescendo in Cierges. Spent ricochets fell around Jed like the first drops of a rain storm.

Soon, members of First and Third Battalion ran out of the town, streaming past the American machine gunners and automatic riflemen who had gone forward in support.

Major LaForge was with his company commanders in a shell hole. A signal lamp blinked from the edge of Cierges. "They're pulling out of the town and returning to the jump off point," LaForge said. The American automatic weapons fire stopped. The lamp blinked again. "They're calling for artillery." To the assembled captains he said, "Get ready to pass the other two battalions through and support their withdrawal."

The company commanders leaped out of the hole and hurried to issue their orders. La Forge picked up a field telephone, its coil of wire trailing back the way they had come. He called for artillery.

The men of First and Third Battalion climbed the ridge and ran into the woods. The machine gun teams and automatic riflemen came next, struggling with their heavy equipment. The First Battalion commander, Major Lawrence sprinted into the woods. "LaForge?"

LaForge waved him over.

"They had Maxims behind every rock and fallen wall," Lawrence said. "I ordered the men back to the jump off point. You better come too."

German explosive and gas shells fell into the woods. American shells impacted at the edge of Cierges.

Second Battalion followed the other two battalions through the woods, donning their masks as they moved past clouds of gas.

Jed ran to the south edge of the woods and took a communications trench running toward the American lines. A shell landed to his right barely outside the trench. The concussion smacked his ears, but he kept going.

The other Americans veered to the sides down traverses and soon he was running alone up the rising terrain into the town of Ivoiry. He sprinted toward a still standing shed and threw himself on the floor. The back wall was missing but half of the battered front wall still stood.

A voice behind him said, "I'm glad someone finally showed up." Clarence Dubman stirred a steaming pot on his rolling kitchen, a ladle in his left hand and a .45 pistol in his right. His unhitched mules munched hay at the other side of the shed.

Jed took off his mask. "Where did you come from?"

"I brought you boys something hot to eat. Since no shells fell in the town, I figured the German's had an artillery observer hidden in one of these buildings. They're across the street and can't see me behind this wall. I've been trying to get a shot at them to stop them shooting at you fellas."

Jed crouched behind a hole in the wall. The house across the street had no roof, and a rangefinder protruded above the front wall.

A German peeked out of a window wearing a radio headset. Dub stepped to his right and fired around the wall. The German ducked out of sight.

"Shit, I missed."

A second German popped up, raised a rifle, and fired at the shed. The bullet pierced the wall and clanged off the pots hanging on the rolling kitchen.

"Enough," Dubman said. He motioned Jed up from his hiding place.

Jed hesitated.

"Come on. Now that I have you to help me, I can take care of them."

Jed moved beside the cook.

"Stir this."

Jed grasped the ladle and automatically stirred as Dub opened a drawer in the side of the rolling kitchen and pulled out a hand grenade. He sprinted across the street, his half-blanket apron fluttering around his knees, and hid behind the corner of the house. The German rifleman leaned out the window and fired a round down the street but Dubman was safely under cover.

The German dropped out of sight.

Dub advanced the few steps to the side of the window, pulled the pin from the grenade, let the spoon fly, and tossed it through the window, diving onto the ground. Jed took cover behind the kitchen. The grenade went off with a muffled blast, smoke and dust boiling out of the window. Dubman leaped to his feet, thrust his pistol through the window, and fired into the house. He sprinted back across the street, took the ladle, and continued to stir the slum.

"Nobody messes with my kitchen. Give me your canteen cup."

Jed gulped the warm stew down. It was mostly potatoes with a little meat and a few onions. It was warm and filling. He poured coffee into the cup, swished it around and drank the resulting swill.

"Thanks, Dub."

"What I'm here for, Jed."

Lieutenant Samis slipped into the shed followed by Bunny and Doody. "What was the commotion over here?"

"Private Dubman eliminated a German artillery observer across the street," Jed said, "with grenade and pistol."

"Steinmetz, you and Dodd go check," Samis said.

Bunny and Doody ran out of the shed.

"Would you like some slum, Lieutenant?"

"Not now, Dubman. When I get back to the main trench, I'll send the men to eat."

Bunny and Doody returned. "There was a German observation post in the house, sir," Bunny said. "Four dead. They had maps, a rangefinder, and a radio. We busted up the rangefinder and radio and brought the maps." Doody handed them to the lieutenant.

"You witnessed this, Martin?"

"Yes, sir," Jed said.

Samis looked at Dubman. "Good job, Private. I'll mention this in my report."

Bunny and Doody dug into the slum.

"Hey, Dub, how come you don't have any greens?" Doody asked.

"They're sending so many men over that there's no space on the ships for spoilable food." He opened a compartment on the kitchen and handed out cans of tomato juice. "The army has bought out half the tomato production back home. They say a can of tomato juice is like a couple of quarts of water for thirst and substitutes for a whole meal. We have a big store of it and I'll be giving it to you a lot."

Jed punched a couple of holes in his can and chugged down the juice.

"Let's go, Martin," Samis said. "Steinmetz and Dodd finish eating and join us in the main trench."

When they got to the squad area Lieutenant Samis and Sergeant Lipsitz rounded up the rest of First Platoon and sent them for chow.

Bunny and Doody arrived and sat on the firing step. Jed slumped next to Bunny and took a lit cigarette from him.

"The attack this morning was a complete waste of time," Bunny said leaning back and staring at the sky. "We're no further along than we were this morning."

Doody was stretched out on the firing step asleep. Zyren and Pricklin sat together on a packing crate. Samis, Lips and Collins sat together closest to the brigade P.C.

German artillery rounds began landing in the rubble of Ivoiry at the rate of three a minute knocking down the remaining walls and kicking up large clouds of dust.

After five minutes two soldiers came down the trench, each holding a stew pot.

"What about the cook?" Jed asked.

"They killed one of his mules," one said as he went by.

"He gave us the slum then got out of there before they blew the shed to shit," the other said.

"Once the Krauts found out their spotters were dead, the town wasn't off limits anymore," Bunny said.

Watkia walked up and set two metal buckets on the ground in front of Bunny.

"Where have you been?"

"I had pressing business, whoremonger."

Bunny blew smoke at Watkia.

Jed looked in the buckets. "What do you have there?"

"Somebody captured a German water-point. I got us a couple of buckets of water, tossed a handful of ground coffee into one and found a burning log to set it on. It's not very strong, but it's the best I can do."

Jed and Bunny pulled out their tin cups and Watkia ladled the weak coffee into them. While they drank, he filled their canteens, then tossed each of them a pack of gum. Jed popped a stick into his mouth. He hadn't brushed his teeth in two days and the minty gum tasted fresh and clean.

Jed sat in the trench at the southwest edge of the Emont Woods with Billings the rifle grenadier as forward observers. Samis, Trask, Bunny, and Brock advanced 300 yards to their left trying to establish contact with the 91st Division which had advanced beyond the 37th and created a gap between the two divisions.

Sergeant Trask had given Jed a mirror which he clipped to his bayonet on the end of his rifle and held it above the trench parapet as a periscope. If the Germans attacked, Billings was to fire a grenade with three red lights as a warning. Then Jed and he were to return to their lines.

Jed checked the woods and the field with its ruined tanks and saw no movement.

He lowered the mirror. His reflection looked like Uncle Enoch as he had looked at the Choctaw Route Station: a three-day beard smudged with charcoal, silver-gray eyes, eyelids edged red by smoke and gas, and a pinched, tired look.

"Someone's coming," Billings said.

Jed raised the mirror. German infantry moved past the dead tanks in a line that extended into the woods.

Jed put the mirror in his pocket. "Give the signal!"

Billings fired a grenade into the air. It erupted into three glowing red balls of fire.

To Jed's left, Samis and the others ran south toward the American line.

A German barrage arrived, marching through the woods ahead of the Germans, shells falling with a sickening roar around Jed and Billings. They ducked under a roofed over section of the trench zigzag.

"Your job is done," Jed said. "Go."

Billings ran out into the main trench. A shell landed in the trench and brightly colored fireballs leaped into the air.

As the German barrage passed to the south Jed stepped out into the main trench and ducked back in horror. The upper half of Billings lay at the bottom of the trench. His lower half hung over the parapet. His grenades had cooked off when the shell exploded.

Germans jumped into the trench on either side. In the zigzag Jed couldn't be seen down the trench in either direction or from above, but he was trapped.

An American barrage began.

A shell landed in the trench to Jed's right. There were stifled screams then nothing.

He looked around the corner. A German machine gun crew lay in the trench bottom.

"Are you all right?" someone said in German from the left side.

Jed answered, *"Wir sind gut."*

A German came through the zigzag, saw Jed, and lunged with his bayonet. Jed parried with his own bayonet then stabbed the man in the chest. The soldier fell, dragging Jed's rifle out of his hands.

A German officer stepped into the half-light and pointed a pistol at him. "It is lucky for you that I do not shoot unarmed prisoners. Give me your identification." He held out his left hand.

Jed reached under his gas mask carrier and unbuttoned his blouse. The officer tensed but Jed told him his pay book was in his shirt pocket.

As Jed reached into his blouse, an artillery shell landed on the roof over the traverse. The German officer flinched and lowered his pistol. Jed side stepped away from the pistol barrel, pulled the Derringer, and shot the German in the head. He shoved the Derringer out of sight and picked up his rifle.

Around the corner to his left a German Maxim machine gun crew had set up next to Billings' body and fired at the American lines. Jed tossed a grenade around the corner. The blast silenced the gun and when he looked the whole crew was down.

Jed ran down the empty trench and turned a corner toward his own lines. American machine gun and rifle bullets hit all around and one hit him in the left forearm. As he ducked into a side trench for cover, German soldiers retreated up the trench and across the ground above. One was hit and splashed unmoving into the trench bottom.

When the Germans had passed, the American fire followed them. Jed put his helmet on the end of his bayonet and held it up so the gunners could see it. He ran the rest of the way to the American trench, dove over the parapet, and collapsed on the firing step.

He lit a cigarette, took a few deep drags, and his shakes subsided.

Sergeant Trask walked up and sat beside him.

Jed handed him his mirror. "Billings is dead, Top."

"You saw it?"

"You can be sure I saw it. Did you find the 91st?"

"We didn't have time to link up but they're there on our left. We pulled back when the Germans attacked. Sorry to leave you stranded but looks like you took charge and handled the situation." Trask stood up. "The Germans are retreating to Cierges and we're going back up and dig in at the north edge of the woods." He hurried away.

Jed slumped back against the trench wall. He was worn out.

Brock appeared. "Looks like you got hit."

Jed rolled up his sleeve. The bullet had left a deep gouge in his arm that was bleeding and starting to ache.

Brock took a sewing kit and a half pint bottle from his haversack. "Take a couple of swigs of this."

"What is it?"

"Cognac and laudanum."

"I don't want any."

"Shut up and drink it."

Jed drank deeply, the cognac covering the bitter taste of the laudanum.

Brock cleaned Jed's wound with iodine, closed the gash with six stitches, and wound a bandage around his arm.

"You're as good as Watkia," Jed said.

"Who do you think taught him?"

Brock's contradictions baffled Jed. The laudanum loosened his tongue. "What is it with you? You hate us but you're the first one to care for anyone who's hurt and in pain. You talk big but then aren't around for trouble."

"Me? Who was it I found cowering in a shell hole pretending to take care of a dead man? You've got nerve calling me a coward. I want to stay alive like you do." Brock took a drink from the bottle. "Once you're dead you're dead, that's it."

"I used to go to church when I was little and they said there's more after this life."

"I was brought up Catholic," Brock said. "Confession wipes out everything and you go to Heaven. Bullshit." He held up the bottle. "This is my confession now." He pointed his finger at Jed. "In the end, you're in the same state you were in before your old man ever poked your mother, you're nothing, no pain, no fear of death."

"Is that why you drink, because you fear death?"

Brock peered at Jed with red-rimmed eyes. "I don't drink because I'm afraid of death. I drink so I don't think about dying."

Lips walked up. "Get ready, we're going over again."

Jed picked up his rifle.

A whistle sounded.

"Let's go," Brock said. He and Jed scrambled out of the trench.

The assault was an anti-climax. An American barrage swept through the Bois Emont and pounded Cierges. Second Battalion advanced without opposition and dug in on the line they had reached that morning.

Captain Brown and Sergeant Trask moved left and finally linked up with elements of the 91st Division. As the sun set, the American line was declared solid. Most of their objectives had been reached without further losses for the platoon although Cierges remained in German hands.

CHAPTER 27

SEPTEMBER 29, 1918
BOIS EMONT, FRANCE – **DAY FOUR**

The next morning First and Third Battalions tried to take Cierges again. It turned out to be a frustrating repeat of the previous day's fight. Jed was glad that Second Battalion was in reserve again.

After the Americans retreated to the ridgeline halfway across no-man's-land the 147th Regiment's commander, Colonel Galbraith, crossed to the woods and approached Major LaForge. "We had the town, Sam," Galbraith said, his voice wheezing, "but with all the gas we couldn't hold it. They have artillery on the high ground to the north directed by observation balloons."

A runner stumbled up, red-faced and panting, and handed a message to the colonel who read it and handed it to La Forge. "This confirms a message I got before the telephone line was shot out. You stay here. We're digging in out there on the ridge." He stuffed his gas mask into its carrier. "Pershing says we stop. We'll be relieved soon." A German shell landed forty feet away. "Where the hell is our artillery?"

Shells rumbled overhead and exploded on the high ground behind Cierges.

"There's your answer, Colonel," LaForge said.

Galbraith hustled forward to the ridgeline.

LaForge ordered Second Battalion to improve their defensive positions. Jed's hole was deep enough. He stayed there all night and tried to sleep, despite the German shelling and intermittent rain showers. He pulled a two-hour stint as sentry after midnight then returned to his hole, cold, thirsty, and miserable.

CHAPTER 28

SEPTEMBER 30, 1918

BOIS EMONT, FRANCE – **DAY FIVE**

In the morning, a company of the 32nd Division relieved Company G.

Lieutenant Samis led First Platoon through the woods, minus Watkia, who had departed before sunup. Red-eyed and whiskered, their khakis saturated with dried mud, their weapons covered in rust, they stumbled through the underbrush, stepped over bloated cadavers, and hurried past blasted machine gun pits. The smell of decay and bitter roast pork set Jed's empty stomach churning.

They approached the large shell hole where Jed had taken care of Mike and Tony. In the bottom of the hole lay three dead horses. A soldier held the bridle of another standing on trembling legs, its breath pitiful moans. A soldier placed the barrel of his Enfield against the horse's head and pulled the trigger. The animal collapsed and four men pushed it to the side into the hole. It tumbled onto its harness mates.

"Hey, son," Doody said, "why are you doin' that?"

"These animals are played out and starving and can't be saved," the soldier said. "Orders are to destroy them."

A half-dozen Negroes in blue denim coveralls shoveled dirt into the hole.

Jed was glad Watkia was not there to hear the horse's dying noises.

North of the tree line of the Montfaucon Woods a new trench had been dug by sanitary troops. Twelve bodies wrapped in shelter halves were lined up next to it. Wooden crosses rested on top of each body.

Chaplain Hewitt, his shock of mud-streaked white hair standing out against the dirt backdrop, worked in the trench helping to finish the dig.

Cain moped around the bodies collecting pay books and writing in a ledger.

Jed approached the shrouded forms. Someone had written the name and unit of the man on the crossbar of each cross and one identity tag was hammered into the wood. Tony DiNiccola, David Lewin, the Joneses, Claggett, Forbes' Chauchat loader, Sergeant McClardy, Billings, Corporal Kraft, and three of his Second Squad men, Cole, Alvis, and Joyner, had gone west.

A large Negro in blue reached into the grave trench and helped the chaplain climb out. Hewitt looked as exhausted as the infantrymen.

"Can we help?" Jed asked.

Hewitt wiped his hands with an empty sandbag and shook his head. "No, son. I won't ask you to suffer the pain of burying men from your platoon. These men will help me."

"We'll take respec'ful care of your friends," the Negro said. "You best move along and recover from your trials."

"Thank you for what you're doing," Jed said. He held out his hand.

The man took Jed's hand, and gave a firm shake. "Thank you, sir."

"Come on," Brock said, "we've wasted enough time here."

Trails had been cleared through the Montfaucon Woods.

They stopped in a clearing where a tantalizing odor replaced the persistent stench of death. A dozen rolling kitchens sat in a line. The squad homed in on a red-headed cook. Jed crowded around with the others.

"Don't jostle me, boys, there's enough to go around," Dubman said.

"Dub, what've you got there?" Jed asked.

"Sirloin steaks, French fried potatoes, canned peas, bread, butter and coffee."

"You still only have one mule," Jed said. "Didn't you get another one?"

"Andy Watkia borrowed the new one." He pointed with his carving knife. "Here he comes now."

Watkia reined in the mule and reached into a sack draped over the mule's neck. He tossed a large cabbage at Doody who caught it and held it high.

"Hallelujah, chop this up and fry it in some steak grease, Dub. It ain't collard greens but it'll do."

They wolfed down the first full meal they had had since the assault started.

After Jed finished eating, he hiked through the woods to a field hospital set up in the ravine they had taken on the first day. More than a hundred wounded men lay moaning among the trees. A steady stream of them were carried into and out of the surgical tents.

Abel West was there making notes on a clipboard.

"Sergeant Major, do you know what happened to Mike O'Kean?"

"They patched up his hip and sent him to a gas hospital."

"Will he be OK?"

"The Champ's in great shape. They'll treat his eyes and he should be ready to go in a couple of weeks. I'll see he gets back to our unit."

CHAPTER 29

OCTOBER 2, 1918
RÉCICOURT, FRANCE

The Stars and Stripes

HOW TO ADOPT AN ORPHAN

A company, detachment, or group of the A.E.F. agrees to adopt a child for a year, contributing 500 francs ($87.72) for its support. The children will be either orphans, the children of French soldiers so seriously crippled that they cannot work, or refugees from the invaded districts...

Photographs and the history of each child will be sent to its adopting unit, which will be notified of the child's whereabouts and advised monthly of its progress.

The Red Cross will determine the disposal of the child. It will be maintained in a French family or sent to a trade or agricultural school.

THE STARS AND STRIPES: FRANCE, FRIDAY, AUGUST 23, 1918, page 3

The battalion bivouacked in the woods for two nights then marched south into Récicourt where they went through the routine delousing and reissue of uniforms and equipment. First Squad was assigned billets in a leaky warehouse along the main street of the town and sat outside eating from a basket of Salvation Army doughnuts and drinking coffee. Bunny held a tin of strawberry jam that he doled out to be spread on the doughnuts.

Several civilians, women and children, moved about the streets of the town.

A young girl walked up the street. She had one of the Salvation Army doughnuts cupped in her hands as though it was a precious egg. She was about thirteen years old and wore the apron, short skirt, and dark stockings of one her age. Her hair was parted in the middle and braided into two pigtail circles under her ears. Her clear lavender eyes were fixed determinedly on the doughnut, the horizontal slash of her mouth vigilant above the delicate point of her chin. She nodded shyly to the Americans and continued to pass by until Jed spoke up. "Hello, mademoiselle. That doughnut seems pretty special to you."

She stopped and looked at him. "It is for Mama," she said in English. "She is ill. I thought she would like a sweet."

Jed nodded. "Very thoughtful of you…?"

"Louise," she said. "My name is Louise Archambeau. I live in the house at the end of the street. Your regimental headquarters is in our kitchen. Mama and I live upstairs.

"My name is Jed." He introduced the others: "Corporal Joe Collins, Andy Watkia, Phil Zyren, Tommy Pricklin, Reb Hill, and Bunny Steinmetz."

She nodded to each in turn. "*Bonsoir*, gentlemen," she said. "Good evening."

"Here…" Bunny applied a drop of strawberry jam to her doughnut and pulled an empty crate between him and Jed. "Why don't you have a seat and eat your doughnut and we'll give you two more for you and your Mama to have later?"

"Oh, but I cannot."

"It's all right," Jed said. "We have plenty."

He glanced at his squad mates who all wore friendly smiles. When he looked back at Louise, she was regarding him, her eyebrow arched in question. He nodded his head.

She sat primly on the edge of the crate, taking a demure bite of the doughnut.

Doody walked up and sat down snagging a pastry on the way by. "I've been down to the shitter takin' care of business. That cabbage did the trick." Doody examined the doughnut. "It ain't greens but it can't hurt any." He finished off the doughnut in two bites, washed it down with a cup of coffee, and pulled a piece of paper out of his blouse pocket. "This was on one of them prisoners the other day." Doody handed the paper to Jed. "It looks a little like those Uncle Sam posters we saw back home. I tried to give it to the captain with the rest of the things we gathered up but he didn't want it so I kept it."

Jed introduced Louise to Doody while unfolding the paper. It was a two-foot by four-foot poster of a German soldier pointing with his left index finger with four lines of print in German at the bottom. Louise leaned over to see more clearly as Jed read the words. "I go to the front—have you already subscribed to the 6th war loan?"

Louise looked wide-eyed at Jed. "*Verstehen Sie Deutsch?*"

"Yes, I understand German. My grandmother taught it to me when I was a little boy."

He explained how he and his aunt used German as their secret code.

"There's more writin' on the back," Doody said.

Jed turned the poster over and read again, "My dearest Erich, I wanted you to see that the people back home support you and the other boys. Win the war quickly and hurry back to me—Mother."

Louise nodded her head. "That is correct."

"How do you know English and German, Louise?"

"We studied English in school. During the occupation, the Germans wanted us to learn what they called their beautiful language because soon everybody would be speaking it. We studied it so that we could keep track of what they were doing. Mostly we did not let them know we understood so much."

Bunny put another dab of jam on her doughnut. "Did the Germans treat you badly?"

Louise looked at Jed. "*Ist es in Ordnung, dass ich ihnen meine Geschichte erzählen?*"

"It's alright to tell us your story."

She took a deep breath and began. "They left us children alone but the officers wanted the older girls and women for things other than cooking and cleaning. My mother is beautiful and the local commander, a colonel, wanted her for himself." Louise hugged her elbows close to her sides and ducked her head. "He beat her and did other things to her. Papa was away at the war so my brother tried to defend her. He stabbed the German colonel with a knife and they took him away and shot him." A tear rolled down her cheek. "The colonel died, and no one bothered Mama again. Then we learned Papa was killed in action. She became ill soon after and is in great pain. The doctor said she has a tumor in her belly." Louise paused, her eyes narrowing and her lips tensing. "I think the Boche colonel put the tumor there."

The men of the squad sat frozen.

Louise wiped the tear away. She dipped her finger into the strawberry jam and touched it to her lips, painting them bright red. She managed a coy smile for Jed and said, "Now, the Americans are here and the Boche must be very afraid. We French are so grateful that you traveled across the ocean to help us." She popped the last of the pastry into her mouth and smiled at all of them in turn, her cheeks puffed out as she chewed.

The sky had darkened as she told her story and a steady rain began. Everyone scrambled to pick up the picnic and dashed indoors, Louise with them. It was a downpour in the warehouse since a large section of the roof was missing. The men tried to find corners where the water wasn't splashing and hung their shelter halves to divert the rain.

Louise said to Jed, "I know of a better place, a barn we own across the street from my house. There were no soldiers there this morning. Come with me."

Jed hesitated. She insisted. Jed relented and draped his raincoat over her shoulders, using his shelter half as a cape for himself. He hoisted his pack and rifle and followed her down the street. She stepped between the puddles, trying to keep her shoes and stockings as dry as possible, and then stopped at the door to a small barn across the street from a two-story house. Camouflage netting covered a radio antenna beside the house.

They entered the barn door and Louise lit a candle. The dim light revealed piles of cots and crates of supplies. The regiment was using the barn for a storehouse and the interior was dry.

Louise opened a door in the side wall into a tool closet that had enough space for one person to stretch out on a cot.

"*Dieses Zimmer ist für Sie.*"

"My room," Jed said. "*Danke,*"

"*Bitte. Du bist mein Freund.*"

"Looks like German is our secret code, too," Jed said. He put a cot in the closet and deposited his equipment on it. He checked a side door beside his closet that led to an alley beside the barn. Before they left, they lit several candles, the yellow glow casting an inviting warm light into the room. "Let's go get the others."

The rain had stopped. As they walked Jed asked Louise, "Why did you single me out to be your friend?"

"You remind me of my brother, Jacques. He had the same gentle voice and silver eyes. He was very brave. I am sure you are also very brave."

Jed shook his head. "I'm still trying to find out if I'm brave."

Jed stopped and kneeled before her taking both of her hands in his. "You shouldn't become too attached to me, Louise," he said. "We'll probably move on soon and I don't want it to hurt you."

She squeezed his hands. "*Gott segne dich*, Jed, God bless you and your friends for helping us."

"You're the reason we came here," Jed said. "You are the future."

They returned to the warehouse and led the others to the barn. The men set up cots and hung their wet gear from hooks and nails attached to the walls.

Outside it rained again.

Sergeant Trask walked through the door followed by Brock. "I saw you guys come in here. Who assigned you to this billet?"

Doody lounged back on his cot. "Squatters' rights, Sarge."

Brock walked over and deposited his gear on a cot near the side door next to Jed's closet. "Good work, Andy."

"It was Louise here who found it for us," Jed said. "The regimental P. C. is in her house across the street. Louise Archambeau, these men are First Sergeant Trask and our section leader, Sergeant Brock."

Louise curtsied, "*Messieurs.*"

Trask touched the brim of his helmet in salute.

Brock nodded.

"I hope my billet's as dry as this," Trask said. "You guys can stay here. I'll square it with Abel." He went out into the weather.

Bunny rummaged in his pack and produced a can of salmon. He placed this in the basket with the remaining three doughnuts and added the rest of the strawberry jam. Jed put in a can of beans and the sixty francs Mike had won for him. Doody, Zyren, and Pricklin put in a few French notes and coins and Watkia added a packet of coffee, a small flagon of cognac, and forty more francs.

Jed looked at him.

Watkia shrugged. "I'm not completely corrupt."

Bunny presented the gift basket to Louise.

"No, *Monsieur* Bunny, I cannot accept this. I have nothing with which to pay."

"You don't owe us anything, Miss Louise. Consider this rent. A warm, dry place to sleep is worth more than gold to a soldier."

She looked at Jed who smiled and nodded his agreement. "Were cutting the middleman out of the adoption process."

"Oh, Jed, Bunny, I cannot thank you enough." Tears welled in her eyes. "Mama is in so much pain she cannot eat the little that we have. Tomorrow I will take this money and look for some medicine for her, perhaps laudanum. If I can ease her pain, I think these things will help to build up her strength." Louise looked around at all of them, a smile defying her tears. "*Merci beaucoup*, gentlemen, I hope you will rest well tonight." She ran out the door and across the street to her house.

The next morning the rain stopped after breakfast and the squad bustled around on various fatigue duties. Jed sat outside the barn on a crate cleaning the rust off of his rifle, his gear spread out to dry. Memories of the last week played in his mind and he sat with his jaw set, shoulders hunched. He often saw Uncle Enoch behaving the same way, stoically going about his chores and keeping to himself.

Sergeant Trask walked up the street. "What are you doing, Martin?"

Jed jumped to his feet. "I'm drying out my things while it's not raining."

"I wish the others would show the same initiative."

Trask started to leave.

"We didn't get a lot of feedback on how we did in the operation, Top."

Trask turned back. "The unit did very well. We achieved most of our objectives."

"On the first day some of us lost contact with the company."

Trask's expression changed to a wry grin. "Everything was confused the first day. The unit regrouped and fought as a cohesive unit the rest of the way."

"I was plenty scared," Jed said.

"Everybody was scared, but you stepped up and did what had to be done. That's all I can ask. Finish cleaning your stuff and report for chow."

"Yes, Top."

Jed darted in out of the rain and lit a candle in the tool closet. The company had spent the afternoon in calisthenics and close order drill and Jed was tired, he needed sleep. The rest of the squad was playing craps in the Second Squad billet.

The cot in the closet took up all the room except for the small space to the side of a work bench where he placed his pack, his rifle propped on top, leaning against the work bench. The door opened outward, and he left it partly open to allow fresh air to circulate into his bedroom. He rolled his shelter half into a pillow, blew out the candle, and stretched out on the cot under his blanket.

The creaking barn door woke him and the yellow light of a lantern lit up the interior of the barn. A small female voice spoke in French. A deeper voice shushed her as the two figures passed the shed door.

Jed threw his blanket back and peeked around the doorway.

Brock pulled a canvas bag from under his cot and hung the lantern and his pistol belt from nails on a support post. Rain dripped through a small crack in the roof and sizzled off the top of the lantern. The shadow behind Brock's bulk obscured the woman. He took several gulps from a bottle of wine and put it down on the floor next to the bag.

The woman asked a question in French.

Brock's answer made Jed gasp, his heart pounding. "Watkia donated laudanum. It will ease Mama's pain. But first, you make me feel good."

He fumbled at the buttons of his pants.

The female backed away from Brock into the light, eyes wide, unable to speak.

It was Louise.

"Don't be shy, honey, your grandmas and mamas do it. It's time you learned the French way of love too."

Jed ripped his bayonet from the scabbard strapped to his pack, stepped forward, and pointed the bayonet at Brock. "Let her go, you son of a bitch!"

Brock stuffed himself back into his pants and turned toward Jed. He waved toward the bayonet. "That's the second time you've drawn that weapon on me."

"And I'm going to run it through you if you don't let her go."

Brock reached toward the support post and drew his pistol. "I've got the right to execute you right here, you sniveling coward."

Jed tensed, ready to lunge forward and stab before Brock could shoot him. Before he could move, Trask appeared through the side door, spun Brock around, and punched him in the face. Brock collapsed onto the floor, the pistol beside him.

Louise ran past Trask toward the main door. Jed dropped the bayonet and scooped her into his arms. She was shaking and crying and began to fight him.

"Alles ist jetzt in Ordnung," Jed said. "Everything is all right now."

He set her on her feet.

Trask loomed over the prostrate Brock the pistol in his trembling hand aimed at Brock's head. He stood there for a long minute then tossed the pistol onto Brock's cot. "You're not getting off that easy, Leo. I won't take the fall to put you out of your misery." He went out the side door.

Louise strode to where Brock was lying spread-eagled on the floor, stepped between his legs and kicked him in the crotch. He didn't respond. She kicked harder. Brock flinched and moaned.

She spat on him. *"Haufen Scheiße!"* She reached down and picked up the bottle of wine, wiped off the top, took a long drink and tossed the bottle onto Brock's stomach where the last of the wine spilled onto his shirt. She picked up the canvas bag, spat on him again, and walked out of the room, her head held high.

Brock's breaths came in shallow gasps, followed by long pauses when he seemed to be dead. "She's only thirteen years old," Jed said to the unconscious Brock. "She's right, though, you are a pile of shit."

The rain dripping on the lantern splashed onto Brock's legs. Jed threw a blanket across the still form. It was something Brock would have done, helping an injured man.

Jed shook his head and went to bed.

Dark dreams came. He turned over onto his side, trying to wipe his mind clear, but Howe's body evaporated in a shell burst and Tony DiNiccola's arm hit him in the chest.

He sat up, awake, clutching the arm to his chest, his blood pounding in his ears.

The arm was his rifle. The weapon had tumbled from its perch against the work bench and landed on his chest as he thrashed in his sleep. His head slowly cleared and his heartbeat returned to normal. He leaned the Enfield more securely in the corner.

He lay back and stared into the darkness.

He needed to talk to Trask.

He put on his raincoat and checked Brock, snoring loudly where he had fallen, then went out into the rain. His first stop was the Salvation Army hut. The staff had gone for the night and Bunny, Collins, and Doody were playing craps with a group of Second Platoon men. They waved Jed over but he shook his head.

Watkia sat by himself in a corner with an array of cognac and wine bottles in front of him. Jed sat down at the table. Watkia drank wine from a tall tumbler and stared at a postcard of a young woman with a sultry smile. Long dark curls caressed her naked breasts. He pulled another picture out of his blouse pocket and placed it next to the postcard. This picture showed a demure young lady with a high lace collar, her hair done up in a prim bun. There was a striking similarity between the two women's faces.

"This is my girl back home," Watkia said, waving at the second picture. "Her name is Elka. She's a good Polish, Catholic girl." He drained his glass and refilled it. "There wasn't time for us to get married, but she sure gave me a sendoff." He picked up the postcard of the naked girl. "This is a French postcard I found. This French whore looks like Elka, except Elka's tits are bigger." He looked at Jed. "Should I compare my girl to a French whore? I mean, she did it with me, why wouldn't she do it with some other guy?" Watkia took another drink. "Bunny tried to take me to a whorehouse, but I said no. If I expect Elka to be faithful, why shouldn't I? What would you do?"

"I'm no expert on women but I've gone out with girls to school dances and picnics. A couple of gals used their hands and their mouths for French love. One from Hot Springs taught me about real sex but that didn't work out." Jed shrugged. "I didn't love any of them but, if you love each other, maybe you should wait."

Watkia put the two pictures together and placed them in his pocket. "I'll survive this war and then go back to Ohio, marry Elka, and start a family right away." He raised his glass to Jed.

Jed grabbed a half full wine bottle, touched Watkia's glass and took four long gulps. He didn't want to be the only sober lonely soldier in this town.

"Have you seen Trask?"

"He came in and got a bottle of cognac an hour ago."

"Do you know where he went?"

"He said he was going to lie down and sink into the mud." Andy folded his arms on the table and rested his head on them.

Jed went back out into the rain. A wagon, its two-mule team miserable in the downpour, was parked a block away. Under the wagon lay Sergeant Trask, face up in the mud, rivulets of rainwater flowing around him. Jed ducked under the wagon and helped Trask sit up.

Trask held out the cognac bottle. Jed shook his head.

"Take a drink, goddammit. You were there. How could you not want a drink?"

Jed took the bottle and drank.

"I finally had him. And I had you for a witness, but I couldn't let him do it, not to a little girl." Trask tipped the bottle, bumping it on the bottom of the wagon. "I could have been court martialed a dozen times for what I let him get away with." He thought for a minute. "If he was killed in combat that would release me from my promise."

"Don't say that, Top."

Trask shook his head. "I don't want him to die, but he'll never change." He tried to lie down but Jed pulled at him until he stood up beside the wagon. Jed threw his raincoat over the two of them and guided Trask down the street.

Abel was standing in the doorway to the senior NCO billet puffing on his pipe. When Jed led Trask through the door, the sergeant major pulled Trask's arm over his shoulder and guided Trask to his cot. They took off his soaked outer clothes and laid him down. "Looks like you boys have been on a soldier's retreat," Abel said as he covered Trask with a blanket.

Lips sat at a table with a deck of cards, a score pad and pencil, coffee mugs, and a two-thirds empty bottle of cognac. Abel sat down and pulled a chair over for Jed.

"Do you want to play cards?"

"No, Sergeant Major."

"A drink...?"

Jed nodded.

Abel pushed a coffee cup toward him and filled it with cognac. "I appreciate you taking care of Trask out there. He would have probably gotten pneumonia."

Jed sipped his drink. "I needed to talk, but he was too far gone to answer questions."

"I suppose it had something to do with Sergeant Brock." Abel met Jed's glance, a cloud of pipe smoke around his head. "Brock and Trask have been going at each other since the Philippines and maybe all their lives."

Lips lit two cigarettes, gave one to Jed, and said, "The night before we shipped out from Camp Lee in Virginia, Brock got roaring drunk and started a brawl in a bar in Petersburg. He figured if he spent a month in jail, we'd sail without him and he'd be able to stay in the States."

"What happened?"

"Trask posted bail with fifty dollars he borrowed from Watkia. We sailed for France, Brock was a no show, the court kept the money, case closed."

Jed shook his head. "There's got to be more..."

Abel raised an eyebrow. "There is." He sat back comfortably in his chair and drained his cup. Lips opened a new bottle and topped off their drinks. "Trask told me you're a good soldier. If he trusts you, we can too."

Abel re-packed his pipe and lit it. "Our unit in the Philippines was fighting the Moros on Jolo Island at a place called Bud Bagsak, Bagsak Mountain, high up against a tall peak. The rebel Moros had retreated to a *cotta*, or fortress, and they made their last stand. I was the supply sergeant and was down at the base camp getting ready to take more ammunition up to the unit, so I didn't see the battle. Trask filled me in later. The terrain limited the Americans and the Philippine Scouts to a frontal assault. The attack went well and about the time our guys forced the main gate a group of Moros counterattacked the left flank. Guess who commanded the left flank?"

"Brock..."

Abel nodded. "Brock's squad stopped the attack but all of his men died." Abel took a drink. "Brock was alone and ran away."

"He could have been shot," Jed said.

"Brock claimed he had orders to go down the mountain and help me bring up more ammo, orders from a lieutenant who was, conveniently, dead."

"He got away free?"

"There's more. On his way down the mountain, Brock came upon a Moro prince and his new bride climbing to join their people at the battle. They fought and Brock killed the prince, no problem there, and he attacked the woman, too."

"A woman—"

"Those Moro females were as fierce as their men. Brock had to defend himself. When Trask came on the scene after the battle, she was breathing her last and died." Abel shook his head. "There was evidence that she'd had sex before she died."

Jed set his cup down hard, splashing cognac. "The rumors are true. Brock raped her. Trask had him."

"Brock claimed he had caught them in the marital act before they attacked him. There were no witnesses but Trask knew Brock was lying."

"What did Trask do?"

"The only thing he could with no witnesses. He beat Brock up. He even shoved Brock's head through a panel of a door. That's how Brock got the scar above his eye."

"That's why Brock hates Trask."

"It goes back farther than that." Abel said. "Brock has had a rough life. His father beat him but then died in prison for killing a man. After his dad's death, he grew up in the back room of a New Orleans whorehouse. The customers kicked him around, too. If Brock killed everybody who abused him, he'd still be in prison."

"Some guys think he'd like to kill Trask," Lips said, "but I don't think so."

"Still," Jed said, "it doesn't explain why Trask never brought him up on charges."

"Trask promised Brock's mother he would keep Brock out of prison," Lips said.

"Why?"

"When you signed in to the unit, you told Cain the men in your family are called by their middle names." Jed nodded. "In Trask and Brock's family they name the boys after their fathers and uncles. Do you know their full names?"

"No, why should I?"

"They are Leslie Leo Trask and Leo Leslie Brock."

"Trask and Brock's family?"

"You're such a dope, Jed." Lips said. "Their mothers are sisters."

Jed sat with his mouth open.

"Keep this story between us," Abel said.

"Yes, Sergeant Major." Jed took a large gulp of cognac.

Trask slept quietly.

"He's feeling no pain," Jed said.

"You're wrong, son. He feels every ounce of pain, right back to Valley Forge."

The skies cleared at noon the next day and the squad sat on cots in front of their quarters smoking pipes and cigarettes. Several officers and NCOs hustled down the street and went into the Archambeau house. Louise crossed the street, stopped in front of Jed, and looked evenly at him.

"How are you feeling, Louise?" he asked in German.

She held her head high, gave a confident nod, then stepped forward and sat beside Jed. "Please tell Herr Andy I am grateful for the medicine." She sighed, her expression glum. "Too bad *he* delivered it." She paused. "Mama feels no pain now, but all she does is sleep." She wiped away a tear. "I fear the worst will happen soon."

Cain slouched up the street and stood before the squad. "We're moving again." He checked his watch. "Headquarters closes in one hour at two o'clock."

Louise stood up. "Where are you going?"

"They won't tell us until we get there. We're supposed to move by truck."

Louise looked at Jed. "But you cannot go."

"I told you we would be moving out soon," he said.

Her composure broke, and she ran into her house crying.

A sheepish Brock, the left side of his face swollen, limped down the street followed by a stern-faced Trask.

"I guess Trask made sure Brock turned up," Bunny said.

"Where'd you get the shiner, Sarge?" Doody asked.

Brock sat down on a cot, his head in his hands, elbows on his knees.

Trask stood beside Cain. "All right, babies, full packs, marching order. Inspection in fifteen minutes, transport should be here in twenty."

The men took ten minutes to pack their gear and then lined up in front of the barn.

Lieutenant Samis strode down the line and Trask called the men to attention.

Samis stopped in front of Doody and shook his head. "Private Dodd, you are a mess."

"I'm a fightin' mess, sir."

Samis moved to Brock who had his helmet pulled low over his black eye. The lieutenant leaned in and sniffed. His eyes narrowed. "One of these days, Sergeant."

Samis paused in front of Jed.

"I'll guarantee his rifle is clean, Lieutenant," Trask said. "I wish the rest of them took care of their equipment like he does."

Samis turned to Trask and accepted his salute. "Inspection complete, Top. I'll inform Captain Brown that his company is ready to travel." He walked down the street.

Louise came out of her house, her face composed. She carried two bottles of wine. She presented one bottle each to Jed and Trask. "We don't have much but this wine may make your travels more comfortable."

Trask tucked his bottle out of sight in his pack.

An army truck slewed around the corner, its rear wheels spinning in the mud, and fishtailed toward Louise and the squad. The panicked Annamese driver stomped on the brakes, locking up the wheels. The truck slid toward Louise.

Brock reacted first. He grabbed Louise around the waist and pulled her onto a cot as the truck bounced through a large pothole and came to rest where Louise had been standing. Jed jumped back and avoided being hit by the front bumper.

The hysterical driver, wailing in the strange song of his native language, backed the truck away, set the brake and dismounted the cab, peering around the truck's fender.

"No fella hurt, here," Trask tried in pidgin, "you fella okay." It was unclear if the driver understood.

Several more trucks turned the corner and slid to a stop in line, avoiding collisions of their own. The drivers got out and analyzed the situation in a language that, to Jed's ear, had only vowels and no hard sounds.

"Transport is here. Form up for departure," Trask said.

The platoon shrugged into their packs.

Three Signal Corps men emerged from the Archambeau house and stripped the camouflage netting from the radio antenna beside the house.

Brock stood up and deposited Louise on her feet. She pushed him away and stood erect, smoothing her dress. "*Merci*," she said and turned toward Jed. "I suppose bad soldiers can do something good," she said in German.

"Thank you for the wine," Jed said. "I'll think of you every day. I hope you'll let me write to you."

Her face lit up. "I must give you my postal code. Some mail is getting through. Do you have a pencil?"

Jed asked Cain for a pencil and a message form. Louise wrote on the form and handed it to Jed. "I will wait every day to hear from you."

Jed wrote his military address on another form and handed it to her. "I'll write to you, I promise."

A bugler sounded "attention".

A soft murmur high in the sky rose to a roar as three airplanes dived, black crosses on their wings.

Samis blew his whistle. "Air attack, take cover."

Two black planes with red noses fired their machine guns sending the Signal Corps men running as bullets spattered around the antenna.

The platoon members scrambled into the barn.

Louise started toward her house, but Jed grabbed and held her.

She struggled. "I have to go to Mama."

Several machine gun bullets hit the lead truck. The truck drivers panicked, jumped into their trucks, and raced out of town.

An American anti-aircraft gun opened fire as the third German plane bored in and dropped two black shapes from its yellow underside. The first bomb hit the radio antenna sending metal bars flying. The next one dropped through the roof of the Archambeau house. Smoke and debris leaped skyward. The German planes swooped up and circled to get out of range of the anti-aircraft fire, the bomber trailing smoke.

Louise broke free and ran toward her house.

The bomber's rear gunner sprayed the street.

Louise collapsed.

Jed went to her. She was unconscious but breathing. A bullet had shattered her left foot below the ankle and two others had hit her left thigh and right shoulder.

Jed picked her up and raced down the block and into the aid station.

A doctor took Louise.

Jed waited until the doctor came back to the door. "She will be all right. The leg and shoulder wounds are superficial, but she may lose part of her left foot."

"Can I see her?" Jed asked.

"They're preparing her for surgery."

Jed tried to push past the doctor, but the medic stood firm.

Watkia ran up. "We're moving out. Top says you come now!"

"I didn't get to say goodbye," Jed said.

"Write her a letter."

They hurried back to the platoon area, formed up, and marched.

Jed walked between Watkia and Collins.

"Louise's mother somehow made it downstairs, but her clothes were on fire," Collins said. "Top and I put out the fire, but it was too late. Some French women came and took her body away then the whole house went up."

Brock limped along without comment. Watkia handed Jed a canteen. The cognac burned, but he gulped more. He couldn't look back at the burning house.

No one spoke.

As they passed an open field at the edge of town, the German bomber lay broken, its burning engines buried in the plowed ground, the fuselage cracked in two, the tail sitting undamaged. The rear gunner was alive.

Jed shed his pack and ran across the field, loading his rifle.

Andy Watkia followed him. "Jed, wait."

The front gunner and the pilot lay pinned in the shattered nose of the craft, both dead. When the rear gunner saw Jed approaching, he swung his machine gun around but when he pulled the trigger the gun didn't fire. He threw up his hands. *"Kamerad"*.

"Not bloody likely." Jed raised his rifle and shot the German in the chest.

The gunner collapsed into the fuselage.

Watkia gripped Jed's shoulder.

Jed hung his head. "Murder in self-defense."

He trudged back to the road where the Asian drivers had regrouped and pulled their trucks up to load the Americans. Jed felt numb. He wanted to get on the truck, drink Louise's wine, and leave this place.

CHAPTER 30

OCTOBER 5, 1918

CHOLOY, FRANCE

They traveled all day on the crowded, muddy roads, passed Verdun, and arrived at the town of Choloy at sundown. They bedded down in an intact barn with only straw for bedding and two lanterns for light. Sergeant Brock went to the farthest corner of the barn, chugged half the contents of a canteen, and slumped in the straw, snoring.

Jed picked the corner farthest away from Brock and piled as much straw as he could against the wall covering it with his blanket. He finished the last of Louise's wine and lay staring into the featureless darkness above the rafters.

Lips came into the barn. "Don't get too comfortable here. In the morning, we march."

"Where to now, Sarge?" Doody asked.

"The Pannes sector if it means anything to you. We'll defend the line our boys established back in September when they pushed the Krauts out of Saint-Mihiel."

Bunny came in the door. He pulled three packs of cigarettes and a bottle of wine from his pack.

"Where have you been?" Lips demanded.

"I took a walk. There's a French girl in a house down the street."

"You're staying right here, Steinmetz." He turned to Collins. "Joe, you still can't control your squad."

Collins glared at Lips.

Bunny shrugged and sat on the floor.

"When's the last time you got laid?" Watkia asked.

Bunny lit a cigarette and settled against his pack. "Do you remember Angelique, the one Samis was squiring around back in Longeville?" Watkia nodded. "Trask found the lieutenant and dragged him away from her to a meeting. So, I took bread, cheese, wine, and five packs of cigarettes over there. Angelique, her mother, and I had a picnic in their kitchen. The mother drank a whole bottle of wine and went upstairs to bed. I guess she trusted me or didn't care." The cloud of smoke hovering over him grew larger. "I don't speak French and she spoke no English, but we finished my bottle and I showed her one of my favorite postcards. She got up and checked on her mother then led me into her room downstairs. I finished the work Samis had started in the afternoon."

"You dog," Reb said.

"Somebody had to take care of her. Samis set her up and her signals were clear." He stubbed his cigarette out in a goldfish tin. "I got nothing against the lieutenant. He leaves us alone and didn't do anything stupid in battle."

Trask appeared at the door. "Reveille is at six o'clock, company formation at seven."

"OK, Top," Lips said as he and Collins doused the lanterns.

Watkia lit a candle and inventoried his belongings.

Jed got up and crawled to where Watkia lay. Andy had laid out several bottles, white envelopes, and a Luger pistol.

"I think I talked to the German you bought that from," Jed said.

"What did he say?"

"He liked the cigarettes but said you could have had the Luger for free."

"A deal is a deal," Watkia said. "Everybody gets something. What do you want?"

"I keep thinking about Louise and that German gunner and I can't sleep."

Andy handed Jed a bottle of cognac.

"Thanks, Andy, how much?"

"You paid me the other night. Thanks for listening, it helped."

Jed turned away.

"Jed, Louise is hurt but not dead and that gunner deserved what he got. You're not to blame. The cognac will help short term but you've got to cope with it long term." He stared into a dark corner of the barn. "Sometimes it takes a long time."

At 6 A.M. the platoon awoke and took a half hour to "shit, shine, and shave" as Doody put it, then lined up for breakfast. Smitty, the mess sergeant, ladled out the beans.

Clarence Dubman appeared in full uniform.

"Why aren't you stirring the pot?" Bunny asked.

"They want me at the formation this morning."

The platoon assembled with the company at 7 A.M.

Captain Brown ordered Jed and Dubman to stand in front of the company.

"COMPANY, attensh-HUT," Captain Brown called.

Colonel Galbraith and Major LaForge approached accompanied by a French colonel and lieutenant. Their blue uniforms contrasted with the dull khaki of the Americans. The French colonel stopped and faced Clarence Dubman, the lieutenant at his elbow holding a small wooden box.

Major LaForge read a citation.

Jed was hung over from half of the bottle of Andy's cognac the night before and didn't pay close attention to the words but heard phrases such as "outnumbered and under enemy fire...", "...single-handed destroyed an enemy observation post with pistol and grenade...", "...returned to preparing hot food...", "...contributed to the morale of his unit...", "...having been mentioned in dispatches at brigade level...", "... Croix de Guerre with bronze star attachment."

The French lieutenant opened the box, and the colonel pulled a bronze cross suspended from a green ribbon with vertical red stripes and a bronze star attached to the ribbon. He pinned the medal to the left pocket flap of Dubman's blouse, placed his hands on Dub's shoulders, and kissed him on both cheeks. He stepped back and Dubman saluted him. The colonel returned the salute and sidestepped in front of Jed.

Major LaForge read again. Jed felt embarrassed and exposed. He didn't want a medal but this time he listened more carefully.

"For gallantry in action, James Jedidiah Martin, Private, Company G, 147th Infantry, 37th Division, who, on September 27, 1918, near Montfaucon, France, assisted two severely wounded comrades to a place of safety under heavy enemy fire, thus saving their lives. Having been mentioned in dispatches at the army level, he is awarded the French Croix de Guerre with bronze palm."

The French colonel repeated the pinning ritual. When the colonel kissed him on the cheeks Jed noticed that the French officer's mess served wine with breakfast.

After returning Jed's salute, the French colonel shook Colonel Galbraith's hand, and the Frenchmen departed.

Captain Brown announced that there would be platoon meetings, and that they would begin their march to Pannes at 8 A.M.

Brown dismissed them.

Several men of the platoon converged around Jed and Dub and wanted to examine the new medals. Jed left the group as soon as he could gracefully manage it and headed toward their billets.

When Jed got there, Brock was waiting. He grabbed Jed by the front of his blouse.

"The French may give you a bit of ribbon but I'm not fooled. You're a coward."

Jed pushed Brock away. "I'm not afraid of you, Brock."

"Then the next time you pull a weapon on me you better use it." He clenched his fists. "I ought to beat the shit out of you right now."

"Do it."

Brock peered into Jed's eyes, hesitated, then sat on a cot and turned his gaze away. "It would be too easy, especially since you don't have the big Mick backing you up." He waved Jed away. "Get out of here. I'm not going to waste my time on you."

Mike had been right. Brock backed down in private without a weapon.

When Jed got back to the barn, the platoon members sat in a semi-circle on the floor facing Lips and Lieutenant Samis. Jed sat beside Bunny who gave him a cigarette. Brock came in and sat in his corner. Fifteen anxious looking men stood along one wall.

"Everyone is here, sir," Lips said.

Samis surveyed the assembly. "I'm proud of the way all of you performed in combat." He looked at Jed. "Congratulations to Private Martin for his medal. He is promoted to Private First Class." Murmurs of approval drowned out Brock's snicker. Bunny slapped Jed on the back.

"More decorations will be presented as soon as they are processed. We are reconstituting the platoon including restoring Second Rifle Squad. Philip Zyren is promoted to Corporal and Thomas Pricklin is promoted to Private First Class. They'll return to Second Rifle Squad with Zyren in command."

Samis paused while their friends congratulated the two men. "We are moving to a new area for us. It's a defensive sector, but that doesn't mean there'll be no action. Headquarters wants active patrolling to maintain combat contact with the enemy. It'll give us a chance to get the new men some experience." He faced the new men lining the wall. "Stick with the veterans, stay low, and become one with the earth. Live in the ground or be buried in it." He checked his watch. "We move out in twenty-five minutes." Samis gestured palm down. "Remain at ease."

Samis left the barn and Lips consulted his clipboard. He looked up and smiled. "Two of our guys are returning from hospital."

Jed's heart flipped. He looked around but his shoulders slumped. Mike wasn't there.

"Lenny Gurr will return to Second Rifle Squad." Gurr stepped out of the shadows at the rear of the barn and sat with Zyren and Pricklin. He held up his right sleeve to display his wound chevron. "Also returning and cured of influenza is Ellie Darnell who'll transfer to Second Squad." Darnell joined his new squad mates.

"What happened to George Walker?" Bunny asked.

The smile left Darnell's face. "He didn't make it."

The room grew quiet.

"We have several replacements from the depot divisions," Lips said. "We're going to plus up the rifle and hand bomber sections first. We expect more replacements when we get to Pannes and will fill out the rifle grenade and automatic rifle sections then." The sergeants of the shorted sections grumbled. Lips held up his hand. "As many as half of the replacements coming over have influenza. You'll all be combat effective before we go into action again so quit bitching." Lips flipped a page on his clipboard and announced, "Wayne Turley, you go to First Rifle Squad, Daniel Ponder, William Danforth, and Lonnie Doyle, you go to Second Rifle Squad." The remaining replacements went to the hand bomber section. "You have ten minutes to get acquainted and then we assemble in full marching order." Lips left the barn.

The new man Turley sat down hesitantly near his new squad.

"Where are you from, Wayne?" Jed asked.

"Champaign, Illinois."

Turley seemed pale and withdrawn.

"Are you feelin' alright?" Doody asked.

"I had a light case of influenza on the ship. When we arrived at Brest, I heard an officer say men were dying about one every ten minutes from influenza and pneumonia. I feel stronger now. I hope I don't let you guys down."

"Pay attention," Bunny said, "and do what we do."

"We even got our own supply master and medic in Andy Watkia, there," Doody said.

"You are so full of shit, Doody," Watkia said.

Lips stuck his head in the door. "Let's go. Take a piss and get your shit together. We move out in five minutes."

Jed followed this advice then formed up with the platoon, marching through intermittent rain and constant mud toward their fate in the Pannes Sector.

CHAPTER 31

OCTOBER 8, 1918

PANNES SECTOR, FRANCE

The march to Pannes was thirty-seven kilometers and should have taken only one day, but because of the congestion on the roads and the bad weather it took two days. They spent a chilly night in a fallow field wrapped in their blankets, had a cold breakfast, and set off at first light.

With two hours of marching to go, they flopped at the side of the road for a ten-minute break.

A squad of Negro Pioneer troops lounged on the other side of the road.

Brock called out, "I thought you boys were digging latrines."

"We reckon we dug plenty, mostly graves," one said. "The way you fightin' soldiers is fallin' down, our shovels will be busy directly." Brock glared at him. "Don't worry Sarge. We'll say a prayer when we shovel dirt on your face."

"Don't do me any favors, boy."

Lieutenant Samis walked up. "Sergeant Brock, come with me."

Brock, his face red, joined a group of officers and NCOs fifty feet up the road.

Reb spat tobacco juice. "I reckon I agree with Sergeant Brock."

Watkia glared at Reb.

"What're you lookin' at?"

"Not much."

"You ain't nothin' but a Yankee Jew boy to me, Watkia, with your loaded dice. Stay out of my way."

"I reckon you got it backwards there, Reb," Doody said. "You ain't made a lot of friends since you got here, but we're not against you if you don't make us so." He leaned back on his pack and closed his eyes.

Sergeant Collins said nothing.

Lieutenant Samis ordered the men back onto the road and they started off.

They marched north for two hours without another break and stopped in the town of Pannes. Dubman arrived with his rolling kitchen and served beans with bacon and coffee.

In the morning, they marched to the front-line trenches where members of the 89th Division hurried to depart.

The tense trench routines slammed back into place, and they began watches and repairs, water bailing, and sandbag filling. There was a one-hour bombardment around noon but the troops huddled in underground shelters and no one was injured.

Jed discovered a sizable hole a shell had gouged under a thick tangle of old barbed wire on the no-man's-land side of the main trench. It was dry. Rain water drained out into an old communication trench.

At midnight Watkia relieved Jed from sentry duty. No patrols were scheduled in their sector.

"I'm going out to be alone," Jed said.

Watkia nodded. "I'll make sure you make it back for Stand-To."

Jed crawled out of the trench and under the wire tangles through the drainage cut. He spread his shelter half on the bottom of the hole and wrapped his blanket around him. No-man's-land reeked but was quiet. The darkness hid its horrors.

The most gruesome aspect of no-man's-land was the presence of abandoned, rotting, corpses. Jed couldn't imagine that the British, French, or Germans were unfeeling about the loss of their friends, but it was too dangerous to retrieve and bury all the bodies. Some had to be left behind. They swelled, were consumed by vermin, and melted into the ground reduced to pale skulls and pieces of bone wrapped in shredded uniforms. All that remained was the sadness in the hearts of women and children, in England, France, Germany, and now, America.

No-man's-land wasn't shelled unless necessary since both sides were likely to have patrols or raids out. It was the eye of the storm in the middle of the relentless shelling of the reserve lines.

Jed felt safe. Here, he had time to think.

CHAPTER 32

OCTOBER 10, 1918

PANNES SECTOR, FRANCE

The four-man patrol spread out in no-man's-land before thick coils of barbed wire stretching into the darkness on either side. The barbed wire glowed, as if alive with electricity, pulsing to the red flashes from an artillery barrage rumbling to the southeast.

Jed, on the left, had Lips' .45 Colt pistol. Bunny, in charge, had a shotgun. Doody carried a large pair of wire cutters, and Turley had a bundle of metal wire stakes bent into a screw shape at the bottom. These were silently screwed into the ground to hold open the gaps in the wire.

Their mission was to cut gaps in the wire that a later patrol would exploit during a reconnaissance of the German lines.

As Doody placed the jaws of the cutters around a wire, two flares blossomed to their right.

"Oh, shit."

The men froze.

Three feet away, on the other side of the wire, three German soldiers stared wide-eyed at the Americans. They wore soft caps, their faces blackened with burned cork and smears of mud as were the Americans. One of them raised a potato masher grenade. Bunny raised his shotgun and shook his head. Another German, with NCO lace on his collar, put out his hand and pushed the grenade down. *"Nein, Max."*

Bunny lowered his shotgun. More flares popped to life replacing those burning out.

"Hello, Fritz," Bunny said.

"Hallo, Sammy," the German sergeant said. *"Haben Sie Amerikanische Zigaretten?"*

The German put two fingers to his lips.

"Cigarettes," Jed said.

Bunny produced a pack and tossed it through a hole in the wire. The sergeant caught it and offered the pack to his men. They each took two, placing them carefully into the pockets of their blouses. He made a motion to toss the pack back but Bunny held up his hand. "Keep it."

The German ducked his head, "*Danke.*"

The third German tossed a felt-covered flask through the hole in the wire. Bunny picked it up, unscrewed the top, and sniffed the contents.

"Whew, strong."

"*Schnapps...*"

Bunny took a drink. He choked a little but immediately took another sip. Turley then Doody took their turns and passed the liquor to Jed. It tasted like the contraband schnapps Herr Kurtz had toasted with. It settled like a small furnace in his belly. Jed capped the flask and reached up to pass it back.

"Keep it," the German said.

Max pointed at Bunny's shotgun. "*Schrotflinte.*"

"You have one of the shotguns, I see," the German sergeant said. "Our government has declared they are illegal. You should not have such an inhumane weapon."

"Come and take it from me."

"*Jetzt töten,*" Max said.

"Periscope off the port bow," Jed said in a low voice. The Americans tensed and raised their weapons.

The German sergeant looked at Jed. "You speak German."

"A little."

"I think, perhaps, more than a little."

Jed shrugged his shoulders.

The sergeant shook his head. "Not now, Max. Maybe we will kill them tomorrow."

"Don't bet on it, Fritzie," Bunny said.

"Don't you bet on it, Uncle Sammy," the German sergeant said.

Turley stared wide-eyed.

The flares burned out, and the night swallowed them. Jed hugged the ground, his eyes dazzled in the afterglow.

More flares lit the area. Jed pushed the pistol safety off and thrust it in front of him.

The Germans were gone.

"They're as dirty and scared as we are," Turley said.

"Don't forget, they want to kill us." Doody said.

"Let's get out of here," Bunny said.

As they neared the American lines a German barrage started. The German Sergeant had changed his mind.

The patrol tumbled into their trenches and hurried past Watkia and Reb.

"What about the password?"

"You never challenged us," Jed said over his shoulder.

"MASSILON," Watkia said.

"ATHENS."

Jed's reply was drowned out as a shell hit near the trench parapet.

Jed checked on Watkia and Reb. They were unhurt.

The four hurried down into the company dugout. Captain Brown, Samis, and Trask were there.

"What happened?" Samis asked.

"There was a German wire patrol out there," Bunny deadpanned. "We avoided them but they must have heard us. As we came back, they started shelling."

The barrage outside stopped.

"Cancel the raid, Sergeant Trask. We'll try again tomorrow night," Brown said.

"Holy shit," Turley said to Jed. "Is that what every patrol is like?"

Jed shrugged. "The unexpected always happens."

CHAPTER 33

OCTOBER 13, 1918

PANNES SECTOR. FRANCE

At 9 P. M., Trask, Brock and Jed crawled from a listening post over the open ground that Jed had crossed three nights before.

"What the hell are we doing, Trask?"

"I told you, Leo, we're going to capture a prisoner."

"The minute the Krauts kill me they'll call the whole thing off."

"Cut the bullshit."

They slinked forward and eventually slid into a trench that the Germans had taken great pains to prepare properly. The walls were sandbagged, and the bottom was covered with muddy duckboards.

Trask and Brock moved forward rounding a left jog in a communication trench going deeper into the German lines. Jed followed and peered around the corner. The jog extended ten feet and then turned right. He backed up twenty feet and kneeled down, covering the main trench with Collins' shotgun.

Nothing happened for fifteen minutes as a silent, dark void enveloped Jed.

Then, shouts of alarm in German, a pistol shot, a shotgun blast, and several more pistol shots. A Mauser spoke. The pistol answered.

The Germans fired illumination flares.

The real world leaped back into Jed's vision. He expected Germans to pour around the bend in the trench and almost fired when a figure appeared.

Brock staggered into view clutching his right side where a red stain spread. He stumbled forward and collapsed on his face in the mud.

Jed kneeled and rolled Brock over. He was still alive, taking ragged breaths through clenched teeth. Mud covered his face and eyes.

"Trask...?" Brock squinted and clutched his wounded side. "I thought I shot you out there. How did you shoot me?"

Jed checked and found a single gunshot wound in Brock's waist.

Brock grabbed Jed by his collar, pulled himself into a sitting position, and stuck his .45 under Jed's chin. "You kept me out of prison, Les, like you promised, but that's been a burden for you." Brock shook his head. "You thought you solved your problems by shooting me, but I'm still here." He winced in pain. "I'm going to solve all my problems by blowing your head off."

Jed tried to break through Brock's delirium. "I'm Jed Martin. I'm here to help you."

Brock focused on Jed but didn't release his grip or lower the pistol. "Martin, the little coward." His mouth curled into a sneer. "So, maybe I did get the great hero and now I can shut you up permanently."

Brock pulled the trigger but the automatic's slide was locked back on an empty magazine. He dropped the pistol and whipped his bolo knife out and stuck it firmly under Jed's chin. "A slit throat is as good as a bullet."

Jed reached into the front of his shirt, pulled the Derringer, and thrust it against Brock's ribs. The small gun bucked in his hand. Brock squinted in pain, watery mud streaming down his face like dirty tears. He collapsed back into the mud and dropped the bolo.

A German ran around the corner. Jed raised the shotgun and fired. The buckshot hit the man in the face. His head exploded, and his steel helmet went flying. He crumpled to his knees then fell forward, his brain lying beside what was left of his head.

Jed had been acting without fear, the calming center wrapping his heart and mind. His senses were acute. In spite of the gun blasts he could hear clearly, see sharply in the shifting light, and smell the stink of mud, gunpowder, and shit.

He moved forward and peered around the bend in the trench. Enemy soldiers called to each other. Jed hurried back to where Brock lay face up in the mud, his body limp and fragile, not breathing. A flare burned out and Brock's figure faded into deep shadow.

Three German signal rockets sizzled into the air followed by illumination flares.

The northeast horizon turned into a continuous glow of orange fire as if the sun was about to rise. He bent to pick Brock up and carry him away as the first of the shells sliced in and landed short.

The next round hit much closer. Dirt and mud rained down. Trench mortars thumped, their dark shapes arcing under the dome of flare light. Jed backed up as far as he could as a shell landed on the edge of the trench above where Brock lay. The wall heaved out and collapsed, burying Brock under a mound of sandbags.

Jed took a half step forward to dig Brock out but dove into a funk hole as another shell whistled in and landed on top of the sandbag pile. Splinters flew and a greasy dust devil spun down the trench.

More flares raced skyward. There was nothing else Jed could do. He climbed out of the trench and started across no-man's-land.

A large shell roared in and landed in the trench where Brock lay. The concussion threw Jed into a shell hole filled with water. He clung to the bottom, slime oozing between his fingers.

As he ran out of air he thought to sink into the slime, to join his mother in the rotting depths. He fought the fear and rose out of the water as a mortar shell landed in front of him. The hot blast smacked his face, and something bit his cheek. He lay submerged, rising and gasping for air at quick intervals until the Germans stopped their barrage. He crawled out of the slimy water and slithered toward the German trench. There was a large hole where Brock had been lying. Duckboards and sandbags had been obliterated. A stinking cloud of gas settled in the trench. His tongue felt like he had a mouth full of gravel.

He thought he saw someone moving in the shifting flare light but it was only rats feasting on bits of flesh.

He turned away and crawled back across no-man's-land to the listening post.

He stopped, listening. No one challenged his approach.

"ATHENS," he said.

"What?"

"ATHENS, you idiot, what's the challenge? Were you asleep, Doody?"

"No. Is that you Jed?"

"It could be the whole German army. Can I come in?"

"Sure."

Jed slid into the listening post and sat between Doody and Reb, shivering.

"You are one big mess," Reb said.

"Did you stir that ruckus up?" Doody asked.

Jed nodded.

"Where's Trask and Brock?"

Jed stared toward the German lines. "Out there."

Lieutenant Samis crawled into the post followed by Lips. "You men keep quiet out here." He noticed Jed. "Private Martin, you're back. Are you alone?"

"Yes, sir."

"Come with me," Samis said. He sent Lips to find Captain Brown.

In the company dugout the lieutenant offered Jed hot coffee. Jed drank some and the shivering subsided.

Watkia appeared. He swabbed Jed's cheek cut and chin nick with iodine and put a small gauze and a piece of tape over each of them. "Try to keep them clean."

Jed shrugged. Andy nodded his head, "Yeah, clean around here is one layer of mud."

Captain Brown arrived. "What is your report, Private Martin?"

Jed took off his knit cap and rubbed his forehead with it. "We reconnoitered their forward trenches with Sergeant Trask and Sergeant Brock out in front out of my sight. They must have run into a German patrol. After an exchange of fire Sergeant Brock returned alone badly wounded. A German attacked me and I shot him."

"What happened to Sergeant Brock?"

"A shell collapsed the trench and buried him in two feet of sandbags and another hit the top of the pile. After I got out of the trench a bigger shell blew a big hole in the trench's bottom. I don't see how anyone could have survived."

"What about Sergeant Trask?" Samis asked.

Jed hadn't seen Brock shoot Trask and didn't believe Brock's fantastic claim about Trask shooting him because Brock's wound wasn't from a shotgun but a rifle.

"I don't know, sir." Jed clasped his arms across his chest, shivering again. "The Germans began a barrage. I had to get out of there."

Brown patted Jed's shoulder. "You did the right thing to save yourself, Private."

Samis spoke up. "Request permission to lead a patrol out to recover Sergeant Brock's body and find Sergeant Trask."

"Permission granted." Captain Brown looked at Jed. "I need for you to show the lieutenant where Sergeant Brock died."

"Yes, sir."

His gut tightened. He had acted in self-defense but had left Brock defenseless against the German artillery.

Jed had killed Brock.

Samis chose Bunny and Zyren for the patrol.

Once again Jed crawled across no-man's-land and arrived at the trench.

The patrol climbed down into the trench scattering rats into hiding.

Samis scanned the area. "Is this where you last saw Sergeant Brock?"

"Yes, sir," Jed pointed, "right where that hole is."

The artillery had obliterated everything.

Bunny leaned toward Jed, "How will Brock show up after this?"

Jed checked the bunker where the rats ran in. There was no one there.

Zyren was halfway down the trench. "There's somebody down there."

A figure crawled out of the shadows. He had no knit cap and blood dripped from a gash at his hairline.

It was Trask.

Jed helped Zyren haul Trask to his feet. They sat him on the firing step. Jed wiped the mud from Trask's forehead, swabbed the gash with iodine, and wrapped Trask's individual bandage around his head.

"Can you walk?" Samis asked Trask.

Trask nodded and, supported by Jed and Zyren, walked to the end of the trench.

"Where's Leo?"

"He's gone west, Sarge," Jed said.

"How?"

"When I found him, he was shot but alive. The German artillery got him." Jed's stomach cramped as he told this half-truth to Trask. "I'm sorry, Top."

"It's not your fault. I let it go on too long."

The group hurried back to the listening post, stopping twice to lie prone in flare light. They were met by Captain Brown, Cain, and Lips.

216

Samis reported what they had found in the trench including the recovery of Trask. "Private Martin's account was borne out by the conditions in the trench."

The tenseness in Jed's stomach eased.

Brown turned to Trask. "How bad are you hurt?"

Trask shook his head. "I'll be all right, sir."

"After you get cleaned up, I'll expect a full written report."

Trask moved away helped by Cain.

Brown turned to Samis. "I expect your written report within the hour, Lieutenant. I want to investigate this patrol before our relief arrives." The captain looked at Jed. "Go get some sleep, Private." Brown walked away followed by Samis.

Lipsitz stood next to Jed.

"Hey, Lips. What's going on with the captain?"

"What are you looking at me for? I don't know anything."

Jed wasn't buying it. Lipsitz was the best-informed man in the platoon.

"The lieutenant gave his opinion. Why an investigation?"

Lips shrugged his shoulders. "Brown doesn't know their background like we do but knows they hate each other. They went on patrol and only one came back, so I guess he's suspicious."

Jed rubbed the back of his tingling neck.

"Why are you worried? Did you see what happened between Brock and Trask?"

"I didn't see anything."

"Then you've got nothing to worry about." Lips considered for a moment then shook his head. "Brock and Trask killing each other is barracks talk. They were cousins."

"Sergeant Trask did once think out loud that if Brock died in combat, it would solve all of his problems, but he was drunk."

Lips' eyes got wide. "You better keep your mouth shut about that." He looked at his watch. "The 28th Division relieves us in twenty-one hours."

Jed sat in his secret hole drinking the second half of Andy's cognac and pondering Lips' comment that the cousins would not try to kill each other. Brock had claimed he'd shot Trask and Trask's grazing wound may have been caused by a pistol, but Brock's claim that Trask had shot him was not true. Brock's wound was from a rifle bullet not Trask's shotgun. Brock might have survived that, but he had forced Jed to shoot him. The German artillery had wiped out the evidence.

The scene played repeatedly in his mind as he finished the cognac and lay back pulling his blanket over him.

A half hour before Stand-To Andy Watkia approached Jed's hideout. "Jed, wake up."

Jed awoke, his head fuzzy from drink and restless sleep. "Come on in, Andy."

Watkia crawled in with a mess tin full of warm beans, a slice of punk, and a tin cup of hot coffee. Jed shook his head.

"Eat this. We march soon."

Jed took a bite.

"There's more to Brock's death than the captain knows, isn't there?"

Andy had trusted Jed with personal information. "Brock was going to slit my throat. I shot him. He could have died from that."

"But the artillery made sure."

"Yes."

"Then everything will be all right."

"Will it?" Jed looked away. "I told you too much."

"I wasn't there. I know nothing. Finish that and report for Stand-To."

Jed ate but fatigue made the food tasteless. Brock's death and the wholesale slaughter around him was taking its toll. He might never sleep easy again.

At 8 P.M. the first men of the 28th Division arrived.

First Platoon formed up on Samis. They moved up a communication trench away from the front, the only illumination a high three-quarter moon.

The march to the blight of Pannes took three hours. Their expected trucks, and the haranguing Annamese drivers, were not there. The Americans continued their weary slog for the rest of the night.

CHAPTER 34

OCTOBER 16, 1918

FOUG, FRANCE

They stumbled into the village of Foug as the sun came up. The sound of distant artillery was nearly drowned out by the shouts of officers and NCOs barking commands as the men lined up and filed into a delousing station.

Jed collapsed and slept all day and, after evening chow, found Watkia sitting on a crate in a darkened alley staring glumly into space, a bottle of cognac in his hand.

"Where's Sergeant Trask?"

"He's in the supply shed two blocks down the street. I wouldn't bother him though. He's taking Brock's loss pretty hard."

"I have to talk to him."

"Suit yourself. Don't say I didn't warn you."

Jed pushed the supply shed door open and yellow light spilled into the street. A stack of packing crates stood in the middle of the floor, a lantern on top, its wick turned low. Trask sat beside the crates, his back to the door.

"Is that you Abel, come to be my Father Confessor?" He reached back with a bottle, not looking. "Make a toast my old war horse. Drink to war and fate and justice."

"No, I..."

"All right, more for me." Trask took a sloppy drink. "You know the story, old boy. I've been a hod carrier in Pittsburgh, and a lumberjack in Kentucky. I've dealt cards, slung hash, dug ditches, and painted houses but I always ended up back in the army. To the infantry!" Trask raised the bottle in salute. "This war is going to be won by the infantry, by God, we filthy, weary, living in mud, eating crud, wet to the bone, dreaming of home. I could write a poem for The Stars and Stripes that would tear their hearts out."

Jed sat on the floor and said nothing.

"Infantry: from the French, *infanterie*: 'A very young person, a knight's page', an infant." Trask hung his head. "It's why we call them babies." He kicked at the straw on the floor. "We turn babies into men then send them to die." He rested his head against the crates. "We sent them against the Moros." Trask stood and paced. "The Moros didn't fear death, they welcomed it as *juramentados*, taking an oath to kill and die."

Trask set the bottle on the floor and drew himself to attention, pulling the bottom of his blouse square and adjusting his overseas cap to the correct angle. "You watch out for those Moros, Abel." He snapped a hand salute, wobbled, and sat back on the floor. "When you start a war, what you want is justice, what you get is a mess."

"But what does it prove?" Jed asked.

"Somebody has to stand up to the bastards, and if only a little of the independence and freedom we bring rubs off on these European dolts, we'll have done something."

Jed spoke up. "The random brutality is what hits me hardest. The dead, torn apart, scattered like trash, men with families, histories, and plans reduced to slush. It's as if they were never born."

Trask's voice was surprisingly gentle. "Somebody will remember. They aren't lost for good." He collapsed onto his back, his eyes full of tears, his blood full of cognac. "Leo was the little brother I never had, Abel. I've been my brother's keeper but I let him get away with too much."

Trask raised the cognac bottle but only managed to pour liquor all over his face. "I can see the suspicion in the captain's eyes. He thinks I wanted Leo dead." He sat up suddenly and stared intently at Jed. "Martin said he was shot but I didn't do it, Abel. I only got one shot off at the Germans. Then I was knocked out. The lousy Kraut artillery killed him. Martin said so."

Jed didn't move.

Trask focused on Jed's face. "You're not Abel. You're Martin, from Arkansas." He grabbed Jed by the front of his blouse. "You said the German artillery got him, right?"

"Yes, the German artillery."

Trask nodded his head and released Jed. "I suppose the best way for Leo to go was in combat. There's honor in it despite all the bad things he did."

"I'm glad you didn't kill him in Récicourt after he attacked Louise."

Trask's eyes were unsteady.

"You're better than him," Jed said. "Killing him would've made you just like him."

Trask's face softened. "Well, now he's gone. It doesn't matter anymore."

The shed door opened and the real Abel stepped into the room followed by Cain.

Trask laughed. "Here are Cain and Abel coming to take me away."

Abel West turned the wick on the lantern up bright. He kneeled beside Trask. "No, old friend. The captain signed the file on Brock: missing, presumed dead, case closed."

"Thanks, Abel." A tear ran down Trask's cheek.

Abel turned to Jed. "Private Martin, the official record backs up your account."

Jed kept his face neutral.

Trask hung his head. "Were you listening before you came in?"

"Yes. The four of us in this room are the only ones who know something may have happened in Récicourt. As for Corporal Goldson and me, we know nothing, right Cain?"

"Yes, Sergeant Major."

"With Sergeant Brock gone, it's a personal matter between you and Private Martin."

"It'll stay that way, Sergeant Major," Jed said.

Abel nodded. "Come here, Cain." The two men tugged Trask to his feet. The first sergeant leaned limply on Abel's shoulder. "We've got to get this big monkey sobered up and fit for duty." He pointed at Jed. "Get back to your squad and prepare your gear. Tomorrow we leave for Belgium."

CHAPTER 35
OCTOBER 17, 1918
DOMGERMAIN, FRANCE

At the company formation the next morning, Captain Brown had mission details. "General Pershing has agreed to attach two American Divisions to the French Army in Belgium. The 37th is one of them. We march to the railhead in three hours and leave by train tomorrow morning for a three or four-day trip. We'll be attached to a French corps under the command of King Albert of Belgium."

Names like Passchendaele, Cambrai, and Ypres were whispered at breakfast: great battles where battalions of Britons and Scots were swallowed whole in some of the fiercest fighting of the war. Excitement and apprehension grew.

They marched to the railhead at Domgermain, France and camped out in a warehouse near the tracks. As they settled in it started to rain.

Lips came in with the platoon's mail and handed an envelope to Jed. It was from Enoch. Jed leaned back on his pack under a lantern and opened the letter.

October 1, 1918
J. Jedidiah Martin
I heard you was all fighting in the Argonne Forrest and, even as you may be real busy, there is something you need to know.
Your Aunt Bess has passed. She was trying to be careful, but she has been complaining of weakness lately and the influenza got her.
I'll bury her at the Methodist church alongside Seth and the memorial to your mother.

I think you boys got out of Camp Pike just in time. There's talk that the Arkansas Board of Health is going to put the whole state under quarantine. Until now the government has been covering up the epidemic to keep up morale for the war effort.

As for me, I live alone so I don't expect to get it.

With Bess gone my heart's not in it to keep the farm going. I'm going to sell it.

I sent along a note Bess wrote to you before she passed. She was feverish when she wrote it so take that into account when you read it.

She loved you dearly,

Enoch

Bessie's letter was written in a shaky hand:

September 29, 1918

My dearest Jed,

I hope you get this all right and that you are not hurt. Enoch says your outfit was in some heavy fighting and your name wasn't among those listed in the newspaper as killed or wounded. Praise God. I hope it's not too terrible for you and you are getting your meals and enough sleep. I pray for you morning and night.

As for me, I don't want to worry you, but I have come down with the influenza. I feel very weak and the chills are worse right now and I'm a bit confused. I wish they could give me something.

I don't want to see Rose just yet it wasn't her fault Seth and Enoch loved us both equal it was so beautiful what we had if I go I don't want Enoch to follow too soon but maybe it will be like it was happy and full of life and love like a dream

A line of ink ran down the page and turned left where it ended in her signature:

Ich liebe dich, mein Sohn,

Gott beschütze dich,
Aunt Bess

Jed sat, his head down, arms limp across his knees, the letters falling from his hands. A scratching choke grabbed his throat. He gulped air and sobbed violently. She had signed off, "I love you, my son, God bless you." His voice croaked as he spoke, softly but urgently, "Oh, God, Bess. I love you too." Another gasp shuddered through his chest. He took a deep breath and stared into a dark corner of the warehouse.

He picked up Enoch's letter, crushed it, and threw it back onto the floor.

He pulled out the German schnapps bottle, drained it, then threw it into the dark corner.

With the liquor burning in his blood and the drumming of the rain on the roof Jed slept. At first, he sank into oblivion, but as the cognac wore off the dreams came: of burning buildings and flooded rivers, bleached skulls and splattering gore. No matter how he turned over or rested his head the images persisted.

He hoped things would be different in Belgium.

When Jed awoke, it was raining harder than ever.

He hurried through his morning cleanup and sought out the squad.

Clarence Dubman had backed his rolling kitchen inside the double doors at the front of the warehouse. Dub handed Jed a cup of coffee.

"Sorry to hear about your aunt."

Jed looked at him.

"One of your boys found your uncle's letter. We're all sorry."

Watkia nodded to Jed. The rest of the squad sat still and silent inside the front door out of the rain.

Jed's stomach rumbled. "What's for breakfast, Dub?"

"All I've got are these potatoes and onions. I found a cow in a barn nearby and traded an old lady a cup of cognac for a bucket of milk."

A pot of water boiled on the burner. "Do you have butter, and salt and pepper?" Dub nodded. "Good. We're having poor Irish potato soup for breakfast."

Jed had Dubman chop the potatoes and onions into bite sizes and place them in the boiling water, adding salt and pepper, until the potatoes were tender and the onions clear. Jed added milk and butter, stirred until the milk was ready to boil, and then removed the pot from the fire.

"Breakfast is ready, boys."

They lined up with their canteen cups and were soon gobbling down the soup.

"Something smells familiar."

Mike stood in the doorway.

Jed rushed forward and grabbed Mike in a bear hug, his heart pounding. "How did you get back here?"

Mike hooked a thumb over his shoulder. "This guy helped."

Abel stood in out of the rain, a staff car behind him. "I drove over to the gas hospital at *Julvécourt* and got him."

"How are you, Mike?" Jed asked.

"They cleaned out my eyes and my hip's healed. I'm ready to go."

"Gosh am I glad to see you. Thanks Sergeant Major for bringing him back."

"I want to keep the unit together with trained men."

"Hey, Dub, you got any more soup?" Mike asked. "I'm hungry. We've been driving since the wee hours."

"Sure, Mike. Sergeant Major, would you like some too?"

"Don't mind if I do."

As they ate their breakfast, the men peppered Mike with questions. Bunny asked about the nurses, Dubman asked about the food, and Watkia asked about Mike's treatment and what amenities there were. Doody sat and stared at Mike, grinning.

Mike pointed at the ribbon on Jed's left pocket flap. "Got a medal?"

"I did what anybody would do."

"Oh, sure," Bunny said. "He ran out into an artillery barrage and brought two wounded guys back who would have died. I don't know if it was brave or crazy."

"The Frogs said heroic," Doody said, "and gave him the Craw Day Gayer. The colonel made him a PFC, too."

"Wow," Mike said, "better than winning a bunch of wine in a boxing match. I knew you had it in you."

"It just happened," Jed said. "I'm not here for medals."

Doody spoke up. "Is your leg healed proper, Champ? I was thinkin', if you're too banged up to box, you're handsome enough, maybe we can get you into those moving pictures you like so much."

225

"Douglas Fairbanks wouldn't let himself be shot." Jed said with a smile.

Doody looked around at the others. "We were talking before he got hurt about turning pro. I'll be his manager."

"You can't manage to stay awake half the time," Bunny said, "how are you going to manage a fighter?"

"Andy is a good businessman. You'll give me some pointers, won't you Andy?"

"Sure, Doody, sure," Watkia said, spooning his soup.

"Will all y'all pitch in a few dollars to help us?"

"Yeah," Bunny said. "Here's One Franc to get you started." He flipped a coin toward Doody.

Watkia snatched it out of the air and slipped it into his blouse pocket. "You better let me take care of the financials," he said.

Doody smiled at Andy. "We're gonna be rich."

When they finished their breakfast, Abel excused himself and Mike and Jed sat in a corner to compare notes. Mike's account was mostly about boredom and wanting to return to the squad. His hip was fine, and he danced around shadow boxing to prove it.

"Oh, I almost forgot. I got a letter from Dickie Decker. He enlisted and was with the 28th Division near a place called Apremont. He killed seven Germans with his fists and a shovel, saved his captain, and they gave him the Distinguished Service Cross." Mike sat down. "In exchange, they took his right leg below the knee. His boxing days are over."

"I'm afraid I have worse news." Jed told Mike about Bessie.

"I'm so sorry, Jed."

"The soup reminds me of her."

Jed told of Louise and how she had lit up the lives of the squad but then been seriously wounded. He explained how Bart and Clay Jones had died together and how Brock had accused him of cowardice because he helped Tony and Mike in the shell hole.

Mike looked around the warehouse. "Where's Brock?"

"Brock is dead," Jed said, "German artillery. All we found was a hole in the ground, nobody could have survived the barrage."

Outside, a train chugged by the warehouse and wheezed to a stop, the cars rattling forward against their couplings.

Lieutenant Samis stepped through the door. "Let's go, men. We leave *tout de suite*."

Doody asked, "Hey, Lieutenant, how did you make out with the little French gal back in Longeville? What was her name?"

Samis flushed. "Miss Farrar is a lovely and virtuous young lady." He stepped back out into the rain.

Doody pointed at Bunny. "Virtuous?"

"She had great virtues," Bunny said, grinning.

"What's that all about?" Mike asked.

"I'll tell you later. It's kinda funny. Let's get ready to sleep in the shit."

They were packed into the forty-and-eights again, camping out on fresh straw thrown over the trampled horse manure. Each boxcar had a case of gold fish and tomato juice for their rations.

The trip lasted four days. Whenever they stopped in a small town, the locals were there to sell sweets and bread and bottles of wine. Most of the time was passed lounging in an alcoholic haze with the squad filling Mike in on their exploits while he was gone.

When the rain stopped, they opened the boxcar doors to a flood of fresh air and sat in the doorway whistling at women and old men policing up the discarded tomato and salmon cans littering the roadbed.

That all changed as they moved into the Belgian countryside. The land had been pulverized by artillery for four years. There was nothing but mud, barren tree trunks, wrecked equipment, and crumbled towns, the land sterilized by years of gas and high explosives. The only color was in sparse patches of coarse slew grass, a depressing flat gray-green. There were no civilians in sight.

Seeing more tortured terrain saddened Jed. He had been overseas only two months, and he was already sick of the place. He couldn't imagine how those who had managed to survive four years of this wretched mess could stand it one minute longer.

Mike's return was the only bright spot and Jed supposed he would have to be content with that, for now.

PART THREE

THE LAST BUCKEYE

**War never slays a bad man in its course,
But the good always!**

—Sophocles

What is our death but a night's sleep?

—Martin Luther

CHAPTER 36

OCTOBER 22, 1918
STADEN, NEAR YPRES, BELGIUM

The train rumbled past the crumbled city of Ypres and crawled to a stop in front of a dilapidated sign announcing that the pile of loose bricks and scrap lumber behind it was the town of Wieltje.

From there, the company marched through terrain covered by shell holes and acres of tangled and rusty barbed wire. That night they pitched pup tents in a barren field where they slept with their helmets over their faces and gloves on their hands to keep from being gnawed by rats that lived in the garbage dumps the passing troops left behind.

After two more days, they reached a town called Staden with intact barns and fresh straw. Jed hand scrubbed his uniform and the Lifebuoy soap continued to do its work. New, clean underclothes felt luxurious against his tortured skin.

The next morning there was a company formation.

Samis, Trask, and Bunny received the French Croix de Guerre for their attempt to link up with the 91st Division on 28 September. Sergeant Brock's War Cross was presented posthumously.

Bunny was promoted to Corporal and given command of First Squad, Joe Collins was promoted to Sergeant and became Rifle Section leader, and Samis was promoted to First Lieutenant.

After the men were dismissed, the squad gathered around Bunny.

"Wait 'til the girls see that medal, Bunny, you'll be drowning in pussy," Watkia said.

"Can you help me lay in a haversack full of rubbers?"

Reb came to attention. "What are your fu'st orders, suh?"

"I suggest we repair to our quarters and inspect the wine brother Watkia brought."

Clarence Dubman stood nearby. "I fried up some doughnuts this morning. Do you boys want some?"

"Dub, you have made it a promotion party," Bunny said. "I'll even raise a glass to Brock." He motioned for quiet as they booed. "He was a bum and a coward but, on that day," he pointed to his Croix de Guerre, "he fought right beside us."

Jed said nothing.

"Come on guys," Bunny threw his arm around Dub's shoulder, "let's go celebrate."

They left Staden the next morning. As they marched further east, the condition of the countryside improved. They left the decrepit mess around Ypres and entered territory where the few patches of destruction seemed recent.

Jed took a deep breath. The constant stench of rot and death was gone, replaced by the familiar, comforting odor of rich wet earth.

They crossed a low ridge and found a medium size town standing intact amidst early fall colors.

"The town of Lichtervelde," Cain said.

The battalion spent the next two days in the surrounding fields practicing maneuvers, hand signals, and techniques for dealing with machine gun nests and strong points, sure signs that there was going to be hard fighting ahead.

CHAPTER 37
OCTOBER 28, 1918
LICHTERVELDE, BELGIUM

In Company G, the constant topic of conversation was the ongoing armistice talks.

The men talked in low voices, not whispering but speaking with subdued bravado, so as not to jinx their hopes and validate their fears. They were saving their energy and resting while they had the chance. There would be another action soon. Some would suffer and some die. This was the entry fee when one became a soldier. They were in the business of making war, and the currency of war is death.

As Jed and Mike walked toward their billets after breakfast, First Sergeant Trask motioned them to join him and the staff of the 147th Regiment under thick camouflage netting. They were arrayed in a semi-circle before a single dignified figure. The Division Commander, General Farnsworth, stood straight, shoulders back, calmly scanning the assembled staff. He nodded toward Jed.

"I see a few junior enlisted men. They are welcome. This information is especially important to them. The men and officers of this division have performed magnificently, with valor and persistence. I couldn't be prouder nor is there a better division in this theater of operations. I find no commander lacking in aggressiveness in the assault and no one lacking in zeal to close with the enemy. We have not been profligate in spending our men's lives but have pushed hard to achieve our objectives."

He scanned the serious faces around him. "The men are concerned about the end of this conflict so they may go home, but do not let rumors of an armistice distract them from their duty." He held up a message. "General Bullard, the Commander of the newly formed Second Army of the American Expeditionary Force, has published orders to his command

and he has generously offered them for our consideration. I read in part: 'The Boche is being run out of France by fighting, not peace talks. The moment we stop fighting he will stop going.'" He lowered the paper. "That goes here in Belgium as well. As we move forward in this campaign, we must maintain our initiative. The best way to ensure the end of the war is to continue to punish the enemy." He paused, "Keep killing them until they quit."

The meeting broke up and Trask stood with Mike and Jed. "As much as I hate this shit, this war might end too soon."

Jed eyes widened. "Too soon? They've been fighting for four years."

"It took us fifteen years to get the Philippines under control. Those little brown Moro bastards were tough. They wouldn't give up and they sure knew how to die. But we finally beat them, and they knew it. Look around you," Trask gestured at the surrounding countryside. "Where are we?"

"Belgium."

"Yes." He pointed to the east. "And over there, Germany."

Jed and Mike stared at him.

"Don't you see? French and Belgian territory is devastated. British and French casualties outnumber German casualties. The German people have been sacrificing, they have rationing, and most of their young men are out here, but their countryside is untouched. They won't accept that they're beat. If we end this now, they'll go home to their beer, sausages, and *frauleins*. The Frogs and Belgies have to rebuild everything. It looks like they're losing the war."

"So, we march all the way to Berlin?" Jed asked.

"You mean fight all the way there," Mike said.

"We're here and are pushing them back toward Germany," Trask said. "We can't stop now."

"And thousands more will die," Jed said.

Trask had a regretful pout. "If we don't finish this the right way, someone will have to do this all over again."

CHAPTER 38

OCTOBER 30, 1918

YPRES-LYS CAMPAIGN

As the Americans moved closer to the front, they avoided marching in the road's center to avoid teams of horses pulling French 75 artillery pieces forward.

They slept in another field and arose on the morning of 30 October to a breakfast of bacon, pancakes, fried potatoes, and coffee.

Lieutenant Samis introduced a young Belgian liaison officer named Lieutenant Lannoye, who wore the red ribbon with green stripes of the Belgian Croix de Guerre. The strain of four years of war showed at the corners of Lannoye's eyes as he briefed them on their mission. "To our east is the Lys River which we control. Further east the Scheldt River. The Boche are in trenches east of the Scheldt with outposts between the rivers in a town called Cruyshautem." To Jed's ears the name sounded like Christ Shoutin. "Our attack will begin tomorrow, October 31st. We will cross the Lys, fight past Cruyshautem, cross the Scheldt, and drive the Germans back toward Germany."

The squad moved east until they came to a well-maintained road running to a bridge crossing the Lys River. They stopped in a small village on the west side of the river and pitched pup tents in an orchard beside cottages whose residents huddled in basements.

Other units of the division crossed the Lys settling into funk holes dug into the west side of a railroad embankment running to the northeast parallel to the river.

Second Battalion was the division reserve. They would eliminate strong points the lead troops bypassed or provide a force to repel any German counterattack.

Jed woke before dawn on October 31 to the turmoil of horses and artillerymen clattering down the road, crossing the bridge, and being arrayed along the road between the Lys River and the railroad embankment.

A thin fog burned off as the sun climbed into a clear sky, revealing open country stretching southeast of the railroad to Cruyshautem on the crest of a ridge, then on past the rain-swollen Scheldt River, where the terrain lifted into rolling, tree-covered hills.

The artillery started with a ground-thumping roar, firing over the embankment.

Whistles sounded and the assault companies surged out of their funk holes and over the embankment, moving at a fast walk. When the first line was far enough advanced the brigade reserve troops climbed over the rail line and followed the lead wave along with the French artillery.

This was the signal for Second Battalion to take up their position in reserve at the railroad embankment.

Second Battalion crossed the Lys River bridge and passed through the village of Olsene. Joyous Belgian citizens appeared from cellars celebrating their liberation.

Jed dove to the ground as a German shell whistled in and landed in a group of five civilians, killing an older man, a woman, and two small children.

Lieutenant Lannoye picked up the remaining wounded child and laid him in the arms of a nearby woman. He yelled something at her in Dutch then at the other civilians who picked up the bodies and carried them into a nearby cottage basement.

Jed and the squad hurried through the town and arranged themselves in the funk holes along the west side of the embankment. The overhead railroad ties and rails provided a sturdy bunker roof.

When the German fire stopped, Jed clambered up and looked over the rails. The French artillery engaged strong points with direct fire, the hammering of machine guns drifted over the green fields, and the puffs of grenade blasts were followed after a few seconds by muffled crumps. Spent German machine gun bullets skittered across the gravel roadbed and glanced off the rails.

By nightfall, the forward troops made it to the base of the ridges to the west and southwest of Cruyshautem and dug in. They reported that some Germans were still in Cruyshautem with machine guns and field pieces while most of the German infantry retreated to the east.

Sporadic enemy artillery fire fell all night. At 3 A.M. a widespread barrage of arsine gas arrived and Jed spent a sleepless night in his gas mask.

CHAPTER 39
NOVEMBER 1, 1918
NEAR CRUYSHAUTEM, BELGIUM

The Stars and Stripes

AUSTRIA AGAIN BIDS FOR PEACE; ITALY ATTACKS

"The Austro-Hungarian Government declares itself, in consequence, prepared, without awaiting the result of other negotiations, to enter into pourparlers regarding peace between Austria-Hungary and the States of the opposing party, and regarding an immediate armistice on all the fronts of Austria-Hungary."

THE STARS AND STRIPES: FRANCE, FRIDAY, NOVEMBER 1, 1918, page 1

At sunrise Jed and Mike sat next to the railroad tracks and watched Belgian civilians, driven out of their cellars by the gas, retreat toward the American rear area with wet towels wound around their heads.

Mike handed Jed an envelope. "If something happens to me…"

Jed handled the envelope as though it was red-hot and stuffed it into his blouse pocket. "Do you have some kind of feeling?"

"No, but I was hit once. Maybe next time it'll be two feet higher."

"I don't have a letter for you. I wasn't sure they would send you back here."

"It's all right. We'll take care of each other."

"I took care of Tony when he was dying, against orders, but I didn't help my best friend. I feel rotten about it. What if…?"

"Then you read the letter." Mike smiled and slapped him gently on the shoulder. "Sometimes you think too much, Jed, but I love you for it."

An hour after noon Second Battalion climbed over the railroad berm and started forward. Once again Jed had a knot in his stomach. He was crossing the doorstep of his mortality, the most precious thing he had, his life, at risk.

The Germans masked the western side of Cruyshautem with smoke and their artillerymen dragged the field pieces away. American troops rushed from their hasty foxholes, charged up the hillside into the smoke, and swept over the ridge and through the town.

Jed and the squad followed them up the slope and when they reached the crest a bypassed German machine gunner fired from a cottage window. Bullets snapped past Jed's head as he dove to the ground. Mike threw a grenade into the window. After the grenade went off several wounded Germans yelled *"Kamerad"* and filed out of the house. Doody took them prisoner.

As the smoke cleared, they watched the American leading elements chase the Germans eastward over the Scheldt River Bridge.

The Germans destroyed the bridge. A number of the enemy trapped on the west side surrendered. Military Police rounded them up and marched them, along with Doody's prisoners, to the American rear.

Engineers constructed hasty bridges made up of downed trees and pieces of houses from a town at the river's edge. The division set up a secure position for two battalions on the eastern bank.

As the sun set, Jed and the rest of the division found shelter in abandoned Belgian houses a half-mile west of the river.

The fighting was over for the day.

In the morning, after breakfast, Mike, Watkia, Doody, and Turley started a dice game on a blanket, playing for small French coins.

"We got off easy yesterday," Jed said. "Lips said nobody in the platoon got hit."

"You're right," Turley said. "Second Platoon had two dead and three wounded."

"I still don't know what we're doin' here," Doody said. "The Germans are running away like they're beat and we're still takin' casualties."

"As long as they fight us, we have to keep fighting them," Mike said. "General Bullard said that the Boche is being run out by fighting, not peace talks."

"You consult with generals, now?" Watkia asked.

Mike smiled and shook his head.

"But when will it all be over?" Doody asked.

"When the last man who's supposed to die here dies," Jed said.

Doody picked up the dice and tossed them.

"Seven out," Watkia said and picked up the coins.

"A lot of us Buckeyes have died," Doody said. "I don't want to be the last one."

Bunny walked in. "We caught a break. The French will relieve us tomorrow and we go to the rear for rest."

"Now you're talkin'!" Doody said.

Bunny shook his head. "Don't get your hopes up. We're the freshest unit in the division and, when we come back, we cross the river first."

"Oh, brother man…" Doody flopped back on the floor.

Jed walked outside and lit a cigarette.

Mike joined him. "What's the matter with you?"

Jed shook his head. "This is worse than I ever imagined."

Mike squeezed his shoulder. "We've come this far. We'll be fine."

Jed nodded, threw the cigarette butt away, and stood staring at the river.

The next day, units of the French 12th Division relieved the 37th, and they marched back across the Lys River to the town of Thielt where they rested, played dice, drank, and talked about the rumored armistice. There were daily drills and inspections and by November 8 they were ready to march east and cross the Scheldt River.

CHAPTER 40

NOVEMBER 9, 1918
SYNGHEM, BELGIUM

The Stars and Stripes

The Allied forces in Belgium were before Ghent on Wednesday. South of that city American divisions had played a prominent part in the advance of the preceding days and liberated many villages to which the Belgian tenants had clung through more than four years of German occupation.

THE STARS AND STRIPES: FRANCE, FRIDAY, NOVEMBER 8, 1918, page 1

In the early evening, the men of Second Battalion marched into Synghem, a small town sitting at the focus of a curve in the Scheldt River, two miles north of where the unit had been relieved six days before. The French had failed to expand the bridgehead the 37th had established and had retreated back across the river and moved into the cul-de-sac at Synghem where the Germans observed them from three sides. The town was being dismantled at the rate of one shell a minute.

The French traveled to the rear amid catcalls and insults. The Buckeyes would re-cross the river in a much more exposed position than before.

After dark, Jed and the squad entered the front room of a house with straw bedding on the floor. They lit candles.

Mike settled gingerly onto the straw. "My hip is killing me. I guess I didn't heal as much as I thought."

"This will be over soon."

"That's right," Watkia said. "This will all be over soon. I'm with Doody, why are we getting ready for another attack? One of those prisoners we took said there's talk of revolution in Berlin and mutiny in the German navy. The Germans are praying for an armistice and the Austrians already surrendered."

A shell landed a block away.

Bunny lit a cigarette. "That Hun gunner ain't quitting."

"Fuck him," Watkia said. "Why don't we sit and wait?"

"We have to keep the pressure on the enemy, Andy," Mike said. "If we stay here and stop fighting, the Germans will have won."

"I don't know, Champ," Doody said. "I'd sure hate to see you get hit again. I want to get you back to the States and start your professional boxing career. You remember I told you I'm his manager," he said to the others.

Jed stood at the front window. Mule-drawn wagons carrying pontoon boats stopped next to a canal flowing in front of the house. The boats would allow the troops to cross the Scheldt. Teddy drove one of the wagons.

Jed started out the door to greet Teddy when the roar of an artillery shell rushed in. Jed dove back inside the house. A shell exploded in the street outside, blew the glass from the window, and snuffed out the candles.

Hideous screams arose from the street.

Jed and the squad ran outside and found engineers and medics tending wounded comrades lying in the road. Old Clem was lying on his side, both of his front legs smashed, his gut torn open, screaming piteously, and kicking his hind legs. The other mule stood unharmed trying to shy away but was still harnessed to its wailing companion.

Teddy kneeled beside Old Clem trying to comfort him.

Andy Watkia ran across the street.

"Stop that dying noise!"

Teddy jumped back as Watkia raised the Luger and shot the mule through the head.

Andy turned toward the other mule.

Jed grabbed his arm. "It's over, Andy."

Watkia screamed, threw the pistol into the canal, and ran into the house.

"Jesus, we got a mule killer on our hands," Reb said.

Jed stepped in front of Reb. "Why don't you shut up—once?"

Reb held Jed's eye for a dozen heartbeats, then blinked and walked away.

Teddy looked at Jed, tears flowing.

"I'm so sorry, Teddy," Jed said.

"It's all right, James Jedidiah, Mister Andy did Old Clem a favor. He was bad hurt."

Mike headed for the house. "Let's get some sleep."

"You go with Michael Sean, James Jedidiah. I'll clean up here."

In the house Andy was lying facing the wall, sobbing. Jed sat down next to him and lit a candle. He unwound his puttees and kicked off his boots.

Watkia sat up, his eyes moist. "It was my father." His lower lip trembled. "I was helping my dad with a wagon load of supplies for our store. I was supposed to hold the mules steady while he set the brake and unhitched the team. The mules spooked, but I was too small to hold them. They jumped forward, and the wagon knocked Dad down. A wagon wheel ran over his guts." Andy covered his eyes and rubbed them with the heels of his palms. "He was pissing blood and moaning with the pain. There was nothing we could do. The doctor gave us bottles of laudanum. I wish I'd had some of those one-quarter grain morphine hypos I carry in my bandage kit." He dropped his hands and his eyes darted around the candle lit room. "I got Laudanum in him and he went to sleep but kept waking up and making a terrible noise—a dying noise."

He wiped his hands again and again on his shirt then covered his face. "I gave him all the Laudanum, and he didn't wake up." He jerked to the right facing the wall. "I was only twelve years old."

Doody rolled over. "Y'all are makin' a powerful racket."

Lipsitz shined a flashlight into the room. "The racket will get louder. They moved the attack up one day to tomorrow. Stand-To is at five-thirty, kick off is seven o'clock. We'll be first to cross the river."

CHAPTER 41
NOVEMBER 10, 1918
SYNGHEM, BELGIUM

At 5 A.M. Lieutenant Samis woke the platoon. The men shaved, took cat baths, and at 5:30 A.M. assembled on the road, passed an inspection, and settled down to wait in the alley beside their house. Dubman set up his kitchen at the end of the alley.

"This slum has meat in it," Jed said.

"It's the mule Andy shot last night," Reb said.

Watkia threw down his mess tin. "Shut up!"

"Well, I've had worse," Mike said.

Doody pointed his spoon at Mike. "I'll make sure your training table is better than this. You take care when we go across. We got a big future ahead of us."

Jed didn't mind Doody worrying over Mike. Jed loved Mike like a brother for his strength, good humor, and loyalty and it was only natural others would befriend him. Mike's time away and sudden return had burned all the jealousy out of Jed.

A half dozen Negro Pioneers in worn denim coveralls walked down the alley carrying shovels, pickaxes, and buckets. They passed by without a word or glance at the squad.

As the last man in line approached, Reb stretched out his legs. The Pioneer stumbled and glared at Reb.

"Watch where you're goin', boy," Reb said.

"Hey, Reb," Watkia said. He had his bayonet out and shook his head. He looked at the Pioneer. "I think it would be best if you rejoined your friends. I apologize, sir, for this uncouth piece of shit."

The other members of the work party stood nearby, their tools at the ready. "You all right there, Poole?"

Poole held his right arm at his side, an open straight razor in his hand. "I don't need some white man to fight my battles for me," he said.

"True, but I still think it best if you went about your business."

Poole thought for a minute then folded the razor, put it in his pocket, and walked out of the alley.

"You ain't got the nerve to use that bayonet, Jew boy," Reb said. "I heard tell you never even fired your rifle."

"Ask Jed over there if I have the nerve."

Reb glanced at Jed.

"He does, I know it firsthand."

Reb glanced between Jed and Watkia then turned away without another word.

Trask appeared at the end of the alley. "We move out in five minutes."

First Platoon hurried to the river and huddled behind shattered walls, near piles of engineer lumber, ropes, pulleys, and other equipment that Teddy and some engineers unloaded from his one-mule wagon.

Lieutenant Samis squatted nearby with the Belgian liaison officer and watched Sergeant Patterson and his engineers secure a pontoon bridge on the opposite bank behind a curtain of smoke and high explosives.

"I guess it won't be so bad if they can't see us," Jed said.

"The Germans have registered this area to the meter," Lannoye said. "They are shooting blind but know where we are."

Artillery splinters zinged overhead.

Teddy took a knee beside Jed. He had a wound stripe on his right cuff.

"Here we are," Jed said.

Teddy nodded.

As the engineers finished securing the bridge, a shell landed in the middle of the work party. All of them went down. A few, including Sergeant Patterson, crawled to cover.

Another shell hit the opposite bank and dislodged the bridge. The current eased the free end of the bridge downstream.

Jed laid down his rifle and shrugged out of his gear. He picked up a coil of rope and dashed onto the bridge.

Damn the river—finish the bridge.

He concentrated on the far end of the swaying bridge and ran. Machine gun bullets splashed around him and footsteps pounded behind him.

He ran faster.

At the end of the bridge Samis caught up with him, a coil of rope over his shoulder. The gap between the bridge and the river bank was forty feet and there was nobody on the other side.

Jed tied one end of the rope to the bridge, wrapped the other end around his waist, and tied it off. Samis did the same.

Jed looked at Samis. "We swim."

He dove into the water and swam hard for the other side.

He was halfway there when a shell landed in the water near him, the concussion rolling him upside down. He kicked toward the sky glow at the surface and started for the bank again.

Samis was already there.

"I thought I'd lost you, Martin. Help me hold her against the current."

Jed pulled the slack out of his own rope but it was all they could do to hold the bridge steady. It wouldn't move back toward the bank.

"We have to anchor it," Samis said.

Jed backed up toward a tree stump. When he let his slack out Samis nearly fell over but Jed got his rope wrapped around the stump and the lieutenant tied his rope to another. The ropes creaked under the strain.

"These ropes won't last long," Jed said.

Jed watched two engineers in a spare pontoon paddle across the river trailing a long rope from the opposite river bank. They stopped at the free end of the bridge, attached the rope and a pulley to it, then paddled to the near bank, jumped out, and looped the rope and another pulley around a tree stump.

Teddy had the other end of the long rope attached to his mule's harness and urged the animal forward drawing the end of the bridge to the riverbank where the engineers secured it.

Jed moved to the riverbank and saluted Teddy. Teddy returned the salute.

The rest of First Platoon streamed across the bridge.

Lannoye and Mike arrived first.

"An incredible feat of bravery, Lieutenant Samis," Lannoye said. "The two of you have saved this whole operation."

Jed was soaked and shivering. Mike wrapped his raincoat around Jed's shoulders and gave him the rest of his equipment. "You're going to make me old before my time if you fall off any more bridges."

"This time I remembered to swim," Jed said.

Jed and Mike joined the squad sitting behind the tree stumps where Watkia sewed up a swelling gash on Sergeant Patterson's neck. The engineer gave Jed thumbs up.

"I thought you was afraid of the water," Doody said.

"I could swim when I was little. I guess it came back to me."

Bunny shook his head. "I still don't know whether you're brave or crazy."

"Both," Jed said. He removed his boots and changed into dry socks, then put on the rest of his equipment.

Captain Brown and Sergeant Trask hurried across the bridge as the smoke screen drifted away and the German gunners concentrated their fire on the rest of Company G stopping their attempt to cross.

Brown surveyed the situation. "Good work on the bridge, Samis but you have another job. Go up there and silence those guns. The woods should screen your movement. Sergeant Trask will go with you."

Samis got the platoon up and led them forward.

The platoon advanced up rising terrain toward the dense woods. To the left beyond the woods the German machine guns fired toward the river.

Samis halted the platoon and conferred with Lieutenant Lannoye and Sergeant Trask. He pointed to a creek running through the woods and down the hill. "Trask, take the rifle and grenade sections up that creek through the woods and prepare to flank those guns. I'll take the rest of the platoon and circle to the left, take cover along the front side of the woods, and draw their fire. You hit them from the flank. Give us a half hour, when Fritz shifts his fire onto us, hit them."

Jed had come to admire Samis who was no longer the boy lieutenant who'd berated Jed for wearing his farmer's hat in the rain back in the Baccarat sector. He was a seasoned officer and a rare survivor among the platoon leaders in the AEF.

Samis led the half platoon to the left followed by the Belgian liaison officer.

Trask waved his men forward. They moved into the woods, on line on either side of the creek, into a clearing that was suddenly swept by machine gun fire.

Corporal Zyren and Tommy Pricklin took the full force of the burst and went down face first into the creek. Jed and the others hugged the ground.

The bomber section sergeant charged from the left but was cut down as he tossed a grenade into the machine gun nest silencing the gun.

Jed rose and stepped over Zyren and Pricklin's still forms. He followed Trask from the woods into a meadow.

The creek swung to the right and formed a trench one hundred yards to the flank of the German guns. The Americans piled in, beneath the fire from the machine guns.

A German artillery shell shrieked in and landed in the middle of the creek. The blast knocked Jed's helmet off and wrenched his rifle from his hands.

Sergeant Trask slumped over, his face submerged at the edge of the creek. Reb pulled him to a sitting position. "He's not bleeding. Whoa, look at the dent in his helmet."

Trask shoved Reb away, flung his helmet off, and held his head in his hands, his eyes squeezed tight. When he opened his eyes, they rolled up, and he passed out. Reb checked him over again. "He's breathing but something sure gave him a knock on the noggin."

Jed was unharmed. His rifle lay broken in two. He retrieved his bayonet.

Doody's left arm and hand was a smashed mess of blood and bone. Reb wrapped a bandage tightly around the wound. Elly Darnell bandaged a gash over Bunny's left ear.

Jed crawled to where Watkia wrapped a bandage around Mike's thigh. "They hit me in the leg again, Jed."

German artillery pasted the woods where Samis was hiding.

He raised his voice, "Everybody stay low and get ready to flank those guns."

Someone moaned nearby. Jed peeked over the bank of the creek. The shell had thrown Sergeant Collins into the space between the creek and the German gun pit.

Lieutenant Lannoye ran from the edge of the woods and hunkered by Jed. "I came to see what damage the artillery has done. I see it was effective. Who is in charge here?"

Trask was unconscious, Watkia was scooping a hole into the creek bank, Bunny and Doody were wounded, and all the other corporals and

PFCs were dead or missing. The two remaining hand bombers were privates. Jed was the only PFC left. "I am, sir."

"Can you hit those guns when we start our diversion?"

Collins moaned louder.

"We have a piece of work to do first, sir." Jed organized Bunny and the able men along the stream bank.

Jed was calm but alert.

He leaped out of the creek bed and ran forward and stopped beside Collins who was holding his belly, trying to keep his intestines from spilling out. Jed picked him up and started back to the ditch. Machine gun bullets snapped around him.

Bunny and the others fired a volley and the machine gun fire stopped.

Jed slid into the creek bed and laid Collins down. Watkia hurried over and began bandaging the corporal's hideous wound.

Trask was propped against the side of the creek bed near Jed. "I'm going to put you in for a gallantry citation."

Jed shook his head. "I'm scared but trying to stay alive and help my friends, Top."

"That's courage." Trask looked at Watkia who hung his head as he gave Collins a shot of morphine. "Anyone still here helping his friends is a hero in my book." He squeezed Watkia's shoulder.

"Helping means killing," Jed said.

"Murder in self-defense," Trask said. "You have to catch the other fellow unaware and kill him before he kills you, even when he can't defend himself. Out here it's legal, expected, and respected." He scrunched his eyes in pain. "Andy, give me that French canteen."

Watkia handed him the double-spout and held up a morphine hypo.

Trask shook his head and took a long drink, the dark liquid running out of the corners of his mouth. He took a deep breath and rubbed his eyes. "We pay a price, though." He gave the canteen to Watkia and passed out again.

Watkia checked his pulse. "He's sleeping."

Jed picked up Trask's shotgun and pouch of shells and put his helmet on with the Buckeye insignia on the back. "There's more killing to do."

Watkia pulled out his picture of Elka and tears welled in his eyes.

"Why don't you stay here and attend to the wounded, Andy?" Jed said. "Get the tags off the dead for the lieutenant's report."

Andy sniffed and nodded, "Thanks, Jed."

Jed crawled to where Lannoye crouched with the unhurt men spaced out along the creek bank: Reb Hill and Wayne Turley from first squad, Lenny Gurr, Elly Darnell, Dan Ponder, Bill Danforth and Lonnie Doyle from second squad, and two bomber privates. Ten combat effective men including Jed, one squad, left from half a platoon. He was still scared but saw everything around him clearly. This was where he was supposed to be.

Jed jacked a shell into the shotgun breech. "Are you guys ready?"

Darnell had a wicked-looking club wrapped in barbed wire and Gurr had a two-foot section of truck axle. Ponder had a bolo knife. The bomber privates had sacks of grenades and pistols. Reb, Turley, Danforth, and Doyle had bayonets fixed.

"Give 'em hell," Mike said.

Jed smiled, shrugged his shoulders, and turned to the Belgian lieutenant. "We're ready, sir."

Rifle grenades arced in and spattered along the parapet of the German machine gun position and Chauchat rounds split the German sandbags. The Germans responded by turning their fire from the river crossing onto the edge of the woods.

Lieutenant Lannoye handed Jed a flare pistol. "Fire this flare when you are in position behind them. We will lift our fire and you can do your business."

Jed thanked the Belgian and was turning away when the lieutenant stopped him.

"Thank you, PFC Martin."

"You know my name?"

The Belgian officer nodded then ran in a crouch out of the creek bed and into the woods to rejoin Samis.

Jed tucked the flare pistol into his belt. He gathered his squad around him. "We'll go after the next salvo of grenades. Bunny, keep your head down. You guys have done enough."

Bunny waved him off.

More rifle grenades landed along the front of the German position and Jed ordered his men up and forward. The closest German gunner swung his gun toward Jed's squad.

Turley collapsed back into the creek.

Bunny shot and killed the gunner.

Jed's men found the shelter of two shell holes halfway to the German gun pit. Bunny's men continued to fire on the German left flank and Samis from the woods. Jed raised the flare pistol and fired it as a heavy barrage impacted along the creek bed and in the woods near Lieutenant Samis.

Jed waved his men forward, and they leaped out of the shell holes. They covered the ground to the Germans in ten seconds and set about doing their "business" as Lannoye had called it. The bombers threw grenades up a communications trench to delay reinforcements. Jed poured shotgun blasts into the gun pits.

Darnell split a German gunner's face with his club but was shot in the head by an officer with a pistol. Jed obliterated the officer's face with a shotgun blast.

The Americans worked their way methodically down the zigzag trenches. Lenny Gurr grinned with delight as he bashed heads with his iron bar. Danforth and Doyle were doing hard work with their bayonets.

A German soldier jumped up in front of Jed. "*Kamerad.*"

Jed pointed his shotgun at the young soldier, whose eyes grew large with terror. Jed didn't care that the man was unarmed. Any live German was a threat. He pulled the shotgun trigger, but the hammer snapped on an empty chamber. He dropped the gun and pulled out his Derringer. The teenager stood shaking, tears running from his eyes. Jed pulled the trigger.

The Derringer didn't fire. Jed had failed to reload it after shooting the German officer and Brock.

The frightened youngster closed his eyes and sobbed in German, *"Oma."*

The word jolted Jed. He stared at the quivering boy, his hands shaking.

When Jed tried to reload the Derringer, digging in his pocket for two more bullets, the German boy picked up his rifle.

Someone stepped up beside Jed and fired. The boy folded into the mud.

Reb stood by Jed working the bolt of his rifle. He spat tobacco. "You're welcome."

As a German charged out of a dugout and thrust at Reb with a bayonet, an American stepped past Reb and butt stroked the German across the face, killing him.

It was Andy Watkia. He looked at Reb. "Fuck you."

"Well, the mule killing Jew boy finally stepped up."

Jed picked up his shotgun. As he loaded it, he said, "Take that bigoted horseshit and cram it, Hill."

Reb tensed and took a step toward Jed.

"You touch me, and you'll spend the rest of the century in the stockade."

Reb worked on the plug of tobacco in his mouth.

"You spit on my boots, you get a broken jaw," Jed said hefting the shotgun.

A German officer stepped out of a dugout and raised a pistol. Ponder was nearby and beheaded him with his bolo.

The machine guns fell silent.

The entire line of Germans stood up and "*Kamerad*" echoed down the trench.

"Cease fire, they're surrendering," Jed commanded. To continue the killing was murder. No claim of self-defense was possible. "It's over. Make sure they don't have any weapons." He loaded the Derringer and put it away.

Samis arrived with the rest of the platoon and took charge of the prisoners.

The squad gathered around Jed as he sat on the trench parapet and passed a pack of cigarettes around. Jed inhaled deeply. His breath shuddered as he exhaled. Lenny Gurr wrapped a bandage around a bullet wound in Bill Danforth's shoulder.

"Those Kraut bastards never had a chance," Doyle said.

"They had a chance," Jed said. "Elly Darnell survived influenza to be here today."

The rest of Company G streamed across the bridge and started up the hill.

Jed threw his cigarette butt into the trench. "Let's go see how the rest of our guys are doing." They dragged themselves off the sandbags, the fatigue of released tension moving them in slow motion.

When they arrived at the creek, stretcher bearers had laid out a line of dead next to the creek. Zyren, Pricklin, and Turley lay on stretchers beside the bomber sergeant. Reb and Lenny Gurr carried Darnell's body and added him to the row of honor.

Jed walked over to Bunny. Sergeant Trask was still sleeping. "Where is Joe Collins?"

"They already sent him down the hill," Bunny said. "Funny enough, they said he'd probably be all right. He'll have a bad scar on his belly, but if he doesn't get an infection, he should be fine."

Jed scanned the area. "Did they take Mike and Doody, too?"

Bunny looked toward the river, not meeting Jed's eyes. "That was a fierce barrage they laid on us Jed, the worst ever."

Jed's insides turned to ice. "What are you saying, Bunny?"

"We can't find Mike or Doody, Jed. They were sitting right where that shell hole is. They should be here somewhere but we can't find them." Tears ran down his face. "I'm sorry, Jed. They're gone."

Jed's legs gave out, and he fell onto his back, staring up at the sky, his mind blank. He couldn't think. He couldn't function.

Mike was gone—like Arliss Howe—evaporated.

Oh, Mike, did your good soul survive?

Jed begged his consciousness to be taken away, anywhere, so he wouldn't have to deal with this reality, but Mike appeared before him, a grin fixed on his face. Jed reached for him but Mike shook his head no and shattered into tiny shining pieces. Jed's mind followed the shards as they dove through a brilliant well of pure silver water into the darkness below.

Andy Watkia called his name.

Jed woke and sat up. He didn't know how long he'd been out. Watkia gave him the blue double-spout, and he drank eagerly, wanting the solace of drunkenness. He was dead inside and wanted to run and jump into the river.

Jed watched impassively as the sanitary detail arrived and picked up the stretchers and carried the blanket-draped forms down the hill. Bunny and Danforth, supporting a dazed Trask, followed them.

He sat and let the wine work. It began to dull the ache, and he guzzled more.

"Go easy, Jed. The captain is coming," Watkia said.

Captain Brown and Cain walked up the hill. The captain had a bandage on his forehead, Cain one around his left hand.

"PFC Martin, are you senior here?" Brown asked.

Jed looked around. "I suppose I am, sir."

"I saw what happened at the bridge. You're a corporal now and I'm putting you and Lieutenant Samis in for decorations. Get your men fed and rested. You'll stay here for the night. The rest of the regiment is moving forward to the town of Beirlegem where they'll dig in. I need you fresh in the morning." The captain moved away.

Jed shook his head. He commanded the only rifle squad left in the platoon, five men plus himself.

Watkia leaned in, "You've got to step up and take care of these guys."

"Mike is gone," Jed said to no one in particular. He kneeled by the hole where Mike had sat and scooped two handfuls of dirt into his haversack.

"We all loved Mike, Jed," Watkia said.

"Not more than me."

Three replacements brought the platoon up to 31 men, a little over half the number authorized by the table of organization. Jed's rifle section was only one squad: Andy Watkia, Reb Hill, Lenny Gurr, Dan Ponder, Lonnie Doyle and the three new men named Buck, Stratton, and White.

The platoon bedded down in the captured German trench. Dubman brought them hot food. Jed found a German blanket, shook most of the cooties off it, and crawled into a dry shell hole outside the trench. He finished off the blue canteen and collapsed into sleep.

At midnight Cain shook him awake. He had news. An armistice would take effect in the morning, November 11, 1918 at 11 A.M. Jed's squad was to do a forward reconnaissance after sunrise. Jed was groggy from the wine but he told Cain he'd have the men ready.

CHAPTER 42

NOVEMBER 11, 1918

NEAR BEIRLEGEM, BELGIUM

As the sun rose behind scudding low clouds most of the 147th Regiment was in billets in the small town of Beirlegem, their farthest point of advance. Jed's rifle squad moved forward through the regimental line and established an observation post in a soggy ditch along the road leading east from the town toward Brussels. They were ordered to hold in place and not advance. They could only fire in self-defense.

Jed ordered the replacements to fill sandbags and build a parapet on the edge of the ditch creating a shallow trench.

After setting the work detail, Jed slumped down in the ditch and stared at the orchard a half-mile away where the Germans were hiding. He hadn't been able to help Mike once again, and, with an armistice, he would be denied his chance for revenge on the men who had taken so much from him.

The Germans appeared and set up a field piece at the edge of the tree line. They loaded the gun and elevated the barrel. A flash of fire belched from the mouth of the gun and a shell wheezed overhead followed by the distance-delayed report of the piece. Several seconds later came the muffled crunch of the shell as it impacted in Beirlegem.

Private Buck looked at Jed, his eyes wide. "What do we do, Corporal Martin?"

Jed regarded him deadpan, "Rifles against artillery? It's a quarter to eleven. This will be over in fifteen minutes. We do nothing."

Buck slumped back. "All that training and marching. We get here and it's over."

"If you'd been here more than a few hours, you'd be glad it's over."

As soon as he said it, Jed wondered if he'd spoken the truth. Did he want it to end? He was sick of killing and seeing his friends die, sick of the mud and the food, sick of the cooties and the rats, sick of randomness and uncertainty. But the war had become all he had. Life here was simple and real, everything else seemed petty and without purpose. What was there for him to go back to, riding mules and watching the sharecroppers pick cotton? He had become a soldier. Everywhere he'd gone over the last six months he'd found the army familiar, comfortable in its routines, always providing a place for him. He fit in, he belonged. He belonged so much that he'd become a killer in a place where killing was common.

He brooded over the orchard where his enemies lay. Jed wanted to do more killing. He didn't want the war to end. He wanted payback for Mike.

An American artillery team galloped up the road pulling a French 75 field piece. They skidded to a stop, unlimbered the gun, and ran it down into the ditch behind the sandbag revetment. An artillery captain stepped off his mount, raised a pair of binoculars, and surveyed the orchard. A corporal set up a range finder and called off the distance to the enemy battery. "Eight hundred yards, sir."

"Lay for direct fire."

Fifteen seconds later the officer pulled the lanyard. The muzzle blast smacked Jed in the face and thumped his chest. The red-hot round screamed toward the orchard and exploded fifty feet short. The artillerymen cranked the barrel up slightly and fired again. The air vibrated as the high explosive sailed away. This one hit directly on the revetment the Germans had thrown up around their field piece.

"This is more like it," Buck said. "The war's not over yet." He flipped up the adjustable sight on his Enfield, set it to the range the gunner had called, and took aim. He fired as the 75 barked again. Buck let out a whoop. Stratton and White followed his lead and fired at the Germans.

Jed's mind raced. The war was ending, but he had unfinished issues. He strode to where Watkia hid behind the sandbags and threw his shotgun down. He snatched Watkia's rifle out of his hands and opened the bolt.

"I don't know if you ever fired this thing, but it's time it was dirtied up."

Watkia sheepishly handed him two five-round strippers. Jed set his sight and thumbed five bullets into the magazine. He slammed the action closed, took aim, and fired. He didn't know if he hit anything but he was doing something. He fired the four remaining rounds and reloaded.

The German gunners furiously cranked their gun barrel down.

The artillery captain crouched low. "Everybody down. Prepare to receive direct fire." The officer looked anxiously at his watch. "It's two minutes to the armistice. Don't be the last man to die in this stinking war."

Jed didn't take cover. He had one last chance to fight back. He leaped over the sandbags, stood in the open, and fired the rifle. "Kill me last. I don't care." He fired again. "You bastards killed my friend."

Fire spewed from the barrel of the German field piece and the shell streaked in and landed ten feet from Jed. He was slammed to the ground by the blast.

When Jed regained his senses, Watkia and Reb leaned over him. A searing pain started in his right leg and stabbed into his lower back.

"Can you move your legs?" Reb asked. Jed moved his right leg. Pain exploded in his thigh.

Watkia gave him a shot of morphine.

Reb tied a bandage around his leg. "You lost a lot of blood, Corp, but I think I got it stopped." The morphine began to work and Jed's pain subsided.

Lying in the mud at the bottom of the ditch, behind a blasted section of sandbags, was the headless body of a soldier.

"Buck," Andy Watkia said.

The sounds of combat had been replaced by something else.

"What's that sound?" Jed asked.

"Church bells in Beirlegem. It's 11:02. I guess we made it through."

We made it through.

But at what cost?

The world destroyed, ending in a whimper.

Jed shivered and his vision grew dim.

Maybe he was the last man.

And he wasn't afraid.

PART FOUR

CALM WATERS

Now to attune my dull soul if I can
To the contentment of this countryside,
Where man is not forever killing man
But quiet days like these calm waters glide.

—Edmund Blunden, CBE, MC

CHAPTER 43

APRIL 5, 1919

LONELY OAK BRIDGE, ELEVEN POINT RIVER,

RANDOLPH COUNTY, ARKANSAS

Jed had awakened on a hospital barge being towed down the North Sea coast to Dunkirk. He felt no pain and soon learned why. The liberal doses of morphine he was given frightened him. He was so doped up he couldn't move and spent most of the trip asleep. When he was awake, he watched the neutral faced nurses and orderlies bustling about and attending a multitude of strangers strapped to cots stacked in every corner. Some men were in worse shape than he. They were never awake and occasionally one would be removed and never return.

After he complained, the nurses gradually reduced, but didn't discontinue, his morphine and kept up the dioxychlor Dakin disinfectant drip into his leg and hip to ward off infection. After a week, he was able to sit up and drink a thin beef broth.

Jed's orderly, with his own wound stripe on his sleeve, told him he was going to be all right. "You're healing fine, Corporal, but you might have a permanent limp."

At one point a Belgian army officer and an American colonel appeared. For helping to save the bridge the Belgian pinned the Belgian Croix de Guerre with Palm to the front of Jed's hospital gown. The American did the same with the Distinguished Service Cross. He also presented a Citation Certificate for Gallantry in Action for saving Collins. Lieutenant Lannoye, Captain Brown, and Sergeant Trask had made the recommendations. When the official party departed, Jed took the medals off and put them in his haversack with the certificate. The memories they evoked were too painful.

At Dunkirk, he stayed to himself and concentrated on his recovery, carefully following the instructions of the orderlies and building his strength.

In January, he was transferred to a hospital at Kerhuon, France, on the heights overlooking the port of Brest. American boxcars took him there, three deep tiers of cots on either side, clean, and attended by efficient and pretty nurses.

At Kerhuon, he convinced the nurses to stop the morphine and found that the wine smuggled into the wards replaced the clutching drug.

A letter was forwarded to him from Bunny. He and Watkia were still in France.

Bunny mentioned that Watkia looked forward to running his family's furniture business and that his cousin Pinard in Canada would soon visit on a regular basis. Prohibition would provide Watkia with another opportunity.

Bunny was excited about finding work in the tire factories in Akron, Ohio. He had some contacts there and would try to get the remaining men from the squad jobs, including Jed. He had heard that homecoming celebrations were planned for the retuning veterans. Jed hoped he would miss them. He was awash with pain and loss and didn't want to celebrate.

A postcard from Enoch arrived, forwarded to Jed by Lipsitz. Mike's dad, Patrick, had died of influenza and, shortly after, Mike's mother committed suicide. Mister Jones had died as well. The bad news kept getting worse.

When he was released from the hospital in March, Jed limped along with other casuals through the military transportation system, across the Atlantic by ship, and by train to Camp Sherman, south of Columbus, Ohio. The army doctors examined him, issued him a walking cane, and released him from service. He traveled by train to Pocahontas wearing his uniform, the left sleeve red discharge chevron indicating that he wasn't AWOL.

Enoch met him at the platform wearing the same suit he'd seen Jed off in, his Philippine service medal still pinned to his left lapel.

Enoch shook Jed's hand.

Neither said a word.

Jed drove the buggy to Bessie's grave beside the Methodist church where she had been married those happy days long ago. The graveside visit was difficult, the two men silent, lost in their thoughts and memories.

Now they sat beneath the lonely old oak, its branches full of spring leaves, Jed rolling a cigarette and Enoch filling his pipe, a jug of moonshine propped between them. The southern sun shone down on the green fields of young cotton and the air was cool in the shade of the resilient old tree.

Jed's cane lay in the grass next to Enoch's.

Jed scratched a match, lit his cigarette, and passed it to Enoch who stoked his pipe and threw the match away. They smoked in silence. The Eleven Point flowed calmly toward the Mississippi River and the Gulf of Mexico. Watching the quiet waters was the most peaceful time Jed had had in a year, yet his heart was troubled and he needed to speak with his uncle.

"You're selling the farm."

"Well, I guess it's mine to sell," Enoch said. "It's time to change, like everything else is changing."

Enoch took a long drag on his pipe and blew the smoke on the breeze following the river's course. "I'm going to give you a quarter of the money I get for the land."

"No, you need the money to live on. I've got most of my travel pay left and a little savings. I'll get by."

Enoch held up his hand. "I insist. After I'm gone, you'll get what's left, anyway."

"What are you going to do?"

"I'm going to Marshall, Texas to live with my cousin John. I'll have more than enough money to last me the rest of my days." He took a drink from the jug. "I don't expect I'll last much longer. The fall I took aggravated my old wound. It didn't heal properly and the doctors don't know what to do. There's a poison deep down in my bones and eventually it'll get to my heart." He paused. "I want you to have your share. This was your home, and you always earned your keep."

Enoch tamped the pipe bowl with a small stick and relit the coals. "Wars have destroyed this family one way or another: Old Jed, your mother, Seth, Bess, this abscess eating me alive in my leg. We all died because of war." He looked at Jed, sadness and acceptance in his eyes. "You're the whole family now, son. I care to see you get started well." There was another aching pause, Enoch's lip quivering. "I'm proud of you."

Enoch had never said anything so nice.

Jed changed the subject. "You're wearing your service medal."

Enoch stared at the river. "I'm proud of my service, despite what it done to me, but I didn't do anything, more or less, than the others did."

"You did plenty, I know, now."

"What about you, decorated by the allies?"

Jed took his medals out of his pocket and handed them to Enoch who examined them and handed them back. "You'll have to tell me about it sometime."

Jed stared at the medals. "Murder in self-defense."

"What?"

"Something my Top Sergeant said."

Enoch nodded. "True enough."

"To service." Jed hoisted the jug, drank and handed it over.

"To service." Enoch drank deeply. He set the jug down and rubbed his leg. "Service extracts a high price for the good you do."

"Is there any good in it?"

"Stopping murdering Moros and Kaiserites gives people peace and freedom."

Jed put the medals away. "It's not enough."

"You won. You came home."

"So many didn't." Jed stared at the grass between his knees.

"The price of survival, Jed, is that you remember for the rest of your life."

They sat and watched the river.

"You wrote to me that Mister Jones died," Jed said. "How did it happen?"

"Car crash soon after his two boys were killed."

"I was with them when they got it," Jed said. "The older boy Bart was trying to help his younger brother who was wounded. A German Maxim got them both."

Enoch knocked the spent coals out of his pipe and reloaded. "When Jones heard about it, he fell apart. His wife took the girls and the little boy and went back to New York. The oldest boy still runs the business." He lifted the jug. "Jones started drinking heavily, shouting 'I sent my sons to die!' while racing his Cadillac around the countryside."

Enoch pointed up to the tree trunk. "See that gash right there? He missed the turn onto the bridge and drove that beautiful car right into this oak. They found him on the hood, his head smashed against the tree trunk."

Pipe smoke billowed. "What are you going to do?"

"A friend is holding a job for me in an Akron, Ohio tire factory." Jed let out a thin stream of smoke. "The future is in the cities, making things, building the country. The world expects big things of us. We went over and made a mark."

"Like I knew you would."

Jed considered this and nodded his head. "You toughened me up because you knew my war would come. I did what they told me to do and survived, a limping, sad veteran like you."

"The price of victory."

Jed took a long drink from the jug his mind relaxed, inhibitions gone.

"You and Aunt Bess always say, 'your mother' when referring to Rose, but never, 'your father', it's always Seth."

Enoch took the jug and drank long and hard, not meeting Jed's gaze. "It's a quirk of language we use, like calling the men by their middle names or Teddy calling everybody by their first two names."

Jed shook his head. "Bessie said the four of you were like different parts of the same person, like it was one marriage. You paired off as you saw fit, and there was nothing you couldn't forgive each other."

"You're getting personal about married peoples' business."

"I think it's *my* business. I think it affects me and who I am."

"Identical twins are always close and the women were sisters. You're making too much of the silly way we talk."

"No, it's like some big family secret." Jed hesitated, needing to go on and not knowing how it would affect his relationship with Enoch. He stubbed his cigarette out in the grass. "Bessie said that you boys were perfectly matched twins but that my eyes were more like yours than Seth's."

Enoch stared into the distance, the tension on his face making Jed wonder if he would burst into tears or a fit of anger.

Enoch lowered his head and let out a deep sigh. "Do you have a question for me?"

"Are you my father?"

Enoch's knuckles were white as he squeezed his pipe.

"I don't rightly know, son."

"But it's possible."

"Yes."

"Probable?"

Enoch closed his eyes and nodded his head.

Jed inhaled, held it for a dozen heartbeats then released it in a rush. He turned to Enoch. "You're a hypocrite. You raised me one way, but the town was right, you all were a bunch of free love Bohemians."

Enoch slapped the ground. "Don't you preach to me. I don't suppose you were reading the Bible to those gals you took into the woods at picnics or into the mule shed."

Jed started to speak but closed his mouth.

"We thought we were inventing a new way to live but when you came along and Bessie miscarried Suzanne, it shocked us back to reality. We couldn't undo the past but could settle down and reenter society, even going to church again. When people didn't accept that we had changed we stopped." He struck a match. "We never cared much for what they thought, anyway." Enoch relit his pipe and tossed the match away. "Whether it was Seth or me you're who you are, and after what you've been through, does it matter?"

Jed stood and limped over to the riverbank standing close to the edge, leaning on his cane and staring into the river. His fear of water had been washed away in the Scheldt.

Enoch's admission had been a shock but not a surprise, and in truth, it didn't matter. Most of those involved were gone.

He watched the water eddying around the bridge pilings. Coming home he'd stood on the fantail of the ship watching the moonlit, swirling wake, and remembered the dream he'd had after Mike's death. He could dive through the shimmering water into the oblivion below but didn't. After all he'd done and seen, it would dishonor those who didn't have a choice in dying.

Enoch was right. His burden, and penance, was that he would remember.

A low rumble broke Jed's reverie, sounding like distant artillery, another storm, like a new war, sneaking over the horizon.

The Great War had simply fizzled out. One minute the men on each side had been mortal enemies, the next they were a bunch of filthy, disillusioned men: veterans. After all the useless death, politicians postponed the boxing match. It would be rescheduled at a later date.

Who was the last man to die?

In the end it didn't matter, there was no last man, only the next man, and another family torn apart.

The Martin family had been whittled down to only Jed.

The O'Kean family had disappeared.

Jed pulled Mike's last letter from his shirt pocket. It was all that remained.

Jed,

I hoped you'd never have to read this. I was planning on standing beside you on the stern of the puke bucket taking us back to the States and throw it into the ocean. That didn't happen.

The good news is you are reading it and are OK. I'm glad for you, Jed. You are my best friend and I miss you and want to get back and help and protect you and the guys.

I know it sounds arrogant, but they looked up to me. They called me a hero for winning those fights, but I was scared every time I went into the ring. I hated getting hit in the head. You don't know how much having you there gave me strength and let me push the fear away. I knew I couldn't let you down because you never let me down. You were always there for me.

We have to do some terrible things. We are soldiers. But remember the people we help. We liberate them and give them a future. That's a grand and noble thing. Somebody has to stand up for freedom.

That somebody is us.

Don't be hard on yourself. You're smart and brave and I know you'll do great things, because you are the future, you and the others who made it through. When you have a moment, remember the ones from the squad who didn't: Timmy Smith, Tony DiNiccola, and me.

Sergeant Brock was a bastard but died in service. That deserves a certain respect, too, the respect he didn't seek in life.

I exist as long as you remember me, Jed, and, according to my faith, I will dwell in the house of the Lord forever.

267

*I'll be waiting to see you again one day, waiting with
your mom and dad and your Aunt Bessie and all the boys,
all of our friends who went west.
But there's no hurry, Jed, we can wait.
Your loving brother, Mike.*

Two streaks of tears ran down Jed's face. He put the letter away and reached into the bottom of his haversack for a handful of the soil he and Mike had fought for. He let the earth sift slowly through his fingers and into the flowing waters. "I'll see you again one day, Mike. I'm sorry I didn't get to say goodbye."

He hooked his cane over his arm and pulled his medals out of his pocket. The vast majority of men didn't get any recognition, only the task of killing and being killed in a desperate mess. But he had been recognized. The brass crosses and colorful ribbons were not for killing people, but for saving lives, for *helping people*, as Bessie would say. They told him that what he'd done was acceptable and not wrong. Maybe Fate had decreed that he'd gone to war for the sole purpose of saving those men and fixing that bridge, nothing more.

He held his cane in one hand and the medals in the other. The cane was pain and sorrow, the medals courage and hope.

He threw the cane into the river. He would need no rocking chair. Jed placed the medals carefully into his pocket, walked back to the tree, and sat down.

He picked up the jug and took a long, burning drink. Rejecting the cane was only the first tiny step. He relied on alcohol to lift his spirits, but as drunk as he got at night, the melancholy returned every morning.

Jed handed the jug to Enoch. "It never goes away, does it?"

Enoch paused before drinking. "It hurts less with the years but the memories never fade. You feel guilty that you lived and so many died."

There was a gray mist in his eyes.

"Seems like only yesterday."

EPILOGUE

THE PRICE OF VICTORY

He who did well in war just,
Earns the right to begin doing well in peace...
—Robert Browning
Luria

CHAPTER 44

APRIL 19, 1919

MARTIN FARM, NEAR BIRDELL, ARKANSAS

Jed sat in the dark in Bessie's overstuffed chair smoking cigarettes and staring out the bay window at the lightning flashes and listening to the thunder. He had drunk nearly a quart of moonshine during the night, trying to find respite from his sadness in sleep, but he sat in wide-eyed exhaustion. He felt no guilt at having shot Brock but regretted all the death he had been forced to mete out in the necessity of staying alive and supporting his friends, too many of them gone.

He slammed the moonshine jar onto the table beside the chair. He had lost everything he loved and everything he hated and tried to fill the emptiness with drink. He hadn't sobered up enough to have a hangover in weeks.

Other than the chair, table, and his bed, the house was empty. When Enoch moved out, he couldn't take the chair where Bessie had spent so many comfortable hours.

There was a knock at the front door.

Jed opened it.

Postman Pinkert was there.

Jed waved him in out of the rain.

"I have a letter for you Mister Martin." Pinkert reached under his slicker and pulled out an envelope. "It's from Ohio. I figured it might be important."

Jed took it and stared at it. It was from Bunny.

"Are you all right, Mister Martin?" Pinkert asked.

Jed didn't answer. He tore the letter open. His knees nearly buckled as he read it.

April 13, 1919
Jed Martin, Martin Farm, Birdell, Arkansas

BROCK IS ALIVE. The SOB says you shot him and left
him for dead but the bullet hit a rib and bounced away.
He claims that he crawled away during the shelling. He
hid in a collapsed dugout and saw you looking for him
then sneaked away. A French woman helped him hide
out, pretending he was her husband.
He's here, doing shit details for Watkia, drinking up all
the pinard, and vowing revenge on you.
Trask and Abel West are here, too, and they're local
police.
There's work for you here in Akron, come soon, but be
careful.
Bunny

Jed's skin tingled. Trask was right, Brock always returned. This time
from the dead. The motion he'd seen in the trench that night was
probably Brock crawling away.

Bunny had added a Post Script:

We located Louise before we shipped out for home, gave
her some money, and made sure the docs were taking
good care of her. She sent you a letter.

March 18, 1919
Jed Martin
C/O Monsieur Bunny

Ich hoffe, dass dieses Schreiben Sie gut findet.
I do hope this letter finds you well, Jed. The boys told me
that you were hurt but will be alright. I am praying for
you.
I am doing well myself. The American doctors cared for
me and my wounds have healed. I lost two toes on my left
foot but they have given me a special shoe and I walk
with only a slight limp.

272

I am living with an older French couple whose son was killed in the war and they are very kind to me. I am also back in school.
I hope you will write to me. I think of you often as my friend and big brother.
Maybe one day I will travel to America and visit you.
Gott beschütze dich,
Dein Freund,
Louise

Jed was cheered that he had an address for Louise and that she was doing well.

He hadn't lost everything after all. He had friends in Ohio, Brock to hate, again, and Louise was alive.

He turned to Pinkert. "I appreciate your making sure our letters and postcards got through. I can't tell you how important those letters were."

"Thank you, Mister Martin." Pinkert went out, mounted his mule, and rode away.

Jed put the letter down, stripped off his clothes, and stepped out into the rain. The cold shower washed over him and he felt the sadness begin to slip away.

The rain stopped, and the sun broke under low clouds to the east.

He went through the front door and started for the stairs, drying off with his dirty clothes. He paused at Bessie's chair, picked up the Mason jar from the table, and, for his breakfast, gulped the moonshine down. He would deal with his craving for alcohol later. The first order of business was to get to his job in Ohio, then deal with Leo Brock.

In his room Jed pulled out his khaki uniform. It bore the Buckeye patch on the left shoulder above the red discharge chevron and gold service stripe at the cuff, corporal's stripes and gold wound chevron on the right sleeve. The red, white, and blue ribbon of the Distinguished Service Cross and the green and red French and Belgian War Cross ribbons stood out on the left breast. He was supposed to discard the uniform but had decided to keep it. He put on civilian clothes, loaded his last two bullets into the Derringer, hung it around his neck, and buttoned it under his shirt. He'd kept it a secret from the army and would keep it a secret from the police, too. His folded uniform, two changes of clothes, seven full jars of moonshine, and a cardboard box containing his medals and $5,000 cash Enoch had given him, went into his duffle bag. He placed the family Bible and Bessie's picture book inside and put Trask's battered Buckeye helmet on top. He drew the closing cord tight and threw the bag over his shoulder. He placed his floppy farmer's hat on his head and walked down the stairs and out the front door, marching down the road to Pocahontas and the train to Ohio.

He'd murdered Brock once.

He hoped he wouldn't have to do it again.

(Keep reading for further information and an additional chapter about Leo Brock.)

In memory of:

Private James Ezra Massey
Company G, Second Battalion, 147th Infantry Regiment,
74th Infantry Brigade, 37th (Buckeye) Division,
American Expeditionary Force
The Great War

AUTHOR'S NOTE

The Last Man To Die is a work of fiction. The dates, times, and places in which the 37th "Buckeye" Division served during The Great War are as accurate as the author can make them and are based on the chronology presented in the official two-volume history of the division: *The Thirty-seventh Division in the World War—1917-1918*, by Ralph D. Cole, Division Historian and W. C. Howells, Assistant Division Historian, Columbus, Ohio, 1926. Activities of the 162nd Depot Brigade in training draftees at Camp Pike, Arkansas are based on general practices revealed by the author's extensive research.

All individuals portrayed below the rank of full colonel are fictional. The actual names of the regimental, brigade, and division commanders are used. Their characterizations and quotations are based on the descriptions, conversations, messages, and photographs contained in the division history.

James Jedidiah Martin is loosely based on the author's maternal grandfather, James Ezra Massey, 2565082, Private, Company G, 147th Infantry Regiment, 37th Division. He was born and raised in Pocahontas, Arkansas and was drafted into the Army in May 1918. He joined the 37th division at Pannes, served in that defensive sector, and took part in the Ypres-Lys operation in Belgium.

He was known throughout his life by his middle name, Ezra.

All other persons and events in the story are the product of the author's imagination, including the Lonely Oak Bridge and the Jones Lumber Company. Any similarity to actual people and events is coincidental. The author makes no representation that any depicted crime or atrocity was committed by any member of the United States Army, the AEF, any allied force, or the Imperial German Army.

As mentioned, great care has been taken to make this account of the 37th Division as historically accurate as possible. One instance requiring the author to exercise literary judgment is in the order of battle of the 147th Regiment on the opening day of the Meuse-Argonne offensive on

26 September 1918. The Division History, Volume II, Chapter VIII, consistently reports the First Battalion of the regiment as being on the right of the regimental sector in the front line position. The history then reports, in separate paragraphs, that the Second Battalion then the Third Battalion was in the front line to the left of the First Battalion. Later, in separate paragraphs, the Third Battalion is reported behind the Machine Gun Battalion (in reserve) then the Second Battalion "went over" as regimental reserve. The author has exercised his judgment that, for dramatic effect, the Second Battalion was in the front line to the left of the regimental sector. Any errors in fact are solely the responsibility of the author.

Bob Colvin
11 November 2020

PARTIAL ROSTER (FICTIONAL)
147th Regiment, 74th Brigade, 37th Infantry Division

Second Battalion
Major Samuel Bryce LaForge - Commander - Cincinnati, OH
Sergeant Major John Able West - "Abel" - Cincinnati, OH
Company G
Captain Louis Tyne Brown - Commander - Cincinnati, OH
Sergeant Leslie Leo Trask - First Sergeant - Cincinnati, OH
Corporal Chaim Goldson - "Cain" - Company Clerk - Parma, OH
Private Clarence Dubman - "Dub" - Company Cook - Akron, OH
First Platoon
2nd Lieutenant George Curtis Samis - Commander - Toledo, OH
Platoon Sergeant - Sidney Aaron Lipsitz - "Lips" - Parma, OH
3rd Section (Riflemen)
Sergeant Leo Leslie Brock - Section Leader - Ashtabula, OH
First Squad
Corporal Joseph Collins - Squad Leader - Cuyahoga Falls, OH
Private 1st Class Anthony DiNiccola - "Tony" - Cincinnati, OH
Private 1st Class Steven Foster Dodd - "Doody" – Kyle, WV
Private 1st Class Andrew Joseph Watkia - "Andy" - Parma, OH
Private Timothy June Smith - "Timmy" - Cleveland, OH
Private Benjamin Lev Steinmetz - "Bunny" - Akron, OH
Private George Arthur Walker - Dayton, OH
Private Elmore Joseph Darnell - "Ellie" - Cincinnati, OH
Private James Jedidiah Martin - "Jed" - Replacement - Birdell, AR
Private Michael Sean O'Kean - "Mike" - Replacement - O'Kean, AR
Private John Stuart Jackson Hill - "Reb" - Replacement - Ivor, VA
Private Wayne Moore Turley - Replacement - Champaign, IL
Private Ralph Webster Buck - Replacement - Pittsburgh, PA
Private Albert Louis Stratton - Replacement - Ocala, FL
Private Theodore Winston White - Replacement - Bisbee, AZ
Second Squad
Corporal David Lee Kraft - Squad Leader - Cincinnati, OH
Private 1st Class Richard Lee Cole - Cincinnati, OH
Private 1st Class Thomas Royce Pricklin - Coshocton, OH
Private 1st Class Philip Law Zyren - Cincinnati, OH
Private Joshua Samuel Alvis - Hamilton, OH
Private Leonard Macey Gurr - "Lenny" - Springfield, OH
Private Arliss Temple Howe - Cincinnati, OH
Private Edwin Michael Joyner - Chillicothe, OH
Private William Paul Danforth - Replacement - Crown Point, IN

Private Lonnie Elwin Doyle - <u>Replacement</u> - Owensboro, KY
Private Daniel Ezra Ponder - <u>Replacement</u> - Stoney Point, AR
Additional personnel
Captain Hubert Arnn Hewitt - Chaplain - Warren, OH
Sergeant Wilbur Duane Patterson - Engineer - Orange, OH
Wagoner Theodore Roosevelt Stains - "Teddy" - Birdell, AR

ACKNOWLEDGEMENTS

The Last Man To Die has taken over a decade to prepare. Thousands of hours of research and writing, over one hundred books read, and thousands of magazine articles and web sites visited, all went into this project, but the most important assistance I received during and after that research was from the people who helped me along the way.

At the very top of the list are my dear friends and colleagues Dave Gjerness, who sadly died in October 2020, and his bride Linda Purdy. Dave was a gifted and creative graphic designer who did award winning work in publishing magazines in Minneapolis, Minnesota and Phoenix, Arizona. His suggestions were always spot on and he was a master of image. Linda, as a school teacher, is a tireless, detailed line editor. She finds things that I overlook even when I'm sure everything is tip-top. Her grasp of human interactions aided me greatly in characterizations. I am forever grateful to both, and deeply sad at Dave's passing.

I am exceedingly grateful that Caroline Stenz joined the team and carried on the work that Dave had started.

Mort Castle, Adjunct Professor of English at Columbia College, Chicago, did a thorough developmental edit of the manuscript. His praise and enthusiasm for the work was heartwarming and his sharply pointed suggestions for improvement were invaluable.

Al Moe, a successful author in his own right, offered valuable tips and wisdom.

I thank Duane Patterson, radio producer extraordinaire and all around good guy, for his facilitation of communication, support, and encouragement.

A hat-tip to John McLeod for additional editorial assistance.

A number of BETA readers helped from beginning to end. They include: Kimberly Cummins, Paul Harry, Samantha Morton, Linda Purdy, George Rapp, and Harry Shepler.

The Language Center at Arizona State University assisted with the French and German languages, Ennio "Mike" Paolicci with Italian, and Michael Beckman and Jeff Dunetz with Hebrew.

Dave Nigh of Estrella Mountain Ranch, Arizona provided a critical website prop.

Jackie Salyards, former director of the Randolph County, Arkansas Library; Pat Lambert of the Randolph County, Arkansas Heritage Museum; James Throgmorton of Camera Corner Studios in Pocahontas, Arkansas; Dewrell Thompson, Director, Randolph County Tourism Association; and Susan Thielemier of The Pocahontas Star Herald all rendered valuable assistance.

Thank you all.

BROCK

MARCH 13, 1919

LAMORVILLE, FRANCE

Brock poured a glass of wine and sat back in his chair on the sidewalk outside the bakery. The owner, Gabrielle, placed a plate with fresh-baked bread and a wedge of cheese in front of him. He nodded his head, a faint smile of thanks at the corner of his mouth. He owed this woman much. Over the past few months, she had hid him from authority and helped improve his Louisiana French, happy to have a man to help her with the bakery. She was handsome, with long brown hair, pale green eyes, and a wide, sensuous mouth. When she took off her bulky baker's apron and cotton dress, her small voluptuous body kept him satisfied—if not content.

During the German occupation she had bartered for flour to keep the bakery open and had stored a ton in a root cellar under the noses of the Germans. He suspected the valuable commodity she had used for barter was the same one he shared now, in the cool evenings, after they put out the candles. Her past did not interest him. The German's were long gone, and the American and French armies were far off to the east in occupation duties.

The village crones whispered but didn't question their living arrangement. Maybe he was the husband who had disappeared into the war and had stopped writing but had come home, wounded. Was he not in his own home? Did he not wear his own clothes?

Since he was the only male in the village younger than 70, and there was concern that so many young men had been killed in the war, two women had brought their twenty-year-old daughters to the bakery. Gabrielle assented to their requests he impregnate them. Brock was excited to his best effort by the fact the older women watched. Gabrielle did not watch.

Each mother had brought her daughter twice more to help ensure results, and they were not disappointed. One of the young women had walked by the bakery yesterday, ignoring him, her belly tight against her dress after five months.

Brock carved off a slice of bread, topping it with a thin piece of the cheese. After the Americans drove the Germans out a small cheese industry had sprung up around twenty cows and there were chickens and pigs. No one starved.

He shifted in his seat. The rifle wound in his right side had healed but his left ribs still nagged him. He hadn't known Martin had a small pistol. The bullet glanced off a rib and, though it hurt like Hell, it didn't do much damage, just knocked him out for a while.

After Martin shot him, he had lain buried under a pile of sandbags. Many shells landed in the trench, but the sandbags protected him from the blast and splinters. He awoke when one landed on top of the pile.

During a lull in the shelling, he dug himself out, crawled into a collapsed dugout entrance, and pushed sandbags toward the entrance to protect him from shellfire. He was just in time. A huge shell exploded where he had lain under the sandbags.

He pushed more sandbags forward to block the entrance and looked out through a gap in the bags. Jed Martin, perched at the top of the trench, peered at the hole where Brock had fallen. When a rat sniffed at his wounds Brock slapped it away and it ran out and down the trench.

When he looked again, Martin had disappeared.

Brock crawled to another dugout further down the trench. He used a bottle of iodine to clean his wounds and covered them with extra bandages he carried in his haversack. What little food he had he ate, emptied his canteen of the water and cognac mixture, and dozed off.

He awoke when he heard a patrol approach and lay silent, listening. They were Americans, one of them calling out Trask's name. There was some excited talk and then subdued discussion. Brock gave them time to get clear then crawled out of his hole and made his way back toward the American rear area, angling away from the route of the patrol.

The techniques of stealth the army had taught him helped him creep along the shattered battle ground at night, hiding and sleeping or playing dead during the day. Once, he had to lie still, feigning death, next to a rotting mule carcass. The American patrol gave the stinking animal a wide berth, but it was all he could do to remain still.

Rations on corpses and rainwater from the gas infested shell holes kept him going. This made him almost as sick as having no alcohol to drink. When he approached the American trenches, he hid for a full day in a small hole beneath a dense tangle of wire.

At night a raiding party crawled into no-man's-land. He smeared mud on his face and slipped out of his hide, inching to a position beside the path the party had taken. They returned three hours later with two prisoners and, as they passed, he fell into file behind them. He crawled into the main trench and someone handed him a cup of warm coffee. He took it and hurried up the communication trenches toward the rear, crossing open country, traveling west into a forest.

Three French soldiers bathed in a stream. Brock filched a small loaf of bread, one of their horizon blue coats, and one of their two-quart canteens. The canteen contained wine mixed with water. The bread and half the canteen contents settled his gassed stomach. Moving along the stream he stole their rowboat and rowed down the river all night.

In the morning he landed near a French village. He removed his uniform blouse and equipment and threw them into the water, washed his face, put the blue jacket on, and stumbled into the town.

Inside a small bakery, a middle-aged woman placed loaves of bread into baskets on a table then went through a door into the kitchen. Brock found a broom and began to sweep the flour and dust on the floor out onto the stoop.

"Bonjour, monsieur." The woman stood in the kitchen door.

"Bonjour, Madame."

He told her in his Louisiana French that he would work for food and a place to sleep. She nodded her assent. When he finished sweeping, she gave him a loaf of bread, a bottle of wine, and two small coins. *"Merci beaucoup...?"*

"Gabrielle."

A pile of clean linen towels sat on the table. He picked up one and replaced it with one coin. She nodded again.

She put him in the storage room with a basin of water and a small bar of soap. He washed, dried with half of the towel, and changed his bandages, using strips from the towel's other half. He made a lumpy bed of sacks of flour more comfortable than any other place he had slept in the past year.

After two days he joined Gabrielle in her bed.

Soon news came that the war had ended. Gabrielle seemed happy to hear this, but a sad resignation still showed on her face.

Most of the Americans not on occupation duty in Germany passed through the area in January and February on their way to St. Mihiel, the French coast, and home. Lamorville was too far off the main road for them to stop there.

He realized he would have to move on. A local boy could show up any day—perhaps even Gabrielle's real husband. He had to leave before that happened.

Pouring another glass of wine, he raised his glass in a cynical salute to his being right all along. Left for dead, less than one month later, they called the whole thing off.

But he had survived.

Tonight, he would have one more night with Gabrielle.

Tomorrow, he would leave.

With stolen equipment and his identity tags and pay book, he would present himself as a casual and find a passage to the States—if he didn't run into any 37th Division men.

He didn't expect a joyous homecoming. He had not been fighting for them but for himself and wanted nothing more than his chance for revenge. There were scores to settle in Ohio and, perhaps, in Arkansas.